F   Clarke, Arthur C.
CLA
       Beyond the fall of
       night

$19.95

DATE			
AG 23 '90			
OC - 2 '90			
NO 21 '90			
JA - 7 '91			
JA - 2 '91			
SE 24 '91			
NO - 8 '91			
AP - 7 '92			
AP 28 '92			
OC 9 '92			
JA 8 '94			
SE 19 '94			

BEYOND THE FALL OF NIGHT

Imperial Earth
Islands in the Sky
The Lion of Comarre
The Lost Worlds of
  2001
The Nine Billion
  Names of God
The Other Side of the
  Sky
Prelude to Mars
Prelude to Space

Reach for Tomorrow
Rendezvous with Rama
The Sands of Mars
The Sentinel
Tales from Planet Earth
Tales from the "White Hart"
Tales of Ten Worlds
2001: A Space Odyssey
2010: Odyssey Two
2061: Odyssey Three
The Wind from the Sun

WITH GENTRY LEE

Cradle   *Rama II*

ALSO BY GREGORY BENFORD

Across the Sea of Suns   *In the Ocean of Night*
Against Infinity   *Jupiter Project*
Artifact   *The Stars in Shroud*
Great Sky River   *Tides of Light*
In Alien Flesh (short stories)   *Timescape*

WITH GORDON EKLUND

Find the Changeling   *If the Stars Are Gods*

WITH WILLIAM ROTSLER

Shiva Descending

WITH DAVID BRIN

Heart of the Comet

EDITED WITH MARTIN H. GREENBERG

Hitler Victorious   *What Might Have Been*
Nuclear War   *(volumes 1 and 2)*

BEYOND THE FALL OF NIGHT

ARTHUR C. CLARKE
AND
GREGORY BENFORD

AN ACE/PUTNAM BOOK
PUBLISHED BY G.P. PUTNAM'S SONS
NEW YORK

AN ACE/PUTNAM BOOK
PUBLISHED BY G. P. PUTNAM'S SONS
Publishers Since 1838
200 Madison Avenue
New York, NY 10016

Library of Congress Cataloging-in-Publication Data

Clarke, Arthur Charles, date.
Beyond the fall of night / Arthur C. Clarke and Gregory Benford.
p.   cm.
"An Ace/Putnam book."
I. Benford, Gregory, date. II. Title.
PR6005.L36B45 1990   89-39736 CIP
823'.914—dc20
ISBN 0-399-13499-9

Printed in the United States of America
1   2   3   4   5   6   7   8   9   10

This book has been printed on acid-free paper.
∞

To Mark Martin and David Brin
For tangy ideas, zesty talk, warm friendship

G.B.

FOREWORD

It is now more than half a century since *Against the Fall of Night* was born, yet the moment of conception is still clear in my memory. Out of nowhere, it seems, the opening image of the novel suddenly appeared to me. It was so vivid that I wrote it down at once, though at the time I had no idea that I would ever develop it any further.

That would have been in 1936, plus or minus a year, and I had written several drafts by late 1940, when I was evacuated with my colleagues in His Majesty's Exchequer and Audit Department to the small North Wales town of Colwyn Bay. Here I finished a 15,000-word version, but for the next five years was somewhat preoccupied with other matters (see *Glide Path*). I started work on· it again in August 1945: whether before or after Hiroshima changed the world, I do not now recall.

The first complete draft was finished by January 1946, and promptly sent to John Campbell at *Astounding Stories*. He took three months to reject it, and I rewrote the ending in July 1946, submitting it again to Campbell. He took another three months to reject the *second* version.

After that, I sent it to my new agent, Scott Meredith, who sold it to *Startling Stories*, where it appeared in November 1948. It was accepted by Gnome Press for hardcover publication in September 1949, and was published in a handsome edition with a jacket by promising new artist, one Kelly Freas (it must have been one of Kelly's earliest commissions; I only hope that he was paid for it!).

Because it was my firstborn, *Against the Fall of Night* always had a special place in my affections, yet I was never completely satisfied with it. The opportunity to make a complete revision came during a long sea voyage from England to Australia, when I joined forces with Mike Wilson and set off on an underwater expedition to the Great Barrier Reef (see *The Coast of Coral*). The much longer and drastically revised novel, *The City and the Stars*, was completed in Queensland between excursions to the Reef and the Torres Strait pearling grounds. It was published by Harcourt, Brace & World in 1956, and has remained in print ever since.

At the time, I assumed that new version would completely replace the older novel, but *Against the Fall of Night* showed no tendency to fade away; indeed, to my slight chagrin, some readers preferred it to its successor, and it has now been reissued several times in paperback (Pyramid Books, 1960: Jove, 1978) as well as in the volume *The Lion of Comarre and Against the Fall of Night* (Harcourt, Brace & World; Victor Gollancz, 1970). One day I would like to conduct a poll to discover which is the more popular version; I have long ago given up trying to decide which is the better one.

The search for a title took almost as long as the writing of the book. I found it at last in a poem of A. E. Housman's, which also inspired the short story *Transience:*

> *What shall I do or write*
> *Against the fall of night?*

The name of my protagonist, Alvin, also gave me many headaches, and I cannot remember when—or why—I decided on it. I did not realize that, at least to American readers, it was faintly humorous, being redolent of a well-known comic strip. However, many years later, the name had two enormously important associations for me. The deep submersible *Alvin* took Ballard and his associates to the wreck of the *Titanic* when it was discovered in 1986. That tragedy, though it occurred five years before I was born (that dates me, doesn't it?) has haunted me all my life. It was the basis of the very first story I ever wrote, a luckily long-lost epic called—wait for it—"Icebergs of Space." I also incorporated it into the novel *Imperial Earth* (1975) and it is the subject of a book that has now occupied me for several years.

Perhaps still stranger, the name Alvin is derived from that of Allyn C. Vine, its principal engineer. And Vine was one of the authors of the famous letter in *Science* (*151* 682–683; 1966) which proposed the construction of the Space Elevator—the subject of my novel *The Fountains of Paradise (1979)*. So the name Alvin had more power than I could possibly have imagined in the late 1930s, and I am happy to salute it.

When the suggestion was made that Gregory Benford should write a sequel continuing the story, I was immediately taken by the idea, because I had long admired Greg's writing—especially his remarkable *Great Sky River*. As it happened, I'd also just met him at NASA headquarters; as Professor of Astrophysics at the University of California, Irvine, he is one of NASA's technical advisers.

I have now read his sequel with great enjoyment, because to me—as it will be to you—it was a voyage of discovery. I had no idea how he would develop the themes and characters I had abandoned so long ago. It's particularly interesting to see how some of the concepts of this half-century-old story are now in the forefront of modern science: I am especially fond of the "Black Sun," which is an obvious description of the now extremely popular Black Holes.

I will say no more about Greg's version—or my own. I'll leave you to enjoy both.

One other aside, though. By a strange coincidence, while almost simultaneously we had the proposal to write the sequel to *Against the Fall of Night,* the excellent Australian science fiction writer Damien Broderick ("The Dreaming Dragons") wrote asking if he could write a sequel to *The City and the Stars*! In view of Greg's project, I reluctantly turned it down—but perhaps in another decade. . . .

Arthur C. Clarke
Colombo, Sri Lanka
May 29, 1989

BEYOND THE FALL OF NIGHT

PART
I

PROLOGUE

Not once in a generation did the voice of the city change as it was changing now. Day and night, age after age, it had never faltered. To myriads of men it had been the first and the last sound they had ever heard. It was part of the city: when it ceased the city would be dead and the desert sands would be settling in the great streets of Diaspar.

Even here, half a mile above the ground, the sudden hush brought Convar out to the balcony. Far below, the moving ways were still sweeping between the great buildings, but now they were thronged with silent crowds. Something had drawn the languid people of the city from their homes: in their thousands they were drifting slowly between the cliffs of colored metal. And then Convar saw that all those myriads of faces were turned toward the sky.

For a moment fear crept into his soul—fear lest after all these ages the Invaders had come again to Earth. Then he too was staring at the sky, entranced by a wonder he had never hoped to see again. He watched for many minutes before he went to fetch his infant son.

The child Alvin was frightened at first. The soaring spires of the city, the moving specks two thousand feet below—these were part of his world, but the thing in the sky was beyond all his experience. It was larger than any of the city's buildings, and its whiteness was so dazzling that it hurt the eye. Though it seemed to be solid, the restless winds were changing its outlines even as he watched.

Once, Alvin knew, the skies of Earth had been filled with strange shapes. Out of space the great ships had come, bearing unknown treasures, to berth at the Port of Diaspar. But that was half a billion years ago: before the beginning of history the Port had been buried by the drifting sand.

Convar's voice was sad when presently he spoke to his son.

"Look at it well, Alvin," he said. "It may be the last the world will ever know. I have only seen one other in all my life, and once they filled the skies of Earth."

They watched in silence, and with them all the thousands in the streets and towers of Diaspar, until the last cloud slowly faded from sight, sucked dry by the hot, parched air of the unending deserts.

1
THE
PRISON
OF
DIASPAR

The lesson was finished. The drowsy whisper of the hypnone rose suddenly in pitch and ceased abruptly on a thrice repeated note of command. Then the machine blurred and vanished, but still Alvin sat staring into nothingness while his mind slipped back through the ages to meet reality again.

Jeserac was the first to speak: his voice was worried and a little uncertain.

"Those are the oldest records in the world, Alvin—the only ones that show Earth as it was before the Invaders came. Very few people indeed have ever seen them."

Slowly the boy turned toward his tutor. There was something in his eyes that worried the old man, and once again Jeserac regretted his action. He began to talk quickly, as if trying to set his own conscience at ease.

"You know that we never talk about the ancient times, and I only showed you those records because you were so anxious to see them. Don't let them upset you: as long as we're happy, does it matter how much of the world we occupy? The people you have been watching had more space, but they were less contented than we."

Was that true? Alvin wondered. He thought once more of the desert lapping around the island that was Diaspar, and his mind returned to the world that Earth had been. He saw again the endless leagues of blue water, greater than the land itself, rolling their waves against golden shores. His ears were still ringing with the boom of breakers stilled these thousand million years. And he remembered the forests and prairies, and the strange beasts that had once shared the world with Man.

All this was gone. Of the oceans, nothing remained but the gray deserts of salt, the winding sheets of Earth. Salt and sand, from Pole to Pole, with only the lights of Diaspar burning in the wilderness that must one day overwhelm them.

And these were the least of the things that Man had lost, for above the desolation the forgotten stars were shining still.

"Jeserac," said Alvin at last, "once I went to the Tower of Loranne. No one lives there anymore, and I could look out over the desert. It was dark, and I couldn't see the ground, but the sky was full of colored lights. I watched them for a long time, but they never moved. So presently I came away. Those were the stars, weren't they?"

Jeserac was alarmed. Exactly how Alvin had got to the Tower of Loranne was a matter for further investigation. The boy's interests were becoming—dangerous.

"Those were the stars," he answered briefly. "What of them?"

"We used to visit them once, didn't we?"

A long pause. Then, "Yes."

"Why did we stop? What *were* the invaders?"

Jeserac rose to his feet. His answer echoed back through all the teachers the world had ever known.

"That's enough for one day, Alvin. Later, when you are older, I'll tell you more—but not now. You already know too much."

Alvin never asked the question again: later, he had no need, for the answer was clear. And there was so much in Diaspar to beguile the mind that for months he could forget that strange yearning he alone seemed to feel.

Diaspar was a world in itself. Here Man had gathered all his treasures, everything that had been saved from the ruin of the past. All the cities that had ever been had given something to Diaspar:

even before the coming of the Invaders its name had been known on the worlds that Man had lost.

Into the building of Diaspar had gone all the skill, all the artistry of the Golden Ages. When the great days were coming to an end, men of genius had remolded the city and given it the machines that made it immortal. Whatever might be forgotten, Diaspar would live and bear the descendants of Man safely down the stream of Time.

They were, perhaps, as contented as any race the world had known, and after their fashion they were happy. They spent their long lives amid beauty that had never been surpassed, for the labor of millions of centuries had been dedicated to the glory of Diaspar.

This was Alvin's world, a world which for ages had been sinking into a gracious decadence. Of this Alvin was still unconscious, for the present was so full of wonder that it was easy to forget the past. There was so much to do, so much to learn before the long centuries of his youth ebbed away.

Music had been the first of the arts to attract him, and for a while he had experimented with many instruments. But this most ancient of all arts was now so complex that it might take a thousand years for him to master all its secrets, and in the end he abandoned his ambitions. He could listen, but he could never create.

For a long time the thought-converter gave him great delight. On its screen he shaped endless patterns of form and color, usually copies—deliberate or otherwise—of the ancient masters. More and more frequently he found himself creating dream landscapes from the vanished Dawn World, and often his thoughts turned wistfully to the records that Jeserac had shown him. So the smoldering flame of his discontent burned slowly toward the level of consciousness, though as yet he was scarcely worried by the vague restlessness he often felt.

But through the months and the years, that restlessness was growing. Once Alvin had been content to share the pleasures and interests of Diaspar, but now he knew that they were not sufficient. His horizons were expanding, and the knowledge that all his life must be bounded by the walls of the city was becoming intolerable to him.

Yet he knew well enough that there was no alternative, for the wastes of the desert covered all the world.

He had seen the desert only a few times in his life, but he knew no one else who had ever seen it at all. His people's fear of the outer world was something he could not understand: to him it held no terror, but only mystery. When he was weary of Diaspar, it called to him as it was calling now.

The moving ways were glittering with life and color as the people of the city went about their affairs. They smiled at Alvin as he worked his way to the central high-speed action. Sometimes they greeted him by name: once it had been flattering to think that he was known to the whole of Diaspar, but now it gave him little pleasure.

In minutes the express channel had swept him away from the crowded heart of the city, and there were few people in sight when it came to a smooth halt against a long platform of brightly colored marble. The moving ways were so much a part of his life that Alvin had never imagined any other form of transport. An engineer of the ancient world would have gone slowly mad trying to understand how a solid roadway could be fixed at both ends while its center traveled at a hundred miles an hour. One day Alvin might be puzzled too, but for the present he accepted his environment as uncritically as all the other citizens of Diaspar.

This area of the city was almost deserted. Although the population of Diaspar had not altered for millennia, it was the custom for families to move at frequent intervals. One day the tide of life would sweep this way again, but the great towers had been lonely now for a hundred thousand years.

The marble platform ended against a wall pierced with brilliantly lighted tunnels. Alvin selected one without hesitation and stepped into it. The peristaltic field seized him at once, and propelled him forward while he lay back luxuriously, watching his surroundings.

It no longer seemed possible that he was in a tunnel far underground. The art that had used all Diaspar for its canvas had been busy here, and above Alvin the skies seemed open to the winds of heaven. All around were the spires of the city, gleaming in the sunlight. It was not the city as he knew it, but the Diaspar of a much earlier age. Although most of the great buildings were familiar, there were subtle differences that added to the interest of the scene. Alvin wished he could linger, but he had never found any way of retarding his progress through the tunnel.

All too soon he was gently set down in a large elliptical chamber, completely surrounded by windows. Through these he could catch tantalizing glimpses of gardens ablaze with brilliant flowers. There were gardens still in Diaspar, but these had existed only in the mind of the artist who conceived them. Certainly there were no such flowers as these in the world today.

Alvin stepped through one of the windows—and the illusion was shattered. He was in a circular passageway curving steeply upward. Beneath his feet the floor began to creep slowly forward, as if eager to lead him to his goal. He walked a few paces until his speed was so great that further effort would be wasted.

The corridor still inclined upward, and in a few hundred feet had curved through a complete right angle. But only logic knew this: to the senses it was now as if one were being hurried along an absolutely level corridor. The fact that he was in reality traveling up a vertical shaft thousands of feet deep gave Alvin no sense of insecurity, for a failure of the polarizing field was unthinkable.

Presently the corridor began to slope "downward" again until once more it had turned through a right angle. The movement of the floor slowed imperceptibly until it came to rest at the end of a long hall lined with mirrors. Alvin was now, he knew, almost at the summit of the Tower of Loranne.

He lingered for a while in the hall of mirrors, for it had a fascination that was unique. There was nothing like it, as far as Alvin knew, in the rest of Diaspar. Through some whim of the artist, only a few of the mirrors reflected the scene as it really was—and even those, Alvin was convinced, were constantly changing their position. The rest certainly reflected *something,* but it was faintly disconcerting to see oneself walking amid ever-changing and quite imaginary surroundings. Alvin wondered what he would do if he saw anyone else approaching him in the mirror-world, but so far the situation had never arisen.

Five minutes later he was in a small, bare room through which a warm wind blew continually. It was part of the tower's ventilating system, and the moving air escaped through a series of wide openings that pierced the wall of the building. Through them one could get a glimpse of the world beyond Diaspar.

It was perhaps too much to say that Diaspar had been deliberately built so that its inhabitants could see nothing of the outer world. Yet it was strange that from nowhere else in the city, as far as Alvin knew, could one see the desert. The outermost towers of Diaspar formed a wall around the city, turning their backs upon the hostile world beyond, and Alvin thought again of his people's strange reluctance to speak or even to think of anything outside their little universe.

Thousands of feet below, the sunlight was taking leave of the desert. The almost horizontal rays made a pattern of light against the eastern wall of the little room, and Alvin's own shadow loomed enormous behind him. He shaded his eyes against the glare and peered down at the land upon which no man had walked for unknown ages.

There was little to see: only the long shadows of the sand dunes and, far to the west, the low range of broken hills beyond which the sun was setting. It was strange to think that of all the millions of living men, he alone had seen this sight.

There was no twilight: with the going of the sun, night swept like a wind across the desert, scattering the stars before it. High in the south burned a strange formation that had puzzled Alvin before—a perfect circle of six colored stars, with a single white giant at its center. Few other stars had such brilliance, for the great suns that had once burned so fiercely in the glory of youth were now guttering to their doom.

For a long time Alvin knelt at the opening, watching the stars fall toward the west. Here in the glimmering darkness, high above the city, his mind seemed to be working with a supernormal clarity. There were still tremendous gaps in his knowledge, but slowly the problem of Diaspar was beginning to reveal itself.

The human race had changed—and he had not. Once, the curiosity and the desire for knowledge which cut him off from the rest of his people had been shared by all the world. Far back in time, millions of years ago, something must have happened that had changed mankind completely. Those unexplained references to the Invaders—did the answer lie there?

It was time he returned. As he rose to leave, Alvin was suddenly struck by a thought that had never occurred to him before. The air vent was almost horizontal, and perhaps a dozen feet long. He had always imagined that it ended in the sheer wall of the tower, but this was a pure assumption. There were, he realized now, several other possibilities. Indeed, it was more than likely that there would be a ledge of some kind beneath the opening, if only for reasons of safety. It was too late to do any exploring now, but tomorrow he would come again. . . .

He was sorry to have to lie to Jeserac, but if the old man disapproved of his eccentricities it was only kindness to conceal the truth. Exactly what he hoped to discover, Alvin could not have said. He knew perfectly well that if by any means he succeeded in leaving Diaspar, he would soon have to return. But the schoolboy excitement of a possible adventure was its own justification.

It was not difficult to work his way along the tunnel, though he could not have done it easily a year before. The thought of a sheer five-thousand-foot drop at the end worried Alvin not at all, for Man had completely lost his fear of heights. And, in fact, the drop was only a matter of a yard onto a wide terrace running right and left athwart the face of the tower.

Alvin scrambled out into the open, the blood pounding in his veins. Before him, no longer framed in a narrow rectangle of stone, lay the whole expanse of the desert. Above, the face of the tower still soared hundreds of feet into the sky. The neighboring buildings stretched away to north and south, an avenue of titans. The Tower of Loranne, Alvin noted with interest, was not the only one with air vents opening toward the desert. For a moment he stood drinking in the tremendous landscape: then he began to examine the ledge on which he was standing.

It was perhaps twenty feet wide, and ended abruptly in a sheer drop to the ground. Alvin, gazing fearlessly over the edge of the precipice, judged that the desert was at least a mile below. There was no hope in that direction.

Far more interesting was the fact that a flight of steps led down from one end of the terrace, apparently to another ledge a few hundred feet below. The steps were cut in the sheer face of the building, and Alvin wondered if they led all the way to the surface. It was an exciting possibility: in his enthusiasm, he overlooked the physical implications of a five-thousand-foot descent.

But the stairway was little more than a hundred feet long. It came to a sudden end against a great block of stone that seemed to have been welded across it. There was no way past: deliberately and thoroughly, the route had been barred.

Alvin approached the obstacle with a sinking heart. He had forgotten the sheer impossibility of climbing a stairway a mile high, if indeed he could have completed the descent, and he felt a baffled annoyance at having come so far only to meet with failure.

He reached the stone, and for the first time saw the message engraved upon it. The letters were archaic, but he could decipher them easily enough. Three times he read the simple inscription: then he sat down on the great stone slabs and gazed at the inaccessible land below.

THERE IS A BETTER WAY.
GIVE MY GREETINGS TO THE KEEPER OF THE RECORDS.

ALAINE OF LYNDAR

2

START
OF THE
SEARCH

Rorden, Keeper of the Records, concealed his surprise when his visitor announced himself. He recognized Alvin at once, and even as the boy was entering had punched out his name on the information machine. Three seconds later, Alvin's personal card was lying in his hand.

According to Jeserac, the duties of the Keeper of the Records were somewhat obscure, but Alvin had expected to find him in the heart of an enormous filing system. He had also—for no reason at all—expected to meet someone quite as old as Jeserac. Instead, he found a middle-aged man in a single room containing perhaps a dozen large machines. Apart from a few papers strewn across the desk, Rorden's greeting was somewhat absentminded, for he was surreptitiously studying Alvin's card.

"Alaine of Lyndar?" he said. "No, I've never heard of him. But we can soon find who he was."

Alvin watched with interest while he punched a set of keys on one of the machines. Almost immediately there came the glow of a synthesizer field, and a slip of paper materialized.

"Alaine seems to have been a predecessor of mine—a *very* long time ago. I thought I knew all the Keepers for the last hundred million years, but he must have been before that. It's so long ago that only his name has been recorded, with no other details at all. Where was that inscription?"

"In the Tower of Loranne," said Alvin after a moment's hesitation.

Another set of keys was punched, but this time the field did not reappear and no paper materialized.

"What are you doing?" asked Alvin. "Where *are* all your records?"

The Keeper laughed.

"That always puzzles people. It would be impossible to keep written records of all the information we need: it's recorded electrically and automatically erased after a certain time, unless there's a special reason for preserving it. If Alaine left any message for posterity, we'll soon discover it."

"How?"

"There's no one in the world who could tell you that. All I know is that this machine is an Associator. If you give it a set of facts, it will hunt through the sum total of human knowledge until it correlates them."

"Doesn't that take a lot of time?"

"Very often. I have sometimes had to wait twenty years for an answer. So won't you sit down?" he added, the crinkles round his eyes belying his solemn voice.

Alvin had never met anyone quite like the Keeper of the Records, and he decided that he liked him. He was tired of being reminded that he was a boy, and it was pleasant to be treated as a real person.

Once again the synthesizer field flickered, and Rorden bent down to read the slip. The message must have been a long one, for it took him several minutes to finish it. Finally he sat down on one of the room's couches, looking at his visitor with eyes which, as Alvin noticed for the first time, were of a most disconcerting shrewdness.

"What does it say?" he burst out at last, unable to contain his curiosity any longer.

Rorden did not reply. Instead, he was the one to ask for information.

"Why do you want to leave Diaspar?" he said quietly.

If Jeserac or his father had asked him that question, Alvin would have found himself floundering in a morass of half-truths or downright lies. But with this man, whom he had met for only a few minutes, there seemed none of the barriers that had cut him off from those he had known all his life.

"I'm not sure," he said, speaking slowly but readily. "I've always felt like this. There's nothing outside Diaspar, I know—but I want to go there all the same."

He looked shyly at Rorden, as if expecting encouragement, but the Keeper's eyes were far away. When at last he again turned to Alvin, there was an expression on his face that the boy could not fully understand, but it held a tinge of sadness that was somewhat disturbing.

No one could have told that Rorden had come to the greatest crisis in his life. For thousands of years he had carried out his duties as the interpreter of the machines, duties requiring little initiative or enterprise. Somewhat apart from the tumult of the city, rather aloof from his fellows, Rorden had lived a happy and contented life. And now this boy had come, disturbing the ghosts of an age that had been dead for millions of centuries, and threatening to shatter his cherished peace of mind.

A few words of discouragement would be enough to destroy the threat, but looking into the anxious, unhappy eyes, Rorden knew that he could never take the easy way. Even without the message from Alaine, his conscience would have forbidden it.

"Alvin," he began, "I know there are many things that have been puzzling you. Most of all, I expect, you have wondered why we now live here in Diaspar when once the whole world was not enough for us."

Alvin nodded, wondering how the other could have read his mind so accurately.

"Well, I'm afraid I cannot answer that question completely. Don't look so disappointed: I haven't finished yet. It all started when Man was fighting the Invaders—whoever or whatever they were. Before that, he had been expanding through the stars, but he was driven back to Earth in wars of which we have no conception.

Perhaps that defeat changed his character, and made him content to pass the rest of his existence on Earth. Or perhaps the Invaders promised to leave him in peace if he would remain on his own planet: we don't know. All that is certain is that he started to develop an intensely centralized culture, of which Diaspar was the final expression.

"At first there were many of the great cities, but in the end Diaspar absorbed them all, for there seems to be some force driving men together as once it drove them to the stars. Few people ever recognize its presence, but we all have a fear of the outer world, and a longing for what is known and understood. That fear may be irrational, or it may have some foundation in history, but it is one of the strongest forces in our lives."

"Then why don't I feel that way?"

"You mean that the thought of leaving Diaspar, where you have everything you need and are among all your friends, doesn't fill you with something like horror?"

"No."

The Keeper smiled wryly.

"I'm afraid I cannot say the same. But at least I can appreciate your point of view, even if I cannot share it. Once I might have felt doubtful about helping you, but not now that I've seen Alaine's message."

"You still haven't told me what it was!"

Rorden laughed.

"I don't intend to do so until you're a good deal older. But I'll tell you what it was about.

"Alaine foresaw that people like you would be born in future ages: he realized that they might attempt to leave Diaspar and he set out to help them. I imagine that whatever way you tried to leave the city, you would meet an inscription directing you to the Keeper of the Records. Knowing that the Keeper would then question his machines, Alaine left a message, buried safely among the thousands and millions of records that exist. It could only be found if the Associator was deliberately looking for it. That message directs any Keeper to assist the inquirer, *even if he disapproves of his quest.* Alaine believed that the human race was becoming decadent, and he wanted to help anyone who might regenerate it. Do you follow all this?"

Alvin nodded gravely and Rorden continued.

"I hope he was wrong. I don't believe that humanity is decadent—it's simply altered. You, of course, will agree with Alaine—but don't do so simply because you think it's fine to be different from everyone else! We are happy: if we have lost anything, we're not aware of it.

"Alaine wrote a good deal in his message, but the important part is this. *There are three ways out of Diaspar.* He does not say where they lead, nor does he give any clues as to how they can be found, though there are some very obscure references I'll have to think about. But even if what he says is true, you are far too young to leave the city. Tomorrow I must speak to your people. No, I won't give you away! But leave me now—I have a good deal to think about."

Rorden felt a little embarrassed by the boy's gratitude. When Alvin had gone, he sat for a while wondering if, after all, he had acted rightly.

There was no doubt that the boy was an atavism—a throwback to the great ages. Every few generations there still appeared minds that were the equal of any the ancient days had known. Born out of their time, they could have little influence on the peacefully dreaming world of Diaspar. The long, slow decline of the human will was too far advanced to be checked by an individual genius, however brilliant. After a few centuries of restlessness, the variants accepted their fate and ceased to struggle against it. When Alvin understood his position, would he too realize that his only hope of happiness lay in conforming with the world? Rorden wondered if, after all, it might not have been kinder in the long run to discourage him. But it was too late now: Alaine had seen to that.

The ancient Keeper of the Records must have been a remarkable man, perhaps an atavism himself. How many times down the ages had other Keepers read that message of his and acted upon it for better or worse? Surely, if there had been any earlier cases, some record would have been made.

Rorden thought intently for a moment: then, slowly at first, but soon with mounting confidence, he began to put question after question to the machines, until every Associator in the room was running at full capacity. By means now beyond the understanding of man, billions upon billions of facts were racing through the scrutinizers. There was nothing to do but wait. . . .

*   *   *

In after years, Alvin was often to marvel at his good fortune. Had the Keeper of the Records been unfriendly, his quest could never have begun. But Rorden, in spite of the years between them, shared something of his own curiosity. In Rorden's case, there was only the desire to uncover lost knowledge: he would never have used it, for he shared with the rest of Diaspar that dread of the outer world which Alvin found so strange. Close though their friendship became, that barrier was always to lie between them.

Alvin's life was now divided into two quite distinct portions. He continued his studies with Jeserac, acquiring the immense and intricate knowledge of people, places and customs without which no one could play any part in the life of the city. Jeserac was a conscientious but a leisurely tutor, and with so many centuries before him he felt no urgency in completing his task. He was, in fact, rather pleased that Alvin should have made friends with Rorden. The Keeper of the Records was regarded with some awe by the rest of Diaspar, for he alone had direct access to all the knowledge of the past.

How enormous and yet how incomplete that knowledge was, Alvin was slowly learning. In spite of the self-canceling circuits which obliterated all information as soon as it was obsolete, the main registers contained a hundred trillion facts at the smallest estimate. Whether there was any limit to the capacity of the machines, Rorden did not know: that knowledge was lost with the secret of their operation.

The Associators were a source of endless wonder to Alvin, who would spend hours setting up questions of their keyboards. It was amusing to discover that people whose names began with "S" had a tendency to live in the eastern part of the city—though the machines hastened to add that the fact had no statistical significance. Alvin quickly accumulated a vast array of similar useless facts which he employed to impress his friends. At the same time, under Rorden's guidance, he was learning all that was known of the Dawn Ages, for Rorden had insisted that it would take years of preparation before he could begin his quest. Alvin had recognized the truth of this, though he sometimes rebelled against it. But after a single attempt, he abandoned any hope of acquiring knowledge prematurely.

He had been alone one day when Rorden was paying one of his rare visits to the administrative center of the city. The temptation had been too strong, and he had ordered the Associators to hunt for Alaine's message.

When Rorden returned, he found a very scared boy trying to discover why all the machines were paralyzed. To Alvin's immense relief, Rorden had only laughed and punched a series of combinations that had cleared the jam. Then he turned to culprit and tried to address him severely.

"Let that be a lesson to you, Alvin! I expected something like this, so I've blocked all the circuits I don't want you to explore. That block will remain until I think it's safe to lift it."

Alvin grinned sheepishly and said nothing. Thereafter he made no more excursions into forbidden realms.

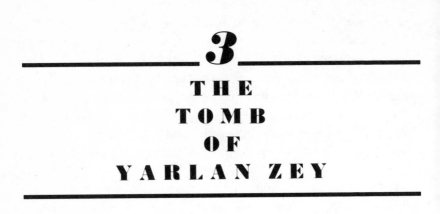

3

THE
TOMB
OF
YARLAN ZEY

Not for three years did Rorden make more than casual references to the purpose of their work. The time had passed quickly enough, for there was so much to learn and the knowledge that his goal was not unattainable gave Alvin patience. Then, one day when they were struggling to reconcile two conflicting maps of the ancient world, the main Associator suddenly began to call for attention.

Rorden hurried to the machine and returned with a long sheet of paper covered with writing. He ran through it quickly and looked at Alvin with a smile.

"We will soon know if the first way is still open," he said quietly.

Alvin jumped from his chair, scattering maps in all directions.

"Where is it?" he cried eagerly.

Rorden laughed and pushed him back into his seat.

"I haven't kept you waiting all this time because I wanted to," he said. "It's true that you were too young to leave Diaspar before, even if we knew how it could be done. But that's not the only reason why you had to wait. The day you came to see me, I set the machines searching through the records to discover if anyone after Alaine's time had tried to leave the city. I thought you might not be the first, and I was right. There have been many others: the last was about fifteen million years ago. They've all been very careful to leave us no clues, and I can see Alaine's influence there. In his message he stressed that only those who searched for themselves should be allowed to find the way, so I've had to explore many blind avenues. I knew that the secret had been hidden carefully—yet not so carefully that it couldn't be found.

"About a year ago I began to concentrate on the idea of transport. It was obvious that Diaspar must have had many links with the rest of the world, and although the Port itself has been buried by the desert for ages, I thought that there might be other means of travel. Right at the beginning I found that the Associators would not answer direct questions: Alaine must have put a block on them just as I once did for your benefit. Unfortunately I can't remove Alaine's block, so I've had to use indirect methods.

"If there was an external transport system, there's certainly no trace of it now. Therefore, if it existed at all, it has been deliberately concealed. I set the Associators to investigate all the major engineering operations carried out in the city since the records began. This is a report on the construction of the central park—*and Alaine has added a note to it himself.* As soon as it encountered his name, of course, the machine knew it had finished the search and called for me."

Rorden glanced at the paper as if rereading part of it again. Then he continued:

"We've always taken it for granted that all the moving ways should converge on the Park: it seems natural for them to do so. But this report states that the Park was built *after* the founding of the city—many millions of years later, in fact. *Therefore the moving ways once led to something else.*"

"An airport, perhaps?"

"No: flying was never allowed over any city, except in very ancient times, before the moving ways were built. Even Diaspar is not as old as that! But listen to Alaine's note:

" 'When the desert buried the Port of Diaspar, the emergency system which had been built against that day was able to carry the remaining transport. It was finally closed down by Yarlan Zey, builder of the Park, having remained almost unused since the Migration.' "

Alvin looked rather puzzled.

"It doesn't tell me a great deal," he complained.

Rorden smiled. "You've been letting the Associators do too much thinking for you," he admonished gently. "Like all of Alaine's statements, it's deliberately obscure lest the wrong people should learn from it. But I think it tells us quite enough. Doesn't the name 'Yarlan Zey' mean anything to you?"

"I think I understand," said Alvin slowly. "You're talking about the Monument?"

"Yes: it's in the exact center of the Park. If you extended the moving ways, they would all meet there. *Perhaps, once upon a time, they did.*"

Alvin was already on his feet.

"Let's go and have a look," he exclaimed.

Rorden shook his head.

"You've seen the Tomb of Yarlan Zey a score of times and noticed nothing unusual about it. Before we rush off, don't you think it would be a good idea to question the machines again?"

Alvin was forced to agree, and while they were waiting began to read the report that the Associator had already produced.

"Rorden," he said at last, "what did Alaine mean when he spoke about the Migration?"

"It's a term often used in the very earliest records," answered Rorden. "It refers to the time when the other cities were decaying and all the human race was moving towards Diaspar."

"Then this 'emergency system,' whatever it is, leads to them?"

"Almost certainly."

Alvin meditated for a while.

"So you think that even if we do find the system, it will only lead to a lot of ruined cities?"

"I doubt if it will even do that," replied Rorden. "When they were abandoned, the machines were closed down and the desert will have covered them by now."

Alvin refused to be discouraged.

"But Alaine must have known that!" he protested. Rorden shrugged his shoulders.

"We're only guessing," he said, "and the Associator hasn't any information at the moment. It may take several hours, but with such a restricted subject we should have all the recorded facts before the end of the day. We'll follow your advice after all."

The screens of the city were down and the sun was shining fiercely, though its rays would have felt strangely weak to a man of the Dawn Ages. Alvin had made this journey a hundred times before, yet now it seemed almost a new adventure. When they came to the end of the moving way, he bent down and examined the surface that had carried them through the city. For the first time in his life, he began to realize something of its wonder. Here it was motionless, yet a hundred yards away it was rushing directly towards him faster than a man could run.

Rorden was watching him, but he misunderstood the boy's curiosity.

"When the Park was built," he said, "I suppose they had to remove the last section of the way. I doubt if you'll learn anything from it."

"I wasn't thinking of that," said Alvin. "I was wondering how the moving ways work."

Rorden looked astonished, for the thought had never occurred to him. Ever since man had lived in cities, they had accepted without thinking the multitudinous services that lay beneath their feet. And when the cities had become completely automatic, they had ceased even to notice that they were there.

"Don't worry about *that*," he said. "I can show you a thousand greater puzzles. Tell me how my Recorders get their information, for example."

So, without a second thought, Rorden dismissed the moving ways—one of the greatest triumphs of human engineering. The long ages of research that had gone to the making of anisotropic matter meant nothing to him. Had he been told that a substance could have the properties of a solid in one dimension and of a liquid in the other two, he would not even have registered surprise.

The Park was almost three miles across, and since every pathway was a curve of some kind all distances were considerably exaggerated. When he had been younger Alvin had spent a great deal of time among the trees and plants of this largest of the city's open spaces. He had explored the whole of it at one time or another, but in later years much of its charm had vanished. Now he understood why: he had seen the ancient records and knew that the Park was only a pale shadow of a beauty that had vanished from the world.

They met many people as they walked through the avenues of ageless trees and over the dwarf perennial grass that never needed trimming. After a while they grew tired of acknowledging greetings, for everyone knew Alvin and almost everyone knew the Keeper of the Records. So they left the paths and wandered through quiet byways almost overshadowed by trees. Sometimes the trunks crowded so closely round them that the great towers of the city were hidden from sight, and for a little while Alvin could imagine he was in the ancient world of which he had so often dreamed.

The Tomb of Yarlan Zey was the only building in the Park. An avenue of the eternal trees led up the low hill on which it stood, its rose-pink columns gleaming in the sunlight. The roof was open to the sky, and the single chamber was paved with great slabs of apparently natural stone. But for geological ages human feet had crossed and recrossed that floor and left no trace upon its inconceivably stubborn material. Alvin and Rorden walked slowly into the chamber, until they came face to face with the statue of Yarlan Zey.

The creator of the great Park sat with slightly downcast eyes, as if examining the plans spread across his knees. His face wore that curiously elusive expression that had baffled the world for so many generations. Some had dismissed it as no more than a whim of the artist's, but to others it seemed that Yarlan Zey was smiling at some secret jest. Now Alvin knew that they had been correct.

Rorden was standing motionless before the statue, as if seeing it for the first time in life. Presently he walked back a few yards and began to examine the great flagstones.

"What are you doing?" asked Alvin.

"Employing a little logic and a great deal of intuition," replied Rorden. He refused to say any more, and Alvin resumed his examination of the statue. He was still doing this when a faint sound behind him attracted his attention. Rorden, his face wreathed in smiles, was slowly sinking into the floor. He began to laugh at the boy's expression.

"I think I know how to reverse this," he said as he disappeared. "If I don't come up immediately, you'll have to pull me out with a gravity polarizer. But I don't think it will be necessary."

The last words were muffled, and, rushing to the edge of the rectangular pit, Alvin saw that his friend was already many feet below the surface. Even as he watched, the shaft deepened swiftly until Rorden had dwindled to a speck no longer recognizable as a human being. Then, to Alvin's relief, the far-off rectangle of light began to expand and the pit shortened until Rorden was standing beside him once more.

For a moment there was a profound silence. Then Rorden smiled and began to speak.

"Logic," he said, "can do wonders if it has something to work upon. This building is so simple that it couldn't conceal anything, and the only possible secret exit must be through the floor. I argued that it would be marked in some way, so I searched until I found a slab that differed from all the rest."

Alvin bent down and examined the floor.

"But it's just the same as all the others!" he protested.

Rorden put his hands on the boy's shoulders and turned him round until he was looking toward the statue. For a moment Alvin stared at it intently. Then he slowly nodded his head.

"I see," he whispered. "So *that* is the secret of Yarlan Zey!"

The eyes of the statue were fixed upon the floor at his feet. There was no mistake. Alvin moved to the next slab, and found that Yarlan Zey was no longer looking toward him.

"Not one person in a thousand would ever notice that unless they were looking for it," said Rorden, "and even then, it would mean nothing to them. At first I felt rather foolish myself, standing on that slab and going through different combinations of control thoughts. Luckily the circuits must be fairly tolerant, and the code thought turned out to be 'Alaine of Lyndar.' I tried 'Yarlan Zey' at first, but it wouldn't work, as I might have guessed. Too many people would

have operated the machine by accident if that trigger thought had
been used."

"It sounds very simple," admitted Alvin, "but I don't think I
would have found it in a thousand years. Is that how the Associators
work?"

Rorden laughed.

"Perhaps," he said. "I sometimes reach the answer before they do,
but they *always* reach it." He paused for a moment. "We'll have to
leave the shaft open: no one is likely to fall down it."

As they sank smoothly into the earth, the rectangle of sky dwindled until it seemed very small and far away. The shaft was lit by
a phosphorescence that was part of the walls, and seemed to be at
least a thousand feet deep. The walls were perfectly smooth and
gave no indication of the machinery that had lowered them.

The doorway at the bottom of the shaft opened automatically as
they stepped toward it. A few paces took them through the short
corridor—and then they were standing, overawed by its immensity,
in a great circular cavern whose walls came together in a graceful,
sweeping curve three hundred feet above their heads. The column
against which they were standing seemed too slender to support the
hundreds of feet of rock above it. Then Alvin noticed that it did not
seem an integral part of the chamber at all, but was clearly of much
later construction. Rorden had come to the same conclusion.

"This column," he said, "was built simply to house the shaft
down which we came. We were right about the moving ways—they
all lead into this place."

Alvin had noticed, without realizing what they were, the great
tunnels that pierced the circumference of the chamber. He could see
that they sloped gently upward, and now he recognized the familiar
gray surface of the moving ways. Here, far beneath the heart of the
city, converged the wonderful transport system that carried all the
traffic of Diaspar. But these were only the severed stumps of the
great roadways: the strange material that gave them life was now
frozen into immobility.

Alvin began to walk toward the nearest of the tunnels. He had
gone only a few paces when he realized that something was happening to the ground beneath his feet. *It was becoming transparent.* A

few more yards, and he seemed to be standing in midair without any visible support. He stopped and stared down into the void beneath.

"Rorden!" he called. "Come and look at this!"

The other joined him, and together they gazed at the marvel beneath their feet. Faintly visible, at an indefinite depth, lay an enormous map—a great network of lines converging toward a spot beneath the central shaft. At first it seemed a confused maze, but after a while Alvin was able to grasp its main outlines. As usual, he had scarcely begun his own analysis before Rorden had finished his.

"The whole of this floor must have been transparent once," said the Keeper of the Records. "When this chamber was sealed and the shaft built, the engineers must have done something to make the center opaque. Do you understand what it is, Alvin?"

"I think so," replied the boy. "It's a map of the transport system, and those little circles must be the other cities of Earth. I can just see names beside them, but they're too faint to read."

"There must have been some form of internal illumination once," said Rorden absently. He was looking toward the walls of the chamber.

"I thought so!" he exclaimed. "Do you see how all these radiating lines lead toward the small tunnels?"

Alvin had noticed that besides the great arches of the moving ways there were innumerable smaller tunnels leading out of the chamber—tunnels that sloped downward instead of up.

Rorden continued without waiting for a reply.

"It was a magnificent system. People would come down the moving ways, select the place they wished to visit, and then follow the appropriate line on the map."

"And what happens then?" said Alvin.

As usual, Rorden refused to speculate.

"I haven't enough information," he answered. "I wish we could read the names of those cities!" he complained, changing the subject abruptly.

Alvin had wandered away and was circumnavigating the central pillar. Presently his voice came to Rorden, slightly muffled and overlaid with echoes from the walls of the chamber.

"What is it?" called Rorden, not wishing to move, because he had nearly deciphered one of the dimly visible groups of characters. But Alvin's voice was insistent, so he went to join him.

Far beneath was the other half of the great map, its faint webwork radiating toward the points of the compass. But this time not all of it was too dim to be clearly seen, for one of the lines, and one only, was brilliantly illuminated. It seemed to have no connection with the rest of the system, and pointed like a gleaming arrow to one of the downward-sloping tunnels. Near its end the line transfixed a circle of golden light, and against that circle was the single word "LYS." That was all.

For a long time Alvin and Rorden stood gazing down at that silent symbol. To Rorden it was no more than another question for his machines, but to Alvin its promise was boundless. He tried to imagine this great chamber as it had been in the ancient days, when air transport had come to an end but the cities of Earth still had commerce one with the other. He thought of the countless millions of years that had passed with the traffic steadily dwindling and the lights on the great map dying one by one, until at last only this single line remained. He wondered how long it had gleamed there among its darkened companions, waiting to guide the steps that never came, until at last Yarlan Zey had sealed the moving ways and closed Diaspar against the world.

That had been hundreds of millions of years ago. Even then, Lys must have lost touch with Diaspar. It seemed impossible that it could have survived: perhaps, after all, the map meant nothing now.

Rorden broke into his reverie at last. He seemed a little nervous and ill at ease.

"It's time we went back," he said. "I don't think we should go any further now."

Alvin recognized the undertones in his friend's voice, and did not argue with him. He was eager to go forward, but realized that it might not be wise without further preparation. Reluctantly he turned again toward the central pillar. As he walked to the opening of the shaft, the floor beneath him gradually clouded into opacity, and the gleaming enigma far below slowly faded from sight.

4

THE
WAY
BENEATH

Now that the way lay open at last before him, Alvin felt a strange reluctance to leave the familiar world of Diaspar. He began to discover that he himself was not immune from the fears he had so often derided in others.

Once or twice Rorden had tried to dissuade him, but the attempt had been halfhearted. It would have seemed strange to a man of the Dawn Ages that neither Alvin nor Rorden saw any danger in what they were doing. For millions of years the world had held nothing that could threaten man, and even Alvin could not imagine types of human beings greatly different from those he knew in Diaspar. That he might be detained against his will was a thought wholly inconceivable to him. At the worst, he could only fail to discover anything.

Three days later, they stood once more in the deserted chamber of the moving ways. Beneath their feet the arrow of light still pointed to Lys—and now they were ready to follow it.

As they stepped into the tunnel, they felt the familiar tug of the peristaltic field and in a moment were being swept effortlessly into the depths. The journey lasted scarcely half a minute: when it ended they were standing at one end of a long, narrow chamber in the form of a half-cylinder. At the far end, two dimly lit tunnels stretched away toward infinity.

Men of almost every civilization that had existed since the Dawn would have found their surroundings completely familiar: yet to Alvin and Rorden they were a glimpse of another world. The purpose of the long, streamlined machine that lay aimed like a projectile at the far tunnel was obvious, but that made it nonetheless novel. Its upper portion was transparent, and looking through the walls Alvin could see rows of luxuriously appointed seats. There was no sign of any entrance, and the whole machine was floating about a foot above a single metal rod that stretched away into the distance, disappearing in one of the tunnels. A few yards away another rod led to the second tunnel, but no machine floated above it. Alvin knew, as surely as if he had been told, that somewhere beneath unknown, far-off Lys, that second machine was waiting in another such chamber as this.

"Well," said Rorden, rather lamely, "are you ready?"

Alvin nodded.

"I wish you'd come," he said—and at once regretted it when he saw the disquiet on the other's face. Rorden was the closest friend he had ever possessed, but he could never break through the barriers that surrounded all his race.

"I'll be back within six hours," Alvin promised, speaking with difficulty, for there was a mysterious tightness in his throat. "Don't bother to wait for me. If I get back early I'll call you—there must be some communicators around here."

It was all very casual and matter-of-fact, Alvin told himself. Yet he could not help jumping when the walls of the machine faded and the beautifully designed interior lay open before his eyes.

Rorden was speaking, rather quickly and jerkily.

"You'll have no difficulty in controlling the machine," he said. "Did you see how it obeyed that thought of mine? I should get inside quickly in case the time delay is fixed."

Alvin stepped aboard, placing his belongings on the nearest seat. He turned to face Rorden, who was standing in the barely visible frame of the doorway. For a moment there was a strained silence while each waited for the other to speak.

The decision was made for them. There was a faint flicker of translucence, and the walls of the machine had closed again. Even as Rorden began to wave farewell, the long cylinder started to ease itself forward. Before it had entered the tunnel, it was already moving faster than a man could run.

Slowly Rorden made his way back to the chamber of the moving ways with its great central pillar. Sunlight was streaming down the open shaft as he rose to the surface. When he emerged again into the Tomb of Yarlan Zey, he was disconcerted, though not surprised, to find a group of curious onlookers gathered around him.

"There's no need to be alarmed," he said gravely. "Someone has to do this every few thousand years, though it hardly seems necessary. The foundations of the city are perfectly stable—they haven't shifted a micron since the Park was built."

He walked briskly away, and as he left the tomb a quick backward glance showed him that the spectators were already dispersing. Rorden knew his fellow citizens well enough to be sure that they would think no more about the incident.

*　　*　　*

Alvin settled back on the upholstery and let his eyes wander round the interior of the machine. For the first time he noticed the indicator board that formed part of the forward wall. It carried the simple message:

LYS

35 MINUTES

Even as he watched, the number changed to "34." That at least was useful information, though because he had no idea of the machine's speed it told him nothing about the length of the journey. The walls of the tunnel were one continual blur of gray, and the only sensation of movement was a very slight vibration he would never have noticed had he not been expecting it.

Diaspar must be many miles away by now, and above him would be the desert with its shifting sand dunes. Perhaps at this very moment he was racing beneath the broken hills he had watched as a child from the Tower of Loranne.

His thoughts came back to Lys, as they had done continually for the past few days. He wondered if it still existed, and once again assured himself that not otherwise would the machine be carrying him there. What sort of city would it be? Somehow the strongest effort of his imagination could only picture another and smaller version of Diaspar.

Suddenly there was a distinct change in the vibration of the machine. It was slowing down—there was no question of that. The time must have passed more quickly than he had thought: somewhat surprised, Alvin glanced at the indicator.

LYS

23 MINUTES

Feeling very puzzled, and a little worried, he pressed his face against the side of the machine. His speed was still blurring the walls of the tunnel into a featureless gray, yet now from time to time he could catch a glimpse of markings that disappeared almost as quickly as they came. And at each appearance, they seemed to remain in his field of vision for a little longer.

Then, without any warning, the walls of the tunnel were snatched away on either side. The machine was passing, still at a very great speed, through an enormous empty space, far larger even than the chamber of the moving ways.

Peering in wonder through the transparent walls, Alvin could glimpse beneath him an intricate network of guiding rods, rods that crossed and crisscrossed to disappear into a maze of tunnels on either side. Overhead, a long row of artificial suns flooded the chamber with light, and silhouetted against the glare he could just make out the frameworks of great carrying machines. The light was so brilliant that it pained the eyes, and Alvin knew that this place had not been intended for Man. What it was intended for became clear a moment later, when his vehicle flashed past row after row of cylinders, lying motionless above their guide-rails. They were larger than the machine in which he was traveling, and Alvin realized that they must be freight transporters. Around them were grouped incomprehensible machines, all silent and stilled.

Almost as quickly as it had appeared, the vast and lonely chamber vanished behind him. Its passing left a feeling of awe in Alvin's mind: for the first time he really understood the meaning of that great, darkened map below Diaspar. The world was more full of wonder than he had ever dreamed.

Alvin glanced again at the indicator. It had not changed: he had taken less than a minute to flash through the great cavern. The machine was accelerating again, although there was still no sense of motion. But on either side the tunnel walls were flowing past at a speed he could not even guess.

It seemed an age before that indefinable change of vibration occurred again. Now the indicator was reading:

LYS

1 MINUTE

and that minute was the longest Alvin had ever known. More and more slowly moved the machine: this was no mere slackening of its speed. It was coming to rest at last.

Smoothly and silently the long cylinder slid out of the tunnel into a cavern that might have been the twin of the one beneath Diaspar. For a moment Alvin was too excited to see anything clearly. His thoughts were jumbled and he could not even control the door, which opened and closed several times before he pulled himself together. As he jumped out of the machine, he caught a last glimpse of the indicator. Its wording had changed and there was something about its message that was very reassuring:

DIASPAR

35 MINUTES

5

THE
LAND
OF LYS

It had been as simple as that. No one could have guessed that he had
made a journey as fateful as any in the history of Man.

As he began to search for a way out of the chamber, Alvin found
the first sign that he was in a civilization very different from the one
he had left. The way to the surface clearly lay through a low, wide
tunnel at one end of the cavern—and leading up through the tunnel
was a flight of steps. Such a thing was almost unknown in Diaspar.
The machines disliked stairways, and the architects of the city had
built ramps or sloping corridors wherever there was a change of
level. Was it possible that there were no machines in Lys? The idea
was so fantastic that Alvin dismissed it at once.

The stairway was very short, and ended against doors that opened
at his approach. As they closed silently behind him, Alvin found
himself in a large cubical room which appeared to have no other exit.
He stood for a moment, a little puzzled, and then began to examine
the opposite wall. As he did so, the doors through which he had
entered opened once more. Feeling somewhat annoyed, Alvin left
the room again—to find himself looking along a vaulted corridor
rising slowly to an archway that framed a semicircle of sky. He
realized that he must have risen many hundreds of feet, but there
had been no sensation of movement. Then he hurried forward up
the slope to the sunlit opening.

He was standing at the brow of a low hill, and for an instant it seemed as if he were once again in the central park of Diaspar. Yet if this was indeed a park, it was too enormous for his mind to grasp. The city he had expected to see was nowhere visible. As far as the eye could reach there was nothing but forest and grass-covered plains.

Then Alvin lifted his eyes to the horizon, and there above the trees, sweeping from right to left in a great arc that encircled the world, was a line of stone which would have dwarfed the mightiest giants of Diaspar. It was so far away that its details were blurred by sheer distance, but there was something about its outlines that Alvin found puzzling. Then his eyes became at last accustomed to the scale of that colossal landscape, and he knew that those far-off walls had not been built by Man.

Time had not conquered everything: Earth still possessed mountains of which she could be proud.

For a long time Alvin stood at the mouth of the tunnel, growing slowly accustomed to the strange world in which he had found himself. Search as he might, nowhere could he see any trace of human life. Yet the road that led down the hillside seemed well kept: he could do no more than accept its guidance.

At the foot of the hill, the road disappeared between great trees that almost hid the sun. As Alvin walked into their shadow, a strange medley of scents and sounds greeted him. The rustle of the wind among the leaves he had known before, but underlying that were a thousand vague noises that conveyed nothing to his mind. Unknown odors assailed him, smells that had been lost even to the memory of his race. The warmth, the profusion of scent and color, and the unseen presences of a million living things, smote him with almost physical violence.

He came upon the lake without any warning. The trees to the right suddenly ended, and before him was a great expanse of water, dotted with tiny islands. Never in his life had Alvin seen such quantities of the precious liquid: he walked to the edge of the lake and let the warm water trickle through his fingers.

The great silver fish that suddenly forced its way through the underwater reeds was the first nonhuman creature he had ever seen.

As it hung in nothingness, its fins a faint blur of motion, Alvin wondered why its shape was so startlingly familiar. Then he remembered the records that Jeserac had shown him as a child, and knew where he had seen those graceful lines before. Logic told him that the resemblance could only be accidental—but logic was wrong.

All through the ages, artists had been inspired by the urgent beauty of the great ships driving from world to world. Once there had been craftsmen who had worked, not with crumbling metal or decaying stone, but with the most imperishable of all materials—flesh and blood and bone. Though they and all their race had been utterly forgotten, one of their dreams had survived the ruins of cities and the wreck of continents.

At last Alvin broke the lake's enchantment and continued along the winding road. The forest closed around him once more, but only for a little while. Presently the road ended, in a great clearing perhaps half a mile wide and twice as long. Now Alvin understood why he had seen no trace of man before.

The clearing was full of low, two-storied buildings, colored in soft shades that rested the eye even in the full glare of the sun. They were of clean, straightforward design, but several were built in a complex architectural style involving the use of fluted columns and gracefully fretted stone. In these buildings, which seemed of great age, the immeasurably ancient device of the pointed arch was used.

As he walked slowly toward the village, Alvin was still struggling to grasp his new surroundings. Nothing was familiar: even the air had changed. And the tall, golden-haired people coming and going among the buildings were very different from the languid citizens of Diaspar.

Alvin had almost reached the village when he saw a group of men coming purposefully toward him. He felt a sudden, heady excitement and the blood pounded in his veins. For an instant there flashed through his mind the memory of all Man's fateful meetings with other races. Then he came to a halt, a few feet away from the others.

They seemed surprised to see him, yet not as surprised as he had expected. Very quickly he understood why. The leader of the party extended his hand in the ancient gesture of friendship.

"We thought it best to meet you here," he said. "Our home is very different from Diaspar, and the walk from the terminus gives visitors a chance to become—acclimatized."

Alvin accepted the outstretched hand, but for a moment was too astonished to reply.

"You knew I was coming?" he gasped at length.

"We always know when the carriers start to move. But we did not expect anyone so young. How did you discover the way?"

"I think we'd better restrain our curiosity, Gerane. Seranis is waiting."

The name "Seranis" was preceded by a word unfamiliar to Alvin. It somehow conveyed an impression of affection, tempered with respect.

Gerane agreed with the speaker and the party began to move into the village. As they walked, Alvin studied the faces around him. They appeared kindly and intelligent: there were none of the signs of boredom, mental strife, and faded brilliance he might have found in a similar group in his own city. To his broadening mind, it seemed that they possessed all that his own people had lost. When they smiled, which was often, they revealed lines of ivory teeth—the pearls that Man had lost and won and lost again in the long story of evolution.

The people of the village watched with frank curiosity as Alvin followed his guides. He was amazed to see not a few children, who stared at him in grave surprise. No other single fact brought home to him so vividly his remoteness from the world he knew. Diaspar had paid, and paid in full, the price of immortality.

The party halted before the largest building Alvin had yet seen. It stood in the center of the village and from a flagpole on its small circular tower a green pennant floated along the breeze.

All but Gerane dropped behind as he entered the building. Inside it was quiet and cool: sunlight filtering through the translucent walls lit up everything with a soft, restful glow. The floor was smooth and resilient, inlaid with fine mosaics. On the walls, an artist of great ability and power had depicted a set of forest scenes. Mingled with these paintings were other murals which conveyed nothing to Alvin's mind, yet were attractive and pleasant to look upon. Let into the wall was something he had hardly expected to see—a visiphone receiver, beautifully made, its idle screen filled with a maze of shifting colors.

They walked together up a short circular stairway that led them out on the flat roof of the building. From this point, the entire village was visible, and Alvin could see that it consisted of about a hundred buildings. In the distance the trees opened out into wide meadows: he could see animals in some of the fields but his knowledge of biology was too slight for him to guess at their nature.

In the shadow of the tower, two people were sitting together at a desk, watching him intently. As they rose to greet him, Alvin saw that one was a stately, very handsome woman whose golden hair was shot through with wisps of gray. This, he knew, must be Seranis. Looking into her eyes, he could sense that wisdom and depth of experience he felt when he was with Rorden and, more rarely, with Jeserac.

The other was a boy a little older than himself in appearance, and Alvin needed no second glance to tell that Seranis must be his mother. The clear-cut features were the same, though the eyes held only friendliness and not that almost frightening wisdom. The hair too was different—black instead of gold—but no one could have mistaken the relationship between them.

Feeling a little overawed, Alvin turned to his guide for support—but Gerane had already vanished. Then Seranis smiled, and his nervousness left him.

"Welcome to Lys," she said. "I am Seranis, and this is my son Theon, who will one day take my place. You are the youngest who has ever come to us from Diaspar: tell me how you found the way."

Haltingly at first, and then with increasing confidence, Alvin began his story. Theon followed his words eagerly, for Diaspar must have been as strange to him as Lys had been to Alvin. But Seranis, Alvin could see, knew all that he was telling her, and once or twice she asked questions which showed that in some things at least her knowledge went beyond his own. When he had finished there was silence for a while. Then Seranis looked at him and said quietly:

"Why did you come to Lys?"

"I wanted to explore the world," he replied. "Everyone told me that there was only desert beyond the city, but I wanted to make sure for myself."

The eyes of Seranis were full of sympathy and even sadness when she spoke again:

"And was that the only reason?"

Alvin hesitated. When he answered, it was not the explorer who spoke, but the boy not long removed from childhood.

"No," he said slowly, "it wasn't the only reason, though I did not know until now. I was lonely."

"Lonely? In Diaspar?"

"Yes," said Alvin. "I am the only child to be born there for seven thousand years."

Those wonderful eyes were still upon him, and, looking into their depths, Alvin had the sudden conviction that Seranis could read his mind. Even as the thought came, he saw an expression of amused surprise pass across her face—and knew that his guess had been correct. Once both men and machines had possessed this power, and the unchanging machines could still read their masters' orders. But in Diaspar, Man himself had lost the gift he had given to his slaves.

Rather quickly, Seranis broke into his thoughts.

"If you are looking for life," she said, "your search has ended. Apart from Diaspar, there is only desert beyond our mountains."

It was strange that Alvin, who had questioned accepted beliefs so often before, did not doubt the words of Seranis. His only reaction was one of sadness that all his teaching had been so nearly true.

"Tell me something about Lys," he asked. "Why have you been cut off from Diaspar for so long, when you know all about us?"

Seranis smiled at his question.

"It's not easy to answer that in a few words, but I'll do my best.

"Because you have lived in Diaspar all your life, you have come to think of Man as a city dweller. That isn't true, Alvin. Since the machines gave us freedom, there has always been a rivalry between two different types of civilization. In the Dawn Ages there were thousands of cities, but a large part of mankind lived in communities like this village of ours.

"We have no records of the founding of Lys, but we know that our remote ancestors disliked city life intensely and would have nothing to do with it. In spite of swift and universal transport, they kept themselves largely apart from the rest of the world and developed an independent culture which was one of the highest the race had ever known.

"Through the ages, as we advanced along our different roads, the gulf between Lys and the cities widened. It was bridged only in times of great crisis: we know that when the Moon was falling, its destruction was planned and carried out by the scientists of Lys. So too was the defense of Earth against the Invaders, whom we held at the Battle of Shalmirane.

"That great ordeal exhausted mankind: one by one the cities died and the desert rolled over them. As the population fell, humanity began the migration which was to make Diaspar the last and greatest of all cities.

"Most of these changes passed us by, but we had our own battle to fight—the battle against the desert. The natural barrier of the mountains was not enough, and many thousands of years passed before we had made our land secure. Far beneath Lys are machines which will give us water as long as the world remains, for the old oceans are still there, miles down in the Earth's crust.

"That, very briefly, is our history. You will see that even in the Dawn Ages we had little to do with the cities, though their people often came into our land. We never hindered them, for many of our greatest men came from Outside, but when the cities were dying we did not wish to be involved in their downfall. With the ending of air transport, there was only one way into Lys—the carrier system from Diaspar. Four hundred million years ago that was closed by mutual agreement. But we have remembered Diaspar, and I do not know why you have forgotten Lys."

Seranis smiled, a little wryly.

"Diaspar has surprised us. We expected it to go the way of all other cities, but instead it has achieved a stable culture that may last as long as Earth. It is not a culture we admire, yet we are glad that those who wish to escape have been able to do so. More than you might think have made the journey, and they have almost all been outstanding men."

Alvin wondered how Seranis could be so sure of her facts, and he did not approve of her attitude toward Diaspar. He had hardly "escaped"—yet, after all, the word was not altogether inaccurate.

Somewhere a great bell vibrated with a throbbing boom that ebbed and died in the still air. Six times it struck, and as the last note faded into silence Alvin realized that the sun was low on the horizon and the eastern sky already held a hint of night.

"I must return to Diaspar," he said. "Rorden is expecting me."

6

THE
LAST
NIAGARA

Seranis looked at him thoughtfully for a moment. Then she rose to her feet and walked toward the stairway.

"Please wait a little while," she said. "I have some business to settle, and Theon, I know, has many questions to ask you."

Then she was gone, and for the next few minutes Theon's barrage of questions drove any other thoughts from his mind. Theon had heard of Diaspar, and had seen records of the cities as they were at the height of their glory, but he could not imagine how their inhabitants had passed their lives. Alvin was amused at many of his questions—until he realized that his own ignorance of Lys was even greater.

Seranis was gone for many minutes, but her expression revealed nothing when she returned.

"We have been talking about you," she said—not explaining who "we" might be: "If you return to Diaspar, the whole city will know about us. Whatever promises you make, the secret could not be kept."

A feeling of slight panic began to creep over Alvin. Seranis must have known his thoughts, for her next words were more reassuring.

"We don't wish to keep you here against your wishes, but if you return to Diaspar we will have to erase all memories of Lys from your mind." She hesitated for a moment. "This has never arisen before: all your predecessors came here to stay."

Alvin was thinking deeply.

"Why should it matter," he said, "if Diaspar does learn about you again? Surely it would be a good thing for both our peoples?"

Seranis looked displeased.

"We don't think so," she said. "If the gates were opened, our land would be flooded with sensation-seekers and the idly curious. As things are now, only the best of your people have ever reached us."

Alvin felt himself becoming steadily more annoyed, but he realized that Seranis' attitude was quite unconscious.

"That isn't true," he said flatly. "Very few of us would ever leave Diaspar. If you let me return, it would make no difference to Lys."

"The decision is not in my hands," replied Seranis, "but I will put it to the Council when it meets three days from now. Until then, you can remain as my guest, and Theon will show you our country."

"I would like to do that," said Alvin, "but Rorden will be waiting for me. He knows where I am, and if I don't come back at once anything may happen."

Seranis smiled slightly.

"We have given that a good deal of thought," she admitted. "There are men working on the problem now—we will see if they have been successful."

Alvin was annoyed at having overlooked something so obvious. He knew that the engineers of the past had built for eternity—his journey to Lys had been proof of that. Yet it gave him a shock when the chromatic mist on the visiphone screen drifted aside to show the familiar outlines of Rorden's room.

The Keeper of the Records looked up from his desk. His eyes lit when he saw Alvin.

"I never expected you to be early," he said—though there was relief behind the jesting words. "Shall I come to meet you?"

While Alvin hesitated, Seranis stepped forward, and Rorden saw her for the first time. His eyes widened and he leaned forward as if to obtain a better view. The movement was as useless as it was automatic: Man had not lost it even though he had used the visi-phone for a thousand million years.

Seranis laid her hands on Alvin's shoulders and began to speak. When she had finished Rorden was silent for a while.

"I'll do my best," he said at length. "As I understand it, the choice lies between sending Alvin back to us under some form of hypno-sis—or returning him with no restrictions at all. But I think I can promise that even if it learns of your existence, Diaspar will con-tinue to ignore you."

"We won't overlook that possibility," Seranis replied with just a trace of pique. Rorden detected it instantly.

"And what of myself?" he asked with a smile. "I know as much as Alvin now."

"Alvin is a boy," replied Seranis quickly, "but you hold an office as ancient as Diaspar. This is not the first time Lys has spoken to the Keeper of the Records, and he has never betrayed our secret yet."

Rorden made no comment: he merely said: "How long do you wish to keep Alvin?"

"At the most, five days. The Council meets three days from now."

"Very well: for the next five days, then, Alvin is extremely busy on some historical research with me. This won't be the first time it's happened—but we'll have to be out if Jeserac calls."

Alvin laughed.

"Poor Jeserac! I seem to spend half my life hiding things from him."

"You've been much less successful than you think," replied Rorden, somewhat disconcertingly. "However I don't expect any trouble. But don't be longer than the five days!"

When the picture had faded, Rorden sat for a while staring at the darkened screen. He had always suspected that the world communi-cation network might still be in existence, but the keys to its opera-tion had been lost and the billions of circuits could never be traced by Man. It was strange to reflect that even now visiphones might be called vainly in the lost cities. Perhaps the time would come when his own receiver would do the same, and there would be no Keeper of the Records to answer the unknown caller. . . .

He began to feel afraid. The immensity of what had happened was slowly dawning upon him. Until now, Rorden had given little thought to the consequences of his actions. His own historical interests, and his affection for Alvin, had been sufficient motive for what he had done. Though he had humored and encouraged Alvin, he had never believed that anything like this could possibly happen.

Despite the centuries between them, the boy's will had always been more powerful than his own. It was too late to do anything about it now: Rorden felt that events were sweeping him along toward a climax utterly beyond his control.

* * *

"Is all this really necessary," said Alvin, "if we are only going to be away for two or three days? After all, we have a synthesizer with us."

"Probably not," answered Theon, throwing the last food containers into the little ground-car. "It may seem an odd custom, but we've never synthesized some of our finest foods—we like to watch them grow. Also, we may meet other parties and it's polite to exchange food with them. Nearly every district has some special product, and Airlee is famous for its peaches. That's why I've put so many aboard—not because I think that even you can eat them all."

Alvin threw his half-eaten peach at Theon, who dodged quickly aside. There came a flicker of iridescence and a faint whirring of invisible wings as Krif descended upon the fruit and began to sip its juices.

Alvin was still not quite used to Krif. It was hard for him to realize that the great insect, though it would come when called and would—sometimes—obey simple orders, was almost wholly mindless. Life, to Alvin, had always been synonymous with intelligence—sometimes intelligence far higher than Man's.

When Krif was resting, his six gauzy wings lay folded along his body, which glittered through them like a jeweled scepter. He was at once the highest and the most beautiful form of insect life the world had ever known—the latest and perhaps last of all the creatures Man had chosen for his companionship.

Lys was full of such surprises, as Alvin was continually learning.

Its inconspicuous but efficient transport system had been equally unexpected. The ground-car apparently worked on the same principle as the machine that had brought him from Diaspar, for it floated in the air a few inches above the turf. Although there was no sign of any guide-rail, Theon told him that the cars could only run on predetermined tracks. All the centers of population were thus linked together, but the remoter parts of the country could only be reached on foot. This state of affairs seemed altogether extraordinary to Alvin, but Theon appeared to think it was an excellent idea.

Apparently Theon had been planning this expedition for a considerable time. Natural history was his chief passion—Krif was only the most spectacular of his many pets—and he hoped to find new types of insect life in the uninhabited southern parts of Lys.

The project had filled Alvin with enthusiasm when he heard of it. He looked forward to seeing more of this wonderful country, and although Theon's interests lay in a different field of knowledge from his own, he felt a kinship for his new companion which not even Rorden had ever awakened.

Theon intended to travel south as far as the machine could go—little more than an hour's journey from Airlee—and the rest of the way they would have to go on foot. Not realizing the full implications of this, Alvin had no objections.

To Alvin, the journey across Lys had a dreamlike unreality. Silent as a ghost, the machine slid across rolling plains and wound its way through forests, never deviating from its invisible track. It traveled perhaps a dozen times as fast as a man could comfortably walk. No one in Lys was ever in a greater hurry than that.

Many times they passed through villages, some larger than Airlee but most built along very similar lines. Alvin was interested to notice subtle but significant differences in clothing and even physical appearance as they moved from one community to the next. The civilization of Lys was composed of hundreds of distinct cultures, each contributing some special talent toward the whole.

Once or twice Theon stopped to speak to friends, but the pauses were brief and it was still morning when the little machine came to rest among the foothills of a heavily wooded mountain. It was not a very large mountain, but Alvin thought it the most tremendous thing he had ever seen.

"This is where we start to walk," said Theon cheerfully, throwing equipment out of the car. "We can't ride any farther."

As he fumbled with the straps that were to convert him into a beast of burden, Alvin looked doubtfully at the great mass of rock before them.

"It's a long way around, isn't it?" he queried.

"We aren't going around," replied Theon. "I want to get to the top before nightfall."

Alvin said nothing. He had been rather afraid of this.

*　　*　　*

"From here," said Theon, raising his voice to make it heard above the thunder of the waterfall, "you can see the whole of Lys."

Alvin could well believe him. To the north lay mile upon mile of forest, broken here and there by clearings and fields and the wandering threads of a hundred rivers. Hidden somewhere in that vast panorama was the village of Airlee. Alvin fancied that he could catch a glimpse of the great lake, but decided that his eyes had tricked him. Still farther north, trees and clearings alike were lost in a mottled carpet of green, rucked here and there by lines of hills. And beyond that, at the very edge of vision, the mountains that hemmed Lys from the desert lay like a bank of distant clouds.

East and west the view was little different, but to the south the mountains seemed only a few miles away. Alvin could see them very clearly, and he realized that they were far higher than the little peak on which he was standing.

But more wonderful even than these was the waterfall. From the sheer face of the mountain a mighty ribbon of water leaped far out over the valley, curving down through space toward the rocks a thousand feet below. There it was lost in a shimmering mist of spray, while up from the depths rose a ceaseless, drumming thunder that reverberated in hollow echoes from the mountain walls. And quivering in the air above the base of the fall was the last rainbow left on Earth.

For long minutes the two boys lay on the edge of the cliff, gazing at this last Niagara and the unknown land beyond. It was very different from the country they had left, for in some indefinable way it seemed deserted and empty. Man had not lived here for many, many years.

Theon answered his friend's unspoken question.

"Once the whole of Lys was inhabited," he said, "but that was a very long time ago. Only the animals live here now."

Indeed, there was nowhere any sign of human life—none of the clearings or well-disciplined rivers that spoke of Man's presence. Only in one spot was there any indication that he had ever lived here, for many miles away a solitary white ruin jutted above the forest roof like a broken fang. Elsewhere, the jungle had returned to its own.

7

THE
CRATER
DWELLER

It was night when Alvin awoke, the utter night of mountain country, terrifying in its intensity. Something had disturbed him, some whisper of sound that had crept into his mind above the dull thunder of the falls. He sat up in the darkness, straining his eyes across the hidden land, while with indrawn breath he listened to the drumming roar of the falls and the faint but unending rustle of life in the trees around him.

Nothing was visible. The starlight was too dim to reveal the miles of country that lay hundreds of feet below: only a jagged line of darker night eclipsing the stars told of the mountains on the southern horizon. In the darkness beside him Alvin heard his friend roll over and sit up.

"What is it?" came a whispered voice.

"I thought I heard a noise."

"What sort of noise?"

"I don't know. Perhaps I was only dreaming."

There was silence while two pairs of eyes peered out into the mystery of night. Then, suddenly, Theon caught his friend's arm.

"Look!" he whispered.

Far to the south glowed a solitary point of light, too low in the heavens to be a star. It was a brilliant white, tinged with violet, and as the boys watched it began to climb the spectrum of intensity, until the eye could no longer bear to look upon it. Then it exploded—and it seemed as if lightning had struck below the rim of the world. For an instant the mountains, and the great land they guarded, were etched with fire against the darkness of the night. Ages later came the echo of a mighty explosion, and in the forest below a sudden wind stirred among the trees. It died away swiftly, and one by one the routed stars crept back into the sky.

For the first time in his life, Alvin knew that fear of the unknown that had been the curse of ancient Man. It was a feeling so strange that for a while he could not even give it a name. In the moment of recognition it vanished and he became himself again.

"What is it?" he whispered.

There was a pause so long that he repeated the question.

"I'm trying to remember," said Theon, and was silent for a while. A little later he spoke again.

"That must be Shalmirane," he said simply.

"Shalmirane! Does it still exist?"

"I'd almost forgotten," replied Theon, "but it's coming back now. Mother once told me that the fortress lies in those mountains. Of course, it's been in ruins for ages, but someone is still supposed to live there."

Shalmirane! To these children of two races, so widely differing in culture and history, this was indeed a name of magic. In all the long story of Earth there had been no greater epic than the defense of Shalmirane against an invader who had conquered all the Universe.

Presently Theon's voice came again out of the darkness.

"The people of the south could tell us more. We will ask them on our way back."

Alvin scarcely heard him: he was deep in his own thoughts, remembering stories that Rorden had told him long ago. The Battle of Shalmirane lay at the dawn of recorded history: it marked the end of the legendary ages of Man's conquests, and the beginning of his long decline. In Shalmirane, if anywhere on Earth, lay the answers to the problems that had tormented him for so many years. But the southern mountains were very far away.

Theon must have shared something of his mother's powers, for he said quietly:

"If we started at dawn, we could reach the fortress by nightfall. I've never been there, but I think I could find the way."

Alvin thought it over. He was tired, his feet were sore, and the muscles of his thighs were aching with the unaccustomed effort. It was very tempting to leave it until another time. Yet there might be no other time, and there was even the possibility that the actinic explosion had been a signal for help.

Beneath the dim light of the failing stars, Alvin wrestled with his thoughts and presently made his decision. Nothing had changed: the mountains resumed their watch over the sleeping land. But a turning-point in history had come and gone, and the human race was moving toward a strange new future.

The sun had just lifted above the eastern wall of Lys when they reached the outskirts of the forest. Here, Nature had returned to her own. Even Theon seemed lost among the gigantic trees that blocked the sunlight and cast pools of shadow on the jungle floor. Fortunately the river from the fall flowed south in a line too straight to be altogether natural, and by keeping to its edge they could avoid the denser undergrowth. A good deal of Theon's time was spent in controlling Krif, who disappeared occasionally into the jungle or went skimming wildly across the water. Even Alvin, to whom everything was still so new, could feel that the forest had a fascination not possessed by the smaller, more cultivated woods of northern Lys. Few trees were alike: most of them were in various stages of devolution and some had reverted through the ages almost to their original, natural forms. Many were obviously not of Earth at all—perhaps not even of the Solar System. Watching like sentinels over the lesser trees were giant sequoias, three and four hundred feet high. They had once been called the oldest things on Earth: they were still a little older than Man.

The river was widening now: ever and again it opened into small lakes, upon which tiny islands lay at anchor. There were insects here, brilliantly colored creatures swinging aimlessly to and fro over the surface of the water. Once, despite Theon's shouts, Krif darted away to join his distant cousins. He disappeared instantly in a cloud of glittering wings, and the sound of angry buzzing floated toward them. A moment later the cloud erupted and Krif came back across the water, almost too quickly for the eye to follow. Thereafter he kept very close to Theon and did not stray again.

Toward evening they caught occasional glimpses of the mountains ahead. The river that had been so faithful a guide was flowing sluggishly now, as if it too were nearing the end of its journey. But it was clear that they could not reach the mountains by nightfall: well before sunset the forest had become so dark that further progress was impossible. The great trees lay in pools of shadow, and a cold wind was sweeping through the leaves. Alvin and Theon settled down for the night beside a giant redwood whose topmost branches were still ablaze with sunlight.

When at last the hidden sun went down, the light still lingered on the dancing waters. The two boys lay in the gathering gloom, watching the river and thinking of all that they had seen. As Alvin fell asleep, he found himself wondering who last had come this way, and how long since.

The sun was high when they left the forest and stood at last before the mountain walls of Lys. Ahead of them the ground rose steeply to the sky in waves of barren rock. Here the river came to an end as spectacular as its beginning, for the ground opened in its path and it sank roaring from sight.

For a moment Theon stood looking at the whirlpool and the broken land beyond. Then he pointed to a gap in the hills.

"Shalmirane lies in that direction," he said confidently. Alvin looked at him in surprise.

"You told me you'd never been here before!"

"I haven't."

"Then how do you know the way?"

Theon looked puzzled.

"I don't know—I've never thought about it before. It must be a kind of instinct, for wherever we go in Lys we always know our way about."

Alvin found this very difficult to believe, and followed Theon with considerable skepticism. They were soon through the gap in the hills, and ahead of them now was a curious plateau with gently sloping sides. After a moment's hesitation, Theon started to climb. Alvin followed, full of doubts, and as he climbed he began to compose a little speech. If the journey proved in vain, Theon would know exactly what he thought of his unerring instinct.

As they approached the summit, the nature of the ground altered abruptly. The lower slopes had consisted of porous, volcanic stone, piled here and there in great mounds of slag. Now the surface turned suddenly to hard sheets of glass, smooth and treacherous, as if the rock had once run in molten rivers down the mountain. The rim of the plateau was almost at their feet. Theon reached it first, and a few seconds later Alvin overtook him and stood speechless at his side. For they stood on the edge, not of the plateau they had expected, but of a giant bowl half a mile deep and three miles in diameter. Ahead of them the ground plunged steeply downward, slowly leveling out at the bottom of the valley and rising again, more and more steeply, to the opposite rim. And although it now lay in the full glare of the sun, the whole of that great depression was ebon black. What material formed the crater the boys could not even guess, but it was black as the rock of a world that had never known a sun. Nor was that all, for lying beneath their feet and ringing the entire crater was a seamless band of metal, some hundred feet wide, tarnished by immeasurable age but still showing no slightest trace of corrosion.

As their eyes grew accustomed to the unearthly scene, Alvin and Theon realized that the blackness of the bowl was not as absolute as they had thought. Here and there, so fugitive that they could only see them indirectly, tiny explosions of light were flickering in the ebon walls. They came at random, vanishing as soon as they were born, like the reflections of stars on a broken sea.

"It's wonderful!" gasped Alvin. "But what is it?"

"It looks like a reflector of some kind."

"I can't imagine that black stuff reflecting anything."

"It's only black to our eyes, remember. We don't know what radiations they used."

"But surely there's more than this! Where *is* the fortress?"

Theon pointed to the level floor of the crater, where lay what Alvin had taken to be a pile of jumbled stones. As he looked again, he could make out an almost obliterated plan behind the grouping of the great blocks. Yes, there lay the ruins of once mighty buildings, overthrown by time.

For the first few hundred yards the walls were too smooth and steep for the boys to stand upright, but after a little while they reached the gentler slopes and could walk without difficulty. Near the bottom of the crater the smooth ebony of its surface ended in a thin layer of soil, which the winds of Lys must have brought here through the ages.

A quarter of a mile away, titanic blocks of stone were piled one upon the other, like the discarded toys of an infant giant. Here, a section of a massive wall was still recognizable: there, two carven obelisks marked what had once been a mighty entrance. Everywhere grew mosses and creeping plants, and tiny stunted trees. Even the wind was hushed.

So Alvin and Theon came to the ruins of Shalmirane. Against those walls, if legend spoke the truth, forces that could shatter a world to dust had flamed and thundered and been utterly defeated. Once these peaceful skies had blazed with fires torn from the hearts of suns, and the mountains of Lys must have quailed like living things beneath the fury of their masters.

No one had ever captured Shalmirane. But now the fortress, the impregnable fortress, had fallen at last—captured and destroyed by the patient tendrils of the ivy and the generations of blindly burrowing worms.

Overawed by its majesty, the two boys walked in silence toward the colossal wreck. They passed into the shadow of a broken wall, and entered a canyon where the mountains of stone had split asunder.

Before them lay a great amphitheater, crossed and crisscrossed with long mounds of rubble that must mark the graves of buried machines. Once the whole of this tremendous space had been vaulted, but the roof had long since collapsed. Yet life must still exist somewhere among the desolation, and Alvin realized that even this ruin might be no more than superficial. The greater part of the fortress would be far underground, beyond the reach of Time.

"We'll have to turn back by noon," said Theon, "so we mustn't stay too long. It would be quicker if we separated. I'll take the eastern half and you can explore this side. Shout if you find anything interesting—but don't get too far away."

So they separated, and Alvin began to climb over the rubble, skirting the larger mounds of stone. Near the center of the arena he came suddenly upon a small circular clearing, thirty or forty feet in diameter. It had been covered with weeds, but they were now blackened and charred by tremendous heat, so that they crumbled to ashes at his approach. At the center of the clearing stood a tripod supporting a polished metal bowl, not unlike a model of Shalmirane itself. It was capable of movement in altitude and azimuth, and a spiral of some transparent substance was supported at its center. Beneath the reflector was welded a black box from which a thin cable wandered away across the ground.

It was clear to Alvin that this machine must be the source of the light, and he began to trace the cable. It was not too easy to follow the slender wire, which had a habit of diving into crevasses and reappearing at unexpected places. Finally he lost it altogether and shouted to Theon to come and help him.

He was crawling under an overhanging rock when a shadow suddenly blotted out the light. Thinking it was his friend, Alvin emerged from the cave and turned to speak. But the words died abruptly on his lips.

Hanging in the air before him was a great dark eye surrounded by a satellite system of smaller eyes. That, at least, was Alvin's first impression: then he realized that he was looking at a complex machine—and it was looking at him.

Alvin broke the painful silence. All his life he had given orders to machines, and although he had never seen anything quite like this creature, he decided that it was probably intelligent.

"Reverse," he ordered experimentally.

Nothing happened.

"Go. Come. Rise. Fall. Advance."

None of the conventional control thought produced any effect. The machine remained contemptuously inactive.

Alvin took a step forward, and the eyes retreated in some haste. Unfortunately their angle of vision seemed somewhat limited, for the machine came to a sudden halt against Theon, who for the last minute had been an interested spectator. With a perfectly human ejaculation, the whole apparatus shot twenty feet into the air, revealing a set of tentacles and jointed limbs clustering round a stubby cylindrical body.

"Come down—we won't hurt you!" called Theon, rubbing a bruise on his chest.

Something spoke: not the passionless, crystal-clear voice of a machine, but the quavering speech of a very old and very tired man.

"Who are you? What are you doing in Shalmirane?"

"My name is Theon, and this is my friend, Alvin of Loronei. We're exploring Southern Lys."

There was a brief pause. When the machine spoke again its voice held an unmistakable note of petulance and annoyance.

"Why can't you leave me in peace? You know how often I've asked to be left alone!"

Theon, usually good-natured, bristled visibly.

"We're from Airlee, and we don't know anything about Shalmirane."

"Besides," Alvin added reproachfully, "we saw your light and thought you might be signaling for help."

It was strange to hear so human a sigh from the coldly impersonal machine.

"A million times I must have signaled now, and all I have ever done is to draw the inquisitive from Lys. But I see you meant no harm. Follow me."

The machine floated slowly away over the broken stones, coming to rest before a dark opening in the ruined wall of the amphitheater. In the shadow of the cave something moved, and a human figure stepped into the sunlight. He was the first physically old man Alvin had ever seen. His head was completely bald, but a thick growth of pure white hair covered all the lower part of his face. A cloak of woven glass was thrown carelessly over his shoulders, and on either side of him floated two more of the strange, many-eyed machines.

8

THE
STORY
OF
SHALMIRANE

There was a brief silence while each side regarded the other. Then
the old man spoke—and the three machines echoed his voice for a
moment until something switched them off.

"So you are from the North, and your people have already forgotten Shalmirane."

"Oh, no!" said Theon quickly. "We've not forgotten. But we
weren't sure that anyone still lived here, and we certainly didn't
know that you wished to be left alone."

The old man did not reply. Moving with a slowness that was
painful to watch, he hobbled through the doorway and disappeared,
the three machines floating silently after him. Alvin and Theon
looked at each other in surprise: they did not like to follow, but their
dismissal—if dismissal it was—had certainly been brusque. They
were starting to argue the matter when one of the machines suddenly reappeared.

"What are you waiting for? Come along!" it ordered. Then it
vanished again.

Alvin shrugged his shoulders.

"We appear to be invited. I think our host's a little eccentric, but
he seems friendly."

From the opening in the wall a wide spiral stairway led down-

ward for a score of feet. It ended in a small circular room from which
several corridors radiated. However, there was no possibility of
confusion, for all the passages save one were blocked with debris.

Alvin and Theon had walked only a few yards when they found
themselves in a large and incredibly untidy room cluttered up with
a bewildering variety of objects. One end of the chamber was occupied by domestic machines—synthesizers, destructors, cleaning
equipment and the like—which one normally expected to be concealed from sight in the walls and floors. Around these were piled
cases of thought records and transcribers, forming pyramids that
reached almost to the ceiling. The whole room was uncomfortably
hot owing to the presence of a dozen perpetual fires scattered about
the floor. Attracted by the radiation, Krif flew toward the nearest
of the metal spheres, stretched his wings luxuriously before it, and
fell instantly asleep.

It was a little while before the boys noticed the old man and his
three machines waiting for them in a small open space which reminded Alvin of a clearing in the jungle. There was a certain
amount of furniture here—a table and three comfortable couches.
One of these was old and shabby, but the others were so conspicu-
ously new that Alvin was certain they had been created in the last
few minutes. Even as he watched, the familiar warning glow of the
synthesizer field flickered over the table and their host waved silently toward it. They thanked him formally and began to sample
the food and drink that had suddenly appeared. Alvin realized that
he had grown a little tired of the unvarying output from Theon's
portable synthesizer and the change was very welcome.

They ate in silence for a while, stealing a glance now and then
at the old man. He seemed sunk in his own thoughts and appeared
to have forgotten them completely—but as soon as they had finished
he looked up and began to question them. When Alvin explained
that he was a native not of Lys but of Diaspar, the old fellow showed
no particular surprise. Theon did his best to deal with the queries:
for one who disliked visitors, their host seemed very anxious to have
news of the outer world. Alvin quickly decided that his earlier
attitude must have been a pose.

Presently he fell silent again. The two boys waited with what patience they could: he had told them nothing of himself or what he was doing in Shalmirane. The light-signal that had drawn them there was still as great a mystery as ever, yet they did not care to ask outright for an explanation. So they sat in an uncomfortable silence, their eyes wandering round that amazing room, finding something new and unexpected at every moment. At last Alvin broke into the old man's reverie.

"We must leave soon," he remarked.

It was not a statement so much as a hint. The wrinkled face turned toward him but the eyes were still very far away. Then the tired, infinitely ancient voice began to speak. It was so quiet and low that at first they could scarcely hear: after a while the old man must have noticed their difficulty, for of a sudden the three machines began once more to echo his words.

Much that he told them they could never understand. Sometimes he used words which were unknown to them: at other times he spoke as if repeating sentences or whole speeches that others must have written long ago. But the main outlines of the story were clear, and they took Alvin's thoughts back to the ages of which he had dreamed since his childhood.

The tale began, like so many others, amid the chaos of the Transition Centuries, when the Invaders had gone but the world was still recovering from its wounds. At that time there appeared in Lys the man who later became known as the Master. He was accompanied by three strange machines—the very ones that were watching them now—which acted as his servants and also possessed definite intelligences of their own. His origin was a secret he never disclosed, and eventually it was assumed that he had come from space, somehow penetrating the blockade of the Invaders. Far away among the stars there might still be islands of humanity which the tide of war had not yet engulfed.

The Master and his machines possessed powers which the world had lost, and around him he gathered a group of men to whom he taught much wisdom. His personality must have been a very striking one, and Alvin could understand dimly the magnetism that had drawn so many to him. From the dying cities, men had come to Lys in their thousands, seeking rest and peace of mind after the years of confusion. Here among the forests and mountains, listening to the Master's words, they found that peace at last.

At the close of his long life the Master had asked his friends to carry him out into the open so that he could watch the stars. He had waited, his strength waning, until the culmination of the Seven Suns. As he died the resolution with which he had kept his secret so long seemed to weaken, and he babbled many things of which countless books were to be written in future ages. Again and again he spoke of the "Great Ones" who had now left the world but who would surely one day return, and he charged his followers to remain to greet them when they came. Those were his last rational words. He was never again conscious of his surroundings, but just before the end he uttered one phrase that revealed part at least of his secret and had come down the ages to haunt the minds of all who heard it: *"It is lovely to watch the colored shadows on the planets of eternal light."* Then he died.

So arose the religion of the Great Ones, for a religion it now became. At the Master's death many of his followers broke away, but others remained faithful to his teachings, which they slowly elaborated through the ages. At first they believed that the Great Ones, whoever they were, would soon return to Earth, but that hope faded with the passing centuries. Yet the brotherhood continued, gathering new members from the lands around, and slowly its strength and power increased until it dominated the whole of Southern Lys.

It was very hard for Alvin to follow the old man's narrative. The words were used so strangely that he could not tell what was truth and what legend—if, indeed, the story held any truth at all. He had only a confused picture of generations of fanatical men, waiting for some great event which they did not understand to take place at some unknown future date.

The Great Ones never returned. Slowly the power of the movement failed, and the people of Lys drove it into the mountains until it took refuge in Shalmirane. Even then the watchers did not lose their faith, but swore that however long the wait they would be

ready when the Great Ones came. Long ago men had learned one
way of defying Time, and the knowledge had survived when so
much else had been lost. Leaving only a few of their number to
watch over Shalmirane, the rest went into the dreamless sleep of
suspended animation.

Their numbers slowly falling as sleepers were awakened to replace those who died, the watchers kept faith with the Master. From
his dying words it seemed certain that the Great Ones lived on the
planets of the Seven Suns, and in later years attempts were made to
send signals into space. Long ago the signaling had become no more
than a meaningless ritual, and now the story was nearing its end. In
a very little while only the three machines would be left in Shalmirane, watching over the bones of the men who had come here so
long ago in a cause that they alone could understand.

The thin voice died away, and Alvin's thoughts returned to the
world he knew. More than ever before the extent of his ignorance
overwhelmed him. A tiny fragment of the past had been illuminated
for a little while, but now the darkness had closed over it again.

The world's history was a mass of such disconnected threads, and
none could say which were important and which were trivial. This
fantastic tale of the Master and the Great Ones might be no more
than another of the countless legends that had somehow survived
from the civilizations of the Dawn. Yet the three machines were
unlike any that Alvin had ever seen. He could not dismiss the whole
story, as he had been tempted to do, as a fable built of self-delusion
upon a foundation of madness.

"These machines," he said abruptly, "surely they've been questioned? If they came to Earth with the Master, they must still know
his secrets."

The old man smiled wearily.

"*They* know," he said, "but they will never speak. The Master saw
to that before he handed over the control. We have tried times
without number, but it is useless."

Alvin understood. He thought of the Associator in Diaspar, and
the seals that Alaine had set upon its knowledge. Even those seals,
he now believed, could be broken in time, and the Master Associator

must be infinitely more complex than these little robot slaves. He wondered if Rorden, so skilled in unraveling the secrets of the past, would be able to wrest the machines' hidden knowledge from them. But Rorden was far away and would never leave Diaspar.

Quite suddenly the plan came fully fledged into his mind. Only a very young person could ever have thought of it, and it taxed even Alvin's self-confidence to the utmost. Yet once the decision had been made, he moved with determination and much cunning to his goal.

He pointed toward the three machines.

"Are they identical?" he asked. "I mean, can each one do everything, or are they specialized in any way?"

The old man looked a little puzzled.

"I've never thought about it," he said. "When I need anything, I ask whichever is most convenient. I don't think there is any difference between them."

"There can't be a great deal of work for them to do now," Alvin continued innocently. Theon looked a little startled, but Alvin carefully avoided his friend's eye. The old man answered guilelessly.

"No," he replied sadly, "Shalmirane is very different now."

Alvin paused in sympathy: then, very quickly, he began to talk. At first the old man did not seem to grasp his proposal: later, when comprehension came, Alvin gave him no time to interrupt. He spoke of the great storehouses of knowledge in Diaspar, and the skill with which the Keeper of the Records could use them. Although the Master's machines had withstood all other inquirers, they might yield their secrets to Rorden's probing. It would be a tragedy if the chance were missed, for it would never come again.

Flushed with the heat of his own oratory, Alvin ended his appeal:

"Lend me one of the machines—you do not need them all. Order it to obey my controls and I will take it to Diaspar. I promise to return it whether the experiment succeeds or not."

Even Theon looked shocked, and an expression of horror came across the old man's face.

"I couldn't do that!" he gasped.

"But why not? Think what we might learn!"

The other shook his head firmly.

"It would be against the Master's wishes."

Alvin was disappointed—disappointed and annoyed. But he was young, and his opponent was old and tired. He began again to go through the argument, shifting his attack and pressing home each advantage. And now for the first time Theon saw an Alvin he had never suspected before—a personality, indeed, that was surprising Alvin himself. The men of the Dawn Ages had never let obstacles bar their way for long, and the willpower and determination that had been their heritage had not yet passed from Earth. Even as a child Alvin had withstood the forces seeking to mold him to the pattern of Diaspar. He was older now, and against him was not the greatest city of the world but only an aged man who sought nothing but rest, and would surely find that soon.

9

MASTER
OF THE
ROBOT

The evening was far advanced when the ground-car slid silently through the last screen of trees and came to rest in the great glade of Airlee. The argument, which had lasted most of the journey, had now died away and peace had been restored. They had never quite come to blows, perhaps because the odds were so unequal. Theon had only Krif to support him, but Alvin could call upon the argus-eyed, many-tentacled machine he still regarded so lovingly.

Theon had not minced his words. He had called his friend a bully and had told Alvin that he should be thoroughly ashamed of himself. But Alvin had only laughed and continued to play with his new toy. He did not know how the transfer had been effected, but he alone could control the robot now, could speak with its voice and see through its eyes. It would obey no one else in all the world.

Seranis was waiting for them in a surprising room which seemed to have no ceiling, though Alvin knew that there was a floor above it. She seemed to be worried and more uncertain than he had ever seen her before, and he remembered the choice that might soon lie before him. Until now he had almost forgotten it. He had believed that, somehow, the Council would resolve the difficulty. Now he realized that its decision might not be to his liking.

The voice of Seranis was troubled when she began to speak, and from her occasional pauses Alvin could tell that she was repeating words already rehearsed.

"Alvin," she began, "there are many things I did not tell you before, but which you must learn now if you are to understand our actions.

"You know one of the reasons for the isolation of our two races. The fear of the Invaders, that dark shadow in the depths of every human mind, turned your people against the world and made them lose themselves in their own dreams. Here in Lys that fear has never been so great, although we bore the burden of the attack. We had a better reason for our actions, and what we did, we did with open eyes.

"Long ago, Alvin, men sought immortality and at last achieved it. They forgot that a world which had banished death must also banish birth. The power to extend his life indefinitely brought contentment to the individual but stagnation to the race. You once told me that you were the only child to be born in Diaspar for seven thousand years—but you have seen how many children we have here in Airlee. Ages ago we sacrificed our immortality, but Diaspar still follows the false dream. That is why our ways parted—*and why they must never meet again.*"

Although the words had been more than half-expected, the blow seemed none the less for its anticipation. Yet Alvin refused to admit the failure of all his plans—half-formed though they were—and only part of his brain was listening to Seranis now. He understood and noted all her words, but the conscious portion of his mind was retracing the road to Diaspar, trying to imagine every obstacle that could be placed in his way.

Seranis was clearly unhappy. Her voice was almost pleading as it spoke, and Alvin knew that she was talking not only to him but to her own son. Theon was watching his mother with a concern which held at least more than a trace of accusation.

"We have no desire to keep you here in Lys against your will, but you must surely realize what it would mean if our people mixed. Between our culture and yours is a gulf as great as any that ever separated Earth from its ancient colonies. Think of this one fact,

Alvin. You and Theon are now of nearly the same age—*but he and I will have been dead for centuries when you are still a boy.*"

The room was very quiet, so quiet that Alvin could hear the strange, plaintive cries of unknown beasts in the fields beyond the village. Presently he said, almost in a whisper:

"What do you want me to do?"

"I have put your case to the Council, as I promised, but the law cannot be altered. You may remain here and become one of us, or you may return to Diaspar. If you do that, we must first reshape the patterns of your mind so that you have no recollection of Lys and never again attempt to reach us."

"And Rorden? He would still know the truth, even if I had forgotten everything."

"We have spoken with Rorden many times since you left. He recognizes the wisdom of our actions."

In that dark moment, it seemed to Alvin that the whole world had turned against him. Though there was much truth in the words of Seranis, he would not recognize it: he saw only the wreck of his still dimly conceived plans, the end of the search for knowledge that had now become the most important thing in his life.

Seranis must have read his thoughts.

"I'll leave you for a while," she said. "But remember—whatever your choice, there can be no turning back."

Theon followed her to the door but Alvin called after him. He looked inquiringly at his mother, who hesitated for a moment and then nodded her head. The door closed silently behind her, and Alvin knew that it would not open again without her consent.

Alvin waited until his racing thoughts were once more under control.

"Theon," he began, "you'll help me, won't you?"

The other nodded but did not speak.

"Then tell me this—how could your people stop me if I tried to run away?"

"That would be easy. If you tried to escape, my mother would take control of your mind. Later, when you became one of us, you would not wish to leave."

"I see. Can you tell if she is watching my mind now?"

Theon looked worried, but his protest answered the question.

"I shouldn't tell you that!"

"But you will, won't you?"

The two boys looked silently at each other for many seconds. Then Theon smiled.

"You can't bully me, you know. Whatever you're planning—and *I* can't read your mind—as soon as you tried to put it into action Mother would take over. She won't let you out of her sight until everything has been settled."

"I know that," said Alvin, "but is she looking into my mind at this moment?"

The other hesitated.

"No, she isn't," he said at last. "I think she's deliberately leaving you alone, so that her thoughts won't influence you."

That was all he needed to know. For the first time Alvin dared to turn his mind upon the only plan that offered any hope. He was far too stubborn to accept either of the alternatives Seranis had offered him, and even if there had been nothing at stake he would have bitterly resisted any attempt to override his will.

In a little while Seranis would return. He could do nothing until they were in the open again, and even then Seranis would be able to control his actions if he attempted to run away. And apart from that, he was sure that many of the villagers could intercept him long before he reached safety.

Very carefully, checking every detail, he traced out the only road that could lead him back to Diaspar on the terms he wished.

Theon warned him when Seranis was near, and he quickly turned his thoughts into harmless channels. It had never been easy for her to understand his mind, and now it seemed to Seranis as if she were far out in space, looking down upon a world veiled with impenetrable clouds. Sometimes there would be a rift in the covering, and for an instant she could catch a glimpse of what lay beneath. She wondered what Alvin was trying to hide from her. For a moment she dipped into her son's mind, but Theon knew nothing of the other's plans. She thought again of the precautions she had taken: as a man may flex his muscles before some great exertion, she ran through the compulsion patterns she might have to use. But there was no trace of her preoccupation as she smiled at Alvin from the doorway.

"Well," she asked, "have you made up your mind?"

Alvin's reply seemed frank enough.

"Yes," he said. "I will return to Diaspar."

"I'm sorry, and I know that Theon will miss you. But perhaps it's best: this is not your world and you must think of your own people."

With a gesture of supreme confidence, she stood aside to let Alvin pass through the door.

"The men who can obliterate your memory of Lys are waiting for you: we expected this decision."

Alvin was glad to see that Seranis was leading him in the direction he wished to go. She did not look back to see if he was following. Her every movement told him: "Try and run away if you like—my mind is more powerful than yours." And he knew that it was perfectly true.

They were clear of the houses when he stopped and turned to his friend.

"Good-bye, Theon," he said, holding out his hands. "Thank you for all you've done. One day I'll be back."

Seranis had stopped and was watching him intently. He smiled at her even while he measured the twenty feet of ground between them.

"I know that you're doing this against your will," he said, "and I don't blame you for it. I don't like what I'm doing, either." (That was not true, he thought. Already he was beginning to enjoy himself.) He glanced quickly around: no one was approaching and Seranis had not moved. She was still watching him, probably trying to probe into his mind. He talked quickly to prevent even the outlines of his plan from shaping among his thoughts.

"I do not believe you are right," he said, so unconscious of his intellectual arrogance that Seranis could not resist a smile. "It's wrong for Lys and Diaspar to remain apart forever: one day they may need each other desperately. So I am going home with all that I have learned—*and I do not think that you can stop me.*"

He waited no longer, and it was just as well. Seranis never moved, but instantly he felt his body slipping from his control. The power that had brushed aside his own will was even greater than he had expected, and he realized that many hidden minds must be aiding Seranis. Helplessly he began to walk back toward the center of the village, and for an awful moment he thought his plans had failed.

Then there came a flash of steel and crystal, and the metal arms closed swiftly around him. His body fought against them, as he had known it must do, but his struggles were useless. The ground fell away beneath him and he caught a glimpse of Theon, frozen by surprise with a foolish smile upon his face.

The robot was carrying him a dozen feet above the ground, much faster than a man could run. It took Seranis only a moment to understand his ruse, and his struggles died away as she relaxed her control. But she was not defeated yet, and presently there happened that which Alvin had feared and done his best to counteract.

There were now two separate entities fighting inside his mind, and one of them was pleading with the robot, begging it to set him down again. The real Alvin waited, breathlessly, resisting only a little against forces he knew he could not hope to fight. He had gambled: there was no way of telling beforehand if the machine could understand orders as complex as those he had given it. Under no circumstances, he had told the robot, must it obey any further commands of his until he was safely inside Diaspar. Those were the orders. If they were obeyed, Alvin had placed his fate beyond the reach of human interference.

Never hesitating, the machine raced on along the path he had so carefully mapped out for it. A part of him was still pleading angrily to be released, but he knew now that he was safe. And presently Seranis understood that too, for the forces inside his brain ceased to war with one another. Once more he was at peace, as ages ago an earlier wanderer had been when, lashed to the mast of his ship, he had heard the song of the Sirens die away across the wine-dark sea.

10

DUPLICATION

"So you see," concluded Alvin, "it will carry out any orders I give, no matter how complicated they are. But as soon as I ask questions about its origin, it simply freezes like that."

The machine was hanging motionless above the Master Associator, its crystal lenses glittering in the silver light like a cluster of jewels. Of all the robots which Rorden had ever met, this was by far the most baffling: he was now almost sure that it had been built by no human civilization. With such eternal servants it was not surprising that the Master's personality had survived the ages.

Alvin's return had raised so many problems that Rorden was almost afraid to think of them. He himself had not found it easy to accept the existence of Lys, with all its implications, and he wondered how Diaspar would react to the new knowledge. Probably the city's immense inertia would cushion the shock: it might well be years before all of its inhabitants fully appreciated the fact that they were no longer alone on Earth.

But if Alvin had his way, things would move much more quickly than that. There were times when Rorden regretted the failure of Seranis' plans—everything would have been so much simpler. The problem was immense, and for the second occasion in his life Rorden could not decide what course of action was correct. He wondered how many more times Alvin would present him with such dilemmas, and smiled a little wryly at the thought. For it would make no difference either way: Alvin would do exactly as he pleased.

As yet, not more than a dozen people outside Alvin's own family knew the truth. His parents, with whom he now had so little in common and often did not see for weeks, still seemed to think that he had merely been to some outlying part of the city. Jeserac had been the only person to react strongly: once the initial shock had worn off he had engaged in a violent quarrel with Rorden, and the two were no longer on speaking terms. Alvin, who had seen this coming for some time, could guess the details but to his disappointment neither of the protagonists would talk about the matter.

Later, there would be time enough to see that Diaspar realized the truth: for the moment Alvin was too interested in the robot to worry about much else. He felt, and his belief was now shared by Rorden, that the tale he had heard in Shalmirane was only a fragment of some far greater story. At first Rorden had been skeptical, and he still believed the "Great Ones" to be no more than another of the world's countless religious myths. Only the robot knew the truth, and it had defied a million centuries of questioning as it was defying them now.

"The trouble is," said Rorden, "that there are no longer any engineers left in the world."

Alvin looked puzzled: although contact with the Keeper of the Records had greatly enlarged his vocabulary, there were thousands of archaic words he did not understand.

"An engineer," explained Rorden, "was a man who designed and built machines. It's impossible for us to imagine an age without robots—but every machine in the world had to be invented at one time or other, and until the Master Robots were built they needed men to look after them. Once the machines could care for themselves, human engineers were no longer required. I think that's a fairly accurate account, though of course it's mostly guesswork. Every machine we possess existed at the beginning of our history, and many had disappeared long before it started."

"Such as flyers and spaceships," interjected Alvin.

"Yes," agreed Rorden, "as well as the great communicators that could reach the stars. All these things vanished when they were no longer needed."

Alvin shook his head.

"I still believe," he said, "that the disappearance of the spaceships can't be explained as easily as that. But to get back to the machine—do you think that the Master Robots could help us? I've never seen one, of course, and don't know much about them."

"Help us? In what way?"

"I'm not quite sure," said Alvin vaguely. "Perhaps they could force it to obey *all* my orders. They repair robots, don't they? I suppose that would be a kind of repair. . . ."

His voice faded away as if he had failed even to convince himself.

Rorden smiled: the idea was too ingenuous for him to put much faith in it. However, this piece of historical research was the first of all Alvin's schemes for which he himself could share much enthusiasm, and he could think of no better plan at the moment.

He walked toward the Associator, above which the robot was still floating as if in studied indifference. As he began, almost automatically, to set up his questions on the great keyboard, he was suddenly struck by a thought so incongruous that he burst out laughing.

Alvin looked at his friend in surprise as Rorden turned toward him.

"Alvin," he said between chuckles, "I'm afraid we still have a lot to learn about machines." He laid his hand on the robot's smooth metal body. "They don't share many human feelings, you know. It wasn't really necessary for us to do all our plotting in whispers."

*   *   *

This world, Alvin knew, had not been made for Man. Under the glare of the trichromatic lights—so dazzling that they pained the eyes—the long, broad corridors seemed to stretch to infinity. Down these great passageways all the robots of Diaspar must come at the end of their patient lives, yet not once in a million years had they echoed to the sound of human feet.

It had not been difficult to locate the maps of the underground

city, the city of machines without which Diaspar could not exist. A
few hundred yards ahead the corridor would open into a circular
chamber more than a mile across, its roof supported by great columns that must also bear the unimaginable weight of Power Center.
Here, if the maps spoke the truth, the Master Robots, greatest of all
machines, kept watch over Diaspar.

The chamber was there, and it was even vaster than Alvin had
imagined—but where were the machines? He paused in wonder at
the tremendous but meaningless panorama beneath him. The corridor ended high in the wall of the chamber—surely the largest cavity
ever built by man—and on either side long ramps swept down to
the distant floor. Covering the whole of that brilliantly lit expanse
were hundreds of great white structures, so unexpected that for a
moment Alvin thought he must be looking down upon a subterranean city. The impression was startlingly vivid and it was one he
never wholly lost. Nowhere at all was the sight he had expected—
the familiar gleam of metal which since the beginning of time Man
had learned to associate with his servants.

Here was the end of an evolution almost as long as Man's. Its
beginning was lost in the mists of the Dawn Ages, when humanity
had first learned the use of power and sent its noisy engines clanking
about the world. Steam, water, wind—all had been harnessed for a
little while and then abandoned. For centuries the energy of matter
had run the world until it too had been superseded, and with each
change the old machines were forgotten and the new ones took their
place. Very slowly, over millions of years, the ideal of the perfect
machine was approached—that ideal which had once been a dream,
then a distant prospect, and at last reality:

No machine may contain any moving parts.

Here was the ultimate expression of that ideal. Its achievement
had taken Man perhaps a thousand million years, and in the hour
of his triumph he had turned his back upon the machine forever.

The robot they were seeking was not as large as many of its
companions, but Alvin and Rorden felt dwarfed when they stood
beneath it. The five tiers with their sweeping horizontal lines gave
the impression of some crouching beast, and looking from it to his

own robot Alvin thought it strange that the same word should be used for both.

Almost three feet from the ground a wide transparent panel ran the whole length of the structure. Alvin pressed his forehead against the smooth, curiously warm material and peered into the machine. At first he saw nothing: then, by shielding his eyes, he could distinguish thousands of faint points of light hanging in nothingness. They were ranged one beyond the other in a three-dimensional lattice, as strange and as meaningless to him as the stars must have been to ancient Man.

Rorden had joined him and together they stared into the brooding monster. Though they watched for many minutes, the colored lights never moved from their places and their brilliance never changed. Presently Alvin broke away from the machine and turned to his friend.

"What are they?" he asked in perplexity.

"If we could look into our own minds," said Rorden, "they would mean as little to us. The robots seem motionless because we cannot see their thoughts."

For the first time Alvin looked at the long avenue of titans with some trace of understanding. All his life he had accepted without question the miracle of the synthesizers, the machines which age after age produced in an unending stream all that the city needed. Thousands of times he had watched that act of creation, never thinking that somewhere must exist the prototype of that which he had seen come into the world.

As a human mind may dwell for a little while upon a single thought, so these greater brains could grasp and hold forever the most intricate ideas. The patterns of all created things were frozen in these eternal minds, needing only the touch of a human will to make them reality.

The world had gone very far since, hour upon hour, the first cavemen had patiently chipped their arrowheads and knives from the stubborn stone.

"Our problem now," said Rorden, "is to get into touch with the creature. It can never have any direct knowledge of Man, for there's no way in which we can affect its consciousness. If my information's correct, there must be an interpreting machine somewhere. That was a type of robot that could convert human instructions into commands that the Master Robots could understand. They were pure intelligence with little memory—just as this is a tremendous memory with relatively little intelligence."

Alvin considered for a moment. Then he pointed to his own robot.

"Why not use it?" he suggested. "Robots have very literal minds. It won't refuse to pass on our instructions, for I doubt if the Master ever thought of this situation."

Rorden laughed.

"I don't suppose he did, but since there's a machine specially built for the job I think it would be best to use it."

The Interpreter was a very small affair, a horseshoe-shaped construction built around a vision screen which lit up as they approached. Of all the machines in this great cavern, it was the only one which had shown any cognizance of Man, and its greeting seemed a little contemptuous. For on the screen appeared the words:

STATE YOUR PROBLEM
PLEASE THINK CLEARLY

Ignoring the implied insult, Alvin began his story. Though he had communicated with robots by speech or thought on countless occasions, he felt now that he was addressing something more than a machine. Lifeless though this creature was, it possessed an intelligence that might be greater than his own. It was a strange thought, but it did not depress him unduly—for of what use was intelligence alone?

His words died away and the silence of that overpowering place crowded back upon them. For a moment the screen was filled with swirling mist, then the haze cleared and the machine replied:

REPAIR IMPOSSIBLE
ROBOT UNKNOWN TYPE

Alvin turned to his friend with a gesture of disappointment, but even as he did so the lettering changed and a second message appeared:

DUPLICATION COMPLETED
PLEASE CHECK AND SIGN

Simultaneously a red light began to flash above a horizontal panel Alvin had not noticed before, and was certain he must have seen had it been there earlier. Puzzled, he bent toward it, but a shout from Rorden made him look around in surprise. The other was pointing toward the great Master Robot, where Alvin had left his own machine a few minutes before.

It had not moved, but it had multiplied. Hanging in the air beside it was a duplicate so exact that Alvin could not tell which was the original and which the copy.

"I was watching when it happened," said Rorden excitedly. "It suddenly seemed to extend, as if millions of replicas had come into existence on either side of it. Then all the images except these two disappeared. The one on the right is the original."

11

THE
COUNCIL

Alvin was still stunned, but slowly he began to realize what must have happened. His robot could not be forced to disobey the orders given it so long ago, but a duplicate could be made with all its knowledge yet with the unbreakable memory-block removed. Beautiful though the solution was, the mind would be unwise to dwell too long upon the powers that made it possible.

The robots moved as one when Alvin called them toward him. Speaking his commands, as he often did for Rorden's benefit, he asked again the question he had put so many times in different forms.

"Can you tell me how your first master reached Shalmirane?"

Rorden wished his mind could intercept the soundless replies, of which he had never been able to catch even a fragment. But this time there was little need, for the glad smile that spread across Alvin's face was sufficient answer.

The boy looked at him triumphantly.

"Number One is just the same," he said, "but Two is willing to talk."

"I think we should wait until we're home again before we begin to ask questions," said Rorden, practical as ever. "We'll need the Associators and Recorders when we start."

Impatient though he was, Alvin had to admit the wisdom of the advice. As he turned to go, Rorden smiled at his eagerness and said quietly:

"Haven't you forgotten something?"

The red light on the Interpreter was still flashing, and its message still glowed on the screen.

PLEASE CHECK AND SIGN

Alvin walked to the machine and examined the panel above which the light was blinking. Set in it was a window of some almost invisible substance, supporting a stylus which passed vertically through it. The point of the stylus rested on a sheet of white material which already bore several signatures and dates. The last of them was almost fifty thousand years ago, and Alvin recognized the name as that of a recent President of the Council. Above it only two other names were visible, neither of which meant anything to him or to Rorden. Nor was this very surprising, for they had been written twenty-three and fifty-seven million years before.

Alvin could see no purpose for this ritual, but he knew that he could never fathom the workings of the minds that had built this place. With a slight feeling of unreality he grasped the stylus and began to write his name. The instrument seemed completely free to move in the horizontal plane, for in that direction the window offered no more resistance than the wall of a soap bubble. Yet his full strength was incapable of moving it vertically: he knew, because he tried.

Carefully he wrote the date and released the stylus. It moved slowly back across the sheet to its original position—and the panel with its winking light was gone.

As Alvin walked away, he wondered why his predecessors had come here and what they had sought from the machine. No doubt, thousands or millions of years in the future, other men would look into that panel and ask themselves: "Who was Alvin of Loronei?" *Or would they?* Perhaps they would exclaim instead: "Look! Here's Alvin's signature!"

The thought was not untypical of him in his present mood, but he knew better than to share it with his friend.

At the entrance to the corridor they looked back across the cave, and the illusion was stronger than ever. Lying beneath them was a dead city of strange white buildings, a city bleached by the fierce light not meant for human eyes. Dead it might be, for it had never lived, but Alvin knew that when Diaspar had passed away these machines would still be here, never turning their minds from the thoughts greater men than he had given them long ago.

They spoke little on the way back through the streets of Diaspar, streets bathed with sunlight which seemed pale and wan after the glare of the machine city. Each in his own way was thinking of the knowledge that would soon be his, and neither had any regard for the beauty of the great towers drifting past, or the curious glances of their fellow citizens.

It was strange, thought Alvin, how everything that had happened to him led up to this moment. He knew well enough that men were makers of their own destinies, yet since he had met Rorden events seemed to have moved automatically toward a predetermined goal. Alaine's message—Lys—Shalmirane—at every stage he might have turned aside with unseeing eyes, but something had led him on. It was pleasant to pretend that Fate had favored him, but his rational mind knew better. Any man might have found the path his footsteps had traced, and countless times in the past ages others must have gone almost as far. He was simply the first to be lucky.

The first to be lucky. The words echoed mockingly in his ears as they stepped through the door of Rorden's chamber. Quietly waiting for them, with hands folded patiently across his lap, was a man wearing a curious garb unlike any that Alvin had ever seen before. He glanced inquiringly at Rorden, and was instantly shocked by the pallor of his friend's face. Then he knew who the visitor was.

He rose as they entered and made a stiff, formal bow. Without a word he handed a small cylinder to Rorden, who took it woodenly and broke the seal. The almost unheard-of rarity of a written message made the silent exchange doubly impressive. When he had finished Rorden returned the cylinder with another slight bow, at which, in spite of his anxiety, Alvin could not resist a smile.

Rorden appeared to have recovered himself quickly, for when he spoke his voice was perfectly normal.

"It seems that the Council would like a word with us, Alvin. I'm afraid we've kept it waiting."

Alvin had guessed as much. The crisis had come sooner—much sooner—than he had expected. He was not, he told himself, afraid of the Council, but the interruption was maddening. His eyes strayed involuntarily to the robots.

"You'll have to leave them behind," said Rorden firmly.

Their eyes met and clashed. Then Alvin glanced at the Messenger.

"Very well," he said quietly.

The party was very silent on its way to the Council Chamber. Alvin was marshaling the arguments he had never properly thought out, believing they would not be needed for many years. He was far more annoyed than alarmed, and he felt angry at himself for being so unprepared.

They waited only a few minutes in the anteroom, but it was long enough for Alvin to wonder why, if he was unafraid, his legs felt so curiously weak. Then the great doors contracted, and they walked toward the twenty men gathered around their famous table.

This, Alvin knew, was the first Council Meeting in his lifetime, and he felt a little flattered as he noticed that there were no empty seats. He had never known that Jeserac was a Council member. At his startled gaze the old man shifted uneasily in his chair and gave him a furtive smile as if to say: "This is nothing to do with me." Most of the other faces Alvin had expected, and only two were quite unknown to him.

The President began to address them in a friendly voice, and looking at the familiar faces before him, Alvin could see no great cause for Rorden's alarm. His confidence began to return: Rorden, he decided, was something of a coward. In that he did his friend less than justice, for although courage had never been one of Rorden's most conspicuous qualities, his worry concerned his ancient office almost as much as himself. Never in history had a Keeper of the Records been relieved of his position: Rorden was very anxious not to create a precedent.

In the few minutes since he had entered the Council Chamber, Alvin's plans had undergone a remarkable change. The speech he had so carefully rehearsed was forgotten: the fine phrases he had been practicing were reluctantly discarded. To his support now had come his most treacherous ally—that sense of the ridiculous which had always made it impossible for him to take very seriously even the most solemn occasions. The Council might meet once in a thousand years: it might control the destinies of Diaspar—but those who sat upon it were only tired old men. Alvin knew Jeserac, and he did not believe that the others would be very different. He felt a disconcerting pity for them and suddenly remembered the words Seranis had spoken to him in Lys: "Ages ago we sacrificed our immortality, but Diaspar still follows the false dream." That in truth these men had done, and he did not believe it had brought them happiness.

So when at the President's invitation Alvin began to describe his journey to Lys, he was to all appearances no more than a boy who had by chance stumbled on a discovery he thought of little importance. There was no hint of any plan or deeper purpose: only natural curiosity had led him out of Diaspar. It might have happened to anyone, yet he contrived to give the impression that he expected a little praise for his cleverness. Of Shalmirane and the robots, he said nothing at all.

It was quite a good performance, though Alvin was the only person who could fully appreciate it. The Council as a whole seemed favorably impressed, but Jeserac wore an expression in which relief struggled with incredulity. At Rorden, Alvin dared not look.

When he had quite finished, there was a brief silence while the Council considered his statement. Then the President spoke again:

"We fully appreciate," he said, choosing his words with obvious care, "that you had the best of motives in what you did. However, you have created a somewhat difficult situation for us. Are you quite sure that your discovery was accidental, and that no one, shall we say, *influenced* you in any way?" His eyes wandered thoughtfully toward Rorden.

For the last time, Alvin yielded to the mischievous promptings of his mind.

"I wouldn't say that," he replied, after an appearance of considerable thought. There was a sudden quickening of interest among the Council members, and Rorden stirred uneasily by his side. Alvin gave his audience a smile that lacked nothing of candor, and added quickly in a guileless voice:

"I'm sure I owe a great deal to my tutor."

At this unexpected and singularly misleading compliment, all eyes were turned upon Jeserac, who became a deep red, started to speak, and then thought better of it. There was an awkward silence until the President stepped into the breach.

"Thank you," he said hastily. "You will remain here while we consider your statement."

There was an audible sigh of relief from Rorden—and that was the last sound Alvin heard for some time. A blanket of silence had descended upon him, and although he could see the Council arguing heatedly, not a word of its deliberations reached him. It was amusing at first, but the spectacle soon became tedious and he was glad when the silence lifted again.

"We have come to the conclusion," said the President, "that there has been an unfortunate mishap for which no one can be held responsible—although we consider that the Keeper of the Records should have informed us sooner of what was happening. However, it is perhaps as well that this dangerous discovery has been made, for we can now take suitable steps to prevent its recurrence. We will deal ourselves with the transport system you have located, and you"—turning to Rorden for the first time—"will ensure that all references to Lys are removed from the Records."

There was a murmur of applause and expressions of satisfaction spread across the faces of the councillors. A difficult situation had been speedily dealt with, they had avoided the unpleasant necessity of reprimanding Rorden, and now they could go their ways again feeling that they, the chief citizens of Diaspar, had done their duty. With reasonably good fortune it might be centuries before the need arose again.

Even Rorden, disappointed though he was for Alvin's sake as well as his own, felt relieved at the outcome. Things might have been very much worse—

A voice he had never heard before cut into his reverie and froze the councillors in their seats, the complacent smiles slowly ebbing from their faces.

"And precisely why are you going to close the way to Lys?"

It was some time before Rorden's mind, unwilling to recognize disaster, would admit that it was Alvin who spoke.

The success of his subterfuge had given Alvin only a moment's satisfaction. Throughout the President's address his anger had been steadily rising as he realized that, despite all his cleverness, his plans were to be thwarted. The feelings he had known in Lys when Seranis had presented her ultimatum came back with redoubled strength. He had won that contest, and the taste of power was still sweet.

This time he had no robot to help him, and he did not know what the outcome would be. But he no longer had any fear of these foolish old men who thought themselves the rulers of Diaspar. He had seen the real rulers of the city, and had spoken to them in the grave silence of their brilliant, buried world. So in his anger and arrogance, Alvin threw away his disguise and the councillors looked in vain for the artless boy who had addressed them a little while ago.

"Why are you going to close the way to Lys?"

There was silence in the Council Room, but the lips of Jeserac twisted into a slow, secret smile. This Alvin was new to him, but it was less alien than the one who had spoken before.

The President chose at first to ignore the challenge. Perhaps he could not bring himself to believe that it was more than an innocent question, however violently it had been expressed.

"That is a matter of high policy which we cannot discuss here," he said pompously, "but Diaspar cannot risk contamination with other cultures." He gave Alvin a benevolent but slightly worried smile.

"It's rather strange," said Alvin coldly, "that in Lys I was told exactly the same thing about Diaspar." He was glad to see the start of annoyance, but gave his audience no time to reply.

"Lys," he continued, "is much larger than Diaspar and its culture is certainly not inferior. It's always known about us but has chosen not to reveal itself—as you put it, to avoid contamination. Isn't it obvious that we are *both* wrong?"

He looked expectantly along the lines of faces, but nowhere was there any understanding of his words. Suddenly his anger against these leaden-eyed old men rose to a crescendo. The blood was throbbing in his cheeks, and though his voice was steadier now it held a note of icy contempt which even the most pacific of the councillors could no longer overlook.

"Our ancestors," began Alvin, "built an empire which reached to the stars. Men came and went at will among all those worlds—and now their descendants are afraid to stir beyond the walls of their city. *Shall I tell you why?*" He paused: there was no movement at all in the great bare room.

"It is because we are afraid—afraid of something that happened at the beginning of history. I was told the truth in Lys, though I had guessed it long ago. Must we always hide like cowards in Diaspar, pretending that nothing else exists—because half a billion years ago the Invaders drove us back to Earth?"

He had put his finger on their secret fear, the fear that he had never shared and whose power he could therefore never understand. Let them do what they pleased: he had spoken the truth.

His anger drained away and he was himself again, as yet only a little alarmed at what he had done. He turned to the President in a last gesture of independence.

"Have I your permission to leave?"

Still no words were spoken, but the slight inclination of the head gave him his release. The great doors expanded before him and not until long after they had closed again did the storm break upon the Council Chamber.

The President waited until the inevitable lull. Then he turned to Jeserac.

"It seems to me," he said, "that we should hear your views first."

Jeserac examined the remark for possible traps. Then he replied: "I think that Diaspar is now losing its most outstanding brain."

"What do you mean?"

"Isn't it obvious? By now young Alvin will be halfway to the Tomb of Yarlan Zey. No, we shouldn't interfere. I shall be very sorry to lose him, though he never cared very much for me." He sighed a little. "For that matter, he never cared a great deal for anyone save Alvin of Loronei."

12

THE
SHIP

Not until an hour later was Rorden able to escape from the Council Chamber. The delay was maddening, and when he reached his rooms he knew it was too late. He paused at the entrance, wondering if Alvin had left any message, and realizing for the first time how empty the years ahead would be.

The message was there, but its contents were totally unexpected. Even when Rorden had read it several times, he was still completely baffled:

"Meet me at once in the Tower of Loranne."

Only once before had he been to the Tower of Loranne, when Alvin had dragged him there to watch the sunset. That was years ago: the experience had been unforgettable but the shadow of night sweeping across the desert had terrified him so much that he had fled, pursued by Alvin's entreaties. He had sworn that he would never go there again. . . .

Yet here he was, in that bleak chamber pierced with the horizontal ventilating shafts. There was no sign of Alvin, but when he called, the boy's voice answered at once.

"I'm on the parapet—come through the center shaft."

Rorden hesitated: there were many things he would much rather do. But a moment later he was standing beside Alvin with his back to the city and the desert stretching endlessly before him.

They looked at each other in silence for a little while. Then Alvin said, rather contritely:

"I hope I didn't get you into trouble."

Rorden was touched, and many truths he was about to utter died abruptly on his lips. Instead he replied:

"The Council was too busy arguing with itself to bother about me." He chuckled. "Jeserac was putting up quite a spirited defense when I left. I'm afraid I misjudged him."

"I'm sorry about Jeserac."

"Perhaps it was an unkind trick to play on the old man, but I think he's rather enjoying himself. After all, there was some truth in your remark. He was the first man to show you the ancient world, and he has rather a guilty conscience."

For the first time, Alvin smiled.

"It's strange," he said, "but until I lost my temper I never really understood what I wanted to do. Whether they like it or not, I'm going to break down the wall between Diaspar and Lys. But that can wait: it's no longer so important now."

Rorden felt a little alarmed.

"What do you mean?" he asked anxiously. For the first time he noticed that only one of the robots was with them on the parapet. "Where's the second machine?"

Slowly Alvin raised his arm and pointed out across the desert, towards the broken hills and the long line of sand dunes, crisscrossed like frozen waves. Far away, Rorden could see the unmistakable gleam of sunlight upon metal.

"We've been waiting for you," said Alvin quietly. "As soon as I left the Council, I went straight to the robots. Whatever happened, I was going to make sure that no one took them away before I'd learned all they could teach me. It didn't take long, for they're not very intelligent and knew less than I'd hoped. *But I have found the secret of the Master.*" He paused for a moment, then pointed again at the almost invisible robot. "Watch!"

The glistening speck soared away from the desert and came to rest perhaps a thousand feet above the ground. At first, not knowing what to expect, Rorden could see no other change. Then, scarcely believing his eyes, he saw that a cloud of dust was slowly rising from the desert.

Nothing is more terrible than movement where no movement should ever be again, but Rorden was beyond surprise or fear when the great sand dunes began to slide apart. Beneath the desert something was stirring like a giant awaking from its sleep, and presently there came to Rorden's ears the rumble of falling earth and the shriek of rock split asunder by irresistible force. Then, suddenly, a great geyser of sand erupted hundreds of feet into the air and the ground was hidden from sight.

Slowly the dust began to settle back into the jagged wound torn across the face of the desert. But Rorden and Alvin still kept their eyes fixed steadfastly upon the open sky, which a little while ago had held only the waiting robot. What Alvin was thinking, Rorden could scarcely imagine. At last he knew what the boy had meant when he had said that nothing else was very important now. The great city behind them and the greater desert before, the timidity of the Council and the pride of Lys—all these seemed trivial matters now.

The covering of earth and rock could blur but could not conceal the proud lines of the ship still ascending from the riven desert. As Rorden watched, it slowly turned toward them until it had foreshortened to a circle. Then, very leisurely, the circle started to expand.

Alvin began to speak, rather quickly, as if the time were short.

"I still do not know who the Master was, or why he came to Earth. The robot gives me the impression that he landed secretly and hid his ship where it could be easily found if he ever needed it again. In all the world there could have been no better hiding place than the Port of Diaspar, which now lies beneath those sands and which even in his age must have been utterly deserted. He may have lived for a while in Diaspar before he went to Shalmirane: the road must still have been open in those days. But he never needed the ship again, and all these ages it has been waiting out there beneath the sands."

The ship was now very close, as the controlling robot guided it toward the parapet. Rorden could see that it was about a hundred feet long and sharply pointed at both ends. There appeared to be no windows or other openings, though the thick layer of earth made it impossible to be certain.

Suddenly they were spattered with dirt as a section of the hull opened outward, and Rorden caught a glimpse of a small, bare room with a second door at its far end. The ship was now hanging only a foot away from the parapet, which it had approached very cautiously like a sensitive, living thing. Rorden had backed away from it as if he were afraid, which indeed was very near the truth. To him the ship symbolized all the terror and mystery of the Universe, and evoked as could no other object the racial fears which for so long had paralyzed the will of the human race. Looking at his friend, Alvin knew very well the thoughts that were passing through his brain. For almost the first time he realized that there were forces in men's minds over which they had no control, and that the Council was deserving of pity rather than contempt.

*   *   *

In utter silence, the ship drew away from the tower. It was strange, Rorden thought, that for the second time in his life he had said good-bye to Alvin. The little, closed world of Diaspar knew only one farewell, and that was for eternity.

The ship was now only a dark stain against the sky, and of a sudden Rorden lost it altogether. He never saw its going, but presently there echoed down from the heavens the most awe-inspiring of all the sounds that Man had ever made—the long-drawn thunder of air falling, mile after mile, into a tunnel drilled suddenly across the sky.

Even when the last echoes had died away into the desert, Rorden never moved. He was thinking of the boy who had gone—wondering, as he had so often done, if he would ever understand that aloof and baffling mind. Alvin would never grow up: to him the whole Universe was a plaything, a puzzle to be unraveled for his own amusement. In his play he had now found the ultimate, deadly toy which might wreck what was left of human civilization—but whatever the outcome, to him it would still be a game.

The sun was now low on the horizon, and a chill wind was blowing from the desert. But still Rorden waited, conquering his fears, and presently for the first time in his life he saw the stars.

* * *

Even in Diaspar, Alvin had never seen such luxury as that which lay before him when the inner door of the airlock slid aside. At first he did not understand its implications: then he began to wonder, rather uneasily, how long this tiny world might be upon its journeying between the stars. There were no controls of any kind, but the large, oval screen which completely covered the far wall would have shown that this was no ordinary room. Ranged in a half-circle before it were three low couches: the rest of the cabin was occupied by two tables, a number of most inviting chairs, and many curious devices which for the moment Alvin could not identify.

When he had made himself comfortable in front of the screen, he looked around for the robots. To his surprise, they had disappeared: then he located them, neatly stowed away in recesses high up beneath the curved ceiling. Their action had been so completely natural that Alvin knew at once the purpose for which they had been intended. He remembered the Master Robots: these were the Interpreters, without which no untrained human mind could control a machine as complex as a spaceship. They had brought the Master to Earth and then, as his servants, followed him into Lys. Now they were ready, as if the intervening eons had never been, to carry out their old duties once again.

Alvin threw them an experimental command, and the great screen shivered into life. Before him was the Tower of Loranne, curiously foreshortened and apparently lying on its side. Further trials gave him views of the sky of the city, and of great expanses of desert. The definition was brilliantly, almost unnaturally, clear, although there seemed to be no actual magnification. Alvin wondered if the ship itself moved as the picture changed, but could think of no way of discovering this. He experimented for a little while until he could obtain any view he wished: then he was ready to start.

"Take me to Lys"—the command was a simple one, but how could the ship obey it when he himself had no idea of the direction?

Alvin had never thought of this, and when it did occur to him the machine was already moving across the desert at a tremendous speed. He shrugged his shoulders, thankfully accepting what he could not understand.

It was difficult to judge the scale of the picture racing up the screen, but many miles must be passing every minute. Not far from the city the color of the ground had changed abruptly to a dull gray, and Alvin knew that he was now passing over the bed of one of the lost oceans. Once Diaspar must have been very near the sea, though there had never been any hint of this even in the most ancient records. Old though the city was, the oceans must have passed away long before its building.

Hundreds of miles later, the ground rose sharply and the desert returned. Once Alvin halted his ship above a curious pattern of intersecting lines, showing faintly through the blanket of sand. For a moment it puzzled him: then he realized that he was looking down on the ruins of some forgotten city. He did not stay for long: it was heartbreaking to think that billions of men had left no other trace of their existence save these furrows in the sand.

The smooth curve of the horizon was breaking up at last, crinkling into mountains that were beneath him almost as soon as they were glimpsed. The machine was slowing now, slowing and falling to earth in a great arc a hundred miles in length. And then below him was Lys, its forests and endless rivers forming a scene of such incomparable beauty that for a while he would go no farther. To the east, the land was shadowed and the great lakes floated upon it like pools of darker night. But toward the sunset, the waters danced and sparkled with light, throwing back toward him such colors as he had never imagined.

It was not difficult to locate Airlee—which was fortunate, for the robots could guide him no farther. Alvin had expected this, and felt glad to have discovered some limits to their powers. After a little experimenting, he brought his ship to rest on the hillside which had given him his first glimpse of Lys. It was quite easy to control the machine: he had only to indicate his general desires and the robots attended to the details. They would, he imagined, probably ignore any dangerous or impossible orders, but he did not intend to try the experiment.

Alvin was fairly certain that no one could have seen his arrival. He thought this rather important, for he had no desire to engage in mental combat with Seranis again. His plans were still somewhat vague, but he was running no risks until he had re-established friendly relations.

The discovery that the original robot would no longer obey him was a considerable shock. When he ordered it from its little compartment it refused to move but lay motionless, watching him dispassionately with its multiple eyes. To Alvin's relief, the replica obeyed him instantly, but no amount of cajoling could make the prototype carry out even the simplest action. Alvin worried for some time before the explanation of the mutiny occurred to him. For all their wonderful skills, the robots were not very intelligent, and the events of the past hour must have been too much for the unfortunate machine. One by one it had seen all the Master's orders defied—those orders which it had obeyed with such singleness of purpose for so many millions of years.

It was too late for regrets now, but Alvin was sorry he had made only a single duplicate. For the borrowed robot had become insane.

Alvin met no one on the road to Airlee. It was strange to sit in the spaceship while his field of vision moved effortlessly along the familiar path and the whispering of the forest sounded in his ears. As yet he was unable to identify himself fully with the robot, and the strain of controlling it was still considerable.

It was nearly dark when he reached Airlee, and the little houses were floating in pools of light. Alvin kept to the shadows and had almost reached Seranis' home before he was discovered. Suddenly there was an angry, high-pitched buzzing and his view was blocked by a flurry of wings. He recoiled involuntarily before the onslaught: then he realized what had happened. Krif did not approve of anything that flew without wings, and only Theon's presence had prevented him from attacking the robot on earlier occasions. Not wishing to hurt the beautiful but stupid creature, Alvin brought the robot to a halt and endured as best he could the blows that seemed to be raining upon him. Though he was sitting in comfort a mile away, he could not avoid flinching and was glad when Theon came out to investigate.

13

THE
CRISIS

At his master's approach Krif departed, still buzzing balefully. In the silence that followed Theon stood looking at the robot for a while. Then he smiled.

"I'm glad you've come back. Or are you still in Diaspar?"

Not for the first time Alvin felt a twinge of envy as he realized how much quicker Theon's mind was than his own.

"No," he said, wondering as he did so how clearly the robot echoed his voice. "I'm in Airlee, not very far away. But I'm staying here for the present."

Theon laughed heartily.

"I think that's just as well," he said. "Mother's forgiven you, but the Central Council hasn't. There's a conference going on indoors now: I have to keep out of the way."

"What are they talking about?"

"I'm not supposed to know, but they asked me all sorts of questions about you. I had to tell them what happened in Shalmirane."

"That doesn't matter very much," replied Alvin. "A good many other things have happened since then. I'd like to have a talk with this Central Council of yours."

"Oh, the whole Council isn't here, naturally. But three of its members have been making inquiries ever since you left."

Alvin smiled. He could well believe it: wherever he went now he seemed to be leaving a trail of consternation behind him.

The comfort and security of the spaceship gave him a confidence he had seldom known before, and he felt complete master of the situation as he followed Theon into the house. The door of the conference room was locked and it was some time before Theon could attract attention. Then the walls slid reluctantly apart, and Alvin moved his robot swiftly forward into the chamber.

The room was the familiar one in which he had had his last interview with Seranis. Overhead the stars were twinkling as if there were no ceiling or upper floor, and once again Alvin wondered how the illusion was achieved. The three councillors froze in their seats as he floated toward them, but only the slightest flicker of surprise crossed Seranis' face.

"Good evening," he said politely, as if this vicarious entry were the most natural thing in the world. "I've decided to come back."

Their surprise exceeded his expectations. One of the councillors, a young man with graying hair, was the first to recover.

"How did you get here?" he gasped.

Alvin thought it wise to evade the question: the way in which it was asked made him suspicious and he wondered if the underground transport system had been put out of action.

"Why, just as I did last time," he lied.

Two of the councillors looked fixedly at the third, who spread his hands in a gesture of baffled resignation. Then the young man who had addressed him before spoke again.

"Didn't you have any—difficulty?"

"None at all," said Alvin, determined to increase their confusion. He saw that he had succeeded.

"I've come back," he continued, "under my own free will, but in view of our previous disagreement I'm remaining out of sight for the moment. If I appear personally, will you promise not to try and restrict my movements again?"

No one said anything for a while and Alvin wondered what thoughts were being exchanged. Then Seranis spoke for them all.

"I imagine that there is little purpose in doing so. Diaspar must know all about us by now."

Alvin flushed slightly at the reproach in her voice.

"Yes, Diaspar knows," he replied. "And Diaspar will have nothing to do with you. It wishes to avoid contamination with an inferior culture."

It was most satisfying to watch the councillors' reactions, and even Seranis colored slightly at his words. If he could make Lys and Diaspar sufficiently annoyed with each other, Alvin realized that his problem would be more than half solved. He was learning, still unconsciously, the lost art of politics.

"But I don't want to stay out here all night," he continued. "Have I your promise?"

Seranis sighed, and a faint smile played about her lips.

"Yes," she said, "We won't attempt to control you again. Though I don't think we were very successful before."

Alvin waited until the robot had returned. Very carefully he gave the machine its instructions and made it repeat them back. Then he left the ship, and the airlock closed silently behind him.

There was a faint whisper of air but no other sound. For a moment a dark shadow blotted out the stars: then the ship was gone. Not until it had vanished did Alvin realize his miscalculation. He had forgotten that the robot's senses were very different from his own, and the night was far darker than he had expected. More than once he lost the path completely, and several times he barely avoided colliding with trees. It was blackest of all in the forest, and once something quite large came towards him through the undergrowth. There was the faintest crackling of twigs, and two emerald eyes were looking steadfastly at him from the level of his waist. He called softly, and an incredibly long tongue rasped across his hand. A moment later a powerful body rubbed affectionately against him and departed without a sound. He had no idea what it could be.

Presently the lights of the village were shining through the trees ahead, but he no longer needed their guidance, for the path beneath his feet had now become a river of dim blue fire. The moss upon which he was walking was luminous and his footprints left dark patches which slowly disappeared behind him. It was a beautiful and entrancing sight, and when Alvin stooped to pluck some of the strange moss it glowed for minutes in his cupped hands before its radiance died.

Theon was waiting for him outside the house, and for the second time he was introduced to the three councillors. He noticed with some annoyance their barely concealed surprise: not appreciating the unfair advantages it gave him, he never cared to be reminded of his youth.

They said little while he refreshed himself, and Alvin wondered what mental notes were being compared. He kept his mind as empty as he could until he had finished: then he began to talk as he had never talked before.

His theme was Diaspar. He painted the city as he had last seen it, dreaming on the breast of the desert, its towers glowing like captive rainbows against the sky. From the treasure-house of memory he recalled the songs that the poets of old had written in praise of Diaspar, and he spoke of the countless men who had burned away their lives to increase its beauty. No one now, he told them, could ever exhaust a hundredth of the city's treasures, however long they lived. For a while he described some of the wonders which the men of Diaspar had wrought: he tried to make them catch a glimpse at least of the loveliness which such artists as Shervane and Perildor had created for men's eternal admiration. And he spoke also of Loronei, whose name he bore, and wondered a little wistfully if it were indeed true that his music was the last sound Earth had ever broadcast to the stars.

They heard him to the end without interruption or questioning. When he had finished it was very late and Alvin felt more tired than he could ever remember. The strain and excitement of the long day had told on him at last, and quite suddenly he fell asleep.

*   *   *

Alvin was still tired when they left the village not long after dawn. Early though it was, they were not the first upon the road. By the lake they overtook the three councillors, and both parties exchanged slightly self-conscious greetings. Alvin knew perfectly well where the Committee of Investigation was going, and thought it would be appreciated if he saved it some trouble. He stopped when they reached the foot of the hill and turned toward his companions.

"I'm afraid I misled you last night," he said cheerfully. "I didn't come to Lys by the old route, so your attempt to close it wasn't really necessary."

The councillors' faces were a study in relief and increased perplexity.

"Then how *did* you get here?" The leader of the Committee spoke, and Alvin could tell that he at least had begun to guess the truth. He wondered if he had intercepted the command his mind had just sent winging across the mountains. But he said nothing, and merely pointed in silence to the northern sky.

Too swift for the eye to follow, a needle of silver light arced across the mountains, leaving a mile-long trail of incandescence. Twenty thousand feet above Lys, it stopped. There was no deceleration, no slow braking of its colossal speed. It came to a halt instantly, so that the eye that had been following it moved on across a quarter of the heavens before the brain could arrest its motion. Down from the skies crashed a mighty peal of thunder, the sound of air battered and smashed by the violence of the ship's passage. A little later the ship itself, gleaming splendidly in the sunlight, came to rest upon the hillside a hundred yards away.

It was difficult to say who was the most surprised, but Alvin was the first to recover. As they walked—very nearly running—toward the spaceship, he wondered if it normally traveled in this abrupt fashion. The thought was disconcerting, although there had been no sensation of movement on his first voyage. Considerably more puzzling, however, was the fact that the day before this resplendent creature had been hidden beneath a thick layer of iron-hard rock. Not until Alvin had reached the ship, and burned his fingers by incautiously resting them on the hull, did he understand what had happened. Near the stern there were still traces of earth, but it had been fused into lava. All the rest had been swept away, leaving uncovered the stubborn metal which neither time nor any natural force could ever touch.

With Theon by his side, Alvin stood in the open door and looked back at the three silent councillors. He wondered what they were thinking, but their expressions gave no hint of their thoughts.

"I have a debt to pay in Shalmirane," he said. "Please tell Seranis we'll be back by noon."

The councillors watched until the ship, now moving quite slowly—for it had only a little way to go—had disappeared into the south. Then the young man who led the group shrugged his shoulders philosophically.

"You've always opposed us for wanting change," he said, "and so far you've won. But I don't think the future lies with either of our parties now. Lys and Diaspar have both come to the end of an era, and we must make the best of it."

There was silence for a little while. Then one of his companions spoke in a very thoughtful voice.

"I know nothing of archeology, but surely that machine was too large to be an ordinary flyer. Do you think it could possibly have been—"

"A spaceship? If so, this *is* a crisis!"

The third man had also been thinking deeply.

"The disappearance of both flyers and spaceships is one of the greatest mysteries of the Interregnum. That machine may be either: for the moment we had better assume the worst. If it is in fact a spaceship, we must at all costs prevent that boy from leaving Earth. There is the danger that he may attract the Invaders again. That would be the end."

A gloomy silence settled over the company until the leader spoke again.

"That machine came from Diaspar," he said slowly. "Someone there must know the truth. I think we had better get in touch with our cousins—if they'll condescend to speak to us."

Sooner than he had any right to expect, the seed that Alvin had planted was beginning to flower.

*   *   *

The mountains were still swimming in shadow when they reached Shalmirane. From their height the great bowl of the fortress looked very small: it seemed impossible that the fate of Earth had once depended on that tiny ebon disk.

When Alvin brought the ship to rest among the ruins, the desolation crowded upon him, chilling his soul. There was no sign of the old man or his machines, and they had some difficulty in finding the entrance to the tunnel. At the top of the stairway Alvin shouted to give warning of their arrival: there was no reply and they moved quietly forward, in case he was asleep.

Sleeping he was, his hands folded peacefully upon his breast. His eyes were open, staring sightlessly up at the massive roof, as if they could see through to the stars beyond. There was a slight smile upon his lips: Death had not come to him as an enemy.

14

OUT
OF THE
SYSTEM

The two robots were beside him, floating motionless in the air. When Alvin tried to approach the body, their tentacles reached out to restrain him, so he came no nearer. There was nothing he could do: as he stood in that silent room he felt an icy wind sweep through his heart. It was the first time he had looked upon the marble face of Death, and he knew that something of his childhood had passed forever.

So this was the end of that strange brotherhood, perhaps the last of its kind the world would know. Deluded though they might have been, these men's lives had not been wholly wasted. As if by a miracle they had saved from the past knowledge that else would have been lost forever. Now their order could go the way of a million other faiths that had once thought themselves eternal.

They left him sleeping in his tomb among the mountains, where no man would disturb him until the end of Time. Guarding his body were the machines which had served him in life and which, Alvin knew, would never leave him now. Locked to his mind, they would wait here for the commands that could never come, until the mountains themselves had crumbled away.

The little four-legged animal which had once served man with the same devotion had been extinct too long for the boys ever to have heard of it.

They walked in silence back to the waiting ship, and presently the fortress was once more a dark lake among the hills. But Alvin did nothing to check the machine: still they rose until the whole of Lys lay spread beneath them, a great green island in an orange sea. Never before had Alvin been so high: when finally they came to rest the whole crescent of the Earth was visible below. Lys was very small now, only a dark shadow against the gray and orange of the desert—but far around the curve of the globe something was glittering like a many-colored jewel. And thus for the first time Theon saw the city of Diaspar.

They sat for a long time watching the Earth turn beneath them. Of all Man's ancient powers this surely was the one he could least afford to lose. Alvin wished he could show the world as he saw it now to the rulers of Lys and Diaspar.

"Theon," he said at last, "do you think that what I'm doing is right?"

The question surprised Theon, who as yet knew nothing of the sudden doubts that sometimes overwhelmed his friend. Nor was it easy to answer dispassionately: like Rorden, though with less cause, Theon felt that his own character was becoming submerged. He was being sucked helplessly into the vortex which Alvin left behind him on his way through life.

"I believe you are right," Theon answered slowly. "Our two peoples have been separated for long enough." That, he thought, was true, though he knew that his own feelings must bias his reply. But Alvin was still worried.

"There's one problem I haven't thought about until now," he continued in a troubled voice, "and that's the difference in our life-spans." He said no more, but each knew what the other was thinking.

"I've been worrying about that a good deal," Theon admitted, "but I think the problem will solve itself when our people get to know each other again. We can't both be right—our lives may be too short and yours are certainly too long. In time there will be a compromise."

Alvin wondered. That way, it was true, lay the only hope, but the ages of transition would be hard indeed. He remembered again those bitter words of Seranis: *"We shall both be dead when you are still a boy."* Very well: he would accept the conditions. Even in Diaspar all friendships lay under the same shadow: whether it was a hundred or a million years away made little difference at the end. The welfare of the race demanded the mingling of the two cultures: in such a cause individual happiness was unimportant. For a moment Alvin saw humanity as something more than the living background of his own life, and he accepted without flinching the unhappiness his choice must one day bring. They never spoke of it again.

Beneath them the world continued on its endless turning. Sensing his friend's mood, Theon said nothing, and presently Alvin broke the silence again.

"When I first left Diaspar," he said, "I did not know what I hoped to find. Lys would have satisfied me once—but now everything on Earth seems so small and unimportant. Each discovery I've made has raised bigger questions and now I'll never be content until I know who the Master was and why he came to Earth. If I ever learn that, then I suppose I'll start to worry about the Great Ones and the Invaders—and so it will go on."

Theon had never seen Alvin in so thoughtful a mood and did not wish to interrupt his soliloquy. He had learned a great deal about his friend in the last few minutes.

"The robot told me," Alvin continued, "that this machine can reach the Seven Suns in less than half a day. Do you think I should go?"

"Do you think I could stop you?" Theon replied quietly.

Alvin smiled.

"That's no answer," he said, "even if it's true. We don't know what's out there in space. The Invaders may have left the Universe, but there may be other intelligences unfriendly to Man."

"Why should there be?" Theon asked. "That's one of the questions our philosophers have been debating for ages. A truly intelligent race is not likely to be unfriendly."

"But the Invaders—?"

Theon pointed to the unending deserts below.

"Once we had an Empire. What have we now that they would covet?"

Alvin was a little surprised at this novel point of view.

"Do all your people think like this?"

"Only a minority. The average person doesn't worry about it, but would probably say that if the Invaders really wanted to destroy Earth they'd have done it ages ago. Only a few people, like Mother, are still afraid of them."

"Things are very different in Diaspar," Alvin said. "My people are great cowards. But it's unfortunate about your Mother—do you think she would stop you coming with me?"

"She most certainly would," Theon replied with emphasis. That Alvin had taken his own assent for granted he scarcely noticed.

Alvin thought for a moment.

"By now she'll have heard about this ship and will know what I intend to do. We mustn't return to Airlee."

"No: that wouldn't be safe. But I have a better plan."

* * *

The little village in which they landed was only a dozen miles from Airlee, but Alvin was surprised to see how greatly it differed in architecture and setting. The houses were several stories in height and had been built along the curve of a lake, looking out across the water. A large number of brightly colored vessels were floating at anchor along the shore: they fascinated Alvin, who had never heard of such things and wondered what they were for.

He waited in the ship while Theon went to see his friends. It was amusing to watch the consternation and amazement of the people crowding round, unaware of the fact that he was observing them from inside the machine. Theon was gone only a few minutes and had some difficulty in reaching the airlock through the inquisitive crowds. He breathed a sigh of relief as the door closed behind him.

"Mother will get the message in two or three minutes. I've not said where we're going, but she'll guess quickly enough. And I've got some news that will interest you."

"What is it?"

"The Central Council is going to hold talks with Diaspar."

"What!"

"It's perfectly true, though the announcement hasn't been made yet. That sort of thing can't be kept secret."

Alvin could appreciate this: he never understood how *anything* was ever kept secret in Lys.

"What are they discussing?"

"Probably ways in which they can stop us leaving. That's why I came back in a hurry."

Alvin smiled a little ruefully.

"So you think that fear may have succeeded where logic and persuasion failed?"

"Quite likely, though you made a real impression on the councillors last night. They were talking for a long time after you went to sleep."

Whatever the cause of this move, Alvin felt very pleased. Diaspar and Lys had both been slow to react, but events were now moving swiftly to their climax. That the climax might have unpleasant consequences for him, Alvin did not greatly mind.

They were very high when he gave the robot its final instructions. The ship had come almost to rest, and the Earth was perhaps a thousand miles below, nearly filling the sky. It looked very uninviting: Alvin wondered how many ships in the past had hovered here for a little while and then continued on their way.

There was an appreciable pause, as if the robot was checking controls and circuits that had not been used for geological ages. Then came a very faint sound, the first that Alvin had ever heard from the machine. It was a tiny humming, which soared swiftly octave by octave until it was lost at the edge of hearing. There was no sense of change or motion, but suddenly he noticed that the stars were drifting across the screen. The Earth reappeared, and rolled past—then appeared again, in a slightly different position. The ship was "hunting," swinging in space like a compass needle seeking the north. For minutes the skies turned and twisted around them, until at last the ship came to rest, a giant projectile aimed at the stars.

Centered in the screen the great ring of the Seven Suns lay in its rainbow-hued beauty. A little of Earth was still visible as a dark crescent edged with the gold and crimson of the sunset. Something was happening now, Alvin knew, beyond all his experience. He waited, gripping his seat, while the seconds drifted by and the Seven Suns glittered on the screen.

There was no sound, only a sudden wrench that seemed to blur the vision—but Earth had vanished as if a giant hand had whipped it away. They were alone in space, alone with the stars and a strangely shrunken sun. Earth was gone as though it had never been.

Again came that wrench, and with it now the faintest murmur of sound, as if for the first time the generators were exerting some appreciable fraction of their power. Yet for a moment it seemed that nothing had happened: then Alvin realized that the sun itself was gone and that the stars were creeping slowly past the ship. He looked back for an instant and saw—nothing. All the heavens behind had vanished utterly, obliterated by a hemisphere of night. Even as he watched, he could see the stars plunge into it, to disappear like sparks falling upon water. The ship was traveling far faster than light, and Alvin knew that the familiar space of Earth and Sun held him no more.

When that sudden, vertiginous wrench came for the third time, his heart almost stopped beating. The strange blurring of vision was unmistakable now: for a moment, his surroundings seemed distorted out of recognition. The meaning of that distortion came to him in a flash of insight he could not explain. *It was real, and no delusion of his eyes.* Somehow he was catching, as he passed through the thin film of the present, a glimpse of the changes that were occurring in the space around him.

At the same instant the murmur of the generators rose to a roar that shook the ship—a sound doubly impressive, for it was the first cry of protest that Alvin had ever heard from a machine. Then it was all over, and the sudden silence seemed to ring in his ears. The great generators had done their work: they would not be needed again until the end of the voyage. The stars ahead flared blue-white and vanished into the ultraviolet. Yet by some magic of Science or Nature the Seven Suns were still visible, though now their positions and colors were subtly changed. The ship was hurtling toward them along a tunnel of darkness, beyond the boundaries of space and time, at a velocity too enormous for the mind to contemplate.

It was hard to believe that they had now been flung out of the solar system at a speed which unless it were checked would soon take them through the heart of the Galaxy and into the greater emptiness beyond. Neither Alvin nor Theon could conceive the real immensity of their journey: the great sagas of exploration had completely changed Man's outlook toward the Universe, and even now, millions of centuries later, the ancient traditions had not wholly died. There had once been a ship, legend whispered, that had circumnavigated the Cosmos between the rising and the setting of the sun. The billions of miles between the stars meant nothing before such speeds. To Alvin this voyage was very little greater, and perhaps less dangerous, than his first journey to Lys.

It was Theon who voiced both their thoughts as the Seven Suns slowly brightened ahead.

"Alvin," he remarked, "that formation can't possibly be natural."

The other nodded.

"I've thought that for years, but it still seems fantastic."

"The system may not have been built by Man," agreed Theon, "but intelligence must have created it. Nature could never have formed that perfect circle of stars, one for each of the primary colors, all equally brilliant. And there's nothing else in the visible Universe like the Central Sun."

"Why should such a thing have been made, then?"

"Oh, I can think of many reasons. Perhaps it's a signal, so that any strange ship entering the Universe will know where to look for life. Perhaps it marks the center of galactic administration. Or perhaps—and somehow I feel that this is the real explanation—it's simply the greatest of all works of art. But it's foolish to speculate now. In a little while we'll know the truth."

15

VANAMONDE

So they waited, lost in their own dreams, while hour by hour the Seven Suns drifted apart until they had filled that strange tunnel of night in which the ship was riding. Then, one by one, the six outer stars vanished at the brink of darkness and at last only the Central Sun was left. Though it could no longer be fully in their space, it still shone with the pearly light that marked it out from all other stars. Minute by minute its brilliance increased, until presently it was no longer a point but a tiny disk. And now the disk was beginning to expand before them—

There was the briefest of warnings: for a moment a deep, bell-like note vibrated through the room. Alvin clenched the arms of his chair, though it was a futile enough gesture.

Once again the great generators exploded into life, and with an abruptness that was almost blinding, the stars reappeared. The ship had dropped back into space, back into the Universe of suns and planets, the natural world where nothing could move more swiftly than light.

They were already within the system of the Seven Suns, for the great ring of colored globes now dominated the sky. And what a sky it was! All the stars they had known, all the familiar constellations, had gone. The Milky Way was no longer a faint band of mist far to one side of the heavens: they were now at the center of creation, and its great circle divided the Universe in twain.

The ship was still moving very swiftly toward the Central Sun, and the six remaining stars of the system were colored beacons ranged around the sky. Not far from the nearest of them were the tiny sparks of circling planets, worlds that must have been of enormous size to be visible over such a distance. It was a sight grander than anything Nature had ever built, and Alvin knew that Theon had been correct. This superb symmetry was a deliberate challenge to the stars scattered aimlessly around it.

The cause of the Central Sun's nacreous light was now clearly visible. The great star, surely one of the most brilliant in the whole Universe, was shrouded in an envelope of gas which softened its radiation and gave it its characteristic color. The surrounding nebula could be seen only indirectly, and it was twisted into strange shapes that eluded the eye. But it was there, and the longer one stared the more extensive it seemed to be.

Alvin wondered where the robot was taking them. Was it following some ancient memory, or were there guiding signals in the space around them? He had left their destination entirely to the machine, and presently he noticed the pale spark of light toward which they were traveling. It was almost lost in the glare of the Central Sun, and around it were the yet fainter gleams of other worlds. Their enormous journey was coming to its end.

The planet was now only a few million miles away, a beautiful sphere of multicolored light. There could be no darkness anywhere upon its surface, for as it turned beneath the Central Sun, the other stars would march one by one across its skies. Alvin now saw very clearly the meaning of the Master's dying words: "It is lovely to watch the colored shadows on the planets of eternal light."

Now they were so close that they could see continents and oceans and a faint haze of atmosphere. Yet there was something puzzling about its markings, and presently they realized that the divisions between land and water were curiously regular. This planet's continents were not as Nature had left them—but how small a task the shaping of a world must have been to those who built its suns!

"Those aren't oceans at all!" Theon exclaimed suddenly. "Look—you can see markings in them!"

Not until the planet was nearer could Alvin see clearly what his friend meant. Then he noticed faint bands and lines along the continental borders, well inside what he had taken to be the limits of the sea. The sight filled him with a sudden doubt, for he knew too well the meaning of those lines. He had seen them once before in the desert beyond Diaspar, and they told him that his journey had been in vain.

"This planet is as dry as Earth," he said dully. "Its water has all gone—those markings are the salt-beds where the seas have evaporated."

"They would never have let that happen," replied Theon. "I think that, after all, we are too late."

His disappointment was so bitter that Alvin did not trust himself to speak again but stared silently at the great world ahead. With impressive slowness the planet turned beneath the ship, and its surface rose majestically to meet them. Now they could see buildings—minute white incrustations everywhere save on the ocean beds themselves.

Once this world had been the center of the Universe. Now it was still, the air was empty and on the ground were none of the scurrying dots that spoke of life. Yet the ship was still sliding purposefully over the frozen sea of stone—a sea which here and there had gathered itself into great waves that challenged the sky.

Presently the ship came to rest, as if the robot had at last traced its memories to their source. Below them was a column of snow-white stone springing from the center of an immense marble amphitheater. Alvin waited for a little while: then, as the machine remained motionless, he directed it to land at the foot of the pillar.

Even until now, Alvin had half hoped to find life on this planet. That hope vanished instantly as he left the airlock. Never before in his life, even in the desolation of Shalmirane, had he been in utter silence. On Earth there was always the murmur of voices, the stir of living creatures, or the sighing of the wind. Here were none of these, nor ever would be again.

Why the machine had brought them to this place there was no way of telling, but Alvin knew that the choice made little difference. The great column of white stone was perhaps twenty times the height of a man, and was set in a circle of metal slightly raised above the level of the plain. It was featureless and of its purpose there was no hint. They might guess, but they would never know, that it had once marked the zero point of all astronomical measurements.

So this, thought Alvin sadly, was the end of all his searching. He knew that it would be useless to visit the other worlds of the Seven Suns. Even if there was still intelligence in the Universe, where could he seek it now? He had seen the stars scattered like dust across the heavens, and he knew that what was left of Time was not enough to explore them all.

Suddenly a feeling of loneliness and oppression such as he had never before experienced seemed to overwhelm him. He could understand now the fear of Diaspar for the great spaces of the Universe, the terror that had made his people gather in the little microcosm of their city. It was hard to admit that, after all, they had been right.

He turned to Theon for support, but Theon was standing, hands tightly clenched, with his brow furrowed and a glazed look in his eyes.

"What's the matter?" Alvin asked in alarm.

Theon was still staring into nothingness as he replied.

"There's something coming. I think we'd better go back to the ship."

* * *

The galaxy had turned many times upon its axis since consciousness first came to Vanamonde. He could recall little of those first eons and the creatures who had tended him then—but he could remember still his desolation when they had gone at last and left him alone among the stars. Down the ages since, he had wandered from sun to sun, slowly evolving and increasing his powers. Once he had dreamed of finding again those who had attended his birth, and though the dream had faded now, it had never wholly died.

On countless worlds he had found the wreckage that life had left behind, but intelligence he had discovered only once—and from the Black Sun he had fled in terror. Yet the Universe was very large, and the search had scarcely begun.

Far away though it was in space and time, the great burst of power from the heart of the Galaxy beckoned to Vanamonde across the light-years. It was utterly unlike the radiation of the stars, and it had appeared in his field of consciousness as suddenly as a meteor trail across a cloudless sky. He moved toward it, to the latest moment of its existence, sloughing from him in the way he knew the dead, unchanging pattern of the past.

He knew this place, for he had been here before. It had been lifeless then, but now it held intelligence. The long metal shape lying upon the plain he could not understand, for it was as strange to him as almost all the things of the physical world. Around it still clung the aura of power that had drawn him across the Universe, but that was of no interest to him now. Carefully, with the delicate nervousness of a wild beast half poised for flight, he reached out toward the two minds he had discovered.

And then he knew that his long search was ended.

16

TWO
MEETINGS

How unthinkable, Rorden thought, this meeting would have seemed only a few days ago. Although he was still technically under a cloud, his presence was so obviously essential that no one had suggested excluding him. The six visitors sat facing the Council, flanked on either side by the co-opted members such as himself. This meant that he could not see their faces, but the expressions opposite were sufficiently instructive.

There was no doubt that Alvin had been right, and the Council was slowly realizing the unpalatable truth. *The delegates from Lys could think almost twice as quickly as the finest minds in Diaspar.* Nor was that their only advantage, for they also showed an extraordinary degree of coordination which Rorden guessed must be due to their telepathic powers. He wondered if they were reading the councillors' thoughts, but decided that they would not have broken the solemn assurance without which this meeting would have been impossible.

Rorden did not think that much progress had been made: for that matter, he did not see how it could be. Alvin had gone into space, and nothing could alter that. The Council, which had not yet fully accepted Lys, still seemed incapable of realizing what had happened. But it was clearly frightened, and so were most of the visitors.

Rorden himself was not as terrified as he had expected: his fears were still there, but he had faced them at last. Something of Alvin's own recklessness—or was it courage?—had changed his outlook and given him new horizons.

The President's question caught him unawares but he recovered himself quickly.

"I think," he said, "it's sheer chance that this situation never arose before. There was nothing we could have done to stop it, for events were always ahead of us." Everyone knew that by "events" he meant Alvin, but there were no comments. "It's futile to bicker about the past: Diaspar and Lys have both made mistakes. When Alvin returns, you may prevent him leaving Earth again—if you can. I don't think you will succeed, for he may have learnt a great deal by then. But if what you fear has happened, there's nothing any of us can do about it. Earth is helpless—as she has been for millions of centuries."

Rorden paused and glanced along the table. His words had pleased no one, nor had he expected them to do so.

"Yet I don't see why we should be so alarmed. Earth is in no greater danger now than she has always been. Why should two boys in a single small ship bring the wrath of the Invaders down upon us again? If we'll be honest with ourselves, we must admit that the Invaders could have destroyed our world ages ago."

There was a shocked silence. This was heresy—but Rorden was interested to notice that two of the visitors seemed to approve.

The President interrupted, frowning heavily.

"Is there not a legend that the Invaders spared Earth itself only on condition that Man never went into space again? And have we not now broken those conditions?"

"Once I too believed that," said Rorden. "We accept many things without question, and this is one of them. But my machines know nothing of legend, only of truth—and there is no historical record of such an agreement. I am convinced that anything so important would have been permanently recorded, as many lesser matters have been."

Alvin, he thought, would have been proud of him now. It was

strange that he should be defending the boy's ideas, when if Alvin himself had been present he might well have been attacking them. One at least of his dreams had come true: the relationship between Lys and Diaspar was still unstable, but it was a beginning. Where, he wondered, was Alvin now?

*   *   *

Alvin had seen or heard nothing, but he did not stop to argue. Only when the airlock had closed behind them did he turn to his friend.

"What was it?" he asked a little breathlessly.

"I don't know: it was something terrific. I think it's still watching us."

"Shall we leave?"

"No: I was frightened at first, but I don't think it will harm us. It seems simply—interested."

Alvin was about to reply when he was suddenly overwhelmed by a sensation unlike any he had ever known before. A warm, tingling glow seemed to spread through his body: it lasted only a few seconds, but when it was gone he was no longer Alvin of Loronei. Something was sharing his brain, overlapping it as one circle may partly cover another. He was conscious, also, of Theon's mind close at hand, equally entangled in whatever creature had descended upon them. The sensation was strange rather than unpleasant, and it gave Alvin his first glimpse of true telepathy—the power which in his race had so degenerated that it could now be used only to control machines.

Alvin had rebelled at once when Seranis had tried to dominate his mind, but he did not struggle against this intrusion. It would have been useless, and he knew that this intelligence, whatever it might be, was not unfriendly. He relaxed completely, accepting without resistance the fact that an infinitely greater intelligence than his own was exploring his mind. But in that belief, he was not wholly right.

One of these minds, Vanamonde saw at once, was more sympathetic and accessible than the other. He could tell that both were filled with wonder at his presence, and that surprised him greatly. It was hard to believe that they could have forgotten: forgetfulness, like mortality, was beyond the comprehension of Vanamonde.

Communication was very difficult: many of the thought-images in their minds were so strange that he could hardly recognize them. He was puzzled and a little frightened by the recurrent fear-pattern of the Invaders; it reminded him of his own emotions when the Black Sun first came into his field of knowledge.

But they knew nothing of the Black Sun, and now their own questions were beginning to form in his mind.

"What are you?"

He gave the only reply he could.

"I am Vanamonde."

There came a pause (how long the pattern of their thoughts took to form!) and then the question was repeated. They had not understood: that was strange, for surely their kind had given him his name for it to be among the memories of his birth. Those memories were very few, and they began strangely at a single point in time, but they were crystal-clear.

Again their tiny thoughts struggled up into his consciousness.

"Who were the Great Ones—are you one of them yourself?"

He did not know: they could scarcely believe him, and their disappointment came sharp and clear across the abyss separating their minds from his. But they were patient and he was glad to help them, for their quest was the same as his and they gave him the first companionship he had ever known.

As long as he lived, Alvin did not believe he would ever again undergo so strange an experience as this soundless conversation. It was hard to believe that he could be little more than a spectator, for he did not care to admit, even to himself, that Theon's mind was so much more powerful than his own. He could only wait and wonder, half dazed by the torrent of thought just beyond the limits of his understanding.

Presently Theon, rather pale and strained, broke off the contact and turned to his friend.

"Alvin," he said, his voice very tired, "there's something strange here. I don't understand it at all."

The news did a little to restore Alvin's self-esteem, and his face must have shown his feelings, for Theon gave a sudden, not unsympathetic laugh.

"I can't discover what this—Vanamonde—is," he continued. "It's a creature of tremendous knowledge, but it seems to have very little intelligence. Of course," he added, "its mind may be of such a different order that we can't understand it—yet somehow I don't believe that is the right explanation."

"Well, what *have* you learned?" asked Alvin with some impatience. "Does it know anything about this place?"

Theon's mind still seemed very far away.

"This city was built by many races, including our own," he said absently. "It can give me facts like that, but it doesn't seem to understand their meaning. I believe it's conscious of the past, without being able to interpret it. Everything that's ever happened seems jumbled together in its mind."

He paused thoughtfully for a moment: then his face lightened.

"There's only one thing to do: somehow or other, we must get Vanamonde to Earth so that our philosophers can study him."

"Would that be safe?" asked Alvin.

"Yes," answered Theon, thinking how uncharacteristic his friend's remark was. "Vanamonde is friendly. More than that, in fact—he seems almost affectionate."

And quite suddenly the thought that all the while had been hovering at the edge of Alvin's consciousness came clearly into view. He remembered Krif and the small animals that were constantly escaping ("It won't happen again, Mother") to annoy Seranis. And he recalled—how long ago that seemed!—the zoological purpose behind their expedition to Shalmirane.

Theon had found a new pet.

17

THE
BLACK
SUN

They landed at noon in the glade of Airlee, with no thought of concealment now. Alvin wondered if ever in human history any ship had brought such a cargo to Earth—if indeed Vanamonde was located in the physical space of the machine. There had been no sign of him on the voyage: Theon believed, and his knowledge was more direct, that only Vanamonde's sphere of attention could be said to have any location in space.

As they left the ship the doors closed softly behind them and a sudden wind tugged at their clothes. Then the machine was only a silver dot falling into the sky, returning to the world where it belonged until Alvin should need it again.

Seranis was waiting for them as Theon had known and Alvin had half expected. She looked at the boys in silence for a while, then said quietly to Alvin:

"You're making life rather complicated for us, aren't you?"

There was no rancor in the words, only a half-humorous resignation and even a dawning approval.

Alvin sensed her meaning at once.

"Then Vanamonde's arrived?"

"Yes, hours ago. Since dawn we have learned more of history than we knew existed."

Alvin looked at her in amazement. Then he understood: it was not hard to imagine what the impact of Vanamonde must have been upon this people, with their keen perceptions and their wonderfully interlocking minds. They had reacted with surprising speed, and he had a sudden incongruous picture of Vanamonde, perhaps a little frightened, surrounded by the eager intellects of Lys.

"Have you discovered what he is?" Alvin asked.

"Yes. That was simple, though we still don't know his origin. He's a pure mentality and his knowledge seems to be unlimited. But he's childish, and I mean that quite literally."

"Of course!" cried Theon. "I should have guessed!"

Alvin looked puzzled and Seranis took pity on him.

"I mean that although Vanamonde has a colossal, perhaps an infinite, mind, he's immature and undeveloped. His actual intelligence is less than that of a human being"—she smiled a little wryly—"though his thought processes are much faster and he learns very quickly. He also has some powers we do not yet understand. The whole of the past seems open to his mind, in a way that's difficult to describe. He must have used that ability to follow your path back to Earth."

Alvin stood in silence, for once somewhat overcome. He realized how right Theon had been to bring Vanamonde to Lys. And he knew how lucky he had been ever to outwit Seranis: that was not something he would do twice in a lifetime.

"Do you mean," he asked, "that Vanamonde has only just been born?"

"By his standards, yes. His actual age is very great, though apparently less than Man's. The extraordinary thing is that he insists that *we* created him, and there's no doubt that his origin is bound up with all the great mysteries of the past."

"What's happening to Vanamonde now?" asked Theon in a slightly possessive voice.

"The historians of Grevarn are questioning him. They are trying to map out the main outlines of the past, but the work will take years. Vanamonde can describe the past in perfect detail, but since he doesn't understand what he sees it's very difficult to work with him."

Alvin wondered how Seranis knew all this: then he realized that probably every waking mind in Lys was watching the progress of the great research. "Rorden should be here," he said, coming to a sudden decision. "I'm going to Diaspar to fetch him." "*And* Jeserac," he added, in a determined afterthought.

* * *

Rorden had never seen a whirlwind, but if one had hit him the experience would have felt perfectly familiar. There were times when his sense of reality ceased to function, and the feeling that everything was a dream became almost overwhelming. This was such a moment now.

He closed his eyes and tried to recall the familiar room in Diaspar which had once been both a part of his personality and a barrier against the outer world. What would he have thought, he wondered, could he have looked into the future when he had first met Alvin and seen the outcome of that encounter? But of one thing he was sure and a little proud: he would not have turned aside.

The boat was moving slowly across the lake with a gentle rocking motion that Rorden found rather pleasant. Why the village of Grevarn had been built on an island he could not imagine: it seemed a most inconvenient arrangement. It was true that the colored houses, which seemed to float at anchor upon the tiny waves, made a scene of almost unreal beauty. That was all very well, thought Rorden, but one couldn't spend the whole of one's life staring at scenery. Then he remembered that this was precisely what many of these eccentric people did.

Eccentric or not, they had minds he could respect. To him the thoughts of Vanamonde were as meaningless as a thousand voices shouting together in some vast, echoing cave. Yet the men of Lys could disentangle them, could record them to be analyzed at leisure. Already the structure of the past, which had once seemed lost forever, was becoming faintly visible. And it was so strange and unexpected that it appeared to bear no resemblance at all to the history that Rorden had always believed.

In a few months he would present his first report to Diaspar.

Though its contents were still uncertain, he knew that it would end forever the sterile isolation of his race. The barriers between Lys and Diaspar would vanish when their origin was understood, and the mingling of the two great cultures would invigorate mankind for ages to come. Yes even this now seemed no more than a minor by-product of the great research that was just beginning. If what Vanamonde had hinted was indeed true, Man's horizons must soon embrace not merely the Earth, but must enfold the stars and reach out to the Galaxies beyond. But of these further vistas it was still too early to be sure.

Calitrax, chief historian of Lys, met them at the little jetty. He was a tall, slightly stooping man, and Rorden wondered how, without the help of the Master Associators, he had ever managed to learn so much in his short life. It did not occur to him that the very absence of such machines was the reason for the wonderful memories he had met in Grevarn.

They walked together beside one of the innumerable canals that made life in the village so hazardous to strangers. Calitrax seemed a little preoccupied, and Rorden knew that part of his mind was still with Vanamonde.

"Have you settled your date-fixing procedure yet?" asked Rorden presently, feeling somewhat neglected.

Calitrax remembered his duties as host and broke contact with obvious reluctance.

"Yes," he said. "It had to be the astronomical method. We think it's accurate to ten thousand years, even back to the Dawn Ages. It could be even better, but that's good enough to mark out the main epochs."

"What about the Invaders? Has Bensor located them?"

"No: he made one attempt but it's hopeless to look for any isolated period. What we're doing now is to go back to the beginning of history and then take cross-sections at regular intervals. We'll link them together by guesswork until we can fill in the details. If only Vanamonde could interpret what he sees! As it is we have to work through masses of irrelevant material."

"I wonder what he thinks about the whole affair: it must all be rather puzzling to him."

"Yes, I suppose it must. But he's very docile and friendly, and I think he's happy, if one can use that word. So Theon believes, and they seem to have a curious sort of affinity. Ah, here's Bensor with the latest ten million years of history. I'll leave you in his hands."

* * *

The Council chamber had altered little since Alvin's last visit, for the seldom-used projection equipment was so inconspicuous that one could easily have overlooked it. There were two empty chairs along the great table: one, he knew, was Jeserac's. But though he was in Lys, Jeserac would be watching this meeting, as would almost all the world.

If Rorden recalled their last appearance in this room, he did not care to mention it. But the councillors certainly remembered, as Alvin could tell by the ambiguous glances he received. He wondered what they would be thinking when they had heard Rorden's story. Already, in a few months, the present had changed out of all recognition—and now they were going to lose the past.

Rorden began to speak. The great ways of Diaspar would be empty of traffic: the city would be hushed as Alvin had known it only once before in his life. It was waiting, waiting for the veil of the past to be lifted again after—if Calitrax was right—more than fifteen hundred million years.

Very briefly, Rorden ran through the accepted history of the race—the history that both Diaspar and Lys had always believed beyond question. He spoke of the unknown peoples of the Dawn Civilizations, who had left behind them nothing but a handful of great names and the fading legends of the Empire. Even at the beginning, so the story went, Man had desired the stars and at last attained them. For millions of years he had expanded across the Galaxy, gathering system after system beneath his sway. Then, out of the darkness beyond the rim of the universe, the Invaders had struck and wrenched from him all that he had won.

The retreat to the solar system had been bitter and must have lasted many ages. Earth itself was barely saved by the fabulous battles that raged round Shalmirane. When all was over, Man was left with only his memories and the world on which he had been born.

Rorden paused: he looked round the great room and smiled slightly as his eyes met Alvin's.

"So much for the tales we have believed since our records began. I must tell you now that they are false—false in every detail—*so false that even now we have not fully reconciled them with the truth.*"

He waited for the full meaning of his words to strike home. Then, speaking slowly and carefully, but after the first few minutes never consulting his notes, he gave the city the knowledge that had been won from the mind of Vanamonde.

It was not even true that Man had reached the stars. The whole of his little empire was bounded by the orbit of Persephone, for interstellar space proved a barrier beyond his power to cross. His entire civilization was huddled round the sun, and was still very young when—the stars reached him.

The impact must have been shattering. Despite his failures, Man had never doubted that one day he would conquer the deeps of space. He believed too that if the Universe held his equals, it did not hold his superiors. Now he knew that both beliefs were wrong, and that out among the stars were minds far greater than his own. For many centuries, first in the ships of other races and later in machines built with borrowed knowledge, Man had explored the Galaxy. Everywhere he found cultures he could understand but could not match, and here and there he encountered minds which would soon have passed altogether beyond his comprehension.

The shock was tremendous, but it proved the making of the race. Sadder and infinitely wiser, Man had returned to the solar system to brood upon the knowledge he had gained. He would accept the challenge, and slowly he evolved a plan which gave hope for the future.

Once, the physical sciences had been Man's greatest interest. Now he turned even more fiercely to genetics and the study of the mind. Whatever the cost, he would drive himself to the limits of his evolution.

The great experiment had consumed the entire energies of the race for millions of years. All that striving, all that sacrifice and toil, became only a handful of words in Rorden's narrative. It had brought Man his greatest victories. He had banished disease: he could live forever if he wished, and in mastering telepathy he had bent the most subtle of all powers to his will.

He was ready to go out again, relying upon his own resources, into the great spaces of the Galaxy. He would meet as an equal the races of the worlds from which he had once turned aside. And he would play his full part in the story of the Universe.

These things he did. From this age, perhaps the most spacious in all history, came the legends of the Empire. It had been an Empire of many races, but this had been forgotten in the drama, too tremendous for tragedy, in which it had come to its end.

The Empire had lasted for at least a billion years. It must have known many crises, perhaps even wars, but all these were lost in the sweep of great races moving together toward maturity.

"We can be proud," continued Rorden, "of the part our ancestors played in this story. Even when they had reached their cultural plateau, they lost none of their initiative. We deal now with conjecture rather than proven fact, but it seems certain that the experiments which were at once the Empire's downfall and its crowning glory were inspired and directed by Man.

"The philosophy underlying these experiments appears to have been this. Contact with other species had shown Man how profoundly a race's world-picture depended upon its physical body and the sense organs with which it was equipped. It was argued that a true picture of the Universe could be attained, if at all, only by a mind which was free from such physical limitations—a pure mentality, in fact. This idea was common among most very ancient religions and was believed by many to be the goal of evolution.

"Largely as a result of the experience gained in his own regeneration, Man suggested that the creation of such beings should be attempted. It was the greatest challenge ever thrown out to intelligence in the Universe, and after centuries of debate it was accepted. All the races of the Galaxy joined together in its fulfillment.

"Half a billion years were to separate the dream from the reality.

Civilizations were to rise and fall, again and yet again the age-long toil of worlds was to be lost, but the goal was never forgotten. One day we may know the full story of this, the greatest sustained effort in all history. Today we only know that its ending was a disaster that almost wrecked the Galaxy.

"Into this period Vanamonde's mind refuses to go. There is a narrow region of time which is blocked to him; but only, we believe, by his own fears. At its beginning we can see the Empire at the summit of its glory, taut with the expectation of coming success. At its end, only a few thousand years later, the Empire is shattered and the stars themselves are dimmed as though drained of their power. Over the Galaxy hangs a pall of fear, a fear with which is linked the name 'the Mad Mind.'

"What must have happened in that short period is not hard to guess. The pure mentality had been created, but it was either insane or, as seems more likely from other sources, was implacably hostile to matter. For centuries it ravaged the Universe until brought under control by forces of which we cannot guess. Whatever weapon the Empire used in its extremity squandered the resources of the stars: from the memories of that conflict spring some, though not all, of the legends of the Invaders. But of this I shall presently say more.

"The Mad Mind could not be destroyed, for it was immortal. It was driven to the edge of the Galaxy and there imprisoned in a way we do not understand. Its prison was a strange artificial star known as the Black Sun, and there it remains to this day. When the Black Sun dies, it will be free again. How far in the future that day lies there is no way of telling."

18

RENAISSANCE

Alvin glanced quickly around the great room, which had become utterly silent. The councillors, for the most part, sat rigid in their seats, staring at Rorden with a trancelike immobility. Even to Alvin, who had already heard the story in fragments, Rorden's narrative still had the excitement of a newly unfolding drama. To the councillors, the impact of his revelations must be overwhelming.

Rorden was speaking again in a quiet, more subdued voice as he described the last days of the Empire. This was the age, Alvin had decided, in which he would have liked to live. There had been adventure then, and a superb and dauntless courage—the courage that can snatch victory from the teeth of disaster.

"Though the Galaxy had been laid waste by the Mad Mind, the resources of the Empire were still enormous, and its spirit was unbroken. With a courage at which we can only marvel, the great experiment was resumed and a search made for the flaw that had caused the catastrophe. There were now, of course, many who opposed the work and predicted further disasters, but they were overruled. The project went ahead and, with the knowledge so bitterly gained, this time it succeeded.

"The new race that was born had a potential intellect that could not even be measured. But it was completely infantile: we do not know if this was expected by its creators, but it seems likely that they knew it to be inevitable. Millions of years would be needed before it reached maturity, and nothing could be done to hasten the process. Vanamonde was the first of these minds: there must be others elsewhere in the Galaxy, but we believe that only a very few were created, for Vanamonde has never encountered any of his fellows.

"The creation of the pure mentalities was the greatest achievement of Galactic civilization: in it Man played a major and perhaps a dominant part. I have made no reference to Earth itself, for its story is too small a thread to be traced in the great tapestry. Since it had always been drained of its most adventurous spirits our planet had inevitably become somewhat conservative, and in the end it opposed the scientists who created Vanamonde. Certainly it played no part at all in the final act.

"The work of the Empire was now finished: the men of that age looked round at the stars they had ravaged in their desperate peril, and they made the decision that might have been expected. They would leave the Universe to Vanamonde.

"The choice was not hard to make, for the Empire had now made the first contacts with a very great and very strange civilization far around the curve of the Cosmos. This civilization, if the hints we can gather are correct, had evolved on the purely physical plane further than had been believed possible. There were, it seemed, more solutions than one to the problem of ultimate intelligence. But this we can only guess: all we know for certain is that within a very short period of time our ancestors and their fellow races have gone upon a journey which we cannot follow. Vanamonde's thoughts seem bounded by the confines of the Galaxy, but through his mind we have watched the beginning of that great adventure—"

* * *

A pale wraith of its former glory, the slowly turning wheel of the Galaxy hangs in nothingness. Throughout its length are the great empty rents which the Mad Mind has torn—wounds that in ages to come the drifting stars will fill. But they will never restore the splendor that has gone.

Man is about to leave his Universe, as once he left his world. And not only Man, but the thousand other races that have worked with him to make the Empire. They have gathered together, here at the edge of the Galaxy, with its whole thickness between them and the goal they will not reach for ages.

The long line of fire strikes across the Universe, leaping from star to star. In a moment of time a thousand suns have died, feeding their energies to the dim and monstrous shape that has torn along the axis of the Galaxy and is now receding into the abyss. . . .

*   *   *

"The Empire had now left the Universe, to meet its destiny elsewhere. When its heirs, the pure mentalities, have reached their full stature we believe it will return again. But that day must still lie far ahead.

"This, in its outlines, is the story of Galactic civilization. Our own history, which we thought so important, is no more than a belated episode which we have not yet examined in detail. But it seems that many of the older, less adventurous races refused to leave their homes. Our direct ancestors were among them. Most of these races fell into decadence and are now extinct: our own world barely escaped the same fate. In the Transition Centuries—which really lasted for millions of years—the knowledge of the past was lost or else deliberately destroyed. The latter seems more probable: we believe that Man sank into a superstitious barbarism during which he distorted history to remove his sense of impotence and failure. The legend of the Invaders is certainly false, and the Battle of Shalmirane is a myth. True, Shalmirane exists, and was one of the greatest weapons ever forged—but it was used against no intelligent enemy. Once the Earth had a single giant satellite, the Moon. When it began to fall, Shalmirane was built to destroy it. Around that destruction have been woven the legends you all know, and there are many such."

Rorden paused, and smiled a little ruefully.

"There are other paradoxes that have not yet been resolved, but the problem is one for the psychologist rather than the historian. Even my records cannot be wholly trusted, and bear clear evidence of tampering in the very remote past.

"Only Diaspar and Lys survived the period of decadence—Diaspar thanks to the perfection of its machines, Lys owing to its partial isolation and the unusual intellectual powers of its people. But both cultures, even when they had struggled back to their former level, were distorted by the fears and myths they had inherited.

"Those fears need haunt us no longer. All down the ages, we have now discovered, there were men who rebelled against them and maintained a tenuous link between Diaspar and Lys. Now the last barriers can be swept aside and our two races can move together into the future—whatever it may bring."

*   *   *

"I wonder what Yarlan Zey would think of this?" said Rorden thoughtfully. "I doubt if he would approve."

The Park had changed considerably, so far very much for the worse. But when the rubble had been cleared away, the road to Lys would be open for all to follow.

"I don't know," Alvin replied. "Though he closed the moving ways, he didn't destroy them as he might very well have done. One day we must discover the whole story behind the Park—and behind Alaine of Lyndar."

"I'm afraid these things will have to wait," said Rorden, "until more important problems have been settled. In any case, I can picture Alaine's mind rather well: once we must have had a good deal in common."

They walked in silence for a few hundred yards, following the edge of the great excavation. The Tomb of Yarlan Zey was now poised on the brink of a chasm, at the bottom of which scores of robots were working furiously.

"By the way," said Alvin abruptly, "did you know that Jeserac is staying in Lys? Jeserac, of all people! He likes it there and won't come back. Of course, that will leave a vacancy on the Council."

"So it will," replied Rorden, as if he had never given the matter any thought. A short time ago he could have imagined very few things more unlikely than a seat on the Council; now it was probably only a matter of time. There would, he reflected, be a good many other resignations in the near future. Several of the older councillors had found themselves unable to face the new problems pouring upon them.

They were now moving up the slope to the Tomb, through the long avenue of eternal trees. At its end, the avenue was blocked by Alvin's ship, looking strangely out of place in these familiar surroundings.

"There," said Rorden suddenly, "is the greatest mystery of all. *Who was the Master?* Where did he get this ship and the three robots?"

"I've been thinking about that," answered Theon. "We know that he came from the Seven Suns, and there might have been a fairly high culture there when civilization on Earth was at its lowest. The ship itself is obviously the work of the Empire.

"I believe that the Master was escaping from his own people. Perhaps he had ideas with which they didn't agree: he was a philosopher, and a rather remarkable one. He found our ancestors friendly but superstitious and tried to educate them, but they misunderstood and distorted his teachings. The Great Ones were no more than the men of the Empire—only it wasn't Earth they had left, but the Universe itself. The Master's disciples didn't understand or didn't believe this, and all their mythology and ritual was founded on that false premise. One day I intend to go into the Master's history and find why he tried to conceal his past. I think it will be a very interesting story."

"We've a good deal to thank him for," said Rorden as they entered the ship. "Without him we would never have learned the truth about the past."

"I'm not so sure," said Alvin. "Sooner or later Vanamonde would have discovered us. And I believe there may be other ships hidden on Earth: one day I mean to find them."

The city was now too distant to be recognized as the work of Man, and the curve of the planet was becoming visible. In a little while they could see the line of twilight, thousands of miles away on its never-ending march across the desert. Above and around were the stars, still brilliant for all the glory they had lost.

For a long time Rorden stared at the desolate panorama he had never seen before. He felt a sudden contemptuous anger for the men of the past who had let Earth's beauty die through their own neglect. If one of Alvin's dreams came true, and the great transmutation plants still existed, it would not be many centuries before the oceans rolled again.

There was so much to do in the years ahead. Rorden knew that he stood between two ages: around him he could feel the pulse of mankind beginning to quicken again. There were great problems to be faced, and Diaspar would face them. The recharting of the past would take centuries, but when it was finished Man would have recovered all that he had lost. And always now in the background would be the great enigma of Vanamonde—

If Calitrax was right, Vanamonde had already evolved more swiftly than his creators had expected, and the philosophers of Lys had great hopes of future cooperation which they would confide to no one. They had become very attached to the childlike supermind, and perhaps they believed that they could foreshorten the eons which his natural evolution would require. But Rorden knew that the ultimate destiny of Vanamonde was something in which Man would play no part. He had dreamed, and he believed the dream was true, that at the end of the Universe Vanamonde and the Mad Mind must meet each other among the corpses of the stars.

Alvin broke into his reverie and Rorden turned from the screen.

"I wanted you to see this," said Alvin quietly. "It may be many centuries before you have another chance."

"You're not leaving Earth?"

"No: even if there are other civilizations in this Galaxy, I doubt if they'd be worth the trouble of finding. And there is so much to do here—"

Alvin looked down at the great deserts, but his eyes saw instead the waters that would be sweeping over them a thousand years from now. Man had rediscovered his world, and he would make it beautiful while he remained upon it. And after that—

"I am going to send this ship out of the Galaxy, to follow the Empire wherever it has gone. The search may take ages, but the robot will never tire. One day our cousins will receive my message, and they'll know that we are waiting for them here on Earth. They will return, and I hope that by then we'll be worthy of them, however great they have become."

Alvin fell silent, staring into the future he had shaped but which he might never see. While Man was rebuilding his world, this ship would be crossing the darkness between the galaxies, and in thousands of years to come it would return. Perhaps he would be there to meet it, but if not, he was well content.

They were now above the Pole, and the planet beneath them was an almost perfect hemisphere. Looking down upon the belt of twilight, Alvin realized that he was seeing at one instant both sunrise and sunset on opposite sides of the world. The symbolism was so perfect and so striking that he was to remember this moment all his life.

* * *

In this Universe the night was falling: the shadows were lengthening toward an east that would not know another dawn. But elsewhere the stars were still young and the light of morning lingered: and along the path he once had followed, Man would one day go again.

PART
II

19
THE
RETURN
OF
EVIL

The naked woman seemed to be dead. The four-winged bird which gyred down from a pale afternoon sky thought as much. It wheeled in lazy eights with the woman at the cross point, keeping the body under its precise gaze. It flapped easily, luxuriating in the loft of thermals from the rocky bluff nearby. Its forewings canted wind into the broad, gossamer-thin hindwings, bringing an ancient pleasure. But then directives ingrained in its deepest genes tugged it back to its assigned task: to find the living humans in this area and summon aid.

The brighter portion of its oddly shaped intelligence decided that this woman, who had not stirred for long minutes, was certainly dead. It made this decision not by reason but by a practical sense set long before it had come to know reason. The pebbles around her head were stained dark and a massive bruise had blossomed over her left ribs like a purple sunrise.

Already the bird had seen over twenty dead humans among the trees, charred to ash, and none living. It decided not to report this body as a possible candidate. That would take valuable time, and members of this curious, unimpressive subspecies of humans were notoriously fragile.

The four-winger had much rugged territory to cover and was

running out of time. It hung for a long moment, indecisive as only a considerable intelligence can be, forewings rising as hindwings fell. Then the four-winger peeled away, eyes scanning every minute speck below.

The afternoon shadows lengthened considerably before the woman stirred, her weak gasping lost beneath the chuckle of the nearby stream. Her breath whistled between broken teeth.

This sound attracted a six-legged mother making her way with two cubs along the muddy bank. The woman's dying might have gained an audience then. But the sleek creatures saw that the woman distinctly resembled those who truly ruled here, though she smelled quite differently.

The mother instructed her cubs to note and always respect that form, now broken but always dangerous. She used a language simple in words but complex in positional grammar, inflections giving layers of meaning. She augmented this with deft signs, using her midlegs.

The family's quick flight downstream sent a tang into a crosswind which in turn roused the interest of a more curious creature. It was distantly descended from the simple raccoon, its pelt a rich symbol-laden swirl of red and auburn. This crafty intelligence quickly assessed the situation from the cover of stingbushes.

It was cautious but not afraid. To it, the most important issue here lay in interlacing the dying woman's jarring presence with the elaborate meaning of its own life. From birth it had integrated each experience with its innate sense of balance and appropriate scale—indeed, this was the sole purpose of its conscious being. Such integration was complete and utterly beyond human ability, but emerged effortlessly, the outcome of events in its evolution scattered through a billion years. The revival of its species a few centuries before had rendered with fidelity a creature in many ways superior to the pitiful figure it now watched intently.

At last, and with proper understanding of the pattern of events which might spread from its actions like the branches of an infinite tree, unending, the raccoonlike beast padded forward. It smelled the woman. There also came the sharp bite of fresh dung nearby where a small predator had passed some hours before, hesitated a moment, and then decided that the woman was a better prospect for tonight, when she would be safely dead. This information rippled atop the usual background flavorings of sunset: a crisp aroma of granite cooling, the sweet perfume of the eternal flowers, a musty odor of fungus drawing water up the hills from the muttering stream.

The woman's swollen skull was the worst problem. The optical disk bulged in both eyes. With long, tapered hands that echoed only faintly their origin in claws, the creature felt the unfamiliar cage of bones beneath the skin and muscle. The right arm was skewed unnaturally awry. Several ribs were cleanly snapped.

This specific form taken from the human spectrum had not existed in the time of the raccoon-creature's origin, so it was an interesting puzzle. The body's design was archaic, a patchwork of temporary solutions to passing problems. Yet evolution had sanctified these cumbersome measures with success in the raw, natural world.

The creature set about healing the body. It did not know how the woman came to be here or that she was in any way special. Gingerly it used techniques that were second nature, massaging points in this body which it knew emitted restoring hormones. It used its elbows—an awkward but unavoidable feature still not bettered in nature—to generate healing vibrations. The soft, swollen contusion in the right temple responded to rhythmic squeezing of the spine. The creature could feel pressures slowly relent and diffuse throughout the woman's head. Her glandular imperatives sluggishly closed internal hemorrhages. Stimuli to the neck and abdomen made her internal organs begin their filtering of the waste-clogged blood.

Dusk brought the rustle of movement to the creature's large ears, but none of the telltale sounds implied danger. The creature sat comfortably beside the sprawled woman and slept, though even then with an alertness the woman could never know. When she began to mutter the creature realized it could understand the slurred words.

"... get away ... keep down ... down ... can't see us ... from the air ..."

Much of her talk was garbled fever dreams. From brief moments of coherence the creature came to understand that the woman had been hunted remorselessly from a flyer, along with her tribe.

The tribe had not escaped. A dry night breeze coming off the hotter plains to the west brought the sickly sweet promise of flesh rotting in tomorrow's sun. The creature closed its nostrils to the smell.

The raccoon-being was pleasantly surprised that it could understand the woman's words. The lands here were filled with life-forms drawn from two billion years of incessant creation, and most of them could not fathom the languages of the others. This woman must have been taught—perhaps by genetic tuning—to comprehend the complex languages more advanced creatures used.

The large creature felt that to engrain such knowledge was an error, a skewed and perhaps arrogant presumption. An early human form such as this might well be confused by such complex, disorienting craft. Language arose from a world view. The rich web of perceptions which had formed her present tongue could scarcely ride easily in her cramped mental confines.

Normally it did not question the deeds of the advanced human forms called the Supras. But this badly mauled woman, her skin lacerated and turgid with deep bruises, raised doubts. Perhaps her injuries stemmed directly from her knowledge.

After some contemplation, however, its innate sense that life was a dusty mirror, reflecting only passing images of truth, told it that this woman was here for no ordinary reason. So it sat and thought and monitored her body's own weak but persistent self-repairing.

The woman lay beneath a night that gradually cleared as cumulus clouds blew in from the west and went on beyond the distant hills, as though hurrying for an appointment they could never meet. The creature sensed rising plumes of water vapor exhaled by the dense jungle and forest. These great moist wedges acted like invisible mountains, forcing inblowing air to rise and rain out its wet burden.

A great luminous band rose on the horizon, so bright and varied that it did not seem to be composed of stars, but rather of ivory and ice. Vast ragged lanes of dust sprawled across swarms of piercing light. These were the shreds of the galactic arm, a last rampart shielding the galactic center.

The raccoon-beast knew that Earth had been deflected toward this central hub long ago, before its own kind had evolved, when Earth was verdant for the first time. The scope of such an undertaking was beyond its comprehension. It dimly sensed that the humans of that time had made the sun pass near another star, one that refused to shine in the night.

A sharp veer around that dead, dark mass had sent the solar system plunging inward toward the great galactic bulge. The sun had crossed lanes of dust as the galaxy rotated, its spiral arms trailing like those of a spinning starfish. The constellations in Earth's nights warped and shifted. Ages passed. Life performed its ceaseless self-contortions. Fresh intelligences arose. Strange, alien minds came from distant suns.

The purposes of that time were shrouded in ambiguity. The sun had followed a stretched ellipse that looped close to the galactic center. A shimmering sphere of light gradually grew in the heavens. To remain near this wheeling beeswarm of ten billion stars, yet another encounter had proved necessary. That time, legend said, the sun had brushed by a giant molecular cloud. Each time, gravity's tugs rearranged the stately glide of the planets. The precision of those soft collisions had been of such delicacy that the new orbits fit the needs of further vast engineering enterprises—the dismantling of whole worlds. Such had humans been, once.

The raccoon-creature found a few planets—those which had survived that epic age of boundless ambition—among the great washes of light that hung above. Innumerable comet tails pointed outward from the sun toward gossamer banks of dim radiance. In such a crowded symphony of sky the slow gavotte of worlds seemed a minor theme.

But tonight the heavens stirred with luminous trouble. Staring upward, the raccoon-creature watched red and orange lights flare and dodge and veer. Soundless and involuted, these were the scribbles of swift combat. The bright traces faded slowly.

They were the first acts of hostility written on this broad sky for nearly a billion years. As before, they arose from the conflicts inherent in the minds of humans—that uneasy anthology of past influences.

Their reptilian subbrains, tucked around the nerve stem, preserved a taste for ritual and violence. Surrounding that, the limbic brain brought an emotional tang to all thoughts—this, an invention of the early mammals. Together, these two ancient remnants gave humans their visceral awareness of the world.

The furry creature which watched the flowering night knew, with a hard-won wisdom buried deep in its genes, that the battle above marked the emergence of something ancient and fearsome. Humanity's neocortex wrapped around the two animal brains in an unsure clasp. In some eras that grip had slipped, unleashing powerful bursts of creativity, of madness, of squandered energy.

The neocortex did hold sway with its gray sagacity, directing its reasoning power outward into the world. But always the deeper minds followed their own rhythms. Some forms of the human species had integrated this triune brain after heroic struggle. Others had engineered the neocortex until it mastered the lower two with complete, unceasing vigilance.

The raccoon-creature had a very different mind, the process of nearly a billion years more of design by both Darwinian winnowing and by careful pruning. Misgivings stirred in that mind now. The broad face wrinkled with complex, unreadable expressions. From its feral legacy it allowed itself a low, moaning growl colored with unease.

Very little of humanity's history had survived the rub of millennia. In any case that tangled record, shot through by discordant voices, would not have been comprehensible to this creature.

Still, it had a deep sense that it was witnessing in the streaked sky not a mere passing incident, but the birth of a savage new age. In the early eras of the human species, simpler minds had identified the dark elements of life with the random tragedies which humans suffered, from storm and disease and nature's myriad calamities. That time lay in the unimaginable past. Now humanity's greatest adversary had emerged again—not the unthinking universe, but itself. And so true evil had returned to the world.

20

THE
UR-HUMANS

The woman dreamed for two days.

She thrashed sometimes, calling out hoarsely, her words slurred just beyond comprehension. The creature had carefully moved her to the shade of some tall trees whose branches formed curious curls like hooks at the very top. It foraged for simple fruit and held slices to the woman's mouth so the juice would trickle down her swollen throat. For itself small animals sufficed, which it caught by simply keeping still for long periods and letting them wander within reach. This was enough, for it knew how to conserve strength while never letting its attention wander from the woman's weak but persistent rhythms of regrowth.

The uses of fantasy are many, and healing is not the least of these. She slept not merely because this was the best way to repair herself. Behind her jerking eyelids a thin layer outside the neocortex brain was rerunning the events which had led to her trauma. This sub-brain integrated emotional and physiological elements, replaying her actions, searching for some fulcrum moment when she might have averted the calamity.

There was some comfort in knowing, finally, that nothing would have changed the outcome. When she reached this conclusion a stiffness left her and to the watching creature her body seemed to soften. Some memories were eventually discarded in this process as too painful to carry, while others were amplified in order to attain a kind of narrative equilibrium. This editing saved her from a burden of remorse and anxiety that, in earlier forms of humanity, would have plagued her for years after.

In the second day she momentarily burst into a slurred song. At dusk she awoke. She looked up into the long, tapered muzzle of her watcher and asked fuzzily, "How many . . . lived?"

"Only you, that I can sense." The creature's voice was low and yet lilting, like a bass note that had worked itself impossibly through the throat of a flute.

"No . . . ?" She was quiet for a time, studying the green moon that swam beyond the mountains.

She said weakly, "The Supras . . ."

"They did this?"

"No, no. I saw some humans, like us, in flyers. The Supras were engaged . . . far away. I thought they would help us."

"They have been busy." It gestured at the southern horizon. In twilight's dim gleaming a fat column of oily smoke stood like an obsidian gravestone.

"What's . . ."

"It has been there since yesterday." The looming distant disaster had strengthened the creature's resolution.

"Ah." She closed her eyes then and subsided into her curious, eyelid-fluttering sleep. For her it was a slippery descent into a labyrinth where twin urges fought, revenge and survival. These two instincts, already ancient before the first hominids walked, rarely married with any security. Yet if she did not feel the pinch of their competition she would not have been by her own judgment a true human.

The next day she got up. Creaking unsteadily, she walked to the stream, where she lay facedown and drank for a long time. One finger was missing from her left hand, but she insisted on helping the creature forage for berries and edible leaves. She spoke little. They took shelter when silvery ships flashed across the sky, but this time there were no rolling booms of distant explosions, as she remembered from before. She did not speak of what had happened and her companion did not ask.

They came upon three humans crisped to ashes and she wept over each. "I never saw weapons before," she said. "Like living flames." "Your enemy took care to thoroughly burn each." She sifted through the shattered bones. "They had strange flyers. Cast down bolts, explosions . . ."

At evening meal she sang again the hypnotic slow song she had pushed up out of her dream-state before, her somber voice hanging on the long notes. Then her eyes abruptly filled and she rushed off into the bushes. Later she sheepishly returned, her mouth attempting a crooked smile, knowing that the need to cover emotion was a quirk of humans and would mean nothing to the raccoon-creature.

On the morning of the third day she broke a long silence with, "I am Cley. Do you use names?"

The creature did not use names among its own kind but knew that humans did, and the animals who mimicked them. "I have been called the Seeker After Patterns."

"Well then, Seeker, I thank you for—"

"Our species are allies. Nothing need be said." Seeker dipped its large head in a way that seemed unnatural to it. Cley realized with a pang that Seeker had studied humans enough to attempt this gesture, invoking humbleness.

"Still, I owe so much."

"My species came long after yours. We benefited from your struggle."

"I doubt we did you much good."

"Life builds upon life. Your kind were but fossils and dust when we walked."

They gathered berries in silence. Seeker could rear up, Centaur-like, or even stand entirely on its hind legs, using its midpaws like clumsy hands. This aided in scooping many small fish from the cold stream rushing over black pebbles. They ate the yellow-green fish without using a fire and stayed well back among the trees. Cley had processed her deep sense of loss through several nights now and the pain of it ebbed, permitting the color to return to her cheeks and no longer robbing her of her sharpness. She and Seeker set out to search the forest further for bodies and this gave her strength despite what she dreaded finding.

She was not married to anyone, male or female, but she knew each person in her tribe intimately. The anonymous charred remains were a blessing, in a way. Apparently some had rotted, then been burned.

They searched systematically through the afternoon, finding only more scorched bodies. Finally they stood looking down into a broad valley, tired, planning where to go next.

"I trust you are all right," a voice said behind them.

Cley whirled. Seeker was already dashing with liquid grace among the nearby trees. A tall, blocky man stood on the outer deck of a brass-colored craft that balanced silently in the air. He had come upon them from behind without even Seeker noticing and this, more than his size and the silent power of his craft, told Cley that she had no chance of getting away. Blinking against the sun glare, she saw that this was a Supra.

"I . . . yes, I am."

"One of our scouts finally admitted that it was not sure all the bodies it saw were dead. I am happy I decided to check upon its work."

As he spoke his ship settled gently near Cley and he stepped off without glancing at the ground. Despite his bulk he moved with unconscious lightness.

"My friend saved me."

"Ah. Can you induce him to return?"

"Seeker! Please come!"

She glimpsed a bulk moving through the nearby bushes, closer than Cley thought the creature could be and coming opposite from the direction Seeker had left. It must be quicker than it looked. There was scarcely a ripple in the foliage but she knew it was there, still cautious. The man smiled slightly and shrugged. "Very well."

"You came to bury my kind?" Cley said bitingly.

"If necessary. I would rather save them."

"Too late for that."

A sadness flickered in his face as he nodded. "The scouts reported some bodies, but all have been burned. You are all I have found—delightfully alive."

His calm mildness was maddening. "Where *were* you Supras? They hounded us, tracked us, killed us all!"

His face showed a quick succession of emotions, each too fleeting for her to read before the next crowded in. Still he said nothing, though his mouth became a tight line and his eyes moistened. He gestured at the pall of smoke that still climbed on the far horizon.

Cley followed his movement and said severely, "I guessed you had to defend your own, but couldn't you have, have . . ."

Her voice trailed away when she saw the pained twinge that constricted his face as her words struck home. Then his mouth thinned again and he nodded. "They attacked new work and old alike. We could not divine what they were about, and when we did, it was too late."

Her anger, stilled for a moment by his vulnerability, returned like an acrid burn in the back of her throat. "We had *nothing* to defend ourselves!"

"Did you think we had weapons?"

"Supras have everything!"

He sighed. "We protect through our laboring machines, through the genius of our past."

"There was fighting in the past. I have heard—"

"The *far* past. Well before your time. We—"

"But *they* knew how. Why didn't you?"

His expression changed again several times with a speed she found baffling. Then a grave sourness shaped his mouth with a sardonic twist. "Tell me who *they* were and perhaps I can answer you."

"They?" She felt sudden doubt. "I thought you would know. They . . . well, they looked more like us . . ."

"Than like me?"

She studied him for a long moment. He was twice her size, with an enormous head. Yet his ears were small and his nose was stubby, like an afterthought. "Yes, they were more our size. Their heads were human and—"

"Ur-human," the man corrected absently, as though he was distracted.

"What?"

"Oh, I am sorry. We term your kind Ur-human, since you are the earliest form available."

Her mouth whitened. "And what do you call yourselves?"

"Ah, humans," he said uncomfortably.

"Well," she said pointedly, "those who burned your city and killed us, they were Ur-human, too."

"Did they have earlobes?"

"I, I can't remember. Things happened fast and—"

"Were their teeth widely spaced, like yours? That was an early modification of the even earlier hominid forms, I gather from my studies with the Keeper of the Records."

"Look, I—"

"Large spacings prevent food from accumulating and decaying. We use that design, as you can see, but also regrow a set every century to compensate for wear. If—"

"You think I had time to think of *that?*"

The man's raptly studious expression vanished as he blinked. "I merely hoped to enlist your aid."

"*You* people run the world, not us."

Soberly he said, "No longer."

She dammed up the bitter torrent within her and said quietly, "Who were they?"

"I don't know. They looked human."

"They weren't like my people."

"Of course not. You possess only those skills appropriate to tending the forests. These people had mastered warring technology that is ancient beyond measure."

He gazed apprehensively at the sky, rubbing his shoulder as though he was stiff. She noticed that his light, loose-fitting jump suit was stained and torn.

"You fought them?"

"As we could. We were surprised and saw only flame, no people."

Seeker spoke from beside them. "The lightning returned here, later, to burn the dead humans."

Both humans were startled. Blinking, the man said, "You are remarkably silent."

Seeker said, "A craft of ours. You found no humans unburned?"

The man frowned. "Not yet."

"I doubt you will," Seeker said. "They are thorough."

Cley asked, "What did they do to your cities?"

"Come." He gave the order without taking his eyes from the sky. His mouth echoed a quick flurry of emotion and he held a palm up to Seeker. "Fine ally, we gather now."

This seemed enough for Seeker. The brass-bright craft tilted momentarily as the creature boarded. Cley went through the wide hatchway and into a simple, comfortable control cabin. The Supra sat down and the ship lifted with scarcely a murmur.

"I am Alvin," he said, as though anyone would know who he was. His casual confidence told her more than the name, and she responded to his questions about the last few days with short, precise answers. She had rarely even seen a Supra and this one was not winning her over.

But as they rose with smooth acceleration Cley gaped, not attempting to hide her surprise. Within moments she saw the lands where she had lived and labored reduced to a mere spot in a vastly larger canvas. She watched the mountains she had admired as a girl reduced to foot soldiers in an army that marched around the curve of the world. Her tribe had known well the green complexity of the forests, but she had not truly comprehended the extent of the Supras' works. Many thin brown rivers flowed through narrow canyons, giving the mountain range the look of a knobby spine from which many nerves trailed into the tan deserts beyond. Brilliant snowcaps crowned the tallest peaks, but these were not, she saw, the source of the countless rivers. Each muddy nerve began abruptly high in a canyon and was busily digging itself in deeper.

Cley pointed and before she could ask Alvin said, "We feed them from tunnels. The great Millennium Lakes lie far underground here."

This landsculpting was only a few centuries old, but already the moist wealth had reclaimed much of the planet's dry midcontinent.

Alvin sat back, indolent as his ship performed a long turn to show her the expanses. She caught a brilliant spark of polished metal far away on the very curve of the planet.

"Diaspar," Alvin said.

"The legend," she whispered.

"It is quite real," he said, running his eyes over the display screens that studied the space around them.

"Did they go there, too?"

"The attackers? No. I have no idea why not."

"Does Diaspar's name come from 'despair'?"

"What?" He sat bolt upright. "No, of course not. Who said it did?"

"It was a joke we made," she said to unknit his eyebrows. "That you Supras had been walled up in there so long—"

"Nonsense! We saved humanity, holding on while the desert encroached. We—"

"And that green spot? Right beside Diaspar?"

"That's Lys."

"Lies? Someone telling lies?"

"No! Look, I do not know what you Ur-humans do for amusement, but I do not find—"

"I was merely recalling some primeval humor."

Alvin shook his head. His eyes never left the screens and she realized he was looking for a sign that the attackers might return again. How they could vanish so readily and elude the Supras she could not fathom. But then, the Earth was large, and in these sprawling lands there were many places to hide.

21

THE
LIBRARY
OF
LIFE

They descended along the spine of snowcapped mountains. Cley was surprised to find that seen this way the soaring peaks were like crumpled sacks carelessly thrown on a tan table, all other detail washed away. She did not know, and Alvin did not tell her, that mountains were passing features, scum stirred up by the slow waltz of continents.

These proudly jutting spires had first broken through an ancient ocean floor as the seas themselves drained away. The birth of the first peaks had been chronicled in a ledger kept by humans, now lost in the recesses of ornate and useless detail which Diaspar still hoarded. These groaning ridges had risen during a time when the greatest of all human religions bloomed on their flanks. That faith had converted the entire world, had plumbed the philosophic depths of the then-human soul, and now was totally forgotten. Only the Keeper of Records knew the name of that belief, and he had not bothered to unveil that dusty era for Alvin. The furious causes and grand illusions of the past were like the ghosts of worn, vanquished mountain ranges, now sunk beneath the seas of sand.

Cley gazed across the broad plains of desert, for so long like the winding sheets of Earth's corpse, now being forced back by forest. Sandy wastes still lapped at the jewel of Diaspar. She saw as they

swept southward that from distant Lys a long finger of a river-valley
pointed into the desert, reaching crookedly toward Diaspar. The
reconquering of the planet proceeded around its girth, and at this
sight a sensation swept over her of sudden lightness, of buoyant,
weightless hope. The loss of her tribe fell away from her for at least
one moment and she basked in the spectacle of her world, seeing for
the first time its intricate wholeness.

Something moved on the far curved horizon and she pointed.
"What's that?"

"Nothing dangerous," Alvin answered. At the limits of her tele-
scoped vision she could make out a long straight line that pointed
nearly straight down. It seemed to move and then she lost it in
distant clouds. Alvin ignored her, brooding, eyes flicking among the
many dense thickets of data that the ship's walls offered him.

"Where are we going?"

He blinked as though returning from some distant place. "To hell
and back."

When she frowned, puzzled, he smiled. "An ancient phrase.
Come, I'll show you that hell does dwell on Earth—for the moment."

They plunged down through a storm wrack that was speeding
around the equator. Clouds fat and purpling with moisture speckled
the air's high expanse. In the last few years she had felt their winds
and rain more often as moisture spread through the parched ecos-
phere.

The ship swooped through decks of thin fog and down, across
vistas of windswept sand. Seeker put its tapered hand in hers and
murmured, "Wait." She shot it a quick questioning glance. Its ban-
dit-mask markings around the large eyes seemed to promise mischievous revelations. Alvin apparently noticed nothing except the walls'
sliding arrays, as though these perspectives of space and vast time
were commonplace.

"See?" He summoned up a continent-wide view of the desert on
a bulkhead. A network of red lines appeared slowly, images building
up like pale blood vessels shown beneath a sallow skin. "The old
subway tunnels, leading to cities that once lived."

"When?"

"More years ago than you could count if you did nothing else throughout your life."

She stared. The display showed wispy lattices of streets beneath the shifting sands, the shadows of cities whose very names were lost. "So many . . ."

"There were vast alternatives to Diaspar then. We did not seize them."

"And now?"

Alvin laughed. "Uncountable! Infinitude!"

To her surprise Seeker spoke, reedy and melodious. "There are more breeds of infinitude than of finiteness."

Alvin raised his eyebrows, startled. "You know of transfinites?"

"You speak of mere mathematics. I refer to your species."

Seeker had not spoken to Alvin since they entered the ship. She saw that the beast was not awed by this sleek, swift artifact. It sat perfectly at ease and nothing escaped its quick, bright eyes.

Alvin pursed his lips. "Just so, sage. Did you know that your kind evolved to keep humans intellectually honest?"

Cley could not read Seeker's expression as it said with a rippling intonation, "So humans think."

Alvin looked disconcerted. "I . . . I suppose we, too, have illusions."

"Truth depends on sense organs," Seeker said with what Cley took to be a kindly tinge to its clipped words. Or was she imposing a human judgment on Seeker's slight crinklings around its slitted eyes, the sharpening of the peaks of its yellow ears?

"We have records of the long discourses between your kind and mine," Alvin began. "I studied them."

"A human library," Seeker said. "Not ours."

Cley saw in Seeker's eyes a gulf, the darkness that would always hang between species. Across hundreds of millions of years words were mere signal flares held up against the encroaching night.

"Yes," Alvin said soberly, "and that is what burns. We know what humans thought and did, but I am coming to see that much history passed outside human ken."

"Much should."

"But we will regain everything," Alvin said severely.

"You cannot regain time."

Alvin nodded with wan fatigue. Cley knew fragments of his history and saw that he had changed in the several centuries since as a daring boy he had altered human fortunes. One of her own people would have passed through wisdom and died in the time this man had enjoyed; another sign of the unknowable distance between the species. Alvin's spirit visibly ebbed, as if this flight had taken him momentarily away from a fact he could not digest.

The ship was landing beside a wall of black that she at first took to be solid. Then she saw ash-gray coils rising through sullen clouds and knew that this was the smoky column she had seen for days.

"The Library of Life," Alvin said. "They attacked it with something like lightning. Bolts that struck and burrowed and hunted. They found the treasure that ages of wearing winds had not discovered."

"An underground library?" Cley asked. Her tribe had once laughed at a Supra who told them of this practice, the attempt to imprison meaning in fixed substance. People who lived and worked in the constant flux of the deep woods saw permanence for the illusion that it was.

"A legacy separated from Diaspar," Alvin said kindly. "The ancients knew its storehouse would not be needed in my crystal city. But the urge to preserve was profound in them and so they buried deeply."

"A recurrent human feature," Seeker said.

"The only way to understand the past," Alvin countered sharply.

"Meaning passes," Seeker said.

"Does transfinite geometry?"

"Geometry signifies. It does not mean."

Alvin grunted with exasperation and kicked open the hatch. The sharp bite of smoke made Cley cough but Alvin took no notice of it. They climbed out into a buzz and clamor of feverish activity. All around the ship worked legions of robots. Supras commanded teams that struggled up from ragged-mouthed tunnels in the desert, carrying long cylinders of gleaming glass.

"We're trying to save the last fragments of the library, but most of it is gone," Alvin said, striding quickly away from the guttural rumble of the enormous fire. Smoke streamed from channels gouged in the desert. These many thin, soot-black wedges made up the enormous pyre that towered above them, filling half the sky.

"What was in there?" Cley asked.

"Frozen life," Seeker said.

"Yes," Alvin said, his glance betraying surprise. "The record of all life's handiwork for over a billion years. Left here, should the race ever need biological stores again."

"Then that which burns," Seeker said, "is the coding."

Alvin nodded bitterly. "A mountain-sized repository of DNA."

"Why was it in the desert?" Cley asked.

"Because there might have come a time when even Diaspar failed, yet humanity went on. So the Keeper says."

The teams of robots moved in precise ranks that even the hubbub of fighting the fires could not fracture. They surged on wheels and legs and tracks, churning the loose soil as they pushed large mounds of grit and gravel into the open troughs where flames still licked. She could see where explosions had ripped open the long trenches. Now the fire scoured the deep veins of the planet's accumulated genetic wisdom, and the robots were like insect teams automatically hurrying to protect their queen, preserving a legacy they could not share. Cley could scarcely take her eyes from the towering pyre where the heritage of numberless extinct species was vanishing into billowing wreaths of carbon.

The machines automatically avoided the three of them as they walked over a low hill and into an open hardpan plain. In oblivious tribute to the perfection he knew in Diaspar, Alvin did not bother to move aside as batallions of robots rushed past them. Seeker flinched visibly at the roar and wind of great machines, dangerously close.

Cley saw that feelers of grass and scrub trees had already advanced here, resurgent life licking at the dead sands. Supras hurried everywhere, ordering columns of machines with quick stabs at hand-held instruments.

"The fight goes no better," Alvin said sourly. "We are trying to snuff it out by burying the flames. But the attackers have used some inventive electromotive fire that survives even burial."

"The arts of strife," a woman commented sardonically.

Cley turned and saw a tall, powerfully built woman some distance away. Yet her voice had seemed close, intimate.

"Alvin!" the woman called and ran toward them. "We have lost a phylum."

Alvin's stern grimace stiffened further. "Something minor, I hope?"

"The Myriasoma."

"The many-bodied? No!" Despair flitted across his face.

Cley asked, "What are they?"

Alvin stared into the distance, emotion flickering in his face. "A form my own species knew, long ago. A composite intelligence which used drones capable of receiving electromagnetic instructions. The creature could disperse itself at will."

Cley looked at the woman uneasily, feeling an odd tension playing at the edge of her perceptions. "I never saw one."

"We had not revived them yet," Alvin said. "Now they are lost."

Seeker said, "Do not be hasty."

Alvin ignored it. "You are sure we lost all?"

"I hoped there would be traces, but . . . yes. All."

Cley heard the woman and simultaneously felt a deeper, resonant voice sounding in her mind. The woman turned to her and said, "You have the talent, yes. Hear."

This time the woman's voice resounded only in Cley's mind, laced with strange, strumming bass notes. *I am Seranis, a Supra who shares this.*

"I, I don't understand," Cley said. She glanced at Seeker and Alvin but could not read their looks.

We have re-created you Ur-humans from the entries in this Library. We further augmented you so that you could understand us through this direct talent.

"But Alvin didn't—"

He is of Diaspar and thus lacks the talent. Only we from Lys have the threads of microwave-active magnetite laid down in skull and brain.

They twine among your—and our—neurological circuitry. When stimulated by electrical activity, these amplify and transmit our thoughts. Seranis took Cley's hands and held them up, palms facing, then slowly brought them to Seranis's temples. Cley felt the voice strengthen. *I am antenna and receiver, as are you.*

"I could never do this before!" Cley said loudly, as if the new talent made her doubt her older voice.

The talent must be stimulated first, since it is not natural to Urhumans. Seranis smiled sardonically. *It might have helped your species in your age. We of Lys have it because for so long we lived for the whole, for our community. This knits us together.*

"And Alvin?"

Diaspar is the master of urban mechanism, Lys of verdant wooded majesty. Their art escapes their boundaries, while ours sings of our time and community. Diaspar rejected the enveloping intimacy of the talent, though it is an unending pleasure. And we of Lys pay the price of mortality for this.

"This talent . . . kills you?"

Seranis smiled wearily. *Yes. Stressed so, inevitably the brain loses structure, substance. This defect of finiteness we share with you Urhumans.*

Cley knew that she was speaking with the person who had brought her kind back into the world, yet she could not decide whether to be angry or grateful. "Then why give it to us, if we did not have it before . . . before you cooked us up from your Library?"

Did a quick flicker of caution pass in the tightening of Seranis's lips? *For now, let me simply say that we know you well enough to savor your kinesthetic joys, your quick and zesty sense of the world. That we lost in Lys.*

Cley thought, *Lost in lies?*

Seranis blinked and Cley knew she had been understood. The little joke came through in even this strange medium.

Somberly Seranis said, *We believed the great lie about invaders, yes. Some say that is why we are so named.*

"Invaders?"

Once both Diaspar and Lys believed that humanity fled the stars, before a horde. But the fact—uncovered by Alvin as he ventured out from Diaspar, to Lys and beyond—is that humanity retreated before the knowledge of greater minds among the stars. We tried to evolve even vaster forces, minds free of matter itself. And succeeded. But exhaustion and fear drove us into a wan recessional as cities died and hopes faded.

An immense sadness ran through these thoughts, long rolling notes that held in Cley's mind like a soulful dirge. These chords were all counterpointed by the pressing world around her—a medley of crackling distant fires, the acrid tang of oily smoke, the hoarse shouts of orders and dismay, the grim grinding of heavy machines.

She realized Alvin was studying her with interest, and remembered that she had spoken his name. Immediately she had a sense of the chasm that had opened between her and anyone who could not catch the silky speed of this talent, its filmy warmth and cloaked meanings.

And it brought more still—pure unbidden sensation. Seranis turned to give a spoken order to a machine and Cley felt an echo of the woman's swivel, the catch of indrawn breath, minute pressures and flexes. Still deeper in Seranis burned a slow, sexual fire. The folk of Lys had kept the roiling passions of early humanity, the carnal joy and longing that flushed the mind with goaty rut, calling up the pulsing urgencies laid down in reptile brains on muddy shores.

Seranis was an adult in a way Alvin would never be. Neither was wrong or right; each subspecies had chosen profoundly different paths.

"Ah, yes," Cley made herself say, jerking her mind out of the hot, cloying satisfactions of this talent. "I, I . . ."

"You need say nothing," Alvin said, smiling. "I envy you. More, I need you."

Ranks of tractor-driven robots roared by them, making talk impossible, slinging pebbles high in the air. Seeker nervously shuffled back and forth, eyeing the gargantuan machines. It had now the look of an animal in strange surroundings, wary and skittish. Cley was concerned for it, but she knew she could do nothing for Seeker without the approval of the Supras.

"Need me?" she asked. "For what?"

Alvin said smoothly, "You are a rarity now. That was why I searched."

The lightning sought our Ur-humans, Seranis put in. *Alvin himself looked for the survivors, but . . .*

Cley glanced from Alvin to Seranis, acutely conscious of their casual ease. They were half again as large as she, their chocolate skins vibrant with health. Seranis, though, showed lines in her face which gave it a grave, crinkled geometry. Their clothes rippled to accommodate each movement. An air of unconscious well-being hovered around their sleek resilience. She glanced down at herself: bruised from her injuries, scratched by bushes, skin creased and scabbed and dirty.

She felt a flickering burst of embarrassment.

I am sorry, Seranis sent with concern. *That was an overlap of my own emotion. Nakedness carries sexual and social signals in Lys.*

Cley asked wonderingly, "The simple baring of skins?" Her people enjoyed the rub of the world on their flesh, but it meant nothing more. For her, passion rose from context, not attire.

Alvin's kind do not feel it, since immortals do not need reproduction.

"They do not sex?"

Seldom. Long ago they altered themselves—a subcurrent added, *(or perhaps the machines did a little pruning)* with a lilting tinge of amber laughter—*to avoid the ferment of sexuality. They banished sexual signaling, all the unconscious signs and gestures. Still, I have this trait, and some of my feelings transmitted to you. I*—

"Never mind," Cley said shortly. She ordinarily felt no shame at all and much preferred her present nudity. Clothes robbed her of freedom and a silky sensitivity.

What *did* bother her was her sudden intense feeling of inferiority. It had come welling up, tagged with the unsettling embarrassment and riding on her knowledge that her kind was so limited. To the Supras she was a living fossil.

She remembered with some satisfaction that Alvin was deaf to the darting talent-currents and so spoke aloud, though already the thick movements of her throat and tongue were beginning to seem brutish and clumsy. "Why are you so concerned for us?"

"You Ur-humans are valuable," Alvin said cautiously.

"Because we can do grunt labor?" Cley asked sarcastically.

"You know you have crafts in dealing with biological systems that we later adaptations do not," Seranis said evenly.

"Oh sure." Cley held up a small finger which she quickly transformed into five different tools—needle, connector, biokey, pruner, linkweb. "This wasn't your add-on?"

"Well," Seranis said carefully, "we did modify a few of them. But Ur-humans had the underlying capabilities."

Cley's mouth twisted with ironic humor. "Good thing you gave me this talent-talk. I can feel that there's something you don't want to tell me."

"You are right." Alvin swept his arms to take in the wall of roiling smoke that stood like a solid, ominous barrier. "We're concerned now because we could lose you all."

"Lose us?"

She caught thoughts from Seranis but the layers were chopped wedges, fogged by meanings she could sense but not decipher. In the instant between *lose* and *us* she felt a long, stretched interval in which gravid blocks of meaning rushed by her. It was as if immense objects swept through a high, vaulted space that she could see only in quilted shadows. She felt then the true depth and speed of Seranis—knew that through this luxuriant talent she was floating in a tiny corner of an immense cathedral of ideas, far from the great transept and unaware of labyrinths forever shrouded. Passages yawned far away, reduced by perspective to small mouths, yet she knew instantly that they were corridors of thought down which she could never venture in her lifetime. The hollow silence of these chilly spaces, all part of Seranis, held unintelligible mystery. These people looked human, despite their size and odd liquid grace, but she suddenly sensed that they were as strange as any beast she had seen in the swelling forests. Yet they stood in the long genetic tradition of her kind and so she owed them some loyalty. Still, the sheer *size* of their minds—

"We could lose you Ur-humans," Alvin said with what she now saw was indulgent patience. "Your species records were obliterated in the attack. All other Ur-humans were burned to a crisp. You, Cley, are the last remaining copy."

22

A
LARGER
TOPOLOGY

She worked for long days in the shattered ruins. The robots cleared the heavy wreckage, but there were innumerable places where human care and common sense could rescue a fragment of the shattered past and she was glad to help. The severed finger on her left hand had regrown but was still stiff and weak so she wanted to exercise it. And she needed time to clear her head, to climb out of an abyss of grief.

The attack had been thorough. Livid bolts had assaulted one wing of the Library with particular attention, she learned. Shafts had descended again and again in brilliant skeins of color, hanging for long moments like a malevolent rainbow whose feet shot electrical arrows into the soil.

That wing had housed the Library of Humanity. The Ur-humans had been the oldest form lodged there, and now they and all the many varieties of humanity that had immediately followed them were lost—except for Cley.

The impact of this was difficult for her to comprehend. The robots gave her awkward, excessive deference. The Supras all paid her polite respect, and she felt their careful protection as she worked. In turn, without being obvious, she watched the Supras commanding their robot legions, but did not know how to read their mood.

Then one day a Supra woman suddenly broke off her task and began to dance. She moved with effortless energy, whirling and tumbling, her feet flashing across the debris of the Library, hands held up as if to clasp the sky. Other Supras took up the dance behind her and in moments they were all moving with stunning speed that did not have any note of rush or frenzy.

Cley knew then that she was watching a refinement of Ur-human rituals that went far beyond anything her tribe had used to defuse inner torments. She could glimpse no pattern to their arabesques, but sensed subtle elements slipping by in each movement. It was eerie to watch several hundred bodies revolve and spring and bounce and glide, all without the merest glance at one another, without song or even faint music. In the total silence she could pick up no signals from the talent; they were utterly quiet, each orbiting in a closed curve. The Supras danced without pause or sign of tiring for the rest of the day and through the night and on well into the next morning.

Cley watched their relentless, driving dances without hope of comprehending. Without meaning to, the Supras told her that she was utterly alone. Seeker was no company, either; it gave the Supras only an occasional glance and soon fell asleep. She longed for her own people and tried to leave the Supra compound, but as she approached the perimeter her skin began to burn and itch intolerably. While the tall, perfect figures whirled through the night she remembered loves and lives now lost down death's funnel, tried to sleep and could not.

And then without a sign or gesture they abruptly stopped . . . looked around at each other . . . and wordlessly returned to work. Their robots started up again and there was never any mention of the matter.

The next day, as work resumed, Seranis took samples of her hair, skin, blood and urine. *For the Library*, Seranis explained.

"But there isn't one anymore."

Come.

Seranis led her and Seeker down through a shattered portal. Cley had lived all her life in the irregular beauties of the forests, where her people labored. She was unprepared for the immense geometries below, the curling subterranean galleries that curved out of sight, the alabaster helicities that tricked her eye into believing that gravity had been routed.

Already we rebuild.

Teams of bronzed robots were tending large, blocky machines that exuded glossy walls. The metallic blue stuff oozed forth and bonded seamlessly, yet when Cley touched it a moment later the slick surface was rock-hard.

"But for what? You've lost the genetic material." She preferred to speak now rather than use the talent, for fear of giving away her true feelings.

We can save your personal DNA, of course, and the few scraps we have recovered here. Other species dwell in the forests. We will need your help in gathering them.

Currents from Seranis gently urged her to use her talent exclusively, but Cley resisted, wanting to keep a distance between them.

"Good. You've read my helix, now let me go out—"

Not yet. We have processes to initiate. To re-create your kind demands guidance from you as well.

"You did it without me before."

With difficulty and error.

"Look, maybe I can find some of my people. You may have missed—"

Alvin is sure none remain.

"He can't be certain. We're good at hiding."

Alvin possesses a surety you cannot know.

Seeker said in its high, melodious voice like sunlight dancing on water, "Alvin moves in his own arc."

Seranis studied the large creature carefully. "You perceive him as a segment of a larger topology?"

Seeker rose up on its hind legs, ropes of muscle sliding under its fur, and gestured with both its forelegs and hands, complex signals Cley could not decipher.

"He first resolved the central opposition between the interior and exterior of Diaspar," Seeker said in its curious, light voice. "This he did by overcoming blocks of cultural narrowness, of unknown history, of his people's agoraphobia, of the computers. This inside-outside opposition he then transformed by breaking out, only to meet its reflection in the oppositions between Lys and Diaspar. To surmount this, his spirit convolved it into the opposition of the provincialism of Earth versus the expansiveness of the galaxy itself. And by confronting the Diaspar computers with a paradox in the blocked memory of one of the service robots of Shalmirane. This act led him outward again, in a starship."

Seranis gaped, the first time Cley had ever seen a Supra impressed. "How could you possibly know—?"

Seeker waved aside her question. "And so beneath the Seven Suns he found another barrier, the vacant cage of something great beyond humanity. This spatial barrier he now confronts in his own mind, and seeks to turn it into a barrier in time."

"I . . . I don't understand . . ." Cley said.

"I do." Seranis studied Seeker warily. "This beast sees our motions in another plane. It has pieced together our conversations and ferreted out much. But what do you mean, a barrier in time?"

Seeker's broad mouth turned downward, the opposite of a human smile. Cley suspected that Seeker was conveying something like ironic amusement, for its eyes darted with a kind of liquid, skipping joy. "Two meanings I offer. He delves backward in time, to evolution's edge, for the Ur-humans. As well, he seeks something outside of time, a new cage."

Cley felt a flash of alarm in Seranis, who stiffly said, "That is nonsense."

"Of course," Seeker said. "But not my nonsense." It made a dry, barking noise that Cley could have sworn was laughter carrying dark filigrees beneath.

Cley felt a surf of consternation roll over the sea-deep swell of Seranis's mind. "And next?" Seranis asked.

"No cage holds forever."

"Will you help us?"

"I have a higher cause," Seeker said quietly.

"I suspected as much." Seranis raised one eyebrow. "Higher than the destiny of intelligent life?"

"Yours is a local intelligence."

"We spread once among the stars—and we can do it again."

"And yet you remain bottled inside your skins."

"As do you," Seranis said with clipped precision.

"You know we differ. You must be able to sense it." Seeker rapped the cranial bulge that capped his snout, as though knocking on a door.

"I can feel something, yes," Seranis said guardedly.

Cley could pick up nothing from Seeker. She shuffled uneasily, lost in the speed and glancing impressions of their conversation.

"You humans have emotions," Seeker said slowly, "but emotions possess you."

Seranis prodded, "And your kind?"

"We have urges which serve other causes."

Seranis nodded, deepening Cley's sensation of enormous shared insights that seemed as unremarkable to the others as the air they breathed. They all lived as ants in the shadow of mountains of millennia, and time's sheer mass shaded every word. Yet no one spoke clearly. Dimly she guessed that the riverrun of ages had somehow blurred all certainties, cast doubt on the very categories of knowing themselves. History held counterexamples to any facile rule. All tales were finally slippery, suspect, so talk darted among somber chasms of ignorance and upjuts of painful memory as old as continents, softening tongues into ambiguity and guile.

Seeker broke the long, strained silence between them. "We are allies at the moment, that we both know."

"I am happy to hear so. I have wondered why you accompanied Cley."

"I wished to save her."

Seranis asked suspiciously, "You just happened along?"

"I was here to learn of fresh dangers which vex my species."

Seranis folded her arms and shifted her weight, an age-old human gesture Cley guessed meant the same to all species: a slightly protective reservation of judgment. "Are you descended from the copies we made?"

"From your Library of Life?" Seeker coughed as though to cover impolite amusement, then showed its yellow teeth in a broad, unreadable grin. "Genetically, yes. But once you released my species, we took up our ancient tasks."

Seranis frowned. "I thought you were originally companions to a species of human now vanished."

"So that species thought."

"That's what the libraries of Diaspar say," Seranis said with a trace of affronted ire.

"Exactly. They were a wise species, even so."

"Ur-human?" Cley asked. She would like to think that her ancestors' saga had included friends like Seeker.

Its large eyes studied her for a long moment. "No, they were a breed which knew the stars differently than you."

"Better?"

"Differently."

"And they're completely lost?" Cley asked quietly, acutely aware of the shrouded masses of history.

"They are gone."

Seranis asked suspiciously, "Gone—or extinct?"

"From your perspective," Seeker said, "there is no difference."

"Seems to me extinction pretty much closes the book on you," Cley said lightly, hoping to dispel the tension which had somehow crept into the conversation.

"Just so," Seranis said evenly. "The stability of this biosphere depends on keeping many species alive. The greater their number, the more rugged Earthlife is, should further disasters befall the planet."

"As they shall," Seeker said, settling effortlessly into its position for walking, a signal that it would talk no more.

Damned animal! Seranis could not shield this thought from Cley, or else did not want to.

They left the Library of Humanity in a seething silence, Seranis deliberately blocking off her talent so that Cley could not catch the slightest prickly fragment of her thoughts.

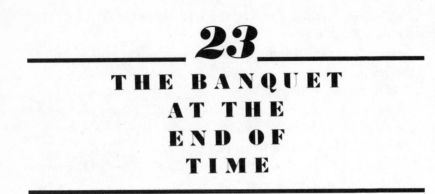

23

THE BANQUET
AT THE
END OF
TIME

That evening Alvin presided over a grand meal for three hundred with Cley as guest of honor. Robots had labored through the day, extruding a large, many-spired banquet hall which seemed to rise up groaning from the soil itself. Its walls were sand-colored but opalescent. Inside, a broad ceiling of overlapping arches looked down on tables that also grew directly from a granite floor. Spiral lines wrapped around the walls, glowing soft blue at the floor and shifting to red as they rose, circling the room, making an eerie effect like a sunset seen above an azure sea. Tricks of perspective led Cley into false corridors and sometimes there appeared to be thousands of other guests eating in the distance. At times holes would gape in the floor and robots would rise through them bearing food, a process she found so unsettling that thereafter she stayed in her seat. Despite the cold night air of the desert the room enjoyed a warm spring breeze scented like the pine forests she knew so well. Her gown scarcely seemed to have substance, caressing her like water, yet covered her from ankle to neck.

They ate grains and vegetables of primordial origin, many dating back to the dawn of humanity. These had already been spread through the emerging biosphere, and this meal was the boon of an ample harvest, brought here from crops throughout the globe. Cley savored the rich sauces and heady aromas but kept her wits about her in conversation with her hosts.

Often their talk went straight by her, arabesques of talent-meaning sliding among percussive verbal punctuations. The Supras of Lys tapered their rapid-fire signals to make them comprehensible to Cley. Those of Diaspar used only the subset of their language which she could follow. They tried to keep the din of layered cross-references simple in deference to her, but gusts of enthusiasm would sweep their ornate conversations into realms of mystifying complexity.

She felt their remorse and anger underlying a stern resolve to recover what they could. Yet Alvin made jokes, even quoting some ancient motto of a scholarly society from the dawn of science. *"Nullius in verba,"* he said dryly, "or 'don't take anyone's word for it.' Makes libraries seem pointless, wouldn't you say?"

Cley shrugged. "I am no student."

"Exactly! Time to stop studying our history. We should reinvent it." Alvin took a long drink from a chalice.

"I'd like to just live my life, thanks," Cley said quietly.

"Ah," he said, "but the true trick is to treasure what we were and have done—without letting it smother us."

Alvin smiled with a dashing exuberance she had not seen among the other Supras. He waved happily as what appeared to be a flock of giant scaly birds flew through the hall, wheeled beautifully, and flew straight through the ceiling without leaving a mark.

Seranis was distracted by a flurry of talent-talk but displayed her skill by simultaneously saying to Cley, "He means that here at the end of a long corridor of time, we should ignore the echoes."

Cley frowned, wishing Seeker had come to this bewildering banquet, but the quiet beast had elected to rest. She was concerned. She could not in all honesty see why Seeker stayed with her when the Supras would probably have let it go. Its laconic replies had antagonized Seranis and that could be dangerous. While Supras had never harmed Ur-humans, she was not sure any such convention governed their relations with distant species. In any case, caution outweighed theory, as mice knew about elephants.

To not seem a complete dunce, she tried to get back into conversation. Alvin was the center of attention, but he looked quickly back at her when she asked, "How can you shrug off history?"

He eyed her closely, as if trying to read something inscrutable. "By studied neglect." He leaned forward, eyes intent and sharp with mirth. The day of dancing seemed to have released him from some burden she could not guess. "History is such detail! Emperors are like the dinosaurs. Their names and antics are unimportant. Only the dates of their appearance and passing can matter."

Someone called from down the table, "The Keeper of Records will scold you!"

Alvin answered, "No, he will not. He knows we hold aloft time's dread weight only by keeping a sense of balance. Otherwise it would crush us."

"We dance on time!" another voice called. "*It's* under *us.*"

Alvin chuckled. "True, in a way. The roll call of empires is dust beneath our feet . . . yet we cling to our old habits. *Those* last."

"We need some human continuity," Cley said reasonably. "My tribe—"

"Yes, a singular invention. When we recalled you all, it was apparent we could not let you resurrect the old imperial habits."

Cley frowned. "Imperial . . . ?"

"Of course," Seranis said. "You do not know." She inhaled a passing spice cloud and while her lungs savored it she sent, *We took your genotype from the Age of Empire, when humanity plundered the solar system and nearly extinguished itself.*

The talent-voice of Seranis carried both a sting of rebuke and the balm of forgiveness. This only irritated Cley, who struggled to hide it.

"My tribe made no . . . war." She had to pause and let her deep-based vocabulary call up the word, for she had never used it before. Comprehending the definition and import of the word took a long moment. With foreboding she permanently tagged it for ready future use.

"That was how we wanted it." Alvin smiled as though he were discussing the weather. "We reasoned that at most you might eventually expand for territory, rather than for political gains and taxes, as in the imperial model."

"We did not realize we were so . . . planned." Cley gritted her teeth, hoping that this would not leak out through her talent. The nakedness of her thoughts was proving to be a nuisance.

"We did not interfere with your basic design, believe me," Seranis said kindly. She offered Cley a tart fruit but seemed unbothered at its refusal. "Your group loyalty is your species' most important way to find an identity. It fosters social warmth. Such patterns persist, from a children's playhouse to a transworld alliance."

"And how do *you* work together?"

Alvin said, "We do not struggle against each other, for such traits have been very nearly edited out of us. But most important, we have the blessing of a higher goal."

"What?" Cley demanded.

"Perhaps *enemy* is a better term than goal. Until now I would have said that history was our true foe, dragging at our heels as we attempted to escape from it. But now we have met an active enemy from out of history itself, and I must say I find myself filled with eagerness."

Alvin was clearly the youngest of these Supras, though Cley could not reliably read the age of any of these bland, perfect faces. "Enemies? Other Supras?"

"No no. You are recalling those people who supposedly fired at you, who killed your tribefellows, who destroyed the Library of Life?"

"Yes." Cley's mouth narrowed with the effort of concealing her hate. Primitive emotions would not go well here.

"They were illusions."

"I saw them!"

"They appeared here, too. I closely examined our records and"— he snapped his fingers—"there they were. Just as you had seen. We were too busy to notice, and so we owe you a vote of thanks."

"They were real!"

"Extensive study of their spectral images show them to be artful refractions of heated air."

Cley looked blank. The sensation of being robbed of a clear enemy was like stepping off a stair in darkness and finding no next step. "Then . . . what . . ."

Alvin leaned back and cupped his hands behind his neck, elbows high. He gazed up at the clear night, seeming to take great joy in the broad sweep of stars. Many comets unfurled their filmy tails, so many they seemed like a flock of arrows aimed at the unseen sun, which had sheltered behind the curve of Earth.

Alvin said slowly, "What heats air? Lightning. But to do it so craftily?"

Seranis looked surprised. Cley saw that Alvin had told none of this to the others, for throughout the great hall the long tables fell silent.

Seranis said, "Electrical currents—that's all lightning is. But to make realistic images . . ."

Cley asked, "All to trick us?"

Alvin clapped his hands together loudly with childlike glee, startling his hushed audience. "Exactly! Such ability!"

Seranis asked quietly, "Already?"

Alvin nodded. "The Mad Mind. It has returned."

A blizzard of talent-talk struck Cley like a blow. The Supras were on their feet, buzzing with speculation. Inside her head percussive waves seemed to amplify the torrent.

Again she felt the labyrinth of their minds, the kinesthetic thrust of ideas streaming past, features blurred beyond comprehension.

Whirlwinds.

A black sun roaring against ruby stars.

Purple geysers on an infinite plain.

The plain shrinking until it was a disk, the black sun at its center.

Stars shredded into phosphorescent tapestries.

For instants the black sun swam at the rim of the beeswarm gossamer galaxy. Next, it buzzed ominously at the very focus of the spiral arms.

She dropped away from darkening thunderheads, fleeing this storm. Tucked herself away. Waited.

Panting with the mental exertion, she wondered what the people of Lys were like when they were alone. Or if they ever were.

Supras, Ur-humans, Seeker—all from different eras in the eon-long explorations of evolution. This desert plain was like a baked-dry display table covered with historical curiosities. What vexed currents worked, when different ages sought to conspire! And she was pinned here, firmly spiked by the bland, all-powerful, condescending reasonableness of the Supras.

Cley pressed her palms to her ears. The din of talent-talk drummed on. As soon as they got through with their labyrinthian logic, they would notice her again.

And talk down to her. Reassure her. Treat her like a vaguely remembered pet.

No wonder they had not recalled the many varieties of dogs and cats, she thought bitterly. Ur-humans had served that purpose quite nicely.

Her people . . . They had labored for the Supras for centuries, tending the flowering biosphere. The Supras had known enough to let them form tribes, to work their own small will upon the forest. But drawn out of that fragile matrix, Cley gasped like an ancient beached fish.

She staggered away, anger clouding her vision. Conflicts that had been building in her burst forth, and she hoped the blizzard of talent-talk hid them. But she could avoid them no longer herself.

She was like a bug here, scuttling at the feet of these distracted supermen. They were kind enough in their cool, lopsided fashion, but their effort to damp their abilities down to her level was visible—and galling. Longing for her own kind brimmed in her.

Her only hope of seeing her kind again lay in these Supras. But a clammy fear clasped her when she tried to think what fresh Ur-humans would be like.

Bodies decanted from some chilly crucible. Her relatives, yes, clones of her. But strangers. Unmarked by life, unreared. They would be her people only in the narrow genetic sense.

Unless somewhere, some Ur-humans lived. *They* would know the tribal intimacies, the shared culture she longed for.

If they existed, she had to find them.

Yet every nuance of the Supras' talk suggested that they would not let her go.

They were not all-powerful—she had to keep reminding herself of that. They gave Seeker an edgy respect, clearly unsure of what it represented.

Their very attainments gave them vulnerabilities. Immortals were enormously cautious; accident could still destroy them. Caution could err. They could have missed some of her kind in the dense woods.

Nobody from the crystal elegances of Diaspar or Lys could be worth a damn at tracking in the wilderness.

Very well, then. She would escape.

24

FLIGHT

Surprise and diversion are tactics best used swiftly. In Cley's case the surprise had to come at the perimeter the Supras had erected around the wrecked Library. Yet she had no idea how to do this.

She confessed her thoughts to Seeker. She was sure that it would not betray her. It seemed unsurprised by her news, or at least to Cley the beast showed no visible reaction, though its fur did stir with amber patterns. She had hoped for some laconic but practical advice. It simply nodded and disappeared into the night.

"Damn," she muttered. Now that she had decided to act, the hopelessness of her situation seemed comic. She was, after all, the least intelligent human here, surrounded by technology as strange to her as magic.

The party continued across the camp. Waves of talent-talk frothed in her mind, making it difficult to think clearly. She hoped this torrent would also provide cover for her plans.

A loud, groaning explosion rolled through the dark. Seeker was suddenly beside her. "Walk," it said.

Shouts, flashes of purple radiance, a chain of hollow pops. Luminescent panels flickered out.

They simply slipped away. Seeker had executed some trick to deflate the screens near the Library and instantly Supras and robots reacted. For all their mastery of science the Supras reacted in near-panic to the noisy folding of the screens. They truncated all standing robot orders and directed every effort toward erecting the defenses again.

Seeker watched warily as they walked unhurriedly across the camp to the side nearest the forest. "The moment was approaching," was all it would say.

"But the robots—"

"They will not expect this now. They never see the moment."

They moved silently out of the Supra camp, keeping to the shadows. Everywhere robots hurried to restore the bulwarks of the Library but took no notice of them.

They reached the forest beneath a moonless sky strung with a necklace of dense stars. Cley tweaked her eyesight to enhance the infrared and bring color forth from the pale glow of a million suns.

They ran steadily for the first hour and then slowed as the terrain steepened. Whatever Seeker had used to gain them freedom would not last for long. She had been restless under the lofty and distracted restrictions of the Supras and she could not for long conceal from them her feelings. She suspected that Seeker had sensed her restlessness and had prepared to get the two of them out, before Seranis could read Cley's intentions and tighten her hold.

After a while all this complication fell away from Cley and she gave herself over to the healing exuberance of the forest. She knew from Supra talk that her kind were not the true, original humans which had come out of the natural forces of far antiquity, but that mattered little. Though her genetic structure could be easily modified, as the inclusion of the thought-talent showed, the Supras had kept her kind true to their origins. The simple enfolding of forest could still reach deeply into her.

Seeker did not slow its rhythmic pace, four legs seeming to slide across the ground while its hands swept obstacles aside for the both of them. "They must be looking for us now," Cley said after a long time of silence.

"Yes. My effect will wear away."

"What was it?"

Seeker looked at her, opened its slanted mouth, but said nothing.
"Is it something I shouldn't know?"

"A thing you cannot know."

"Oh." She was used to Supras making her feel stupid. Seeker,
whose kind had come well over a hundred million years after Ur-
humans, made nothing of its abilities, but this somehow made them
seem more daunting.

"They can find us, though," she said. "Supras have so many
tricks."

"We must seek concealment. Something more works in the sky."
She looked up and saw only a low fog. She puffed heavily with
the effort of keeping up with Seeker as they plowed through dense
thickets. "Why can't they see us right away?"

"We swim in the bath of life."

With each step the statement became more true. They moved
deep into the embrace of a land bustling with transformation. Fungi
and lichen coated every exposed rock. This thick, festering paint
worked with visible energy, bubbling and fuming as it ate stone and
belched digestive gases into a hovering mist. Where they had done
their work webbed grasses already thrived.

Cley stepped gingerly through a barren area speckled with bile-
green splotches, afraid one might attack her feet with its acidic
eagerness. Not all the vapors that hung over the fevered landscape
were mere bioproducts intended to salt the atmosphere with trace
elements. Buzzing mites abruptly rose from a stand of moldyweed
and swarmed around them. For a terrified moment she batted them
off until Seeker said calmly, "Stand still. They are thirsty."

The cloud was opalescent, its members each like a tiny flying chip
of ice that refracted pale starlight. Yet they seemed clever, buzzing
with encased fervor and quick skill. They banked in elaborate turns
around her. She realized she must seem like a mountain of chemical
cropland. "What do they—"

"Do not speak. They will smell your stomach lining and plunge
down your throat."

She shut up and closed her nostrils as well. The clasping cartilage
in her nose had been useful in staving off water losses in the desert

of an ancient Earth only dimly remembered by even the Keeper of Records. Now it kept out drumming mites as she held her breath for long, aching moments, wondering what the succulent scent of her digestive acids was. She squeezed her eyes shut, gritting her teeth. If she could only have the luxury of screaming, just once—

The fog hesitated, buzzed angrily, and then purred away in search of more tasty banquets.

"They seek to find and alter," Seeker said. "Not merely eat."

"How can you tell?" she asked wonderingly.

"In my age there were many forms which lived by chemical craft. They work on molecules themselves, transforming crude minerals into elegant usefuls."

Cley shivered. "They make my skin crawl."

"These are obviously designed to aid the lichen in their gnawing, preparing the ground for life."

"I never saw them before."

"They ferret out their molecular cuisine at the edge of the forest. Your kind inhabited the deep woods."

"I hope—"

"No more talk. Quickly now."

They ran hard. Seeker stopped often and crouched forward, listening to the ground. Cley needed the time to adjust her blood chemistry. The rhythms of walking helped key in hormonal cues to stop her menstrual cycle and increase endurance. She kept glancing at the sky where the galactic center was rising. Its gossamer radiance was unwelcome; she felt exposed.

Loping along a steep hillside, Seeker said, "They come now."

"The Supras?" she asked.

"More than them."

"You can tell that from listening to—"

Seeker crouched, its snout narrowing, ears flaring. It was absolutely still and then was instantly moving, even faster this time. She ran to catch up. "What—"

"Ahead," it called.

Her breath rasped as they struggled up a narrow draw. A deep bass note seemed to come from everywhere until she realized that she felt it through her feet. A peak above them cracked open with a groan and abruptly a geyser shot straight up. Tons of water spewed high in the air and showered down. Fat raindrops pelted them.

Seeker called, "A fresh river. The rock strain has grown for days and so I sought the outbreak. It will afford momentary shelter."

The droplets hammered at Cley. Seeker made an urgent sign. Through the spray of water overhead she saw rainbow shards of radiance cascade across the sky.

"Searching," Seeker said.

"Who is?"

"What, not who. That which destroyed the Library."

They watched as a filigree of incandescence stretched and waxed. Through the geyser's mist the shifting webbed patterns glowed like a design cast over all humanity. Cley had seen this beautiful tapestry before—seen it descend and bring stinging death to all she loved. Its elegant coldness struck into her heart with leaden solidity. She had managed to put aside the horror but now here it was again. Those luminiscent tendrils had tracked and burned and nearly killed her and she longed to find a way to strike back. *War.* The ancient word sang in her thumping pulse, in flared nostrils, in dry taut lips.

She stood with her clothes sticking to her in the hammering rain, hoping that this momentary fountain had saved them. How long could the mists shield them?

But now among the flexing lightning darted amber dots—craft of the Supras, spreading out from the Library. She had long expected to see them pursuing her, but they were not searching the ground. Instead they moved in formations around the gaudy luminescent ripples.

Seeker looked bedraggled, its coat dark with the wet. "Down," it said firmly.

They scrambled into a shallow cave. The river-forming geyser spread a canopy of fog, but Cley adjusted her sight to bring up the faint images she could make out through the wisps. She and Seeker watched the intricate dodge and swerve of Supra ships as they sought to enclose and smother the downward-lancing glows.

"Water will hide us for a while," Seeker said.

"Are they after the Library again?"

"No. They seem to—there."

A streamer broke through an amber pouch spun by Supra ships. It plunged earthward and in a dazzling burst split into fingers of prickly light. These raced over the mountains and down into valleys like rivulets of a tormented river in the air. One orange filament raced nearby, ripe with crackling ferocity. It dwelled a moment along the way they had come, as if sniffing for a trail, and then darted away, leaving only a diminishing flurry of furious pops.

The Supras seemed to have caged in the remaining bright lacings. The thrusts broke into colors and roiled about the sky like quick, caged fire turned back by flashes from the Supras.

Then the sky ebbed as if a presence had left it. The amber Supra ships drifted back toward the Library.

"We are fortunate," Seeker said.

Cley said, "That was a cute trick with the water."

"I doubted it would work."

"You gambled our lives on—?"

"Yes."

"Good thing you don't make mistakes."

"Oh, I do." Seeker sighed with something like weariness. "To live is to err."

Cley frowned. "C'mon, Seeker! You have some help, some connection."

"I am as mortal as you."

"What're you connected to?" she persisted.

It lifted one amber shoulder in a gesture she could not read. "Everything. And the nothing. It is difficult to talk about in this constricted language. And pointless."

"Well, anyway, that'll keep the Supras busy. They've already figured out how to fight the lightning."

"It searched for us, knowing we had escaped."

"How could it?"

"It is intelligence free of matter and has ways we cannot know."

Already Seeker moved on, slipping on some gravel and sprawling, sending pebbles rattling downslope. But it got back up, fatigue showing in its eyes, and moved on in a way that was once called "dogged," but now had no such description, for there were no longer any dogs.

Scrambling over the ridgerock, Seeker added, "And should not know."

25

BIOLOGIC

They made good time. The geyser sent feathery clouds along the backbone of the mountain range. These thickened and burst with rain. The air's ferment hid them and brought moist swarming scents.

The parched Earth needed more than the water so long hidden in deep lakes. Through the roll of hundreds of millions of years its skin of soil had disappeared, broken by sunlight and baked into vapor. The Supras had loosed upon these dry expanses the lichen, which could eat stone and fart organic paste. Legions of intricately designed, self-reproducing cells then burrowed into the noxious waste. Within moments such a microbe corps could secrete a rich mire of bacteria, tiny fungi, rotifers. Musty soil grew, the fruit of microscopic victories and stalemates waged in every handful of sand around the globe. Soil itself flourished like a ripe plant.

Seeker said they should skirt along these working perimeters of the forest. The biting vapors made Cley cough, but she understood that the shifting brown fogs also cloaked their movements against discovery from above. The night sky had cleared of Supra ships.

They slipped into the shadows of the enveloping woods, but Cley felt uneasy. Soon they looked down on the spreading network of narrow valleys they had traversed. She could see the grasp of life had grown even since she had observed it from Alvin's flyer.

Broad green patches lay ready to serve as natural solar-energy stations. Already some followed the snaking lines of newborn streams, growths cunningly spreading through the agency of animals. Such plants used animals often, following ancient precept. Long ago the flowers had recruited legions of six-legged insects and two-legged primates to serve them. Tasty nectar and fruit seduced many into propagating seeds. The flowers' radiant beauty charmed first humans and later other animals into careful service, weeding out all but the lovely from gardens; a weed, after all, was simply a plant without guile.

But it was the grasses that had held humanity most firmly in thrall for so long, and now they returned as well. Already great plains of wheat, corn and rice stretched between the forks of river-valleys, tended by animals long bred for the task. Humanity had delegated the tasks of irrigation and soil care. As the Supras had revived species, they re-created the clever, narrowly focused intelligences harbored in large rodents. These had proved much more efficient groomers of the grasses than the old, cumbersome technology of tractors and fertilizers.

Cley felt more at home now as they trekked through dense woods. She kindled her hormones and food reserves to fend off sleep and kept up the steady pace needed to stay with Seeker, who showed no signs of fatigue. The forest resembled no terrain that had ever existed before. Assembled from the legacy of a perpetually fecund biosphere, it boasted forms separated by a billion years. The Supras had reactivated the vast index of genotypes in the Library with some skill. Few predators found easy prey, and seldom did a plant not find some welcoming ground after the lichen had made their mulch.

Still, all had to struggle and adjust. The sun's luminosity had risen by more than ten percent since the dawn of humanity. The rub of tides on shorelines had further slowed the planet's whirl, lengthening the day by a fourth. Life had faced steadily longer, hotter days as the crust itself drifted and broke. In the Era of Oceans the wreckage of continental collisions had driven up fresh mountains and opened deep sutures in the seabeds—all as patient backdrop to the frantic buzz of life's adjustments to these immense constraints. Species rose and died because of minute tunings of their genetic texts.

And all the hurried succession and passionate ferment was a drama played out before the gaze of humanity—which had its own agenda.

Over the past billion years the very cycles of life on Earth had followed rhythms laid down by governing intelligences. For so long had Nature been a collaboration between Humanity and Evolution that the effects were inseparable. Yet Cley was startled when they came upon a valley of silent, trudging figures.

"Caution," Seeker whispered.

They were crossing a foggy lowland ripe with the thick fragrance of soil-making lichen. Out of the mist came shambling shadows. Cley and Seeker struck a defensive pose, back to back, for the stubby forms were suddenly all around them. Cley switched to infrared to isolate movements against the pale, cloudy background and found the figures too cool to be visible. Ghostly, moving warily, they seemed to spring everywhere from the ground.

"Robots?" she whispered, wishing for a weapon.

"No." Seeker peered closely at the slow, ponderous shapes. "Plants."

"What?" Cley heard now the *squish squish* as limbs labored to move.

"See—they unhinge from their elders."

In the murky light Cley and Seeker watched the slow, deliberate pods separate from the trunks of great trees. "Plants led, once," Seeker said. "From sea to land, so animals could follow. Flowers made a home for insects—invented them, in my view."

"But why . . . ?"

"Every step was an improvement in reproduction," Seeker said. "Here is another."

"I never heard—"

"This came long after my time, as I came after yours."

Plants had long suffered at the appetites of rodents and birds, who ate a thousand of the seeds for each one they accidentally scattered. Yet plants held great power over their animal parasites; the replacement of ferns by better adapted broad-leaved trees had quickly ended the reign of the dinosaurs. Plants' age-old strategy lay in improving their reproduction, and throughout the Age of Mammals this meant hijacking animals to spread their seeds. When ponderous evolution finally found an avenue of escape from this wastefulness, plants elected to copy the primates' care in tending to their young.

Cley approached one of the stubby, prickly things. It was thick at the base and moved by jerking forward broad, rough appendages like roots. They looked like wobbly pineapples out for a slow stroll. Each great tree exfoliated several walkers, which then moved onto wetter ground enjoying better sunlight. Cley thought of eating one, for the resemblence to pineapples was striking, but their sharp thorns smelled to Seeker of poison. Farther up the valley they found a giant bush busily dispatching its progeny as rolling balls, which sought moist bottomland and warmth.

They kept to the deep canyons. Cloaking mist gave some shelter from the Supra patrols, which now crisscrossed the sky. "They do not know this luxuriance well," Seeker remarked, clicking its sharp teeth with satisfaction. "Nor do their robots."

Cley saw the truth in this, though she had always assumed that the mechanical wonders were of an innately higher order. Humanity had long managed the planet, tended the self-regulating soup of soil and air, of ocean and rich continents. Finally, exhausted and directionless, they had handed this task over to the robots, only to find after more millions of stately years that the robots were intrinsically cautious, perhaps even to a fault.

Evolution shaped intelligences born in silicon and metal as surely and steadily as it did those minds which arose from carbon and enzymes. The robots had changed, yet kept to their ingrained Mandate of Man: to sustain the species against the wearing of the world. It had been the robots, then, who decided that they could not indefinitely manage a planet moist with organic possibility. A miserly element in them decreed that the organic realm should be reduced to a minimum. They had persuaded the leaders of the crumbling human cities to retreat, to let the robots suck Earth's already dwindling water into vast basaltic caverns.

So the Supras' servants had for hundreds of millions of years managed a simple, desiccated Earth.

"Machines feared the small, persistent things," Seeker explained that night. "Life's subtle turns." They had camped around a bristling bush that gave off warmth against the chilly fogs.

"Couldn't they adjust those?" Cley asked. She had seen the routine miracles of the robots. It was difficult to believe those impassive, methodical presences could not master even this rich world with their steady precision.

"You can swallow the most fatal poisons indefinitely if they are in a few parts per trillion," Seeker said slowly.

As she grew to know this beast it had come to seem more approachable, less strange. Yet a cool intelligence lurked behind its eyes and she never quite knew how to take what it said. This ready use of numbers, for instance, was a sudden veer from its usual eloquent brevity.

"The robots must know that."

"True, but consider ozone. A poisonous gas, blue, very explosive—and a thin skin of it over the air determines everything."

Cley nodded. Through the long afternoon of Earth the ozone layer had been leached away countless times. Humanity's excesses had depleted the ozone again and again. Oscillations in the sun's luminosity had wrenched the entire atmospheric balance. Once a great meteor had penetrated humanity's shields when they had fallen into neglect, and very nearly destroyed civilization. All this lay buried in ancient record.

Seeker yawned. "The robots worried over managing such delicate matters. So they simplified their problem."

"They seem in control here."

"They fear what they cannot master."

"But they did master much—Alvin made them revive the biosphere."

"And bring the chaos of biologic."

Seeker lay back with a strange thin grin and scratched its ample blue belly. Wreaths of jade mist curled ripely over the heat bush. Small animals had ventured into a circle around the black shrub as its steady warmth crept through the air. Few animals feared either Cley or Seeker; all species had for so long been clients and partners. They even seemed to understand Seeker's lazy talk. Cley suspected they were hypnotized by the luxuriant singing tones of Seeker's voice, ready yet eloquent. The circle had relaxed as though the bush was a campfire. A true fire, of course, would have risked detection by the Supras.

Cley listened as Seeker described the world view of its kind. Long after the Ur-humans, some beasts had risen to intelligence and had engraved in their own genes elements of racial memory. To instill in wise species a concern for their fragile world it had been the custom for many millions of years to "hard-wire" a respect for evolution and one's place in it. This had become a social cement as deeply necessary as religion had been to the earliest human forms, and even in the Ur-humans.

"Many organisms lorded over the Earth," Seeker said, "beginning with gray slimes, moving on to pasty blind worms, and then to giant oblivious reptiles—and all three persisted longer than you Ur-humans." Seeker snorted so loudly it alarmed her. "We do not know if the dinosaurs had religion."

"And your kind?"

"I worship what exists."

"Look, our tribe chose not to try to learn all that dead history—we had a job to do."

"And a good one."

"Right," she said with flustered pride. "Tuning the forests so they'd make it in spite of all this junk in the air, the plants slugging it out with each other—this isn't a biosphere yet, it's a riot!"

"But a fruitful one." Eyes twinkling, it fished a piece of fruit from some hidden pouch of its fleshy fur. Seeker grinned, a ferocious sight. The moods of the beast were easier for her to read now and she shared its quirky mirth.

And she saw Seeker's argument. The robots had helped humanity accent its intelligence and ensure the immortality of all in Diaspar. But to make the world work the robots had to run a skimpy, dry biosphere whose sole pinnacle was a palsied, stultified Man.

A fat, ratlike thing with six legs ventured nearer the bush. Instantly a black cord whipped through the damp air and wrapped around the squealing prey. A surge dragged the big rodent into a

maw that suddenly opened near the bush's roots. After it closed on
its supper Cley could hear the strangled cries for several moments.
Evolution was still at work, pruning failures from the gene pool
with unblinking patience.

26

PINWHEEL

Next morning the fog began to clear. Seeker kept studying the sky. They had made steady progress climbing the flanks of the saw-toothed mountain range, and now the terrain and rich fauna resembled the territory where Cley had grown up. She searched the distant ridgelines for hints of lookouts. Hers was not the only tribe of Ur-humans, and someone else might have escaped, despite Alvin's certainty. She asked Seeker to tune its nose to human tangs, but no traces stirred the fitful breezes.

Twice they sought cover when flying foxes glided over. By this time surely the Supras would have sent their birds to reconnoiter, but neither her nor Seeker's even sharper vision could make out any of the ponderous, wide-winged silhouettes.

They were watching a vast covey of the diaphanous silvery foxes bank and swoop down the valley currents when Seeker motioned to her. Distant rumblings came, as though the mountains above them rubbed against a coarse sky. The foxes reacted, drawing in their formation like silver leaves assembling a tree.

Blue striations frenzied the air. The few remaining clouds dissipated in a cyclonic churn.

Cley said, "What—"

Sheets of yellow light shot overhead. A wall of sound followed, knocking Cley against Seeker. She found herself facedown among leaves without any memory of getting there.

All around them the forest was crushed, as though something had trampled it in haste. Deep booms faded slowly.

An eerie silence settled. Cley got up and inspected the wrenched trees, gagging at fumes from a split stinkbush. Two flying foxes lay side by side, as though mated in death. Their glassy eyes still were open and jerked erratically in their narrow, bony heads.

"Their brains still struggle," Seeker said. "But in vain."

"What *was* that?"

"Like the assault before on your people?"

"Yes . . . but this time"—she swept her hand to the horizon of mangled forest—"it smashed everything!"

"These foxes took the brunt of it for us."

"Yes, poor things . . ." Her voice trailed off as the animals' bright eyes slowed, dimmed, then closed.

"It does not know precisely where we are, so it sends generous slabs of electrical energy to do their work."

Seeker gently folded the two foxes into its palm and made a slow, grave gesture, as if offering them to the sky. When Seeker lowered its claws Cley could not see the foxes and they were not on the ground or anywhere nearby.

"What—"

Seeker said crisply, "I judge we should shelter for a while."

They climbed swiftly up the rough rise to a large stand of the tallest trees Cley had ever seen. Long, fingerlike branches reached far up into the air, hooking over at the very end. She felt exposed by moving to higher ground, closer to the sky that spat death. From here she could see distant banks of purple clouds that roiled with spokes of virulent light. Filaments of orange arced down along long curves.

"Following the magnetic field of Earth," Seeker said when she pointed them out. "Probing."

Cley saw why the Supras had sent no searching birds. Far away quick darts of blue and orange appeared over the Library of Life. In her mind she felt a dim sense of frenzied struggle.

"The talent," she said. Seeker looked quizzically at her. "I can feel
. . . emotion." She remembered Seeker's remark, *You have emotions,
emotions possess you.* What must it be like to not feel those surges?
Or did Seeker sense something utterly different? "The Supras are
fighting . . . worried . . . afraid."

"The being above keeps them busy while it searches."

They moved on quickly. Cley wanted to get over the highest peak
and work her way along the broad-shouldered mountains toward
where she had lived. She had the image of it all in her head from
the flight with Alvin and she felt a powerful urge to return to the
familiar.

When she said this Seeker replied flatly, "They would seek you
there in time."

"So? They'll look everywhere."

"True," Seeker said, and she thought she had won a small point.

Seeker sniffed the wind and pointed with its twitching nose.
"Come this way."

"Why?" Her home grounds lay the opposite way.

"You wished to find Ur-humans."

"My people?"

"Not yet."

"Damn it, I want *my* kind."

"This way lies your only hope of eventual community."

"Seeker, you know what I want," she said plaintively.

"I know what you need."

She kicked at a rock, feeling frustrated, confused, exhausted.
"And what's that?"

"You need to come this way."

They moved at a steady trot. Cley had always been a good runner,
but Seeker got ahead without showing signs of effort. When she
caught up it had stopped beside a very large tree and was sniffing
around the roots. Seeker took its time, moving cautiously, and Cley
knew enough by now to let it have its way.

A large bush nearby gave off an aroma of cooked meat, and Cley
watched it uneasily. A small mudskipper rat with an enlarged head
came foraging by, smart enough to know that Cley and Seeker were

usually no threat to it. It caught the meat smell and slowed, tantalized. The bush popped and spear seeds embedded in the rat. It yelped and scampered away. Another victory for the plants; the rat would carry the seed, nurturing it in return for its narcotic sap, until it died. Then a fresh bush would grow from the rat's body.

She considered catching the rat for meat, and not incidentally for the narcotic, but Seeker said, "Come."

Somehow it had opened the side of the tree. This was no surprise to Cley, whose people sheltered in the many trees bioteched for just such use. She entered and soon the bark closed upon them, leaving only a wan phosphorescent glow from the walls to guide them. The tree was hollow. There were vertical compartments connected by ramps and clamplike growths all along the walls. Some creature had nearly filled the compartments with large containers, grainy packages of rough cellulose.

"Storage," was all Seeker would say in answer to her questions. They climbed up through ten compartments nearly filled with stacks of oblong, crusty containers, until they came to a large vault, completely empty, with a wide transparent wall. Cley thumped it and the heavy, waxy stuff gave with a soft resistance. She watched the still trees outside, all stately cylinders pointing up into a sky that flickered with traceries of quick luminescence.

This place might be safer; she let herself relax slightly. She took out a knife and gouged the wall. A piece came off with some work and tasted surprisingly good. She ate awhile and Seeker took some. Patches on the walls, ceiling and floor were sticky, without apparent scheme. The compartment smelled of resin and damp wood.

She chanced to glance out the big window as she chewed and that was why she saw it coming.

Something like a stick poked down through high clouds, swelling as it approached, so that she saw it was enormously long. Its ribbed sinews were knobbed like the vertebrae of a huge spine. Groans and splitting cracks boomed down so loudly that she could hear them here, inside. Curving as it plunged, the great round stalk speared through the sky like an accusing finger. And, as she watched, the very end of it curved further, like a finger beckoning upward.

"Time to lie down," Seeker said mildly.

A sonic boom slammed through the forest. She hastily flattened herself on the resilient green floor of the compartment and gazed up through the big window.

"It's falling on us!" she cried.

"Its feat is to forever fall and forever recover."

"It'll smash these—"

"Lie still."

She realized that *this* was the thin, distant movement she had seen on the horizon from Alvin's flyer. Graphite-dark cords wound across the deep mahogany of the huge, trunklike thing. Fingers of ropy vine unfolded from its tip as it plunged straight downward. The vines flung themselves toward the treetops. Some snagged in the branches there.

A hard thump ran through their tree.

She just had time to see the thick vines snatch at the branches of neighboring trees, grip, and tighten.

The broad nub seemed to hang in air, as if contemplating the green skin of the planet below it and selecting what it liked. It drifted eastward for one heartbeat.

Heavy acceleration pressed her into the soft floor. They were yanked aloft. Popping strain flooded their compartment with creaks and snaps and low groans.

Out the window she could see a nearby tree speed ahead. Its roots had curled beneath it, dropping brown clods behind. In another tree, branches sheared off where several thick vines had clutched together; it tumbled away to crash into the forest below.

She could only lie mutely, struggling to breathe, as a flock of tree trunks rose beside them, drawn to the great beckoning finger that now retracted up into the sky with gathering speed. It swept them eastward as trees lashed in air turbulence, as if shaking themselves free of the constraints of dirt and gravity.

Against the steadily increasing tension the ribbed and polished vines managed to retract. They drew their cargo trees into a snug fitting at the base of the blunt, curving rod.

"What's . . . it . . ."

"Pinwheel," Seeker said. "The center rides high in space, and it spins as it orbits. The ends rotate down through the air and kiss the Earth."

Seeker's calm, melodious voice helped stave off her rising panic. They were tilting as they rose. Cloud banks rushed at them, shrouded the nearby trunks in ghostly white—and shredded away as they shot higher. She glimpsed the underside of the pinwheel itself, where corded bunches of wiry strands held the vines in place.

"We spin against Earth's pull, but will slip free."

Seeker's words gave her an image of an enormous rod which slowly dipped down into the planet's air, one tip touching the surface at the same moment that the other end was farthest out in space. Such a vast thing would be far longer than the thickness of Earth's air itself, a creation like a small, slender world unto itself.

Rolling bass wrenchings strummed through the walls and floor. Her heart thudded painfully and wind whistled in her ears.

The strain of withstanding the steadily rising acceleration warped the vines. They stretched and twisted but held the long, tubular trees tight to the underside. She saw that the nub was festooned with shrubs and brush. The Pinwheel stretched away into blue-black vistas as the air thinned around them. The wind in their compartment wailed and she sucked in air, fearing that there was a leak.

But Seeker patted her outstretched hand and she glanced at the great beast. Its eyes were closed as though asleep. This startled her and a long moment passed before she guessed that Seeker could have done this before, that this was not some colossal accident they had blundered into. As if in reply Seeker licked its lips, exposing black gums and pointed yellow teeth.

Her ears popped. She looked outward again, through the slow buffeting of tree trunks. "Upward" was now tilted away from the darkening bowl of sky, but still along the chestnut-brown length of the Pinwheel, as they rotated with it. Black shrubs dotted the great expanse that dwindled away, gray laminations making the perspective even starker. Cross-struts of cedar-red tied the long strips into an interlocking network that twisted visibly in the howling gale that tore along it.

Once they smacked into the nearest tree and a branch almost

punched through the window, but their tree wrenched aside and the impact slammed against the wall.

Her ears popped again and her breath came raggedly. Along the great strips of lighter wood, walnut-colored edges rose. They canted, sculpting the wind—and the roaring gale subsided, the twisting and wrenching lessened. Pops and creaks still rang out but she felt a subtle loosening in the coupled structure.

The last thin haze of atmosphere faded into star-sprinkled black. She felt that an invisible, implacable enemy sat on her chest and would forever, talking to her in a language of wrenching low bass notes. Cold, thin air stung her nostrils but there was enough if she labored to fill her lungs.

The ample curve of the planet rose serenely at the base of the window as she panted. Its smooth ivory cloud decks seemed near enough to touch . . . but she could not raise her arms.

Along the tapering length of the Pinwheel, slow, lazy undulations were marching. They came toward her, growing in height. When the first arrived it gave the nub a hard snap and the trees thrashed on their vine-teathers. The turbulence which the entire Pinwheel felt had summed into these waves, which dissipated in the whip-crack at its ends. Tree trunks thumped and battered but their pressure held.

Seeker licked its lips again without opening its eyes.

They revolved higher. She could see the complete expanse of the Pinwheel. It curved slightly, tapering away, like an infinite highway unconcerned with the impossibility of surmounting the will of planets. Vines wrapped along it and near the middle a green forest flourished.

The far end was a needle-thin line. As she watched, its point plunged into the atmosphere. Undulations from this shock raced back toward her. When these reached her the buffetings were mild, for the trees were now tied snugly against the underside of the Pinwheel's nub end.

Deep, solemn notes beat through the walls. The entire Pinwheel was like a huge instrument strummed by wind and gravity, the waves singing a strange song that sounded through her bones.

The Pinwheel was now framed against the whole expanse of

Earth. Cley still felt strong acceleration into the compartment's floor, but it was lesser now as gravity countered the centrifugal whirl. Their air, too, thickened as the tree's walls exuded a sweet-scented, moist vapor.

The spectacle of her world, spread out in silent majesty, struck her. They were nearing the top of their ascent, the Pinwheel pointing vertically, as if to bury itself in the heart of the planet.

The Pinwheel throbbed. She had felt its many adjustments and percussive changes as it struggled against both elements, air and vacuum. Only a short while ago she had thought that the ravenous green, eating at the pale deserts, waged an epic struggle. Now she witnessed an unending whirl of immeasurably greater difficulty.

And in a glance she knew that the Earth itself and the Pinwheel were two similar systems, brothers of vastly different scales.

The Pinwheel was like a tree, quite certainly alive and yet 99 percent dead. Trees were spires of dead wood, cellulose used by the ancestors of the living cells that made its bark.

Earth, too, was a thin skin of verdant life atop a huge bulk of rocks. But far down in the magma were elements of the ancestral hordes which had come before. The slide and smack of whole continents rode on a slippery base of limestone, layers built up from an infinitude of seashell carcasses. All living systems, in the large, were a skin wrapped around the dead.

"Good-bye," Seeker said, getting up awkwardly. Even its strength was barely equal to the centrifugal thrust.

"What! You're not leaving?"

"We both are."

A loud bang. Cley felt herself falling. She kicked out in her fright and only managed to propel herself into the ceiling. She struck on her neck wrong and painfully rebounded. Her mind kept telling herself she was falling, despite the evidence of her eyes—and then some ancient subsystem of her mind cut in, and she automatically quieted.

She was not truly falling, except in a sense used by physicists. She was merely weightless, bouncing about the compartment before Seeker's amused yawn.

"We're free!"

"For a bit."

"What?"

"See ahead."

Their vines had slipped off. Freed, their tree shot away from the Pinwheel. They went out on a tangent to its great circle of revolution. Already the nub was a shrinking spot on the huge, curved tree that hung between air and space. She had an impression of the Pinwheel dipping its mouth into the rich swamp of Earth's air, drinking its fill alternately from one side of itself and then the other.

But what kept it going, against the constant drag of those fierce winds? She was sure it had some enormous skill to solve that problem, but there was no sign what that might be.

She looked out, along the curve of Earth. Ahead was a dark-brown splotch on the star-littered blackness.

"A friend," Seeker said. "There."

27

JONAH

They rose with surprising speed. The Pinwheel whirled away, its grandiose gyre casting long shadows along its woody length.

Despite the winds it suffered, bushes clung to its flanks. The upper end, which they had just left, now rotated down toward the coming twilight. Its midpoint was thickest and oval, following a circular orbit a third of Earth's radius above the surface. At its furthest extension, groaning and popping with the strain, the great log had reached a distance two-thirds of the Earth's radius out into the cold of space.

They had been flung off at better than thirteen kilometers per second. This was enough to take the trees to other planets, though that was not their destination. They shot ahead of the nub, watching it turn downward with stately resolution, as though gravely bowing to necessity by returning to the planet which held it in bondage.

Its lot was to be forever the mediator between two great oceans which others would sail in serenity, while it knew only the ceaseless tumult of the air and the biting cold of vacuum.

Cley watched silently, clinging to one of the sticky patches on the compartment's walls. There was a solemn majesty to the Pinwheel, a remorseless resignation to the dip of its leading arm into the battering winds. She saw the snug pocket where they had been moored show a flare of ivory light—plasma conjured up by the shock of re-entry. Yet the great arm plunged on, momentum's captive, for its next touchdown.

She saw why it had momentarily hung steady over the forest; at bottom, the rotation nearly canceled the orbital velocity. Craft on such a scale bespoke enormous control, and she asked in a whisper, "Is it intelligent?"

"Of course," Seeker said. "And quite old."

"To do *that* . . ."

"Forever moving, forever going nowhere."

"What thoughts, what *dreams* it must have."

"It is a different form of intelligence from you—neither greater nor lesser."

"Who made it?"

"It made itself, in part."

"How can anything *that* big . . . ?"

Seeker spun itself playfully in air, clicking its teeth in a disjointed rhythm. It seemed uninterested in answering her.

"Alvin and the others made it, right?"

Seeker yelped in high amusement. "Time is more reliable than intelligence."

"Somebody planned that thing."

"Some body? Yes, the body plans—not the mind."

"Huh? No, I mean—"

"In far antiquity there were beasts designed to forage for icesteroids among the cold spaces beyond the planets. *—ooof!*— They knew enough of genecraft to modify themselves. *—ah!*— Perhaps they met other life-forms which came from other stars—I do not know. *—uh!*— I doubt that this matters; time's hand shaped some such creatures into this. *—oof!*—" Seeker seldom spoke so long, and it had managed this time to punctuate each sentence with a bounce from the walls.

"Creatures that gobbled ice?"

Seeker settled onto a sticky patch, held on with two legs, and fanned its remaining legs and arms into the air. "They were sent to seek such, then spiral it into the inner worlds."

"Water for Earth?"

"By that time the robots had decreed a dry planet. The outer icesteroid halo was employed elsewhere."

"Why not use spaceships?"

"Of metal? They do not reproduce."

"These things'd give birth, out there in the cold?"

"Slowly, yes."

"How'd they make Pinwheel? It's not an ice-eater, I can tell that much."

"Time is deep. Circumstance has worked on it. More so than upon your kind."

"Is it smarter?"

"You humans return to that subject always. Different, not greater."

Embarrassed without quite knowing why, Cley said, "I figured it must be smarter than me, to do all that."

"It flies like a bird, without bother. And thinks long, as befits a thing from the great slow spaces."

"*How* does it fly? The wind alone—" The question spoken, she saw the answer. As the other arm of Pinwheel rose to the top of its circular arc, she could make out thin plumes of white jetting behind it. She had seen Supra craft do that, leaving a line of cloud in their wake.

"Consider it a tree that flies," Seeker said.

"Huh? Trees have roots."

"Trees walk, why not fly? We are guests inside a flying tree."

"Ummm. What's it eat?"

"Some from air, some—" Seeker gestured ahead, along their trajectory. They shot above and away from the spinning, curved colossus. And Cley saw a thin haze now hanging against the black of space, dimmer than stars but more plentiful. There was a halo around the Earth, fireflies drawn to the planet's immense ripe glow. Beyond the nightline the gossamer halo hung like a wreath above Earth's shadow.

One mote grew as they sped on. It swelled into a complex structure of struts and half-swollen balloons. It had sinews like knotty walnut. Fleshy vines webbed its intersections. Cley tried to imagine Pinwheel digesting this oddity and decided she would have to see it to believe.

But this minor issue faded as she peered ahead. Other trees like theirs lay fore and aft, some spinning slightly, others tumbling. But all were headed toward a thing that reminded her of a pineapple, prickly with spikes and fur. Around this slowly revolving thing a haze of pale motes clustered.

"All that . . . alive?"

"In a way. Are robots alive?"

"No, of course—are those robots?"

"Not of metal, no. But even robots can make copies of themselves."

Cley said with exasperation, "You know what I mean when something's alive."

"I am deficient in that."

"Well, if you don't know, I can't tell you," she said irritably.

"Good."

"What?"

"Talk is a trick for taking the mystery out of the world."

Cley did not know what to say and decided to let sleeping mysteries lie. Their tree convoy was approaching the fog-glow swathing the pineapple.

Gravity imposes flat floors, straight walls, rectangular rigidities. Weightlessness allows the ample symmetries of the cylinder and sphere. In the swarm of objects, large and small, Cley saw an expressive freedom of effortless new geometries. Necessity dictates form, and the myriad spokes and limbs that jutted from the many shells and rough skins conformed to the demands of momentum.

She watched an orange sphere extend a thin stalk into a nearby array of cylinders. It began to spin about the stalk. This gave it stability so that the stalk punched surely through the thin walls of its prey. Cley wondered how the sphere spun itself up, and suspected that internal fluids had to counterrotate. But was this an attack? The odd array of rubbery columns did not behave like a victim. Instead, it gathered around the sphere. Slow stems embraced and pulses worked along their crusted brown lengths. Cley wondered if she was watching an exchange, the cylinders throbbing energetically to negotiate a biochemical transaction.

Their flotilla of trees cut through the insectlike haze of life, passing near myriad forms that sometimes veered to avoid them. Some, though, tried to catch them. These had angular shapes, needle-nosed and surprisingly quick. But the trees still plunged on, outstripping pursuit, directly into the barnacled pineapple.

But she saw now that only parts of the huge thing seemed solid. There were large caps at the ends which looked firm enough, but the main body revealed more and more detail as they approached. Sunlight glinted from multifaceted specks until Cley realized that these were a multitude of spindly growths projected out from a central axis. She could see the axis buried deep in the profusion of stalks and webbing, like a bulbous brown root.

She stopped thinking of it as a pineapple and substituted "prickly pear." As they came in above the lime-green crown at one end of the "pear" a wave passed across it. The sudden flash made her blink and shield her eyes. Her iris corrected swiftly to let her see through the glare. The wave had stopped neatly halfway across the cap, one side still green, the other a chrome-bright sheen. The piercing shine reminded her of how hard sunlight was, unfiltered by air.

"It swims," Seeker said.

"Where?"

"Or better to say, it paces its cage."

"I . . ." Cley began, then remembered Seeker's remark about words robbing mystery. She saw that the shiny half would reflect sunlight, giving the prickly pear a small push from that side. As it rotated, the wave of color-change swept around the dome, keeping the thrust always in the same direction.

"Hold to the wall," Seeker said.

"Who, what's—oh."

The spectacle had distracted her from their approach. She had unconsciously expected the trees to slow. Now the fibrous wealth of stalks sticking out from the axis grew alarmingly fast. They were headed into a clotted region of interlaced strands.

In the absolute clarity of space she saw smaller and smaller features, many not attached to the prickly pear at all, but hovering like feasting insects. She realized only then the true scale of the complexity they sped toward. The prickly pear was as large as a mountain. Their tree was a matchstick plunging headfirst into it.

The lead tree struck a broad tan web. It stretched this membrane and then rebounded—but did not bounce off. Instead, the huge catcher's mitt damped the bounce into rippling waves. Then a second tree struck near the web's edge, sending more circular waves racing away. A third, a fourth—and then it was their turn.

Seeker said nothing. A sudden, sickening tug reminded her of acceleration's liabilities, then reversed, sending her stomach aflutter. The lurching lasted a long moment and then they were at rest. Out the window she could see other trees embed themselves in the web, felt their impacts make the net bob erratically.

When the tossing had damped away she said shakily, "Rough . . . landing."

"The price of passage. The Pinwheel pays its momentum debt this way," Seeker said, detaching itself from the stick-pad.

"Debt? For what?"

"For the momentum it in turn receives back, as it takes on passengers."

Cley blinked. "People go down in the Pinwheel, too?"

"It runs both ways."

"Well, sure, but—" She had simply not imagined that anyone would brave the descent through the atmosphere, ending up hanging by the tail of the great space-tree as it hesitated, straining, above the ground. How did they jump off? Cley felt herself getting overwhelmed by complexities. She focused on the present. "Look, who's this momentum debt paid *to?*"

"Our host."

"What *is* this?"

"A Jonah."

"What's that mean?"

"A truly ancient term. Your friend Alvin could no doubt tell you its origin."

"He's not my friend—we're cousins, a billion years removed."
Cley smiled ironically, then frowned as she felt long, slow pulses
surge through the walls of their tree. "Say, what's a Jonah do?"

"It desires to swallow us."

28

LEVIATHAN

Creatures were already busy in the compartments. Many-legged, scarcely more than anthologies of ebony sticks and ropy muscle strung together by gray gristle, they poked and shoved the cargo adroitly into long processions.

Though they were quick and able, Cley sensed that these were in a true sense not single individuals; they no more had lives of their own than did a cast-off cell marooned from her own skin.

She and Seeker followed the flow of cargo out the main port, the entrance they had used in the forest only two hours before. They floated out into a confusing melange of spiderlike workers, oblong packages, and forking tubular passages that led away into green profusion.

Cley was surprised at how quickly she had adjusted to the strangeness of zero gravity. Like many abilities which seemed natural once they are learned, like the complex trick of walking itself, weightlessness reflexes had been "hard-wired" into her kind. Had she paused a moment to reflect, this would have been yet another reminder that she could not possibly represent the planet-bound earliest humans.

But she did not reflect. She launched herself through the moist air of the great shafts, rebounding with eager zest from the rubbery walls. The spiders ignored her. Several jostled her in their mechanical haste to carry away what appeared to be a kind of inverted tree. Its outside was hard bark, forming a hollow, thick-walled container open at top and bottom. Inside sprouted fine gray branches, meeting at the center in large, pendulous blue fruit.

She hungrily reached for one, only to have a spider slap her away with a vicious kick. Seeker, though, lazily picked two of them and the spiders back-pedaled in air to avoid it. She wondered what musk or gestures Seeker had used; the beast seemed scarcely awake, much less concerned.

They ate, juice hanging in droplets in the humid air. Canyons of light beckoned in all directions. Cley tugged on a nearby transparent tube as big as she was, through which an amber fluid gurgled. From this anchorage she could orient herself in the confusing welter of brown spokes, green foliage, gray shafts and knobby protrusions. Their tree-ship hung in the embrace of filmy leaves. From the hard vacuum of space the tree had apparently been propelled through a translucent passage which Cley could see, already retracting back toward the catcher's mitt that had stopped them. Small animals scampered along knotted cables and flaking vines, chirruping, squealing, venting visible yellow farts. Everywhere was animation, a sense that nothing dwelled too long..

"Come," Seeker said. It cast off smoothly and Cley followed down a wide-mouthed, olive-green tube. She was surprised to find that she could see through its walls.

Sunlight filtered through an enchanted canopy. Clouds formed from mere wisps, made droplets, and eager leaves sucked them in. She was kept busy watching the slow-motion but perpetual rhythm of this place until Seeker darted away, out of the tube, and into a vast volume dominated by a hollow half-sphere of green moss. The other hemisphere, she saw, was transparent. It let in a bar of yellow sunlight which had been reflected and refracted far down into the living maze around them.

Seeker headed straight for the mossy bowl and attached itself to a low plant. Cley awkwardly bounced off the resilient moss, snatched at a spindly tree, and finally reached Seeker. It was eating crimson bulbs that grew profusely. Cley tried some and liked the rich, grainy taste. But her irritation grew as her hunger dwindled. Seeker seemed about to go to sleep when she said, "You brought us here on purpose, didn't you?"

"Surely." Seeker lazily blinked.

Angered by this display of unconcern, Cley shouted, "I wanted to find my people!"

"They are gone."

"*You* say that, all-powerful *Alvin* said that, but I want to look for them."

"Alvin and his kind are good at a few things. Among them is acquiring information. I believe their search was thorough."

"They missed me!"

"Only for a while."

"You said I could find people like me if I followed you."

"So I believe."

"I still want to see for myself!"

"The price of seeing will be death," Seeker said quietly.

"We've done fine so far."

"A numerical series can have many terms yet be finite."

"But—but—" Cley wanted to express her dismay at being snatched away from everything she knew, but pride forced her to say, "—something in the sky wants to kill me, right? So to get away we go into the sky? Nonsense!"

"I see you are unsettled." Seeker folded its hands across its belly in a gesture that somehow conveyed contrition. "Still, we must flee as far and as fast as we can."

"Why *we*?"

"You would be helpless without me."

Cley's mouth twisted, irritation and self-mockery mingling. "Guess so, up here. In the woods we'd be even."

Seeker said nothing and Cley realized it was being diplomatic. In truth, despite all her experience and skills, Seeker had moved through mixed terrains with an unconscious assurance and craft she envied. "Where do we go, then?"

"For now, the moon."

"The . . ." She had assumed they were arcing above the Earth but would return to it at some distant point. She knew the Supras went to other worlds, too, but she had never heard of her own kind doing so. ". . . for what?"

"We must move outward and be careful."

"To save our skins?"

"Your skin."

"Guess you don't have skin, just fur."

"It does not seek my fur."

"And who is *it?*"

Seeker leaned back and arranged itself, all six limbs folded in a comfortable cross-legged posture. It began to speak, soft and melodiously, of times so distant that the very names of their eras had passed away. The great heavy-pelted beast told her of how humanity had met greater intelligences in the vault of stars, and had fallen back, recoiling at the blow to its deepest pride. They had tried to create a higher mentality, and their failure was as vast as their intention. They had made the Mad Mind, a being embodied without need of inscribing patterns on matter. And it had proved malignant beyond measure. Only heroic struggle had managed to capture and restrain the Mad Mind. To cage it firmly had been the work of millions, exhausting lifetimes.

And still the race had striven on, conjuring up a counter to the Mad Mind named Vanamonde. Both dwelled in the depths of far space. But with that last grand act some light had gone out of humanity. Later species of humans had retreated, letting their machines steal the variety and tang from their world, until only the lights of Diaspar burned in the sands that would one day overwhelm all.

"Cowardly," Cley said.

"Vain pride," Seeker said.

"Why? That makes no sense."

"To think that humans were the pinnacle of creation?"

"Oh. I see."

Cley was subdued for most of the voyage to the moon. She had known a bit of Seeker's story, for it was a tribal fable. But the Mad Mind was older now than the mountains she had roved, a gauzy myth told by the Supras. They spoke, too, of Vanamonde, but that equally tenuous entity was said to be strung among the crush of stars and radiant clouds.

The moon swam green and opulent as they looped outward. Jonah's slight spin gave an obliging purchase to the outer segments of the great vessel, and Cley ventured with Seeker through verdant labyrinths to watch their approach. The lunar landscape was a jagged creation of sharp mountains and colossal waterfalls. These stark contrasts had been shaped by light elements hauled sunward in comets. A film a few molecules thick sat atop the lunar air, holding in a thick mix of gases. The film had permanent holes allowing spacecraft and spaceborn life access, the whole arrangement kept buoyant by steady replenishment from belching volcanoes. This trap offset the moon's feebler gravitational grasp so well that it lost less of its air than did the Earth.

The beckoning moon hung nearly directly sunward and so was nearly drowned in shadow until Jonah began to curve toward its far side. For this passing moment the sun, moon and Earth were aligned in geometric perfection, before plunging back along their complicated courses. Cley watched this moment of uncanny, simple equilibrium and felt the paradox that balance and stillness lay at the heart of all change.

"See," Seeker said. "Storms."

Cley looked down into the murk and whirl of the bottled lunar air, but the disturbance lay above that sharp division. In the blackness over both poles snaked filaments of blushing orange.

"Damn." Cley whispered, as though the helical strands could hear. "The Mad Mind?"

"It probes for us. I had thought it would forage elsewhere first."

Seeker pointed with its ears at what seemed to Cley to be empty space around Earth. Seeker described how the Earth's magnetic domain is compressed by the wind from the sun, and streams out in the wake. She blinked her eyes up into ultraviolet and caught the delicate shimmer of a huge volume around the planet. She witnessed a province she had never suspected, the realm dominated by the planet's blooming magnetic fields. It was a gossamer ball, crumpled in on the sun side, stretched and slimmed by the wind from the sun into tapering tail. Arcades of momentary fretwork grew and died in the rubbery architecture of the magnetosphere, and she knew that these, too, were the footprints of the Mad Mind. "It's searching there."

"It relishes the bands of magnetic field," Seeker said somberly. "I hoped it would seek us only in that realm."

"But it has spread here, too."

"It must."

Cley felt a cold shudder. Immense forces lumbered through these colossal spaces, and she was a woman born to pad the quiet paths of sheltered forests, to prune and plant and catch the savor of the sighing wind. This was not her place.

"It's able to punch through the air blanket?" she asked.

Seeker simply poked one ear at the lunar south pole. She shifted down into the infrared and saw faint plumes geyser below the hard curve of the atmosphere. Orange sparks worked there.

"It's already breached the air layer." She bit her lip and nearly lost her hold on a branch.

"And can hunt and prey at will, once inside. It follows the lunar magnetic-field lines where it wishes." Seeker cast off without warning, kicked against an enormous orchid, and shot down a connecting tube.

"Hey, wait!"

She caught up in an ellipsoidal vault where an army of the black spiders was assembling ranks of oval containers. In the dizzying activity she could barely keep up with Seeker. Larger animals shot by her, some big enough to swat her with a single flipper or snap her in two with a beak, but all ignored her. A fever pitch resounded through the noisy blur. Seeker had stopped, though, and was sunning itself just beneath the upper dome.

"What can we do? Ride back to Earth?"

"I had thought to catch the vessel which now approaches."

She saw through the dome a smaller version of their Jonah, arcing up from one of the portal holes in the air layer. Seeker had said the Jonah was one of the indentured of its species, caged in an endless cycle between Earth and moon. The smaller Jonah dipped into the lunar air, enjoying some tiny freedom. She felt a trace of pity for such living vessels, but then she saw something which banished minor troubles. A great mass came into view, closing with them from a higher orbit.

"What's . . ."

"We approach a momentary mating."

"Mating? They actually . . . in flight?"

"They are always in flight."

"But . . . that thing, it's so *huge.*"

"It is a Leviathan. Jonahs are its spawn. As it swoops closest to the sun, desires well in it, as they have for ages past. We shall simply take advantage of the joy of merging."

As the great bulk glided effortlessly toward them she surveyed its mottled blue-green skin, the tangled jungles it held to the sun's eternal nourishing blare.

Cley could not help but smile. "I think I prefer my lust in smaller doses."

29

EDITING
THE
SUN

Grand beings communicate through emissaries. Slow, ponderous oscillations began to course through the Jonah. Cley saw a watery bubble pop into space from the Jonah's leathery skin nearby. It wobbled, seeking definition, and made itself into an ellipsoid.

"Hurry," Seeker said. "Departure."

Seeker adroitly tugged her along through green labyrinths. When they came to the flared mouth of what seemed to be a giant hollow root, it shoved her ahead. She tumbled head over heels and smacked into a softly resilient pad. Velvet-fine hairs oozing white sap stuck to her. A sharp, meaty flavor clung in her nose. She felt light-headed and realized that the air was thick with vapor that formed and dissolved and met again in billowing, translucent sheets. Seeker slapped away a rubbery blob as big as a man but seemed unconcerned. A hissing began. They were drifting down the bore of a narrowing tube. The walls glowed with pearly softness and she felt the sap cloaking her feet and back.

Seeker snagged a shimmering plate and launched it like an ancient discus toward her. The sticky stuff wrapped around her and Seeker slapped the other end against a denser strand. They gathered speed in a swirl of refracting light. Cley held her breath, frightened by the hectic hiss around them.

"What—" she began, but a soft cool ball of sap caught against her mouth when she breathed in. She blew it away and felt Seeker next to her as the wall glow ebbed. The ribbed tube ahead flexed, bulged—and they shot through into the hard glare of space. The Jonah had blown a rubbery bubble. A sap envelope enclosed them, quickly making a perfect sphere.

"The Jonah is making love to the Leviathan," Seeker said, holding her firmly.

"We're seeds?"

"So we have deceived it, yes."

"What happens when something tries to hatch us?"

"We disregard the invitation."

Such politeness seemed doubtful; they were closing with the broad speckled underbelly, the Jonah already dwindling behind. The speckles were clusters of ruby-dark froth. The Leviathan was at least ten times the size of the Jonah, giving the sex act an air of comedy. As they approached she felt new fear at the enormity of it; this creature was the size of a small mountain range.

This time they donated momentum to their new host through a web of bubbles that seemed to pop and re-form as they plunged through, each impact a small buffeting that sent Cley bouncing off the elastic walls of their own seed-sphere.

When they came to rest a large needle expertly jabbed at their bubble. The ruby light gave a hellish, threatening cast to everything. The needle entered, seemed to sniff around, its sharp point moving powerfully and quite capable, Cley saw, of skewering them both— and Seeker raised a leg and urinated directly onto it. The needle jerked back and fled.

"No, thank you," Seeker said. Their bubble popped, releasing them.

Again Seeker led her through a dizzy maze of verdant growths, following clues she could not see. "Where're we going?"

"To find the Captain."

"Somebody guides this?"

"Doesn't your body guide you?"

"Well, where's this Leviathan going?"

"To the outer worlds."

"You think we're safe here for now?"

"We are safe nowhere. But here we hide in numbers."

"You figure the Mad Mind can't be sure where I am? It tracked me pretty well so far."

"Here there are many more complex forms than you. They will smother your traces."

"What about this talent of mine? Can't this Mind pick up my, well, my 'smell'?"

"That is possible."

"Damn! Wish Seranis hadn't provoked mine to activity."

"She had to."

Cley had been following Seeker closely, scrambling to keep up as they bounced from rubbery walls and glided down curved passageways, deeper into the Leviathan. Seeker's remark made her stop for a moment, gasping in the sweet, cloying air. "*Had* to?"

"You will need it. And the talent takes time to grow."

Cley wanted to bellow out her frustration at the speed and confusion of events, but she knew by now that Seeker would only give her its savage, black-lipped grin. Seeker slowed and veered into crowded layers of great broad leaves. These seemed to attach to branches, but the scale was so large Cley could not see where the gradually thickening, dark brown wood ended. Among the leaves scampered and leaped many small creatures.

She found that without her noticing any transition somehow this zone had gained a slight gravity. She fell from one leaf to another, slid down to a third, and landed on a catlike creature. It died in her hands, provoking a pang of guilt. The cat had wings and sleek orange fur. Seeker came ambling along a thin branch, saw the bird-cat, and with a few movements skinned it and plucked off gobbets of meat.

The goal of finding the Captain faded as both grew hungry. It slowly dawned on Cley that this immense inner territory was not some comfortable green lounge for passengers. It was a world, intact and with its own purposes.

Passengers were in no way special. They had to compete for advantages and food. This point came clear when they chanced upon a large beast lying partly dismembered on a branch. Seeker stopped, pensively studying the savaged hulk. Cley saw that the fur markings, snout and wide teeth resembled Seeker's.

"Your, uh, kind?"

"We had common origins."

Cley could not read anything resembling sadness in Seeker's face. "How many of you are there?"

"Not enough. Though the numbers mean nothing."

"You knew this one?"

"I mingled genetic information with it."

"Oh! I'm sorry, I . . ."

Seeker kicked at the carcass, which was now attracting a cloud of scavenger mites. "It was an enemy."

"After you, ah, 'mingled'—? I mean . . ."

"Before and after."

"But then why did you—I mean, usually we don't . . ."

Seeker gave Cley a glance which combined a fierce scowl with a tongue-lolling grin. "We never think of one thing at a time."

"Even during sex?" Cley laughed. "Do you have children?"

"Two litters."

"Seeker! You're female? I never imagined!"

"Not female as you are."

"Well, you're certainly not male if you bear litters."

"Simple sex like yours was a passing adaptation."

Cley chuckled. "Seeker, sounds like you're missing a lot of fun."

"Humans are noted as sexual connoisseurs with enlarged organs."

"Ummmm. I'll take that as a compliment."

A faint scurrying distracted Cley. She pushed aside a huge fern bough and saw a human shape moving away from them. "Hey!" she called.

The silhouette looked back and turned away.

"Hey, stop! I'm friendly."

But the profile blended into the greens and browns and was gone. Cley ran after it. After blundering along limbs and down trunks she stopped, listening, and heard nothing more than a sigh of breeze and the cooing calls of unknown birds.

Seeker had followed her. "You wished to mate?"

"Huh? No, we're not always thinking about that. Is that what you think? I just wanted to talk to him."

Seeker said, "You will find no one."

"Who was that? Say, that wasn't an illusion, was it? Like those who killed my tribe and that Alvin said were just images?"

"No, that was the Captain."

Cley felt a surge of pride. *Humans* ran this huge thing.

"Alvin said my kind was all gone, except for me."

"They are."

"So this Captain is some other kind? Supra?"

"No. I do not think you truly wish to explore such matters. They are immaterial—"

"Look, I'm *alone*. If I can find *any* kind of human, I will."

Seeker tilted its massive head back, raising and lowering its brow ridges in a way that Cley found vaguely unsettling. "We have other pursuits."

"If you won't help me, I'll find the Captain myself."

"Good."

Cley didn't understand this reply, but she was used to that with Seeker. She grimaced, knowing how hard it would be to find anything in this vast place.

Seeker said nothing more and seemed to be distracted. They worked their way upward against the light centripetal gravity and finally stood on a broad slope made only of great leaves. Sunlight streamed fierce and golden from an open sky that framed the shrinking moon. Cley knew that when the Earth had come alive, over five billion years ago, it had begun wrapping itself in a membrane it made of tailored air and water, for the general purpose of editing the sun. Buried deep in Earth's forest, she had never bothered to think of other planets, but now she saw that the moon too had learned this skill from Earth. There was something fresh and vibrant about the filmed moon, as though it had not shared the long withering imposed by the Supras' robots. Where once *maria* meant the dark blotches of volcanic flows, now true seas lapped at rugged mountains with snow-dappled peaks. Now Earth's spreading voracious green seemed to mimic its junior companion in exuberant disequilibrium.

Seeker bent and pressed an ear against a purple stalk. It nibbled at the young shoots breaking through the slick bark but also seemed to be listening. Then it sat up and said, "We are bound for Venus."

"What's that?"

"The planet next out from Earth, second from the sun."

"Can we live there?"

"I expect the question will be whether we can avoid death there."

With that Seeker fell asleep and Cley, wary of the tangled jungle, did not venture away. She watched the Earth and moon shrink, twin planets brimming against the timeless blaze of the galaxy.

She knew instinctively that the moon was not merely a sheltered greenhouse maintained by constant outside management. Who would tend it, after all? For long eons humankind had been locked into its desert fastnesses. No, the ripeness came from organisms adapting to a material environment which was in turn made by other organisms. To imagine otherwise—as ancient humans had— was to see the world as a game with fixed rules, like human sports, strict and static. Yet even planets had to yield to the press of suns.

The sun had burned hydrogen for nearly five billion years before Earth evolved a species which could understand that simple fact, and its implications. Fusing hydrogen made helium, a gaseous ash that settled to the sun's core. Helium holds in radiation better than hydrogen and so drove the core temperature higher. In turn hydrogen burned more fiercely. The sun grew hotter. Unlike campfires, solar furnaces blaze brighter as their ash gathers.

Earthlife had escaped this dead hand of physics . . . for a while. Long before humans emerged, a blanket of carbon dioxide had helped warm the Earth. As the sun grew hotter, though, life thinned that blanket to keep a comfortable clime.

But carbon dioxide was also the medium through which the rich energy of the sun's fusing hydrogen became transmuted into living matter. It was also the fundamental food for photosynthesis. Thinning the carbon dioxide blanket threatened that essential reaction. So a jot of time after the evolution of humans—a mere hundred million years—the air had such skimpy carbon dioxide that all of the plant kingdom was imperiled.

At that point the biota of Earth could have radically adjusted their chemical rhythms. Other planets had passed through this knothole before and survived. But the intelligences which thronged that era, including the forerunners of Seeker, had intervened.

Moving the Earth further from the solar furnace would offset the steady banking of the inner fires. This led to the great maneuvers which rearranged the planets, opening them to fresh uses.

All this lay buried in Diaspar's dusty records and crossed Cley's thoughts only as a filligree of myth. The much-embellished stories her tribe had told around campfires taught such things through parable and grandiose yarns. Her kind were not studious in the strict sense of the term, but their forest crafts had needed an underpinning of sage myth, the "feel" of why and how biospheres were knit and fed. Some lore was even hard-wired in Cley at the level of instinctive comprehension.

So the cloud-wreathed beauty of the twin worlds made her breath catch, her heart race with a love which was perhaps the hallmark of true intelligence. As Seeker slept she watched specks climb above the sharp-edged air of Luna to meet other dabs in a slow, grand gavotte. Another Jonah approached from Earth. Motes converged on it from eccentric orbits about the moon. She adjusted her eyes to pick out the seeping infrared glow that spoke of internal warmth, and saw a greater cloud, a snapshot of teeming beeswarm wealth. Streamers swung between Earth and moon, endless transactions of species. A thinner rivulet broke away from the figure-eight orbits that linked the twins. It trickled inward and Cley—holding a hand against the sun's glare—saw that it looped toward a thick swarm that clustered about the sun itself.

She felt then both awe, that fear of immensity, and loneliness. She wished her clan could see this, wished that there were other minds of her cut and shape to share this spectacle.

Her attention was so riveted on the unfolding sky that she did not hear the stealthy approach of scraping paws. But she did catch the jostle as something launched itself in the weak gravity.

The shape came at her from behind. She got only a snatched instant to see it, a thing of sleek-jacketed black and flagrant reds. It was hinged like a bat at the wings and slung with ball-bearing agility in its swiveling, three-legged attack.

Claws snatched at the air where Cley had been.

She had ducked and shot sideways, rebounding from a barnacled branch. Instead of fleeing into unknown leafy wilderness, where a pack of the attackers might well be waiting, she launched herself back into the silent, sleek thing.

This it had not expected. It had just seen Seeker and was trying to decide if this new development was a threat or an unexpected banquet.

Cley hit it amidships. A leg snapped; weightlessness makes for flimsy construction. She had flicked two of her fingers into needles, usually used for the fine treatment of ailing creatures. They plunged into the flared red ears of the attacker, puncturing the enlarged eardrums which were its principal sensory organ. The creature departed, a squawking blur of pain and anger.

Cley landed on a wide branch, hands ready. She trembled with a mixture of eagerness and fear which a billion years of selection had still retained as fundamental to the human constitution. The foliage replied to her intent wariness with silent indifference.

Seeker awoke, stretching and yawning. "More food?"

30

THE
CAPTAIN
OF
CLOUDS

They sighted the Supra ship their third day out. It came flaring into view from Earthside, as Cley now thought of the aft layers of the Leviathan.

She and Seeker spent much of their time there, enjoying the view of the steadily shrinking green moon, resting among a tangle of enormous flowerlike growths. Near the moon a yellow star grew swiftly. It became a sleek, silver ship balancing on a thin torch flame.

This had just registered with Cley when Seeker jerked her back behind an overarching stamen. "Do not move," it whispered.

The slim craft darted around the Leviathan as though it were sniffing, its nose turning and swiveling despite being glossy metal. The torch ebbed and fine jets sent it zooming beyond view along the bulk of the Leviathan. Cley felt a shadowy presence, like a sound just beyond recognition. The Supra ship returned, prowling close enough to the prickly growths to risk colliding with upper stems.

Seeker put both of its large, padded hands on Cley's face. Seeker had done this before, to soothe Cley when her anxieties refused to let her sleep. Now the pressure of those rough palms, covered with fine black hair, sent a calming thread through her. She knew what the touch implied: let her mind go blank. That way her talent would transmit as little as possible. Any Supra aboard the ship who had come from Lys could pick up her thoughts, but only if they were focused clearly into perceptible messages. Or so Cley hoped.

The ship held absolutely still for a long while, as if deciding whether to venture inside. The cloud of spaceborne life that surrounded the Leviathan had drawn away from the ship, perhaps fearing the ship's rockets. Its exact cylindrical symmetries and severe gleam seemed strange and malevolent among the drifting swarms, hard and enclosed, giving nothing away. Suddenly the yellow blowtorch ignited again, sending the life-forms skittering away. The ship vanished in moments, heading out from the sun.

"Must've guessed I was running this way," Cley said.

"They try every fleeting possibility."

Seeker seemed concerned, though she was seldom sure what meanings attached to its quick frowns, fur-ripplings and teeth displays.

"I felt something . . ."

"They sought your thought-smell."

"Didn't know I had one."

"It is distinctive."

"You can smell it?"

"In your species many memories are lodged near the brain's receptors for smell. Scents then evoke memories. I do not share this property."

"So?" Sometimes Seeker's roundabout manner irked her. She was not sure whether it was suggesting much by saying little, or simply amusing itself.

"A Supra can remember the savor of your thinking. This act of recollection calls up your talent, makes it stronger."

"Just by remembering, they make *me* transmit better?"

"Something like that."

Cley could not match this with the odd, scratchy presence she had felt. "Well, they're gone now."

"They may return."

"You've got the talent, don't you?"

"If you cannot tell, then I suppose I do not."

"Well, yeah, I sure can't pick up anything from you. But—"

"Let us move away from here. The ship could try again."

They left the flower zone where they had foraged for a day, supping on thick nectar. Cley did not register a transition but somehow they came into a region with light centrifugal gravity. This was not as simple an inner geometry as the Jonah's. Internal portions of Leviathan spun on unseen axes, and streams flowed along sloping hillsides. The local gravity was never more than a subtle touch, but it gave shape and order to the rampant vegetation.

They came into a vast chamber with teeming platforms, passageways, tunnels, balustrades, antechambers, all thronged with small animals moving on intent paths. It was a central station for a system of tubes that seemed to sprout everywhere, even high up the walls. The moist air above was crisscrossed by great shafts of filtered sunlight rising from sources near the floor, up to a distant arched ceiling decorated astonishingly—as if to say that this vault was the fulcrum of all—with a projected view of the starscape outside. The galactic center glowed brilliantly.

Yet all the busy grandeur of this place did not intimidate her; it was even inviting. The scurrying animals were intelligent, in their way, going about swift tasks without giving her more than a glance. Humans were apparently uninteresting, maybe not even unusual— though she doubted that many Supras used Leviathans to journey, given their swift ships.

She did not dwell on the Supra pursuit. The momentum of events carried her further from her lands, and she had resolved to plunge forward rather than endlessly fret. Perhaps she could find Ur-humans somewhere out here, as Seeker had said.

Her hunting skills reawakened as she followed Seeker in its unhurried but quick foraging. Seeker ate a lot and seemed to savor the pursuit of small prey for sport, though it devoured mostly plants. It especially enjoyed ripping big fronds to shreds, picking out packets of ripe red seeds.

The ferment of tangled life around them, extending in all three dimensions throughout Leviathan, captivated Cley. It was so unlike the Supras' carefully tuned projects. As she immersed herself in this complex wealth she understood what had irked and daunted her about the Supras. Their air of superiority had been tolerable, but in their grave manner she felt a cold brush with something she could not name.

Alvin had been even amusing at times, but the others were leaden and solemn. Seranis had shown Cley their art, and it had been cloaked with images of decay. Cley knew in her bones that this was a fashion, even if shaped by the weight of drowsy centuries, not a rule of nature. Entropy increased, surely, and would doom even the glowing stars. But without the sun's abundance no light would have kindled life. The biota were like skilled accountants, living on the flow of energy, paying all required taxes but never neglecting a loophole. Burning fat in Cley's blood generated entropy, but she managed to excrete entropy even faster in waste heat and waste matter—a miraculous, improbable, but perfectly legal dodging of the second law of thermodynamics.

She, like whole planets, shed excrement and pollution. But the pollution of one was the meat of another, and she was beginning to see that this truth worked on the interplanetary scale. Surely it worked a persistent magic in Leviathan, and would soon enough on Earth. The Supras had troubled her because they still resonated with the bleak, fixed compass of Diaspar. Alvin did not know life, that spark which hangs between two eternities. In a deep sense the Supras were immortal but not alive.

She banished these thoughts with a shiver. They trekked through the light gravity of this inner vault, eating berries that swung from animal-snagging palm trees. The sharp fronds could slice off an arm, but Seeker showed her how to confuse the tree's ropy reflexes long enough to snatch berries. They hiked for two days along a broad beach, Seeker catching the yellow fish that thronged the lake. Through clouds Cley could see the lake curling over their heads, kilometers away, describing the vast curve of a rotating cylinder.

"Why do we keep moving so much?" Cley asked when Seeker marched resolutely on despite gathering gloom. Blades of sunlight ebbed and flowed in the huge cylindrical vault like tides of light.

"We hide among life."

"You figure the Supras're still looking for me?"

"They have gone."

"Your own mysterious wisdom tells you that?"

Seeker showed its sparkling teeth, recently cleaned by steaks of yellow fish. "The Supras continue outward."

"Great. Let's go back to Leviathan's skin, then. I liked the view."

Actually she wanted to search for the Captain. She had glimpsed humans near the transparent blisters and each time they had seemed to evaporate into the humid jungle before she could pursue.

Seeker did not comment on her desire to find humans and would not help track them, though she suspected it could sense the smallest animals which swung or padded through the layers of green. For three days they worked their way along these lakes, stopping only to swim and surf. This zone of Leviathan was spinning, yielding curious spiral waves in the lake that worked up and down the shore.

Two more days, by Cley's inner clock, brought them to the skin. Again Cley could not sense when they left the region of spingravity. Fogs had hampered their way, blowing into the Leviathan's recesses, bringing moisture along the paths of the great blades of reflected sunlight that plunged along wide shafts.

Seeker taught her one of its favorite games. They perched in one of the translucent bubbles in Leviathan's outer reaches, waiting. In the utter vacuum outside strange forms glided and worked. Shelled things like abalone attached themselves to Leviathan's skin. Sometimes they mistakenly triggered a reflex that made the slick skin double-fold inward. When one slipped inside, Seeker would crack it open between its hard-soled feet and gulp the shell's inhabitant with lip-smacking relish.

Long, black creatures crawled over Leviathan, grazing on the photosynthetic mats which grew everywhere. Cley could see these dark algae mottling the carbuncled skin, occasionally puffing out spores. The grazers slurped up the brown goo and moved on, the cattle of the skies.

Seeker tried to entice one close to the translucent layer, whirling and grimacing to attract its attention. The vacuum cow turned its slitted dark eyes toward this display. Bovine curiosity brought it closer. Seeker grabbed for it, stretching the tough, waxy wall with its hands and feet. It managed to hang on to the grazer through the thin skin. Grunting and growling, Seeker was strong enough to pluck the struggling cow inward against the atmospheric pressure pushing the envelope out.

For a moment Cley thought Seeker would manage to drag the grazer far enough in to trigger the folding instability and pluck it through. Seeker yelped with tenor joy. But then the vacuum cow spurted steam, wriggled, and jetted away.

Seeker gnashed its teeth. "Devilish things."

"Yeah, looked appetizing."

"They are a great delicacy," Seeker said.

"Pretty resistant, though."

When Clay stopped laughing at the expression on Seeker's face she glanced to the side—and was startled to find standing there a human form. But only a form, for this was like nothing she had ever seen.

The face worked with expression, frowns and smiles and wild flaring eyes, all fidgeting and dissolving. The thing seemed demented. Then she saw that she had been imposing her own need to find expression, impose order. In fact the skittering storms rippled and fought all through the body. Colors and shapes were but passing approximations.

The form took a tentative step toward Cley. She bit her lip. The body jiggled and warped like a bad image projected on a wobbly screen. But this was no illusion. Its lumpy foot brushed aside a stem as it took another step. The fidgeting skin seemed like a mulatto wash that blurred and shifted as the body moved.

She realized that she could see *through* the thing. Plants behind it appeared as flickering images. She heard a slight thrumming as it raised an arm with one smooth unnatural motion, not the hinged pull of muscles at the pivots of shoulder and elbow.

"Aurrouugh," it said, a sound like stones rattling in a jug.

"It is imitating you, as it did before," Seeker said.

"What *is* it?"

"The Captain."

"But—it's—"

"Not all of the Captain, of course."

"What does he—does it—want?"

"I do not know. Often it manifests itself in the form of a new passenger, as a kind of politeness. To learn something it cannot otherwise know."

The shape said, "Yooou waaanteed by maaaany."

Cley pursed her lips. "Yes, many want to find me."

"Yooou musssst lee—vah."

"I, I can't leave. And why should I?"

"Daaaanger. To meee."

"You? What are you?"

The shape stretched its arms up to encompass all the surrounding growth. Its arms ended in stumps, though momentarily a finger or two would sprout at the ends, flutter, and then ease back into the constant flow of the body.

"Everything? You're everything?" Cley asked.

"Wooorld."

Seeker said, "It is the Leviathan. This composite intelligence directs its many parts and lesser minds."

Cley gaped. "Every part of it adds to its intelligence?"

"Alvin thought the Phylum Myriasoma was extinct," Seeker said. "He would be happy to see that he is wrong yet again."

Cley smiled despite her tingling fear. "Supras don't like news like that."

As she watched, the Captain's legs dissolved into a swarm of bits. Each was the size of a thumb and swam in the air with stubby wings. The Captain was an assembly that moved incessantly, each flyer brushing the other but capable of flitting away at any moment. The individual members looked like a bizarre mixture of bird and insect. Each had four eyes, two on opposite sides of their cylindrical bodies and one each at top and bottom.

Cley heard the Captain then in her mind. The thrumming whisper of wings she had heard was echoed by a soft flurry of thoughts in her mind.

You are a danger to me.

"You? The ship?"

I am the world.

And so it must seem to this thing, she realized. It somehow governed the immense complexity of the Leviathan and at some level must *be* the Leviathan, its mind instead of merely its brain. Yet each moment a flying thumb shot away on some mission and others came to merge into the standing, rippling cloud. Beneath its clear message she felt the buzzing of quicksilver thought, the infinitude of transactions the Leviathan must make to keep so vast an enterprise going. It was as though she could listen to the individual negotiations between her own blood cells and the walls of her veins, the acids of her stomach, the sour biles of her liver.

Cley thought precisely, slowly, *How can you be self-aware? You change all the time.*

The shape let its right arm fall off, scattering into clumps that then departed on new tasks. *I do not need to feel myself intact, as you do.*

So how do I know who's talking? Cley countered.

The Captain answered, *I speak for the moment. A little while later I shall speak for that time.*

Cley glanced at Seeker but it was watching with only distant interest. She thought, *Will that be the same* you?

How could you tell? Or I? I always find that your kind of intelligence is obsessed with knowing what you are.

Cley smiled. *Seems a reasonable question.*

Not reasonable. Reason cannot tell you deep things.

Cley watched as the shape gradually decomposed into an oblong cloud of the thumb-things. It had made its polite gesture and now relaxed into a wobbly sphere, perhaps to bring its individual elements closer while lowering its surface area. *Are you afraid of me?* she asked impishly.

My parts know fear. Hunger and desire, as well. They are a species, like you. But I am another kind of being, and can elude attack by dispersing. I do not know fear for myself but I do know caution. I cannot die but I can be hurt.

Cley thought of the honeybees she had tended in the forest—satisfying, sweaty labor that now seemed to have happened a very long time ago. Bees had fewer than ten thousand neurons, she knew, yet did complex tasks. How much more intelligent would be a single arm of this cloud-Captain, when its thumb-things united to merge their minds?

Not hurt by anybody like me, I assume?

The swarm churned. *Yes. I am not vulnerable to destruction of special parts, as are you. Merely by taking away your head, for example, I could leach life from you, rob you of all you know. But each part of me contains some of my intelligence and feels what a part of the world feels.*

Cley felt suddenly the strangeness of this thing hanging before her, bulging and working with sluggish patience as it pondered the Leviathan's intricacies. Another phylum? No, something more— another kingdom of life, a development beyond beings forever separated into inevitable loneliness. In a way she envied it. Each thumb-flyer knew the press of competition, of hunger and longing, but the composite would rise above that raw turbulence, into realms she could not even guess. She glanced at Seeker again and saw that its expression was not of indifference, but of reverence. Seeker had not wanted her to seek the Captain because it was, even for Seeker, a holy being.

I speak to you now because the world cannot tolerate you, the Captain sent.

How come you ran away before? Cley asked.

I needed time to speak to my brothers.

Other Leviathans? As she framed the thought the Captain's answer came: *Other worlds.*

Was there something beyond Leviathans? Cley started to ask but the Captain said, *I now understand many recent events and your connection with them. There is an entity called the Mad Mind and it searches for you.*

I know.

Then know this—

In a flooded single moment a torrent of sensations, ideas, and conclusions forked through her. She had for an instant the perception of what the mind before her was truly like. The layers of its logic were translucent, so that every fact shone through to illuminate the lacing of concepts on another level. And that light in turn refracted through the lattice of mind, shedding its fitful glow on assumptions lying beneath.

This was thought without the constraint of the staged human brains. That a property had emerged in the billion years since the era of Ur-humans and now showed the limitations of evolution's blind methods. Rapid selection pressure operated on what already existed, adding capability to minds rather than snipping away parts which worked imperfectly. The human brain was always retrofitted, and showed its origins in its cumbersome workings. The Captain had arisen from a different mechanism.

But this realization was only a filament tossing on the surge that swamped her. She sagged with the weight of what the Captain had given her, stunned as though by a blow. She was dimly conscious of Seeker leaping forward to cradle her. Then the air clouded with ebony striations and she felt herself dwindling beneath a great dark weight.

31

SKYSHARKS

"You can speak it?" Seeker asked, its tilted chin and rippling amber fur patterns showing concern.

"I, I think so." Cley had slept for many hours. When she revived, Seeker had brought her a banquet of berries and fruits and thick, meaty leaves. Now she tried to explain what she had sensed in the brief collision of minds. Like Seranis, the Captain sent information faster and at greater depth than Cley could handle.

"But didn't you feel it, too?" she asked.

"I do not have your talent."

"What did the Captain do after I fainted?"

"Scattered like a bird swarm into which a hunter has fired a shot."

"Huh. Maybe it didn't know how to tell me without overloading me."

"Perhaps. I have seen Captains before. This was different. Ah—"

Seeker snagged a ratlike creature which was passing and bit off its fat tail. The rat squealed and hissed and Seeker put it gently back down. As the rat scampered away Seeker munched on the tail. "A delicacy," it explained. "They grow tasty tails so that the rest of them is let go."

"It'll live?"

"Within days it will sport another luscious tail." Seeker smacked its lips at a morsel, holding out the last to Cley.

"No rat's ass for me, thanks. You were saying something about the Captain?"

"It was odd."

"How?"

"I have never seen one worried before."

Cley bit her lip, memories stirring. She had felt filigrees of the Captain's anxiety. Already the sharp, vibrant images were trickling away. She suspected that her kind of intelligence was simply unable to file and categorize the massive infusion she had received, and so was sloughing it off.

"The Supras it could deal with," she said. "It's afraid of the Mad Mind, though."

Seeker nodded. "The Mind has fully arrived, then."

"Fully?"

"All components knit together."

"I caught something about that from the Captain." She frowned, troubled, eyes distant. "Sheets of fine copper wire wrapping around blue flames . . ."

"Where?"

"Somewhere further out from here. Where it's cold, dark. There was a feeling of the Mad Mind spreading over whole stars. Suns . . . like campfires."

"It is expanding." Seeker clashed its claws together, a gesture of sly menace which somehow made it look professorial.

She told Seeker what she had glimpsed. Much of it was a tapestry of rediscovered history.

The Mad Mind had been confined to the warped space-time near a huge Black Hole. Only the restraining curvature there could hold the Mind in place for long. This had been done eons ago, a feat accomplished by humanity in collaboration with elements and beings she could not begin to describe. Around the Black Hole orbited a disk made of infalling matter, flattened into a thin plate, spinning endlessly. The inner edge of the disk was gnawed into incandescent ferocity by the compressive clawing of the Black Hole's great tidal gradients. There the Mad Mind had been held by the swirl and knots of vexed space-time. Matter perpetually entered the disk at its outer rim, as dust clouds and even stars were drawn inward by friction and the shredding effects of the Black Hole's grip.

The Mad Mind had been forced to perpetually swim upstream against this flux of matter in the disk. If it relented, the Mind would have been carried by the flow to the very inner edge of the disk. There it would have been sucked further in, spiraling down into the hole.

That had been the prison and torture of the Mad Mind. It had been able to spare nothing in its struggle to survive. And that is all that had saved the rest of the galaxy from its strange wrath.

"But it escaped," Seeker said.

"It . . . diffused." The odd word popped into her head, summoned by the fading images from the Captain. "It is made of magnetic fields, and they diffused across the conducting disk. That took a very long time, but the Mind managed it."

"Where was the Black Hole?" Seeker asked.

"It was the biggest humanity could find—the hole at the center of the galaxy."

They both looked out through the transparent pressure membrane. The vibrant glow of a million suns wreathed the center of the galaxy in beeswarm majesty. Yet at the center of all that glare dwelt an utter darkness, they knew. Ten billion years of galactic progression had fed the Black Hole. Stars which swooped too close to it were stripped and sucked in. Each dying sun added to the compact darkness, the dynamical center about which a hundred billion stars rotated in the gavotte of the galaxy.

Cley whispered, "Then moving the solar system here, near the galactic center, was part of the scheme to trap the Mad Mind?"

Seeker said, "It must have been."

"Wouldn't it be safer to get as far away as possible?"

"Yes. But not responsible."

"So humanity brought the sun and planets here as a kind of guard?"

"That is one possibility. Our star may have been moved here to challenge the Mad Mind when it emerged."

"How can we?"

"With difficulty."

"That's one possibility, you said. What's another?"

"That we were placed here as a sentinel, to warn others."

"Who?"

"I do not know."

"Hard to warn somebody when you don't know who that might be."

"There is yet one more possibility."

"What?"

"That we are here as a sacrifice."

Cley said nothing. Seeker went on. "Perhaps if the Mad Mind finds and destroys its imprisoners, it will be content."

The casual way Seeker said this chilled Cley. "What's all this *about?*"

"Perhaps the Supras know."

"Well then, let *them* fight the Mind. I want out of it."

"There is no way out."

"Well, moving further from the sun sure doesn't seem so smart. That's where the Mind is accumulating itself."

Seeker studied the stars, bright holes punched in the pervading night. "Your talent made you too easy to find on Earth. Here you blend into the many mind-voices."

Cley opened her mouth to disagree and stopped, feeling a light, keening note sound through her thoughts. She blinked. It was a hunting call, a flavor that eons had not erased, as though from some quick bird swooping down through velvet air, eyes intent on scampering prey below.

She glanced back at the smoldering glow of the galactic center. Against it were black shapes, angular and swift, growing. Not metal, like Supra ships, but green and brown and gray.

"Call the Captain!" she said.

"I have," Seeker said.

As Cley watched the approaching sleek creatures she saw that they were larger than the usual spaceborne life she had known, and that it was far too late to avoid them, even if Leviathan could have readily turned its great bulk.

Skysharks, Cley thought, the word leaping up from her buried vocabulary. The term fit, though she did not know its origin. They were elegantly molded for speed, with jets for venting gases. Solar sails gave added thrust, but the lead skyshark had reeled in its sails as it approached, retracting the silvery sheets into pouches in its side. Cupped parabolas fore and aft showed that it had evolved radar senses; these, too, collapsed moments before contact, saving themselves from the fray.

The first of them came lancing into the Leviathan without attempting to brake. It slammed into the skin aft of the blister that held Seeker and Cley. They could see it gouge a great hole in the puckered skin.

The skysharks were large, muscular, powerful. Cley watched the first few plow into the mottled hide of the Leviathan and wondered why they would risk such damage merely for food. But then her ears popped.

"They're breaking the seals!"

"Yes," Seeker said calmly, "such is their strategy."

"But they'll kill everything aboard."

"They penetrate inward a few layers. This lets the outrushing air bring to them the smaller animals."

Cley watched a skyshark back away from the jagged wound it had made. A wind blew the backdrop of stars around, the only evidence of escaping air. Then flecks and motes came from the wound, a geyser of helpless wriggling prey. The skyshark caught each with its quick, wide mouth, seeming to inhale them.

Cley had to remind herself that these gliding shapes and their cool, soundless, artful movements were actually a savage attack, remorseless and efficient. Vacuum gave even death a quality of silent grace. Yet the beauty of threat shone through, a quality shared alike by the grizzly, falcon and rattler.

Her ears popped again. "If we lose all our air . . ."

"We should not," Seeker said, though it was plainly worried, its coat running with swarthy spirals. "Membranes close to limit the loss."

"Good," Cley said uncertainly. But as she spoke a wind rose, sucking dry leaves into a cyclone about them.

"That should not happen," Seeker said stiffly.

"Look."

Outside two skysharks were wriggling into older gouges. Air had ceased to stream from them, so the beasts could enter easily. Others withdrew from the rents they had torn after only a few vicious bites. They jetted along the broad sweep of skin, seeking other weak points. In their tails were nozzled and gimbled chambers. She saw a bright flame as hydrogen peroxide and catalase combined in these, puffs and streamers pushing them adroitly along the rumpled brown hide.

From the gaping gashes where skysharks had entered came fresh puffs of air. Some carried animals tumbling in the thinning gale, and skysharks snapped these up eagerly.

"The ones that went inside—they must be tearing up those membranes," Cley said. "Sucks out the protected areas."

Seeker braced itself against the steadily gathering winds. "A modified tactic. Even if those inside perish, their fellows benefit from the added game. Good for the species overall, despite the sacrifice of a few."

"Yeah, but what'll we *do?*"

"Come."

Seeker launched itself away and Cley followed. Between bounces off trunks and bowers, Seeker curled up into a ball to minimize the pull of the howling gale. Cley copied this, narrowing her eyes against the rain of leaves and bark and twigs that raked her.

Seeker led her along a zigzag path just beneath the Leviathan's skin. Despite the whirling winds she heard the yelps and cries of animals. A catlike creature lost its grip on a tubular root and pinwheeled away. A triangular mat with legs caroomed off Seeker and ricocheted from Cley before whirling into the madhouse mist.

They came to a system like a heart, with veins and arteries stretching away in all directions. The wind moaned and gathered itself here with a promise of worse to come. The open wounds behind them were probably tearing further, she guessed, evacuating more and more of the Leviathan. For the first time it occurred to Cley that even this colossal creature could perhaps die, its fluids and air bled into space.

She hurried after Seeker. A gray cloud streamed by them, headed toward the sighing breezes. Cley recognized this flight of thumb-sized flyers which had made up the Captain, now streaming to defend its ship. There might even be more than one Captain, or a crew of the anthology-beings. Or perhaps the distinction of individual entities was meaningless.

Ahead was a zone of gauzy, translucent surfaces lit by phosphorescent streaks. Seeker grabbed a sheet of the waxy stuff, which seemed to be a great membrane upon which pollen caught. Even in the chaos of drifting debris Cley could see that this was part of an enormous plant. They were at the tip of a great pistil. Seeker was wrenching off a slab of its sticky walls. Above this was a broad transparent dome which brought sunlight streaming into the leathery bud of the plant. Its inner bulb had mirrored surfaces which reflected the intense sunlight into bright blades, sending illumination deep into the inner recesses of the Leviathan.

She took this in at a glance. Then Seeker yanked her into position on the bulb wall, where her feet caught in sticky goo. Seeker barked orders and Cley followed them, fashioning the tough sheet into a pyramidal shape. Seeker stuck the edges together with the wall adhesive. It turned down the last side, leaving them inside the pyramid. They drifted toward the transparent ceiling, moving on an eddy of the slowly building winds. Seeker crouched at an apex of the pyramid. It touched the ceiling and did something quickly to the wall—and they passed through, into naked space.

"This will last for only a while," Seeker said.

"Till we run out of air," Cley said.

"If that long."

The advantage of living construction material was that it grew together, encouraged by an adhesive, becoming tighter than any manufactured seal. Nature loved the smooth and seamless. Soon their pyramid held firm and snug.

They drifted away from Leviathan. Cley hoped the skysharks would ignore them, and indeed the predators were nuzzling greedily at the raw wounds amidships. Around Leviathan was a swarm of debris. Into this cloud came spaceborne life of every description. Some were smaller predators who scavenged on whatever the skysharks left. Others spread great gossamer sheets to catch the air which poured forth from the Leviathan's wounds. Small creatures billowed into great gas bags, fat with rare wealth. Limpets crawled eagerly along the crusty hide toward the rents. When they arrived they caught streamers of fluid that spouted irregularly into the vacuum.

This was a riotous harvest for some; Cley could see joy in the excited darting of thin-shelled beetles who snatched at the tumbling fragments of once-glorious ferns. The wounds created fountains that shot motley clouds of plant and animal life into a gathering crowd of eager consumers, their appetites quickened by the bounty of gushing air.

"Hope they don't fancy our taste," Cley said.

Her mouth was dry and she had long since passed the point of fear. Now she simply watched. Gargantuan forces had a way of rendering her pensive, reflective. This trait had been more effective in the survival of Ur-humans than outright aggression or conspicuous gallantry and it did not fail her now. Visible fear would have attracted attention. They drifted among the myriad spaceborne forms, perhaps too strange a vessel to encourage ready attack; even hungry predators wisely select food they know.

"Do you think they will kill Leviathan?" Cley asked.

"Mountains do not fear ants," Seeker answered.

"But they're gutting it!"

"They cannot persist for long inside the mountain. For the spaceborne, air in plenty is a quick poison."

"Oxygen?"

"It kindles the fires that animate us. Too much, and . . ."

Seeker pointed. Now curls of smoke trickled from the ragged wounds. The puffs of air had thinned but they carried black streamers.

"The skysharks can forage inside until the air makes their innards burn." Seeker watched the spectacle with almost scholarly interest.

"They die, so that others can eat the Leviathan?"

"Apparently. Though I suspect this behavior has other purposes, as well."

"All this pillaging? It's awful."

"Yes. Many have died. But not those for whom this raid was intended."

"Who's that?"

"Us."

32

THE
LIVING
BRIDGE

They waited out the attack. Wispy shreds of smoke thinned as the Leviathan healed its internal ruptures, damming the torrent of air. The remaining skysharks glided with easy menace over the Leviathan's skin, but did not rip and gouge it. They ignored the periodic rings of plant life around Leviathan's middle. Apparently these thick-skinned, ropy growths had developed poisons or other defenses, and were left to spread their leathery leaves to the sun, oblivious to the assault on Leviathan's body.

The skysharks fed first on debris. Then they sensed Cley and Seeker and converged. Their mouths gaped, showing spiky blue teeth. Clay felt ominous, silent presences in her mind, like the sudden press of chilled glass on her face. Seeker said, "Hate them."

"You do?"

"No, *you* hate them. That will protect us."

"I—"

"*Now.*"

She let go some of her bottled-in emotions, envisioning them as a sharp spear lanced directly at the nearest skyshark. This time she felt her transmission as a bright spark of virulent orange. The skyshark wriggled, turned, fled.

"Good. Do that whenever one approaches."

"Why doesn't Leviathan keep them off this way?"

"In packs they damp and defend against Leviathan thought patterns. But it taxes them greatly, for they are not very intelligent. When foraging among the helpless outgushed life, that defense mode is shut off."

Already the skysharks were roaming further from the Leviathan, catching up with creatures and plant shreds blown away. Their angular bodies bulged, bellies still throbbing with the struggles of their ingested banquets. Fore and aft, appendages unfolded from their warty hides. Parabolic antennas blossomed and scanned with patient, metronomic vigilance. Cley suspected there were species which preyed on these sleek hunters, too, though to look at these mean, moving appetites, she could not imagine how they could be vulnerable.

"So you think they're after us?"

"They seldom assault a Leviathan; the losses are too heavy. Usually it is a tactic of desperation, when pickings elsewhere are lean."

"Well, maybe it's been a bad year."

"They were not thinned by hunger. No, they were directed to do this."

"By the Mad Mind?"

"It must be."

Cley felt an icy apprehension. "Then it knows where I am."

"I suspect it is probing, trying whatever idea occurs."

"It killed a lot of creatures, doing this."

"It cares nothing for that."

Their jury-rigged bubble was clouding with moisture. Cley rubbed the surface to see better, forgetting the skysharks and beginning to wonder how they could survive for long out here, Mad Mind or no. Seeker seemed unbothered. It spread its hindquarters, assuming the posture which meant it intended to excrete, and Cley said, "Seeker! Not now."

"But I must."

"Look, we're going to suffocate out here unless—"

Seeker farted loudly and shat a thin stream directly onto the nearest wall. "Take a deep breath," it said.

Cley caught just a taint of the smell—and then her ears popped. Seeker's excrement had eaten a small hole in their protection. Vacuum sucked the brown slime away.

Cley grabbed for the nearest wall as a gathering breeze plucked at her hair. Sudden fear darted through her and she sucked in air greedily, finding it already thinner. In the far wall a small hole shrieked its banshee protest. The wall shot toward her. She struck it, rebounded in the sudden chill. Seeker's fur abruptly filled her face and she clutched a handful.

She would have demanded an explanation but that would have taken air. Seeker surged, carrying her along with muscular agility. Her ears felt as though daggers were thrust into her eardrums. Seeker dug its claws into the walls, wedging the two of them into a corner. She struggled to see what was happening.

Their draining air made a thin, screaming rocket, thrusting them back toward the Leviathan. They passed into its shadow.

She saw a raw wound in the skin nearby. A pale pink membrane slid out from its edges. The gouge looked like a majestically closing eye, hurt and red-rimmed. They were headed nearly directly toward the slowly narrowing rent.

Seeker lunged away. This momentarily altered the direction of the jetting air. Then Seeker slammed against the far wall and the jet swung again. This midcourse correction took them straight through the closing iris of the gouge.

They struck a large, soft fern and bounced among a confused net of branches. The pink membrane sealed shut above them, puckering along the seam.

Cley could hold her breath no longer. She exhaled, coughed, and sucked in thin but warm air. She breathed greedily, blinking.

Around them small scurryings and slidings began. The Leviathan had already begun to secure and revive itself.

"How . . . how'd you *do* that?"

"A simple problem in dynamics." Seeker yawned.

They lived for two days in the segmented chambers of this zone. Armies of small, insectlike workers thronged everywhere, patching and pruning. The pink membrane thickened just enough to keep in air securely, but allowed in beams of sunlight which hastened re-growth. Cley found food and rested, watching the crowds of hurry-ing workers. Through the transparent membrane she could see the spaceborne life outside, and at last understood their role.

Small crawler forms healed the torn skin with their sticky leav-ings. Others seemed to ferry materials from distant parts of Levia-than to the many lacerations. Strange oblong creatures scooted in from distant places, trailing bags of fluids and large seeds.

She slowly caught the sense of Leviathan, its interlocking myster-ies. The carcass of a skyshark, gutted by its own internal fires, became food for the regrowth of myriad plants. The armies which distributed skyshark parts showed no malice or vindictive anger as they tore the body to shreds, sometimes stopping to eat a morsel. They were intent upon their labors, no more.

Though much could be repaired, clearly the great world-creature was badly hurt. Long chasms yawned where skysharks had ruptured enclosed pressure zones, spilling wealth. Whole regions were gray with death. The reek of bodies drove Cley and Seeker from the once-tranquil groves of ropy, banyanlike trees.

But the true sign of the enormous damage came when Cley felt a slow, steady gravity pushing her toward the aft layers.

"We're moving," she said.

"We must." Seeker was carefully picking the briars from a pretty bunch of red berries. It assured her that the thorns were quite tasty, whereas the berries were poison; the bush was a master of sly decep-tion.

"Where to?"

"Jove. Events accelerate."

"Is the Leviathan dying?"

"No, but its pain is vast. It seeks succor."

"From this Jove thing?"

"No, though it expends its fluids to take us there. It can receive the aid of its many friends as we travel."

"Us? We're so important?"

When Seeker said nothing, Cley scrambled away. After getting lost three times she found a translucent bubble that gave an aft view.

Long pearly plumes jetted from Leviathan. They came from tapered, warty growths that Cley was sure did not poke from Leviathan before. They had been grown with startling speed, and somehow linked to a chemical system which was fed in turn by the Leviathan's internal chemistry. Her nose prickled at the scent of peroxide, and the thunder of steady detonations made nearby boughs tremble.

Even as the immense bulk accelerated, Cley could see groups of spacelife detach themselves and spurt away. Some species seemed to be abandoning ship, perhaps sensing that something dangerous lay ahead. They spread broad silvery sails which reflected images of the shrinking sun. Others had sails of utter dull black, and Cley guessed that these might be the natural prey of skysharks. Reflections would attract unwanted attention, so these oddly shaped creatures deployed parachute-shaped sails which absorbed sunlight, and then contrived to shed the build-up of heat through thin, broad cooling vanes.

Such adaptations led to every conceivable arrangement of surfaces. Creatures like abstract paintings were quite workable here, where gravity had no hand in fashioning evolution's pressures. Their struts, sheets, tubes and decks made use of every geometric advantage. Pivots as apparently fragile as a flower stem served to turn vast planes and sails. Transparent veins carried fluids of green and ivory.

Yet as these fled the wounded giant, others flocked in. Great arrays swooped to meet the Leviathan, things that looked to Cley like no more than spindly arrays of green toothpicks. Nonetheless these unlikely-looking assemblies decelerated, attached themselves to the Leviathan, and off-loaded cargoes. It struck Cley that the Leviathan played a role with no easy human analogy. It cycled among worlds, yet was no simple ship. Fleets of spaceborne life exchanged food and seeds and doubtless much more, all by intersecting Leviathan's orbit, hammering out biological bargains, and then returning to the black depths where they eked out a living. Leviathan was ambassador, matchmaker, general store and funeral director, and many other unfathomable roles as well.

Yet the vast beast was deeply damaged, and a fevered note of anxiety layered the air around Cley. She idly turned away from the sunlit spectacle of the aft zones and just had time to glimpse a small, ruddy disk coming into view. Then the hackles on her neck rose and she whirled, already knowing what she would see.

You brought this upon me, the Captain sent.

It towered above her. Its thumb-sized components hovered as though full of repressed energy, giving the stretched human shape the appearance of a warped statue across which dappled light fell, like the shadows of leaves stirred by fitfull breezes.

"I didn't know the skysharks even existed. You've got to understand, I—"

I understand much. Toleration is what I lack.

Cley ached to flee. But how could she elude this angry, swift swarm? Better to keep it talking. "It wasn't my idea to come here."

The elongated human form bulged. Its left arm merged with the body. She sensed a massive threat behind these surges, underlined by spikes of anger that shot through the murky talent-voice of the Captain. *Nor mine. I shall rid myself of you.*

"I'll leave as soon as I can."

The Mad Mind sends tendrils everywhere. They snake into me.

"Do you think it can find me?"

The constantly shifting form curled its legs up into the body, as though its components had to be brought closer to ponder this point. *Soon, yes. It probes me.*

"How much time do I have left?"

It would have tracked you by now, were it not opposed by another and similar skill. I cannot predict the outcome of such large collisions.

Cley tried to make herself think of this thing as a community of parts, not simply an organism. But the moving cloud seemed to purposefully make itself humanlike enough to send disturbing, atavistic fears strumming through her. And she wondered if that, too, was its intention.

"What other 'skill'? Another magnetic mind?"

Similar in power, and winging on the flexings of the fields. It is called Vanamonde.

"Is it dangerous to you?" Despite herself Cley edged away from the shifting fog of creatures. She resolved to stand straight and undaunted in the slight pseudogravity of Leviathan's acceleration, to show no sign of her inner fear. But how much could the Captain sense from her unshielded thoughts?

I do not know. I despise all such human inventions.

This startled her out of her apprehension. "Vanamonde—we made it?"

In typical human fashion, as a corrective to your earlier error—the Mad Mind.

"Look, even Leviathans must make mistakes," Cley said giddily.

Ours do not remain, encased in the lace of magnetic fields, while the galaxy turns upon itself again and again. Our errors die.

The cloud-Captain buzzed and fretted with agitation. Its head lifted into the air, its mouth gaping like a bullet hole that ran completely through the head, so that Cley could see the vegetation beyond. Angry waves roiled up and down the torso.

"So we build things to last," Cley said with airy abandon. She was *not* going to let this talking fog intimidate her. "Can't blame us, can you?"

Why should we not?

"We don't last long ourselves. Not ur-humans, anyway. Our creations have to do our living for us."

Nor should you endure. Time once honored your kind. Now it drags you in its wake.

Despite her fear, this rankled Cley. "Oh, really? You seem pretty scared of stuff we made."

The Captain lost its human shape entirely, exploding like shrapnel into the air. Components buzzed angrily around Cley. She stood absolutely still, remembering the time on Earth when she had sealed her nostrils against a cloud. But that would be of no use here. She stared straight ahead and kept her mind as steady as she could. Small and limited her brain might be, but she wasn't going to give the maddened cloud any satisfaction. The Captain's flyers brushed her like a heavy moist handclasp—insistent, clammy, repulsive. Tiny voices shrieked and howled in her mind and slapping her hands over her ears would be no help.

"You will kindly go about your task," Seeker's voice came cutting through.

Cley jumped, startled by the smooth, almost liquid quality to the sound. Seeker hung by one claw from a strand, peering at the center of the ire-fog. "Now," it added.

Slowly the components steadied, whirling in a cyclone about both Seeker and Cley, but keeping a respectful distance. *I suffer agony for you!*

"As you should," Seeker replied, "for you must."

Be gone!

"In due time," Seeker said.

With that the components streaked away, as if called by numberless tasks. Cley felt a spark of compassion for the strange things, and their even stranger sum. She supposed in some way she was also an anthology being, and her cells suffered in silence for her. But the Captain was a different order of thing, more open to both joy and agony in a way she could not express but felt deeply through the talent.

"Thanks," she said in a whisper, her throat still tight.

Seeker coasted to a light landing near the transparent bubble. "Even a great being can harm in a moment of self-loss."

"Getting mad, that's self-loss? Funny term."

"For Leviathan, the pain is of a different quality than you can feel. Never think that you can sense its sacrifice."

Cley did not know what to say to that. She had seen the terrible damage, the shriveled zones, the creatures which had died as their blood boiled, and worse.

"Meanwhile," Seeker said in the way it had of changing the subject without notice, "enjoy the view."

The ruddy disk was much larger now. It was a planet of silver seas and rough brown cloud-shrouded continents. As they approached it rapidly Cley saw that a circle hung over the equator like a belt. It seemed to be held aloft above the atmosphere by great towers.

These thin stalks were like the Pinwheel she had ridden, but fixed. Their centers orbited, with feet planted in the soil, while their heads met the great ring that girded the planet. Each tower could remain erect by itself, and perhaps they had stood alone once. Now the ring linked each to the others, making the array steady.

Leviathan was intended to sweep by the great circle, Seeker told her. Even at this distance Cley could see compartments sliding up and down the towers, connecting the spaceborne to the worldborne. And larger shapes shot along the ring itself, bringing their stores to the tower nearest their eventual destination. This was how the Leviathan and its myriad passengers merged their fortunes with the spreading green surface below. Some towers plunged into the silver seas, while others stood at the summits of enormous mountains.

"What is this place?" Cley asked.

"Mars," Seeker answered.

"What about Venus?"

Seeker gestured at a blue-white dot. "Nearby. We do not need it now, so I directed the Captain to bring us veering close to Mars. We shall gain momentum, stealing from the planet's hoard, and hasten on."

"Either we're moving very fast, or these places aren't very far apart."

"Both. All the ancient worlds are now clustered in a narrow zone around the sun, each finding its comfortable distance from the fire."

"Looks better off than Earth."

"True, for no humans have meddled with it for over a billion years. Once it too was desert."

This Cley flatly refused to believe, for Mars was a carpet of rich convolutions. Without the Supras and their desert-loving robots, she imagined, Earth might have been like this. "Can we live there?"

"We must pass on. It is too dangerous for us."

Seeker pointed. Along the ring, filaments of orange and blue twisted. They shot up and down the towers, as though seeking a way in. Cley could make out the texture of the towers now and with surprise saw that they were the same woody layers as the Pinwheel—indeed, that the entire ring system was a like living, balanced suspension bridge, cantilevered by Mars out into the great abyss of vacuum.

Cley whispered, "Lightning."

"It searches," Seeker said.

She could see magnetic storms rolling in from beyond Mars, blowing against the ring like surf from an immense ocean. "Can it damage the ring?"

"It may destroy all of that great creature, if it thinks you are there."

"The Mad Mind is everywhere!"

"Spreading, always spreading. When we left Earth it had penetrated sunward only momentarily, and at great cost. Now it hunts amid the worlds. It roves and probes and has even learned to muster packs like the skysharks."

"Things are getting worse fast."

"This is as we wish," Seeker said mildly.

"Huh? Why?"

"If it hid among the stars we could ever be sure of its demise."

Cley shook her head. "You think you can kill it?"

"Not I."

"Who can?"

"Everyone, or no one."

•

33

THE
LIVING
CONTINENTS

They arced starward.

The original solar system had been a hostile realm, with all worlds but Earth ranging from the dead to the murderous. Then came the fabled, eon-old reworking. That had left Earth as the nearest child of the sun, Venus next, and then Mars. All were ripe gardens now.

Beyond Mars lay the true center of the great system, the Jove complex. Its gargantuan hub had once been the planet Jupiter. The swollen, simmering superplanet which now sat at the center of Jove glowed with a wan infrared sunshine of its own. It had fattened itself by gobbling up the masses of ancient Uranus and Neptune. The collisions of those worlds had been one of the spectacular events in human history, though it lay so far in the past now that little record remained, even in Diaspar.

After its deep atmosphere had calmed, bulging Jupiter's steady glow had warmed the chilly wastes of its moons. Then Saturn, cycled through many near-miss passes around Jupiter, had been stripped of much of its mass. This gauzy bounty was spread among the ancient moons. A shrunken Saturn of cool blue oceans now orbited Jupiter. After all this prodigious gravitational engineering, the Saturnian rings were replaced, and looked exactly like the originals.

The baked rock of Mercury had arrived then, spun outward from the sun by innumerable kinematic minuets. Light liquids from Saturn pelted the hardpan plains of Mercury for a thousand years, and now the once barren world swung also around Jupiter, brimming with a curious pink and orange air.

All this had come about through adroit gravitational encounters consuming millennia. Carefully tuned, each world now harbored some life, though of very different forms. The Jove system hung at the edge of the sun's life zone, Jupiter adding just enough ruddy glow to make all the salvaged mass of the ancient gas giant planets useful. Beyond Jove wove only the orbits of rubble and ice, and further still, comets under cultivation.

Cley watched with foreboding the approach of the Jove system's grand gavotte. About her the Leviathan regrew itself, but the springlike fervor of its renewal did not lighten her mood. Seeker was of little help; it dozed often and seemed unworried about the coming conflict. To distract herself, she peered from the transparent blisters, trying to fathom the unfolding intricacies outside.

She had to overcome a habit of thought ingrained in all planet-borne life. Space was not mere emptiness, but the mated assets of energy, matter, and room. Planets, in contrast, were inconvenient sites, important mostly because on their busy surfaces life had begun. After all, unruly atmospheres whip up dust, block sunlight, rust metals, hammer with their winds, overheat and chill. Gravity forced even simple landrovers to use much of their bodies just to stand up. Even airless worlds robbed their surfaces of sunlight half the time. And nothing was negotiable: planets gave a fixed day and night, gravity and atmosphere.

In contrast, sunlight flooded the weatherless calm of space. Flimsy sheets could collect high-quality energy undimmed by roiling air. Cups could sip from the light brush of particles spewed out by the sun. Asteroids offered mass without gravity's demanding grip. Just as an origin in tidepools did not mean that shallow water was the best place for later life, planets inevitably became backwaters as well.

Biological diversity demands room for variation, and space had an abundance of sheer volume to offer the first spaceborne organisms. These had sported tough but flexible skins, light and tight, stingy with internal gas and liquids. Evolution used their fresh, weightless geometries to design shrewd alternatives to the simple guts and spines of the Earthborne.

Cley expected to see fewer of the freeroving spaceforms as the Leviathan glided outward. Instead, the abundance and pace of life quickened. Though sunlight fell with the square of distance from the sun, the available volume rose as the cube. Evolution's blind craft had filled this swelling niche with myriad forms. Spindly, full-sailed, baroquely elegant, they swooped around the Leviathan.

Her explorations took her into odd portions of the Leviathan, along shallow lakes and even across a shadowy, bowl-shaped desert. She found a chunky iceball the size of a foothill, covered with harvesting animals. The Leviathan had captured this comet nucleus and was paying out its fluid wealth with miserly care.

She paid a price for her excursions. Humans had not been privileged among species here since well before Diaspar was a dream. Twice she narrowly escaped being a meal for predators which looked very much like animated thornbushes. She found Seeker just where she had left it days before, and the beast tended to her cuts, bites and scratches.

"Why are you helping me, Seeker After Patterns?" she asked as it licked a cut.

It took its time answering, concentrating on pressing its nose along a livid slash made by the sharp-leaved bushes. When it looked up, the cut had sealed so well only a hairline mark remained.

"To strengthen you."

"Well, it's working. Weightlessness has given me muscles I didn't know I had."

"Not your body. Your talent."

She blinked in the pale yellow sunlight that slanted through the bowers. "I was wondering why I keep hearing things. That last thornbush—"

"You caught its hunt-pleasure."

"Good thing, too. It was fast."

"Can you sense any humans now?"

"No, there aren't . . ." She frowned. "Wait, something . . . Why, it's like . . ."

"Supras."

"How'd you know?"

"The time is drawing close."

"Time for what?"

"The struggle."

"You weren't just giving this talent a chance to grow, were you? You're taking me somewhere, too."

"To Jove."

"Sure, but I mean . . . oh, I see. That's where it'll happen."

"Humans have difficulty in understanding that Earth is not important now. The system's center of life is Jove."

"So the Mad Mind has to win there."

"There may be no winning."

"Well, I know what losing will be like." Cley thought of the scorched and mangled bodies of all the people she had ever loved.

"It is because we do not know what losing would be like that we resist."

"Really? Look, it stomped on us as if we were bugs."

"To it, you are."

"And to you?"

"Do not insects have many uses? In my view they are far more seemly in the currents of life than, say, just another species of the Chordata."

"Cor what?"

"Those who have spinal cords."

Irked, Cley said, "Well, aren't you just another spinal type?"

"True enough. I did not say I was more important than you."

"You compared us Ur-humans—*me*, since I'm all that's left—with bugs!"

"With no insects, soon there would be no humans."

Exasperated, Cley puffed noisily, sending her hair up in a dancing plume. "The Supras sure got along without them, living in Diaspar."

"The Supras are not of your species."

"Not human?"

"Not truly." Seeker finished ministering to her wounds and gave her an affectionate lick.

Cley eased her blouse gingerly over her cuts. "I have to admit I pretty much felt that way myself."

"They cannot be true companions to you."

"They're the only thing left."

"Perhaps not, after we are done."

Cley sighed. "I'm just concentrating on avoiding that Mad Mind."

"It will not care so greatly about you after you have served."

"Served? Fought, you mean?"

"Both."

She felt a light trill streak through her mind. At first she confused it with warbling birdsong, but then she recalled the sensation of blinding, swift thought, conversations whipped to a cyclonic pitch. "Supras. They're coming."

She felt their presence now as several tiny skittering notes in the back of her mind, mouse-small and bee-quick. "What'll we do?"

"Nothing."

"They're getting close."

"It is time they did."

Seeker gestured at the intricate whirl of light visible through a high, arching dome above the tangled greenery. Beyond Jupiter's original large moons there now circled rich Mercury and shrunken Saturn. Each was a different hue. But these radiant dabs swam among washes of bright magenta and burnt-gold—single life-forms larger than continents. Seeker had described some of these in far more detail than Cley could follow. They all seemed to be complex variations on the age-old craft of negotiating sunlight and chemicals into beautiful structures. Seeker implied that these were intelligences utterly different from Earthborne kinds, and she struggled with the notion that what appeared to be enormous gardens could harbor minds superior to her own.

Cley lay back and listened to the steadily strengthening Supra talk. She could not distinguish words, but a thin edge of worry and alarm came through clearly.

Languidly she dozed and listened and thought. The smears of light that swung throughout the great orbiting disk of Jove reminded her of sea mats formed at the shorelines of ancient Earth. She had learned of them through tribal legend, much of which dealt with the lean perspectives of life.

Sandwiched between layers of grit and grime, even those earliest life-forms had found a way to make war. Why should matters be different now? Some microbe mat three billion years before had used sunlight to split water, liberating deadly oxygen. They had poisoned their rivals by excreting the gas. The battle had raged across broad beaches bordered by a brown sea. The victorious mats had enjoyed their momentary triumph beneath a pink sky. But this fresh gaseous resource in turn allowed new, more complex life to begin and thrive and eventually drive the algae mats nearly to extinction.

So it had been with space. Planetary life had leaped into the vast new realm, first using simple machines, and later, deliberately engineered life-forms. The machines had proved to be like the first algae, which excreted oxygen to poison their neighbors. Once begun in space, nothing could stop the deft hand of Darwin from fashioning the human designs into subtler instruments. For a billion years life had teemed and fought and learned amid harsh vacuum and sunlight's glare.

In time the space-dwelling machines were driven into narrow enclaves, like the early algae mats. Out here, bordering the realm of ice, machines had finally wedded with plants to make anthology creatures. This desperate compromise had saved them. Cley had seen several of them enter the Leviathan—beings which looked to her like mossy furniture or animated steel buildings.

Sometime long ago, spaceborne life had begun to compete for materials with the planetary life zones. After all, most of the light elements in the solar system lay in the outer planets and in the cometary nuclei far beyond Pluto. In this competition the planets were hopelessly outclassed.

From the perspective of space, Cley thought, planetary life even looked like those ancient algae mats—flat, trapped in a thin wedge of air, unaware of the great stretching spaces beyond. And now the mats survived only in dark enclaves on Earth, cowering before the ravages of oxygen.

Given a billion years, planetborne life had done better than the mats. Slowly the planetary biospheres forged connections to space-borne life through great beasts like the Pinwheel, the Jonah, the Leviathan.

But was this only a momentary pause, a temporary bargain struck before the planets became completely irrelevant?

Or—the thought struck her solidly—were they already?

34

HOMO
TECHNOLOGICUS

The Supras boarded the Leviathan after protracted negotiation. The Captain appeared before Seeker and Cley, buzzing madly, alarmed for some reason Cley could not understand. She had to reassure the Captain three times that she was indeed the primitive human form the Supras sought.

Only then did the Captain let the Supras board and it was some time before Alvin appeared, alone, thrashing his way through the luxuriant greenery. He was tired and disheveled, his usually immaculate one-piece suit stained and dirty.

Then Clay saw that his left arm was missing below the elbow.

"What—how—"

"Some trouble with a minor agency," Alvin said, voice thin and tight.

She rushed to him. Felt the stub of his arm. The flesh at the elbow was deeply bruised and mottled with livid yellow and orange spots.

"A little snarly thing," he said, sitting carefully in a vine netting. "Came at me as we entered this enormous beast."

"An animal?"

"A concoction of the Mad Mind."

"What—"

"I killed it."

"What can I do? Didn't you bleed? What—"

"Let it go," he said, waving her away, mustering more strength in his voice.

"But you're hurt. I—"

"My arm will take care of itself." He grimaced for an instant but then recovered with visible effort.

She moved to help him but he turned, keeping the severed arm away from her. She frowned with concern. "Well, at least take something for the pain."

"I could release . . ." a twinge shook him ". . . my own endorphins if I chose. But it would slow regrowth."

The stump of the arm had already formed a protruding mass of pale cells at its tip. Cley watched Alvin's flesh slowly begin to extrude from his elbow. The arm seemed to build itself layer by layer as it bulged outward. Stubs of bare white bone first inched forth. Then ligaments and tendons accumulated along the bones, fed by swarms of migrating cells like moving, busy lichen. A wave of denser cartilage followed, cementing attachments with fibers that wove themselves as she watched. Then layers of skin fattened in the wake of growth, first a column of pink and then darker shades. Already Alvin's arm was several centimeters longer. Sweat drenched his clothes but he clenched his teeth and said nothing, muscles standing out in his neck.

Cley sat beside him, fetching water when he asked. A long while passed. He ate some red nuts when she offered them but refused any more food. He seemed to summon up the materials and energy for regrowth from his own tissues. His strong legs seemed to deflate slightly, as though flesh was dissolving and migrating to his wounded arm. His entire body turned a ruddy pink, flushed with blood. Muscles jerked and filigrees of color washed over his skin. He moaned occasionally but managed to contain his torment, breathing shallowly.

His hand formed with quick rushes of matted gray cells. They flowed directly from his veins, moving to the working surface and making mats. These gathered into the fine network of muscles that made the human hand such a marvel of evolution's art. She watched as though this were a living anatomy lesson. Bones grew to their fine tips, followed by a wash of cloaking cells. Blue waves of cells settled into place as muscle. Stringy, yellow fat filled in spaces. Fresh skin had begun to wrap the thumb and fingers before Alvin blinked and seemed to be returning to full consciousness. White slabs hardened to make his fingernails, their tips nicely rounded.

"I . . . I never saw such," Cley said.

"Usually we would take more time."

"You must be exhausted. I could *see* your body stealing tissues to build your arm."

"Borrowing."

"My people have some ability like that, but nothing nearly—"

"We must talk."

Seeker appeared nearby. Where had it been all this time? Cley wondered.

Alvin seemed to shake off the torpor which had possessed him. He stretched his arm experimentally and joints popped in his wrist and fingers. For a moment he reminded Cley of a teenager testing his newfound strength. Then he crisply glanced at Seeker and said, "So."

"So what?" Cley countered. She felt at the edges of perception a darting conversation.

Alvin shook his head and said to Seeker, "You promised you would help keep her safe."

Seeker yawned. "I did."

"But you did not have permission to take her away from us. And certainly not to escape into space."

Cley had expected anger from Alvin, not this air of precise displeasure. She was not surprised that Seeker had struck some kind of deal with them back on Earth, though. Seeker enjoyed wriggling through the interstices of language.

Seeker said, "I did not need permission."

"I should think—"

"After all, who could give it?" Seeker asked lazily.

"She is of *our* kind. That gives us rights—"

"You are Homo Technologicus. She is Ur-human, several species removed from you."

Alvin pursed his lips. "Still, we are more nearly related than you."

"Are you so sure?" Seeker grinned owlishly. "I span the genetic heritage of many earlier forms."

"I am quite confident that if I read your helix I could easily find many more differences—"

"Listen, you two," Cley broke in. "*I* wanted to get away from that Library. So I left. Seeker was just along for company."

Alvin looked at her for a long moment and then said calmly, "At least you are safe and have made the journey to where we need you."

"You intended to bring me here yourself?" Cley asked.

"Yes, in a ship."

Cley's temper flared despite her efforts to maintain the easy calm of a Supra. "What? I could have zipped out here in a ship?"

"Well, yes." Alvin seemed surprised at her question.

She whirled to confront Seeker. "You made me go through all this?"

Seeker worked its mouth awkwardly. "I perceived that as the correct course."

"It was damned dangerous. And you didn't even consult me!"

"You did not know enough to judge," Seeker said uncertainly.

"*I*'ll decide that!"

Seeker backed away. "Perhaps I erred."

"*Perhaps?* You—"

"Do not be hasty," Alvin said mildly. "This animal is clever, and in this case it showed foresight. It was lucky for you that I did not convey you outward by our planned route. We thought it intact. Yet several craft carrying needed Ur-human passengers were destroyed after leaving Earth, and you could well have been among them."

"What?" Cley's flare of anger guttered out. "My people?" Cley was so excited she lost her grip on a vine and had to catch herself.

"Not exactly. We grew them from your helix."

"You mean they're—they're *me?*"

"Some, yes. Others we varied slightly, to get the proper mix of abilities."

Cley had feared the Supras would do this. Would such cooked-up

Ur-humans be zombies, shorn of culture, mockeries of her kind? Such disquiets had propelled her to escape.

"I . . . I want to see them."

"You can when all this is over."

"No! I have a right to be with my own kind."

"Are you not content with our company?" Alvin gestured and Cley saw that while she was so intent a group of Supras had quietly infiltrated the bowers around them. Seranis stood nearby, one eyebrow cocked, studying the leafy cascades with evident distaste. Her clothes had been torn and blackened—in the same engagement as Alvin? Already the rips were healing. Smudges dissolved, digested by the glossy fibers.

Cley sighed. "I'm out of my depth with you Supras. You aren't human."

We are more than human, in your manner of speaking, Seranis sent.

"If you have any sense of justice, you'll let me see my people."

Justice will come in time, Seranis sent with a tinge of blithe unconcern.

Cley looked at Seeker but it seemed to be absorbed in picking mites from its pelt. "How long will that be?" she asked.

"Our struggle has already begun," Alvin said. "It is best that you stay with us for the time being."

Cley blinked. "The fight's already going on?"

"In a sense it has been going on for long before your own birth," Alvin said, cooly gentle.

Cley saw the chinks in his armor now, though—a tilt of his solemn mouth, a refractory glint to his eyes. "Where?"

"The final engagement has begun on the outer rim of the solar system. It now converges here, where the strength of the Jovian magnetic fields can shelter us somewhat, and our reserves are greatest."

Cley suddenly felt strongly the skittering, frayed skein of talent-talk that flitted among the Supras from Lys. Time had enlarged her ability, for she could now trace faint threads of flittering ideas, currents and implications that came and went in gossamer instants.

"What can I do in all this? I—"

As if years of preparation had focused on a single point in time, an answer leaped through her mind. Seranis was the channel for this, Cley felt, but she had a sense of an assembly of voices behind the massive intrusion. A wedge of thought drove itself through her. They were telling her much, but it was like trying to take a drink from a firehose.

"I . . . I don't understand . . ."

"It will take a while to unsort itself in your mind, I'm told," Alvin said.

"So much . . . What is the Black Sun?"

"An ancient term. 'Black Hole' is a better one." Alvin carefully chose his words, obviously talking down to her. "Our legends held that the Mad Mind was imprisoned at the edge of the galaxy, when in fact the Black Hole sits at the center."

"Pretty big error."

"A flaw in notation, apparently." His earnest precision reminded her that his first love had been Diaspar's library. "History was correct about the Mind's devastation, though. It knows a way to eat the plasma veils which hang in the galactic arms, leaving great rents where suns should glow. Legend held that the Mind and Vanamonde would meet among the corpses of the stars, but we find now that the collision must occur here, near Earth, where matters started and must finally end."

Cley shook her head, trying to clear it. "I can't possibly amount to much in all this."

"So I would have said as well, once." Alvin had settled on a branch and even in the low spin-gravity the lines in his face sagged. "But you do matter. You Ur-humans had a hand, along with more advanced human forms and alien races, in making both magnetic entities."

"Us? Impossible."

"I admit it seems extremely unlikely. Yet the deep records of Diaspar are clear, if read closely."

"How could we make something like smart lightning?"

"You may come to understand that in the fray that approaches."

"Well, even if we helped make Vanamonde, what's that matter now? I don't know anything about it."

Alvin looked at Seeker, but the big creature seemed unconcerned.

Cley got the feeling that all this was running more or less as Seeker expected, and it was never one to trouble itself with assisting the inevitable.

Alvin spread his hands. "Deep in Vanamonde lies a set of assumptions, of world view. They depend on the kinesthetic senses of Ur-humans, upon your perceptual space."

"What's that?"

"What matters is that we cannot duplicate such things."

"Come on," Cley said bitterly. "I know I'm dumber than anyone here, but that doesn't mean you can—"

We do not delude you. Seranis gazed at Cley somberly. *The makeup of a being circumscribes its perceptions. That cannot be duplicated artificially. We tried, yes—and failed.*

Alvin said, "We find communicating with Vanamonde exceedingly difficult. We have struggled for centuries to no avail."

"Why?" Cley asked. "I thought you people could do anything."

We cannot transcend our world view, any more than you can, Seranis sent.

"That is always true of a single species," Seeker said casually.

Alvin's forehead knitted with annoyance. "And you?"

"There has been some tinkering since your time," Seeker said.

"This *is* our time!" Alvin said sharply.

Seeker leaned back and did not reply.

"Look," Cley said, "how do you talk to Vanamonde?"

"Badly. To reach it we must step through the thicket of the Ur-human mind-set."

"Thicket?" Cley asked.

"A swamp is perhaps a better term. It is ingrained in Vanamonde's being."

"It has some of *us* in it?" Cley felt a spurt of elation. This was at least some mark her kind had left in the great ruined architecture of time.

"In the growing struggle, speed is essential. To link our own abilities with Vanamonde requires connections only you and your kind can make."

Cley's eyes narrowed suspiciously. "The Ur-humans you manufactured?"

"Yes, they will be used. Seranis and the others of Lys have schooled them in the talent, a labor of great difficulty in such a short time."

"You're manufacturing us, *using* us like, like—"

"Of course." Alvin was unbothered. "That is in the nature of the hierarchy of species."

"You have no right!"

"And we have no wrong."

Seeker made a rude noise and twisted its mouth into an unreadable shape. Clay realized that it conveyed human expressions only when it wished to.

"There is no moral issue here," Alvin went on, casting an irritated glance at Seeker. "These matters transcend the concept of rights. Those ideas attach to strategies societies use to maintain order and station. As concepts they have no validity in the transactions across the gulf that separates us." Alvin smiled, as though he knew this was the sort of thing Ur-humans did to take the edge off a stark statement.

Cley said, "That's incredible. We have an obligation to each other, to treat everyone as holding natural rights."

Natural to what? Seranis sent.

Cley answered, *To anything and anybody who can think.*

Think what? These are not times like those in which your kind evolved. Now there are many beings, large and small, who carry self-awareness.

Cley covered her own inner confusion with, *Then they have to be accorded their own dignity.*

Dignity does not mean they can step outside the inherent ordering ordained by evolution's hand. Seranis gave Clay a look of concern, but in her striations of quick thought there was an underlayer of annoyed impatience.

"Look, I have to think about all this," Cley said.

Alvin said, "There is no time for the kind of thinking you do. The moment is upon us."

Cley turned to Seeker. "What should I do?"

Seeker smacked its lips as though hungry. "I do not subscribe to their ideas. Or to yours. Both are too simple."

"Seeker, I need support from you."

"Your actions I can assist, perhaps," it said. "It is true, as the Supras say, that your innate abilities are needed."

"No, I didn't mean help with their fight. I want you to—well, tell them they're wrong, that they're treating my people like, like *animals.*"

"I am an animal. They do not treat me as you."

"You're not an animal!"

"I am not remotely human."

"But you're, you're . . ."

"I am like you when I need to be. But that is to accomplish an end."

"What end?" Cley asked, her confusion deepening.

"To bring you here at this time. To unite you with Ur-humans, as I promised." It glanced at Alvin and Seranis. "I knew the Supras would probably fail to do so."

Across Alvin's face flitted an expression Cley could not read, but the nearest equivalent was a mixture of irritation and surprised respect. Alvin said warily to Seeker, "It would have been simple to bring you here, had the Mad Mind not managed to learn how to enter our ships. And you could not have known it would understand that so quickly, much less that it could find these Ur-humans among all the ships we have."

"I could not?" Seeker grinned.

Cley felt something pass between Seeker and the Supras, a darting note of complex thought. "Seeker! You have the talent."

"Not your talent. But no matter." Seeker turned to Cley. "I believe this issue must be resolved now, so I shall do it."

Alvin said sternly, "I cannot allow so crucial a matter to—"

"Do as they say," Seeker said to Cley.

"But I—"

"If you wish to think in terms of the structure of rights, then consider a point." Seeker brought a nut toward its mouth but fumbled and dropped it. "The others of your kind—and I do not believe they are your 'people,' for they are not yet people at all—will certainly die if you do not."

Alvin scowled. "You can't be sure of that."

Seeker did not immediately answer. Instead it pulled the carcass of a small rodent from a snag in its pelt and began to casually gnaw on it. The Supras all looked askance at this. Cley remembered how delicate and rarefied their own food had been, like eating clouds.

Seeker licked the carcass sensuously and said, "You remember the era of simple laws?"

Alvin frowned. "What? Oh, you mean the age when science discovered all the laws governing the relations between particles and fields? That time is of no relevance now."

Seeker closed one eye and let one side of its face go slack, as if it could slip halfway into sleep. Cley wondered if this was some arcane joke.

Seeker said, "The Ur-humans found all such laws. But to know how gravity pulls upon a body does not mean even in principle that you can foresee how many such bodies will move. The prediction of any real system is beyond the final, exact reach of science."

Alvin nodded, but Cley could tell that he did not see where this subject led. Neither did she. And time was running out, she thought with irritation, while these two argued over grand principles.

"True," Alvin said, "but that is ancient philosophy. Quantum uncertainty, chaos—these forever screen precise knowledge of the future from our eyes."

Still with one eye closed, Seeker said "And what if this were not so?"

"Then we Supras would have discovered that long ago," Alvin insisted. "Such knowledge would reside in the lore of Diaspar."

Seeker blinked with both eyes and animation returned fully to its face. At the same moment Cley felt a burst of talent-talk like unrecognizable bass notes. Some Supras stirred uneasily. She realized that Seeker had complied—it had sent some sort of message while carrying on this lofty discussion.

Seeker said, "Much has been discovered since strata of learning were laid down in Diaspar."

A note of doubt entered Alvin's voice. "The humans who came after our kind, those who left—they found such ability?"

Seeker said, "No. That is not open to your order of being."

"Beast, are there higher orders which know science?" Alvin looked around at his fellow Supras, who seemed distantly amused by this conversation.

Seeker said, "None you can readily see standing before you."

"Magnetic minds, then? Even they merely use science," Alvin said. "They do not truly comprehend it."

"There are other methods of comprehension which come out of the sum of species."

Alvin's head jerked with surprise. "But we are discussing the fundamental limits on knowledge!"

"This 'knowledge' of yours is also a category," Seeker said, "much like 'rights.' It does not translate between species."

"I cannot understand how that can be," Alvin said primly.

"Exactly," Seeker said.

35

THE
PRISON OF
TIME

The strange conversation between Seeker and the Supras wound on as Cley tried to think.

In the end she saw that she had no choice. She had to take part in whatever was to come, no matter how little the gargantuan events had to do with her own fortunes. Her folk had begun to fade already in her memory, crowded out by the jarring, swift events since they had been burned into oblivion by the Mad Mind. She felt now the totality of what that vicious act had meant. To murder not merely people but *a* people, a species. Was she becoming more like the Supras now, that such an abstraction could touch her, arouse what Alvin would no doubt term her "animal spirits"?

Still, she could not readily feel that the Supras and their cosmic games mattered to what she still thought of as "real" people, her own. She sensed that this attitude itself was perhaps a symptom of her kind—but if so, then so be it, she thought adamantly.

The Supras seemed pleased with her decision. Seeker gave no sign of reaction. After all her agonizing, she was surprised that nothing happened immediately. They swooped in toward the disk of life and worlds that was the Jove complex. Trains of space biota came and went from the Leviathan, carrying out intricate exchanges.

In the moments when Alvin and Seranis were not occupied with tasks, she learned more from them. She recalled when Seranis had let go her constraints, flooding Cley's mind with unsorted impressions and thoughts. Cley then slept long hours, fitfully, sweating, letting her brain do much of the unscrambling. She had learned not to resist. Each time she awoke, surprises awaited, fresh ideas brimming within her.

She spent some time watching the scintillant majesty of Jove, but she now understood that this was not the outer limit to the living solar system. She had been misled by her own eyes.

Earthborne life saw through a narrow slit of the spectrum. Time had pruned planetary life to take advantage of the flux that most ably penetrated the atmosphere, preferring the ample flux of green light. No Earthbound life ever used the lazy, meter-long wavelengths of the radio.

So they could not witness the roll of great plasma clouds which fill the great spiral arms. Seen with a large radio eye, the abyss between suns shows knots and puckerings, swirls and crevasses. The wind that blows outward from suns stirs these outer fogs. Only an eye larger than Leviathan itself could perceive the incandescent richness that hides in those reaches. The beings which swam there gave forth great booming calls and live through the adroit weaving of electrical currents.

Cley realized this after a long sleep, the knowledge coming to her almost casually, like an old memory. She would never see these knots of ionized matter trapped by magnetic pinches, smoldering and hissing with soft energies beyond the seeing of anything born in flesh.

Yet she recalled, through Seranis, the vast flaring of plasma veins, the electromagnetic arteries and organs. Light required a week to span these beings. Bodies so vast must be run by delegation, so the intelligences which had evolved to govern such bulk resembled parliaments more than dictatorships.

She caught a glimmer of how such beings regarded her kind: tiny assemblies powered by the clumsy building up and tearing down of molecules. How much cleaner was the clear rush of electromotive forces!

But then her perceptions dwindled back to her own level, the borrowed memories faded, and she understood.

"Seeker!" she called. "The Mad Mind—humans didn't make it from scratch, did they?"

"Not wholly, no." Seeker had been quiet for a long time, its long face mysteriously calm.

"I caught pictures from Seranis, pictures of magnetic things that seem to live naturally."

Seeker smiled wolfishly. "They are our allies."

Alvin spoke from behind her. "And ones we desperately need."

Cley demanded, "Why didn't you tell me?"

"Because I did not know, not fully. The knowledge . . ." Alvin's normally strong voice faltered. He looked more tired and pensive than before. "No, it was not knowledge. I discounted Vanamonde's testimony when it told us of these magnetic beings. Our Keeper of Records said there were none such. After all, there were no references throughout all of the Records." He smiled wanly. "Now we are wiser. It was smug legend that I knew, the arrogance of Diaspar as vast as its truths."

Cley said slowly, "Humans somehow trapped one of those magnetic creatures?"

Alvin settled onto a sloping, crusty branch, his shoulders sagging. "Humans have a reach which exceeds our grasp."

"The Mad Mind got away?"

He nodded. "And somehow, from its associations with humans, learned to perform feats which no other magnetic being knew. It ravaged enormous territories, slaughtered magnetic structures."

"Until someone trapped it again. This Galactic civilization I keep hearing about?" This talk was unsettling. She started a small fire to cook supper.

"Galactic civilization was once majestic," Alvin said. "It made the pure mentalities like Vanamonde, building on the magnetic beings." Alvin seemed heartened now. "Seeker, what do you think of galactic civilization?"

"I think it would be a good idea," Seeker answered very softly.

"But it exists!"

"Does it? You keep looking at the parts—this or that species or phylum, fleshy or magnetic. Consider the whole."

"The whole what? The Empire left our known universe, leaving—"

"Leaving rooms for newer forms to grow. Very polite, I would say. It was certainly no tragedy."

Alvin frowned. "For humans it was. We—"

Cley stopped listening, taking shelter in the familiar rituals of cooking. Something in the human mind liked the reassuring order of repetition, she supposed. Alvin kept talking, explaining facets of sciences she could not even identify, but she let him run on. The man was troubled, hanging on to his own image of what human action meant. It was better to let his spill of words carry away frustration, the most ancient of human consolations. She cooked three large snakes, blackened with a crust of spices, and offered him one.

To his credit he did not even show hesitation. "A curious custom," he remarked, after biting into a muscular yellow chunk. Its savor seasoned the air. "That such a simple procedure brings out the raw power of the meat."

"You've never cooked before?"

"Our machines do that."

"How can machines know what tastes good?"

Alvin explained, "They have something better: good taste."

"Ha!"

Alvin looked offended. "Diaspar has programs handed down from the greatest chefs."

"I'd rather stir the coals and turn the meat myself."

"You do not trust machines?"

"Only so far as I have to."

"But it was an Ur-human subspecies that set us on the road of technology."

She spat out a piece of gristle. "Has its limits, though. Think it's done you a lot of good?"

Alvin looked blank. "It kept us alive."

"It kept you in a bottle, like a museum exhibit. Only nobody came to see."

Alvin frowned. "And I broke out."

Cley liked the way the flickering firelight cooked flavors and heat into the air, clasping them all in a perfumed veil. Something deeply human responded to this woodsmoke redolence. It touched Alvin, smoothed his face. Seeker sucked in the smoky bouquet, licking the air.

"Did you ever wonder why nobody ever came to visit the museum?"

Alvin looked startled. "Why, no."

"Maybe they were too busy getting things done," she said.

"Out here?"

She could see that no matter how intelligent these Supras were, they also had values and associations that were virtually hard-wired into them. "Sure. Look at that—" She gestured at the translucent bowl above, where Jove spun like a colossal living firework. "—And tell me dried-up old Earth was a better idea."

Alvin said nothing for a long time. Then, "I see. I had thought that human destiny turned upon the pivot of Diaspar."

"It did," Seeker said. Alvin twitched as though something had prodded him; Cley suspected he had forgotten that Seeker was there. "But that is only a partial story."

Alvin looked penetratingly at Seeker. "I have long suspected that you represent something . . . unknown. I extensively interrogated the archives of Diaspar about your species. You evolved during a time when humans were relatively unambitious."

Seeker said softly, "They had done great damage to themselves. Remorse tinged them. But only for a while."

Alvin nodded. "Still, our records did not show such a high intelligence as you display."

"You still think of traits lodged in individuals, in species," Seeker said.

"Well, of course. That defines species, nearly."

Seeker asked, "And if a trait is shared among many species simultaneously?"

Alvin shook his head. "By telepathy, like that of Lys?"

"Or more advanced."

"Well, that might alter the character of intelligence, granted."

Alvin's face took on his librarian's precise, pensive cast, his cheeks hollowing as though he contracted into himself. "I wonder if such talents could arise naturally."

"They do," Seeker said. "I am a member of a larger system. So are you, but you do not communicate well—a typical characteristic of early evolved intelligences."

Alvin's mouth turned up in an irked curve. "People seem to feel I speak fairly clearly."

"People do, yes."

Alvin smiled stiffly. "We re-created you ourselves, made you whole from the Library of Life. Sometimes I think we erred somehow."

"Oh no!" Seeker barked happily. "It was your best idea."

"The records say you were solely suited for Earth."

"Wrong," Seeker said.

"That would explain why you move so easily in space."

"Not entirely." Seeker's eyes danced merrily.

"You have other connections?"

"With everything. Don't you?"

Alvin shrugged uncomfortably. "I don't think so."

"Then do not think so much."

Cley laughed, but at the back of her mind a growing tenor cry demanded attention. "Something's . . ."

Seeker nodded. "Yes."

She felt the Supras of Lys now, Seranis just one among many cascading voices. They formed tight links, some in their ships, some in this Leviathan, others dispersed among Jonahs and Leviathans and the churning life-mats of the Jove system.

"How quickly does it approach?" Alvin asked urgently. The earlier mood was broken, his doubts momentarily dispelled. Now he was cool efficiency.

"I can't tell." Cley frowned. "There are refractions. . . . Is it possible that the Mad Mind can move even faster than light?"

"That is but one of its achievements," Alvin said, concern creasing his forehead. "We humans attained that long ago, but only for small volumes, ships. The Mad Mind was limited, as are the magnetic beings. This great fact ordains that the linking of the natural magnetic minds proceeds slowly across the galaxy. Nothing so large can move faster than light. Or so we thought."

"That's how the Mind finally got out of the Black Sun, isn't it?" Cley asked. She caught thin shouts of alarm in her mind.

"It used the quantum vacuum," Alvin said. His cheeks hollowed again with a cast of relief. The chance to be secure in his knowledge, Cley guessed.

Alvin leaned forward, his eyes soft as he peered into the dying firelight. "On average, empty space has zero energy. But by enclosing a volume with a sphere of conducting plasma, the Mad Mind prevented the creation of waves with wavelengths larger than that volume. These missing waves gave the vacuum a net negative energy, and allowed formation of a wormhole in space-time. All such processes are ruled by probabilities requiring great calculation. Yet through that hole the Mad Mind slithered."

"To our solar system," Cley concluded.

"Never before has a magnetic mind done this," Alvin said. "It escaped from the prison of time—a feat on such a scale that even the Empire did not anticipate."

Seeker whispered, "Coincidence, Alvin?" This was the first time Cley had ever heard Seeker use the name. There was a tinge of pity in the beast's voice, or what she took for that.

Alvin's head jerked up. He flicked a suspicious glance at Seeker. "The thought occurred to us, too. Why should the Mad Mind emerge now?"

"Just as you're getting free of Earth again?" Cley asked.

"Exactly," Alvin said. "So we studied all the physical evidence. Observed the path of damage the Mad Mind has wrecked as it left the galactic center." He hesitated. "And made a guess."

Seeker said, "It was you."

Alvin's eyes shifted away from the waning fire, as though he sought refuge in the gloom surrounding them. "Perhaps so. I found Vanamonde. The exuberance of Vanamonde was so great at being discovered! That sent magnetosonic twists through the whorls of an entire galactic arm. These reached the Mad Mind in its cage. To see ancient foes reuniting again sent it into a rage, a malevolence so strong that it exerted itself supremely. And forced its exit."

They sat silently for a long moment. The inky recesses of the Leviathan were unrelieved by the distant promise of stars.

Cley said finally, "You didn't know. All the lore of Diaspar did not warn you."

He smiled mirthlessly. "But I did it. All the same."

Cley said, "That Empire might have troubled their mighty selves to make a jail that held."

Alvin shook his head. "There is none better in this space-time."

"Well, damn it, at least they shouldn't have just left it as a problem to be solved by *us.*"

Seeker lifted its snout, seeming to listen to something far away. Then it said, "*Shoulds* and *mights* are of no consequence. The problem has arrived."

THE
HERESY OF
HUMANISM

In the end it was like nothing she had expected or feared.

She lay in a comfortable vine mat in the Leviathan, alone, eyes closed. She felt nothing of it, or of her body.

The struggle raged red through landscapes of her mind.

The link with the Supras smoothed the harsh, glancing edges. Still, the cauldron of sensations was only a fragment of the broadening perspectives which opened for her in the hours and then days of the conflict.

She had anticipated great flares of phosphorescent energy, climactic storms of magnetic violence. There were some, but these were merely sideshow illuminations dancing around the major conflict like heat lightning on a far horizon.

For Cley the struggle called upon her kinesthetic senses—overloaded and strained and fractured, splitting her into shards of disembodied perception. This was all she was capable of grasping.

Yet each splinter was intensely vibrant, encompassing.

She felt herself running, once. The pleasant heady rush of sliding muscles, of speed-shot perspectives dwindling, of slick velocities—and then she was in cold inky oblivion, her sun blocked by moving mountains. These moist shadows coiled with acrid odors. Harsh, abrasive air thrust up her nostrils.

The ground—like a plain of lead-gray ball bearings—slid by below her invisible feet, tossing like a storm-streaked, grainy sea. Sweet tastes swarmed up her sinuses, burst wetly green—and she tumbled into another bath of rushing impressions. Of receding depths. And then of oily forces working across her skin. It went on and on, a riverrun she could not stanch or fathom.

But at times she did sense pale immensities working at great distances, like icebergs emerging from a hurricane-racked ocean.

Dimly she caught shreds of a childlike mind, incomparably large, and recognized Vanamonde. It had prowled the solar system, she saw, blunting the attacks of the Mad Mind. She owed it her life, for surely the Mind would otherwise have found her on her outward voyage.

Beneath the ragged waves that washed her she felt infinitesimal currents, tiny piping voices. She recognized these as the recently grown Ur-humans, unformed personalities speckled by dots of kinesthetic tension.

They were all like elemental units in an enormous circuit, serving as components which relayed messages and forces they could no more recognize than a copper wire knows what an electron is.

And Seeker was there. Not the Seeker she knew, but something strange and many-footed, immense, running with timeless grace over the seamless gray plain.

Or was it many Seekers?—the entire species, a kind which had come long after the Ur-humans and yet was equally ancient now, a race which had strived and lost and strived again, endured and gone on silently, peering forward with a hollow barking laugh, still powerful and always asking as life must, and still dangerous and still coming.

And something more.

Seeker. It was engaged somehow at levels she could only glimpse. Seeker struggled in what seemed to Cley to be a crystal sphere— luminous, living. Yet the mote glaring at the sphere's center was a star.

She felt the plasma beings then. Nets of fields and ionized gas slipped fishlike through blackness. They converged on the Jove system. Great slow-twisting blue lightning worked through the orbiting rafts of life there. The mere backwash of this passing struggle scorched broad carpets of spacelife. Lances ruptured beings the size of whole worlds.

The biting pain of it made Cley twist and scream. Her eyes opened once to find her fingernails embedded in her palms, crimson blood streaking her arms. But she could not stop.

Her eyes squeezed shut against her will. A swelling seized her. She felt herself extended, warping the space around her as though she were herself a giant sun, bending rays of light.

She knew this meant she had somehow been incorporated into Vanamonde. But instantly another presence lapped at her mind. She felt herself tucked up into a cranny, snug—then yanked out, spilling into hot, inky murk.

The Mad Mind had her. It squeezed, as though she were moist fruit and would spit out seeds.

—an orange, crusty with age, browned and pitted, covered by white maggots sucking at the inner wealth.—

She saw this suddenly. Her mouth watered. She had to cleanse the slimy maggots before she could eat. She sent down fire and washed the orange in burnt-gold flame. Screaming, the maggots burst open.

—and the orange was a planet.—

Seared and pure and wiped free of the very atmosphere which had sustained the soft maggots.

—and the maggots, singed to oblivion—

They had been four-footed, scaly, quick of mind. But not quick enough. They had barely comprehended what rushed at them out of the maw at the center of the galaxy.

Cley was the orange and then the fire and then the maggots and then, with long strangled gasps, the fire again.

It was good to be the fire. Good to leap and fry and crackle and leap again.

Better by far than to crawl and mew and suck and shit and die.

Better, yes, to float and stream and tingle with blue-white fires. To hang in curtains between the stars and be greater than any sun that had ever flared. To roar at the jeweled stars.

Better to *know* and shimmer and reek. To rasp against the puny clots of knotted magnetic fields, butt into their slow waltzes. To jab and hurt and keep on hurting when the magnetic kernels had ground beneath you, broken, were dust.

Better to be a moving appetite again, an intelligence bigger than solar systems. Pleasure seethed in its self-stink, more raw and muscular with every gathering moment.

—and she broke away from it for a moment, into what seemed to be cool open space, empty of the skittering violence.—

Ah! she thought with buoyant relief.

But it was merely another part of the Mad Mind. Oily and slick and snakelike, it slid itself over her. Into her ears. Up her vagina. Deep, deep probing for her ovaries. Down her throat, prodding with a fluid insistence.

A stench rose and bit into her. Its sharp beak cut and that was when she understood a flicker of what the outside struggle was about.

She suddenly knew that she now could *feel* abstractions. The partition between thought and sensation, so fundamental to being human, was blown to tatters by the Mind's mad gale.

Trapped, she understood.

The Mad Mind held that this universe was one of many expanding bubbles adrift inside a meta-universe. Ours was but one of the possibilities in a cosmos beyond counting.

The great adventure of advanced life-forms, it believed, was to transcend the mere bubble which we saw as our universe. Perhaps there were civilizations of unimaginable essence, around the very curve of the cosmos. The Mad Mind wished to create a tunnel which would prick a hole in our universe-bubble and extend into others.

Slimy blackness crept like fingers. Easeful ideas soothed into her.

The Galactic Empire, she saw, had been a festering pile of insects. When she stopped to see them better they were of all shapes, chittering, filled with meaningless jabber.

Long ago some of these vermin had slipped away, she remembered, through the veils beyond the galaxy. Out, flying through strings of galaxies, across traceries of light. Spanning the great vaults and voids where few luminous sparks stirred.

Those Empire maggots had vanished, leaving dregs to slump into petrified cities: Diaspar. Lys.

And elsewhere in the spiral arms, other races had dwindled into self-obsessed stasis.

But should the holy, enduring fire follow the Empire across the curve of this universe? Should the Mind pursue?

She knew instantly that such goals were paltry. The stuff of maggot-minds.

No—far grander to escape the binds of this universe entirely. Not merely voyage in it. Not simply skim around the sloping warp.

Cley struggled but could find no way through the cloying hot ink that oozed into her throat, her bowels.

She faintly felt that these turgid sensations were in fact ideas. She could not comprehend them as cool abstractions. They reeked and banged, cut and seared, rubbed and poked at her.

And on this stage ideas moved as monstrous actors, capable of anything.

She understood now—as quickly as she could frame the question—what the Madness cloaking her wanted. It desired to create deep wells in space-time. Compression of matter to achieve this in turn required the cooperation of many magnetic minds—for in the end, only intelligence coolly divorced from matter could truly control it.

The risk of such a venture was the destruction of the entire galaxy. Fresh matter had to be created and compacted. This could curve space-time enough to trap the galaxy into a self-contracting sphere, cut off from the universe even as it bled downward into a yawning gravitational pit.

The galaxy could not accept such danger. The magnetic minds had debated the wisdom of such a venture while the Mad Mind was confined. Their discussion had been dispassionate, for they were not threatened. Magnetic intelligences could follow the Mad Mind beyond such geometric oblivion, since they were not tied to the fate of mere matter.

But the galaxy brimmed with lesser life. And in the last billion years, as humanity slept in Diaspar, life had integrated.

Near most stars teemed countless entities, bound to planets or orbiting them. Further out, between the suns, the magnetic structures looked down on this with a slow, brooding spirit. Their inability to transcend the speed of light except in tiny spots meant that these most vast of all intelligences spoke slowly across the chasms of the galactic arms.

Yet slowly, slowly, through these links a true Galactic Mind had arisen. It had been driven to more complex levels of perception by the sure knowledge that eventually the Mad Mind would escape.

So the magnetic beasts could not abandon the matter-born to extinction. They had ruled against the Mad Mind's experiment before, and now they moved to crush the newrisen Mind before it could carry out the compression of mass.

Cley saw this in a passing instant of struggle, while she swam in a milky satin fog—and then immeasurably later, through sheets the colors of blood and brass. She was like a blind ship adrift, with only the gyroscope of her senses of any use.

The pain began then.

It soared through her. If she had once thought of herself and the other Ur-humans as elements in an electrical circuit, now she understood what this could mean.

The agony was timeless. Her jaws strained open, tongue stuck straight out, pink and burning. Her eyes bulged, though still squeezed shut by a giant hand which pinched her nose. She was terrified and then went beyond that to a longing, a need for extinction simply to escape the terror. Her agony was featureless. No tick of time consoled her. Her previous life, memories, pleasures—all dwindled into nothing beside the giant flinty mountain of her pain.

She longed to scream. *Alvin!* Muscles refused to unlock in her throat, her face. Timeless excruciation made her into a statue.

And then without transition she was standing, water cascading all over her, her hair bunched atop her head, her shoulders and breasts white with soapy smears. Her prickly flesh shimmered and melted and her nipples were fat spigots. They snagged bubbles and dripped rich drops. The air eagerly lapped these teardrops as they fell. Her eyes were closed but she could see a pulse flutter in her throat, satin moistness slither over her pendulous breasts.

She knew that this, too, was part of the Mind. Or a last brushing kiss from it. For it was genuinely mad, and contained within it a skein that humans would see as love, or hate, or malignant resolve. But these were categories evolved for a species. They no more described another class of being than violins and drums describe a storm.

Some of its madness was human. Lodged in magnetic helices lay the mentality of Man. Several races had made the Mind and each left a signature.

The Mind's ambition, to escape the bands of space-time itself, was born of humanity. And lacing through the pain were streaks of ancient guilt.

Alvin had known this, she saw. That was some of the weight he carried.

The Mind had come from a substrate of magnetic beings, too. She felt them now, ponderous and eerie.

They brimmed throughout the solar system. Their intelligences were neither higher nor lower than humans', for they were not born from evolutionary forces which had driven humanity to solve problems. They had survived by altering their perceptions. How this happened Cley could not fathom.

But for a sliding instant she caught a glimpse of humanity, from their view.

A great eagle hung in black space, near a sulfurous planet, its wings flapping long and lazy. Diamond-sharp eyes glinted. The beak hung slightly open, as though about to call out a booming song. She watched the flex of the immense feathers for a while as muscles bulged beneath the wings. Only then did she see that the bird flew between the planet behind it and toward a sun in the distance, a star red and hairy with immense chromatic flares.

And across the span of the immense wings nestled small, fevered mites. At one wingtip rose pyramids. Mountains capped in white framed broad plains, which in turn lead to silvery, spiky cities. Across the wingspan lay ages of greatness and long nights of despair. But always the ferment, the jutting towers of boundless ambition, the dusty ruins brought by wear and failure. At the far wingtip a fogged land lay, just beyond her ability to make out detail.

Humanity. All who had ever carried the gleam kindled behind the searching eyes—they were there.

Gathered in time's long tapestry, aback the eagle. They milled and fought and saw only their limited moment. They did not know that they flew between unreadable spheres, in the perfumed air of vast night.

As the bird flapped past her, it turned. The glinting black eyes looked at her once, the beak opened slightly. Then it turned away and flew on. Intent. Resolute.

There came a moment like an immense word on the verge of being spoken.

And then it was over.

She sat up. The vines holding her were like rasping hot breaths. She vomited violently. Coughed. Gasped.

Brown blood had caked thick and crusty at her wrists. Her fingernails had snapped off. The tips were buried in her palms. Numbly Cley licked them clean.

"Have a rat," Seeker said. It held up a green morsel on a forked stick.

Alvin!

She shook her head and was sick again.

"It's done," Seeker said.

"I . . . Who won?"

"We did."

"What . . . what . . ."

"Losses?" Seeker paused as though listening to a pleasant distant song. "Billions of lives. Billions of loves, which is another way to count."

She closed her eyes and felt a strange dry echo of Seeker's voice. This was Seeker's talent. Through it she witnessed the gray, blasted wastes that stretched throughout the solar system. Bodies crushed and scorched. Leviathans boiling away their guts into vacuum. Moons melted to slag.

"The Mad Mind?"

"Eaten by us," Seeker said.

"Us?"

"Life. The Galactic Mind."

She still caught frayed strands of Seeker's ebbing vision. "You see it all, don't you?"

"Only within the solar system. The speed of light constrains."

"All life? On all the worlds?"

"And between them."

"How can you do that?"

Seeker pricked up its outsized ears. Waves of amber and yellow chased each other around its pelt. "Like this."

"Well, what's *that?*"

"This."

In a glimmering she saw fragile, lonely Earth, now the most blighted of all the worlds. But it had been diminished by humans, she saw; the Mad Mind had not injured it. Sentinel Earth had played its role and now could return to obscurity. Or greatness.

"What will happen to it?" Cley asked quietly. Her body ached but she put that fact aside.

"Earth? I imagine the Supras will dream on there." Seeker nipped at the rat with obvious relish.

"Just dream?"

Seeker shook one paw, which it had just burned on the cooking stick. It whimpered at the pain. Cley saw by the hollow look to Seeker's eyes that it had suffered much since she last saw it, but the animal gave no hint in its speech. "Human dreams can be powerful, as we have just witnessed," it said.

For a long moment Cley then saw, through Seeker's strangely boundless talent, the Earth shrink into insignificance. It became a speck inside a great sphere—the same glowing ball she had seen in the struggle.

"What is it?"

"An oasis."

"The whole solar system?"

"An oasis biome, one of billions strewn through the galaxy. Between them live only the magnetic minds. And passing small travelers bound upon their journeys, of course."

"This is your 'higher cause,' isn't it? When Alvin asked if you would help defend human destiny?"

Seeker farted loudly. "He was guilty of the heresy of humanism."

"How can that be heresy?"

"The narcissistic devotion to things human? 'Man is the measure of all things?' Easily."

"Well, he has to speak for his species."

"His genus, you mean, if you would include yourself."

Cley frowned. "I don't know how close to them I am. Or what use they'll have for me now."

"You share the samenesses of your order, which are perhaps the most important."

"Order?"

"The order of primates. A useful intermediate step. You possess the general property of seeing events in close focus. Your ears hear sounds proportional to the logarithm of the intensity. Otherwise you could not hear a bee hum and still tolerate a handclap next to your ear. Or see both by moonlight and at high noon; your eyesight is the same."

"Those are all damn useful," Cley said defensively. She could not see Seeker's point.

"True, but you also consider time the same way. Your logarithmic perception stresses the present, diminishing the past or the future. What happened at breakfast clamors for attention alongside the origin of the universe."

Cley shrugged. "Hell, we have to survive."

"Yes, and hell is what you would bear if you had continued with your heresy."

She shot Seeker an inquiring look. These were grave words, but Seeker rolled lazily and swung from two vines, using them to cavort in midair with flips and turns and airy leaps. Between its huffs and puffs it said, "You would have prevented our oasis biome from integrating, with your grandiose plans."

Cley felt a spurt of irritation. Who was *this* animal, to deride humanity's billion-year history? "Look, I might not like Alvin and the rest all that much, but—"

"Your trouble is that contrary to the logarithmic time sense, evolution proceeds exponentially. And the argument of the exponent is the complexity of life-forms."

"And what's *that* mean?" Cley asked, determined to sail through this airy talk on a practical tack.

"One-celled organisms took a billion years to learn the trick of marrying into two or more. From dinosaurs to Ur-humans took only a hundred million. And then intelligent machines—admittedly, a short-lived experiment—required only a thousand." Seeker did a flip and caught itself on a limb, its tongue lolling.

"You don't seem all that advanced beyond us," Cley said.

"How would you tell? If my kind had evolved into clouds, I couldn't have the fun of this, could I?" Seeker gulped down the rest of the rat.

"Or the fun of dragging me all the way across the solar system?"

"There is duty, too."

"To what?"

"To the system solar. The biome."

"I—" she began, but then a piercing cry burst through her mind.

It was Seranis. Her talent-wail broke like a wave of hopeless grief, discordance boiling with shards of sound.

Cley scrambled away, driven by the mournful, grating power. She nearly collided with a man in the foliage. He gazed blankly at her. Something in his expressionless face reminded her suddenly of her father.

"Who're you?" she asked.

"I have . . . no name."

"Well, what—" and then she fully sensed him. Ur-human, a tiny speck of talent-talk purring in him.

You were one of those links I felt, she sent.

Yes. Those of us here . . . have gathered. We are afraid. His feelings were curiously flat and without fervor.

You're like a child.

I am like us. The talent-voice carried no rancor and his face was smooth and unmarked, though that of a full-grown man.

She looked beyond him and saw a dozen like him, men and women of the same height and body-type. *You're me!*

In a way, he sent mildly.

From the Ur-humans came a tide of bland assent. They were untouched by time and trouble.

The struggle, how was it? she asked.

A woman sent, *Such fun! We had never done anything like that.*

"Well, you won't again," Cley said aloud. She preferred the concrete feel of speech to the sensation of dropping stones down a deep well. "But look, what—"

Then she saw the body. The Ur-humans carried it between them in the light gravity. "Alvin!"

Seranis followed the corpse, her face stony, body stiff, emitting no talent-trace at all now.

Cley asked the man, "What happened?"

"He . . . gave . . . too much." The man-child's throat sounded raw and unused, as though he had seldom spoken before.

Cley gazed into Alvin's open eyes. A blue pattern of burst veins gave them the look of small, trapped seas.

Seranis came last, following the smooth, bland Ur-humans. She said and sent nothing.

Cley looked at Alvin's troubled, fractured eyes and tried to imagine what he had finally faced. She knew suddenly that he had somehow freed her from the Mad Mind's grip. And his cost had been to have his own mind burned away, the brain itself fused.

He had dignity in death and she felt a pang of loss. He had been strange but majestic, in his way. Seeker was wrong; the Supras were still essentially human, though she would never be able to define just what that meant.

In a moment only a heartbeat long she sensed something beyond the kinesthetic effects she had ridden, beyond the explanations she had glimpsed. The coiling complications of ambition, the crazed scheme to tunnel out of their own space-time. . . .

That was part of it, yes.

But she remembered the algae mats of earth's first oceans, billions of years ago. They lived on in the guts of animals, bacteria hiding in dark places where chemistry still kindled without oxygen. She recalled that her own tribe had used them as yeasty agents in the brewing of beer. If such bacteria could think, what would it make of the frothy spume of beer? As catalysts they were certainly taking part in processes transcending themselves, yielding benefits they could not imagine. If they could somehow know, they might well feel immeasurably exalted.

But to those who brewed beer's casual delights, the bacteria were unimaginably far beneath the realm of importance, mere dregs of evolution. And whatever dim perceptions the algae could muster would hardly resemble the true nature of the talk and laughter and argument which swirled through the minds that felt the pleasant effects of that beer.

Her own understandings of what the past struggle had been about—could they be similar? Valid, perhaps, but dwarfed by the unknowable abyss that separated her species from the purposes of entities enormously removed.

Could that bear somehow on what Seeker meant about logarithmic time and exponential growth? That she could not even imagine such a gulf?

The thought caught her for only a single dizzying instant. Then it was gone and she was back in the comfortable, linear progression of events she knew.

She turned away from the body. The Ur-humans milled uncertainly around her. "Seeker, I . . . these people. My people."

"So they are," Seeker said noncommittally at her side.

"Can I have them? I mean, take them back?" She gestured up at the transparent dome where the tired but receptive Earth still spun.

"Of course. The Supras could not help them."

"I'll try to bring up just a few of them at first," Cley said cautiously. The enormity of becoming mother to a race struck her. "See how it goes."

"No one tests the depth of a river with both feet," Seeker said.

Seranis had gone on, solemn and silent, not looking back. Cley wondered if she would ever see the Supras again.

The Ur-humans all studied Cley. "Do you think there'll be a place for them?"

"If you make one."

"And you?"

"This is my place." It fanned a greasy claw at the quiet immensities above.

"The—what did you call it?—system solar?"

Seeker's ears flexed and changed from cinnamon to burnt yellow. "She gave birth to humankind and is a third as old as the universe itself. She is the source of life everlasting."

"And you—you're her agent, aren't you?"

Seeker nodded and laughed. Or at least Cley thought it did. She was never really sure of these things, and perhaps that was for the best.

"I suppose it's reassuring, being part of something so large."

Seeker said, "Indeed. Alvin knew of her. But he described her as endless chains of regulatory messages between the worlds, of intricate feedback, and so missed the point."

"What point?"

"Alvin saw only metabolism. He missed purpose." Seeker produced another rat and began to eat.

"Was it 'her'—your system solar—that really destroyed the Mad Mind?"

"Of course."

"What about the Supras?"

"They did as they must. We helped sculpt their uses."

"Which is it?—'she' did it or 'we' did it?"

"Both."

Cley sighed. "Well, did we humans matter at all?"

"Of course. Though not as you imagine."

"You helped me because of your biome, didn't you?"

Seeker seemed to catch the disappointment in her voice. "Truly. But I came to love you. You are an element I had not comprehended."

To cover her emotions (a very human mannerism, she thought wryly) Cley said lightly, "Just doing my part in the system solar."

Seeker said with a grave scowl, "As you did."

"Hey, c'mon, I did have other motives."

"They were incidental." Seeker lunged at a passing bird, missed, and tumbled into a tangle of vines. Cley laughed. Was this the

super-being she had seen roving among the planets during the battle? The same creature that now wrestled with vines, sputtering in
irritation? Or was there really a contradiction?

"This biome—how come you're so loyal to it?"

"It is the highest form which can evolve from this universe—so
far." Seeker kept twisting around in the thick vines to no avail. Even
so, it continued in an even, measured tone, "The biome has been
implicit in the governing laws since the beginning, and arose here
first as intricate networks on ancient Earth."

"So Alvin had part of it right after all."

Seeker thrashed around, getting itself caught tighter. "Only a
narrow view."

"You said once you had contact with everything."

Seeker shook its head in frustration. "Everything and the nothing."

"What's 'the nothing'?"

Seeker bit into a vine and tore it loose. "When a thinking being
chooses to not think for a while."

"The subconscious?"

"The transconscious. Separation into isolated beings is a feature
of evolution in the human era and before. I am a fragment of the
self-awareness that arose from that early web, and now grows
apace."

"Sounds pretty exalted, Seeker After Patterns."

"You are part of it, too," Seeker said softly.

"I don't feel all that cosmic right this minute," Cley said, beginning to notice many aches. Her palms throbbed. She wondered if
the Supras had any medical miracles handy.

"The biome is ordinary. Not a big abstraction." Seeker wrestled
free of the vines.

"And you're a housekeeper for the system solar?" Cley smiled
ruefully.

"In a way. I voyaged once to another biome, and—"

Cley was startled. "Another star?"

"Yes. I journeyed to speak with that far biome. Quite different,
it was."

"What's a biome say to another?"

"Little, at first. I had difficulties."

"I thought Seeker After Patterns could do anything."

Seeker made its barking laugh. "Only what my planets allow us."

"They sent you?"

"Yes. Eventually the biomes strewn through the spiral arms will connect. There is much work to be done, to understand those strange beings."

"Biomes are beings?"

"Of course. Evolution proceeds beyond the scope of individuals now, or of species and phyla. Biomes are different orders of beings."

As it said this Seeker no longer looked like an amiable pet. She sensed quiet, eerie powers in it.

"Seeker, you speak as if you *are* the system solar."

"So we do."

Cley chuckled and cuffed Seeker beneath its ample, matted chin. "Well, so much for words. Whatever won this, and at whatever cost, we're alive."

"Far more important that the biome lives."

"Yes, thank God."

"You are welcome," said Seeker.